SUNSET AND SAWDUST

'A word-perfect picture' *Daily Mirror*

'Joe Lansdale is the poet laureate of the East Texas backwoods and this new semi-historical romp through dirt roads, deadbeat cops and unshaven villain land evokes the 1930s with the rawness and pungency of Steinbeck's California sagas' *Guardian*

'An enjoyable, good-humoured story' *Sunday Telegraph*

'This is entertaining stuff' *The List*

CAPTAINS OUTRAGEOUS

'Fast paced and extremely funny, *Captains Outrageous* sees Joe Lansdale writing at his very best' *Crime Time*

'Colourful, profane and with an injection of black humour that borders on bad taste, this is another high-octane race through the Texas badlands, with a rising body count and thrills galore. A rewarding romp' *Guardian*

'What is . . . remarkable about the Texan is that the quantity doesn't affect the quality of his work, which remains remarkably high . . . a finely developed sense of the ludicrous . . . the humour usually adds to, rather than detracts from, the suspense'

Glasgow Herald

'It's vintage stuff, a heady mix of brawling, smut and general waywardness from a consistently entertaining writer' *Uncut*

'Real in-your-face stuff and not for those of a sensitive disposition. But it does give rise to many a belly laugh' *Irish Times*

Joe R. Lansdale has written more than a dozen novels and edited several anthologies. He has received the British Fantasy Award, the American Mystery Award, six Bram Stoker Awards and the 2001 Edgar Allan Poe Award for Best Novel from the Mystery Writers of America. He lives in East Texas with his wife, son and daughter. He maintains a website at www.joerlansdale.com.

By Joe R. Lansdale

HAP COLLINS AND LEONARD PINE NOVELS
Savage Season
Mucho Mojo
The Two-Bear Mambo
Bad Chili
Rumble Tumble
Captains Outrageous

OTHER NOVELS
Cold in July
Freezer Burn
The Bottoms
Sunset and Sawdust

SUNSET AND SAWDUST

Joe R. Lansdale

PHOENIX

A PHOENIX PAPERBACK

First published in Great Britain in 2004
by Weidenfeld & Nicolson
This paperback edition published in 2005
by Phoenix,
an imprint of Orion Books Ltd,
Orion House, 5 Upper St Martin's Lane,
London WC2H 9EA

First published in the USA in 2004
by Alfred A. Knopf, a division of Random House, Inc.

1 3 5 7 9 10 8 6 4 2

A CIP catalogue record for this book
is available from the British Library.

ISBN 0 75381 993 7

Printed and bound in Great Britain by
Clays Ltd, St Ives plc

www.orionbooks.co.uk

For Kasey

In East Texas, lies, legend, and reality are all the same.

H. COLLINS
lifelong East Texas resident

SUNSET AND SAWDUST

1

On the afternoon it rained frogs, sun perch, and minnows, Sunset discovered she could take a beating good as Three-Fingered Jack. Unlike Jack, who had taken his in the sunshine, she took hers in her own home at the tail end of a cyclone, the windows rattling, the roof lifting, the hardwood floor cold as stone.

She was on her back wearing only the top half of her dress, because the bottom half had been ripped away when Pete, during the process of beating her, had stepped on it, and the dress, rotten as politics, had torn and left her clothed only from waist to shoulders.

It went through her mind that she was down to two dresses now, and that she hated to see this one go, as it, though faded, had a flowery pattern she liked and the colors blended well with the stains.

But this was a passing thought. She was mostly thinking: How can I stop him from hitting me? She was trying to do this by holding her hands up, but he was beating them down, and her own arms and hands flying back into her face were doing near the damage his fists might have.

Finally, he hammered her to the floor, followed her down, spread her legs, went to tearing and clawing off the rest of her clothes.

When the top of her dress ripped open and he jerked loose one side of her bra, revealing her, he said, "There's that tittie." His speech was slurred and his breath seemed to bleed alcohol.

3

He raked at her undergarments, tore them and tossed them. When he snapped his gun belt free, he tossed it nearby, and while he was on her, tugging at his zipper, trying to put the mule in the barn, Sunset reached over and slipped his .38 revolver from its holster, and without him being aware, put it to his head, gave him one in the temple.

When she pulled the trigger the shot was loud as Gabriel blowing her up to heaven, but it was Pete who went to heaven. Or departed anyway. Sunset liked to think he got a nice chair in hell, right next to the oven.

But in that moment, the shot made her scream, once, sharp and hard as if she had taken the bullet, or as if she had just received a slap on the bottom at birth.

Pete went limp, not only in the organ he had intended to use, but all over. He said not a word. No "Ouch," "Oh shit," or "Can you believe that?" Things he liked to say under normal circumstances, moments of surprise and duress.

He just took the hot load, cut a fart near loud as the .38 shot, collapsed, and rode on out on Death's black horse.

If it wasn't bad enough she had lost her dress, underclothes, and dignity, now all the windows on the east side shook like Marley's chains, then exploded. The door leaped apart as if it had never been anything other than a loosely connected puzzle, and the wind took the roof away.

She lay there on her back, fragments of clothes fastened to her body, her old flat-heeled shoes still on her feet, a piece of window glass poking out of her shoulder, Pete lying heavy against her. She still had the gun in her hand. The shot had gone in small and hadn't come out big like she expected. It must have been a bad load, jumping around in his brain, making jelly of it. Blood ran from the wound, out of his nose and onto her.

4

She rolled him off and looked at him. No mistaking. He wasn't going to recover from this.

"Surprised you, didn't I?" Sunset said.

She studied Pete for a long moment, then started to scream as if a banshee were inside of her. But it wasn't screaming you would have heard if you had been in the other room. It was loud enough, but the storm was louder. The house rocked, squeaked, squealed, and whined.

Then, except for the floor, two ugly chairs, an iron cookstove, Sunset and the dead man, it was all sucked up and thrown lickety-split on down country.

Sunset, screaming, clung to the floor while the storm raved on.

The moment the storm passed, the sky turned clear and the sun poked out and stoked up the heat. It was as if the cool wind and rain had never been.

Sunset stood up, weak and bleeding, fragments of her clothes falling from her. She pulled the piece of glass from her shoulder. It came out smooth without causing too much damage, hardly any blood.

Naked, except for her shoes and the gun she was holding, she wandered off of what remained of her house, stumbled down the muddy clay road in front of the place, frogs, minnows, and perch hopping and flapping beneath her shoes.

She felt as lost as Cain after he killed Abel.

She saw Pete's car, turned over and smashed up, bent in half between two big oak trees as if it had been made of wet licorice. Nearby, his wooden filing cabinet was burst open and there were files all over the place.

Fatefully, she came across one of her curtains, made from a flour sack and dyed blue. It had wrapped itself around a scrub tree limb and was hanging there like it was on the arm of a valet.

Sunset draped it around the lower part of her body, pulled her long red hair down over her breasts, started down the road again, mud squishing around her shoes.

Stooping to yank a mashed frog from the bottom of her shoe, she looked up to see the colored knife sharpener, Uncle Riley, coming down the road with his two mules and wagon. Uncle Riley's son, Tommy, was walking alongside him, spearing sun perch from the ground with a sharp stick, flipping them into the wagon bed.

Uncle Riley pulled on the reins when he saw her, said, "Oh, hell. Now I ain't looking, Miss White Woman. Really. And Tommy, he ain't neither. We ain't seeing a thing."

But Tommy was seeing plenty. Sunset's breasts were poking through her red hair, and Tommy had never seen breasts before, white or black, except those of his mama when suckling, but that was a long-lost memory.

Sunset, at that moment, didn't care who saw what. She was bleeding from nose and mouth and her eyes were starting to swell shut. She felt as if she had been set on fire and put out with a yard rake.

"Uncle Riley," she said, "it's me, Sunset. I been beat."

"Oh, Lord, chile, you sure have. I'm gonna get down and help you. Don't shoot at nothing now, you hear?"

Sunset staggered to one knee, tried to get up, couldn't.

Uncle Riley, who was six-four and forty-four, weighed two-twenty and had a slick bald head he covered with a droopy hat, climbed down from the wagon, took off his work shirt, kept his head turned as he walked toward her.

Uncle Riley put the shirt over Sunset's shoulders. She dropped the curtain and pulled the shirt shut and buttoned it with her free hand. All this from where she knelt on one knee.

6

She tried again to get up, but couldn't. Uncle Riley lifted her into his arms easy as a child. She clung to the pistol as if it were a part of her hand.

He carried her to the wagon and set her on the seat, climbed up beside her. "Now I ain't touching on you, Miss Sunset."

"It's okay, Uncle Riley. You've been a real gentleman."

Tommy, who was standing beside the wagon with a fish stuck on the end of his pointed stick, had yet to close his mouth.

"Get on up here," Uncle Riley said.

Tommy climbed in the back of the wagon with the fish they had been collecting. They were scattered from one end of the wagon bed to the other, and in places they were ankle deep. Uncle Riley had seen the rain of fish as a bonus from God. Fish to eat, fish to salt and smoke for later. They had even gathered a few frogs because Tommy's mama, the midwife, Cary, liked frog legs.

Now Tommy wondered if the fish would keep because it was turning hot again and they were having to haul around this beat-up, big-tittied white woman. What in heaven's name were they going to do with her?

Tommy thought: Her hair is so long and red and wild it looks like tumbling fire. He smiled to himself. Good Lord, he had seen fish rain from the skies and he had seen a white woman's tits. It had been a special day.

"Miss Sunset, I haul you around like this, they gonna kill me," Uncle Riley said.

"Not with me with you they won't."

Sunset heard her mouth say the right things, but she felt as if it were all a dream. She scratched a place behind her ear with the barrel of the .38.

"Missy, they ain't gonna believe me. They ain't gonna believe you."

"They'll believe me."

7

"My cousin Jim, he just seen a white woman bending over in her yard, taking hanging clothes from a basket, and though there wasn't nothing to see cause she had her clothes on and he was up on the road, a white man seen him look at her, and for that, the word got around and them Kluxers took Jim out and castrated him, poured turpentine on the cuts."

"I tell you, it'll be okay."

"What's your husband, Mr. Pete, gonna say?"

"He ain't gonna say nothing, Uncle Riley. I blew his brains out."

"Oh, my goodness."

"Take me to my mother-in-law's."

"Sure you want to go to your mama-in-law's?" Uncle Riley said.

"My daughter's there. Ain't got nowhere else to go."

"Don't know Miss Marilyn gonna take kindly to you shooting her boy."

"I'll cross that bridge when I get to it. Oh, God, what is Karen going to think?"

"She surely loves her daddy."

"She does."

"They gonna castrate me and my boy."

"No, they're not. I'll see to it. For heaven's sake, Uncle Riley, I've known you all my life. Your wife helped deliver my baby."

"White folks forget them things when they want to. And with this Depression on, people just meaner anyhow."

The storm had come so fast and furious, it was hard to accept all the sunlight and heat, but already the fish in the back of the wagon were beginning to smell.

The leather harnesses creaked and the oat-and-hay-stoked bellies of the mules made strange gurgling and trumpeting sounds. From time to time the mules lifted their tails and farted or did their business, jerked their heads and snatched at greenery, and there was plenty of it, because the trail was narrow and the limbs of trees poked out over it, tempting the mules with their leaves.

The wagon squeaked and jostled along the muddy road and the steam from the mud drying rose up in thin wisps and there was a smell like pottery firing in a kiln. The sun burned and gnawed at Sunset's wounds and bruises.

"I feel like I'm gonna pass out," Sunset said.

"Don't do that, now, Miss Sunset. It bad enough you near naked riding along with a nigger, you don't need to have your head on my shoulder."

Sunset dipped her head and the feeling passed. When she sat back up and started to wipe her forehead with the back of her hand, she realized the gun was still in it.

"Maybe I ought to leave this with you?"

"No, ma'am. You don't want to leave that gun with me. Next thing I know, I'm the one done shot him."

"I'll explain."

"White folks find him dead, then see me, they gonna want a nigger anyhow. They see Mr. Pete's gun in my wagon, and him being a lawman and all, me and this boy be strung up faster than you can say, 'Let's get us a nigger.'"

"All right," Sunset said. "I thank you and Tommy, I truly do."

"Besides, you might need that gun when you tell Miss Marilyn what you done did. And you don't need it for her, you might need it for her husband, Mr. Jones."

"When I tell my daughter, I might want to use it on myself."

"Don't talk like that now."

"I can't believe I did it."

"He beat on you like that, Miss Sunset, he deserved killing. I ain't got no truck with a man beats on a woman. You done what you had to do."

"I could have just shot him in the leg or the foot, I guess."

"You done what you had to do." Uncle Riley studied her face. "Damn, Miss Sunset, ain't seen a beating that bad since he whupped up on Three-Fingered Jack. You remember that?"

"I do."

"Boy, he beat that man like he stole something."

"He did. My husband's girlfriend."

"Guess I ought not to have brought that up."

"He taught me how to shoot, Uncle Riley. Can you believe that? Taught me how to shoot a pistol, shotgun and rifle. Taught me until he thought maybe I was getting too good. After we married, he didn't want me to do nothing . . . I can't believe I shot him. I could have just got hit and he'd have got what he wanted and it'd been over. Wouldn't have been the first time. Karen would have a daddy. Thing is, though, he could have had what he wanted without all that, Uncle Riley. I'd have given in without all that. All he'd have to have done was talk sweet. But he liked it rough, even if he didn't have to. I think he was sweet to his girlfriends, but me, he beat."

"Don't talk to me about that, girl. I don't need to hear about it."

"He was bad enough about such, but when he drank, he was mean as a cottonmouth."

"Your hair sure is red," Tommy said.

"Damn, boy," Uncle Riley said. "Miss Sunset don't need you talking about her hair right now. Get on back there and sort them fish out or something."

"They all the same."

"Well, count them, boy."

"It's all right, Uncle Riley. Yeah, Tommy. It's red. My mama used to say red as sunset, so that's what people call me."

"That ain't your name?" Tommy asked.

"It is now. In the Bible they wrote Carrie Lynn Beck. But everyone called me Sunset. Got married I became Jones."

Sunset burst into tears.

"Go on back there now and sit down," Uncle Riley told Tommy.

"I didn't do nothing," Tommy said.

"Boy, you want your ass shined? Go back there."

Tommy moved back a ways, sat down amidst the fish. They were still damp and wet against his pants and he didn't like it, but he sat. He knew he had pushed about as far as he could push, and the next push the wagon would stop and he'd have his daddy's hand across the seat of his pants, or worse, he'd have to go break off his own switch for his daddy to use.

As they went the day died, the woods thinned on either side and you could hear the scream of the saw from the mill, could hear movement of men and mules and oxen and dragged trees, the rattle and gunning of lumber trucks.

"They see me and you, it gonna be bad," Uncle Riley said.

"It'll be all right," Sunset said.

"Tommy, you get on out of the wagon, go off in them trees. I'll come back for you."

Tommy dropped over the side, wandered into the woods.

"I ain't gonna let nothing happen to you," Sunset said. "They'll hang me and you both, they bother you. I still got five rounds in this gun."

"Hanging you with me don't make me feel no better, Miss Sunset. Dead is dead."

"All right. Let me off here. I can walk the rest of the way."

Uncle Riley shook his head. "That might look worse, someone see you get off the wagon, they might get me before you can make sure word gets around good. 'Sides, you can hardly sit up."

Sunset lifted her head, saw the pine trees on either side of them had been chopped off evenly at the tops by the storm. It was like the Grim Reaper of Trees had taken their heads with his scythe.

Rolling into the lumber camp, Sunset saw sweaty men working and mud-splattered mules jangling their harnesses, dragging logs toward the mill. And there were long log wagons coming from deep in the woods drawn by rows of great plodding oxen.

The great round saw in the mill screeched as it chewed trees, and there was the sound of the planing saw as it shaped lumber. The air was full of the sweet sap smell of fresh sawed East Texas pine. Out of a long chute connected to the mill houses came puffs of gnawed wood that floated down on top of a mound of sawdust made dark by time and weather.

All about were broken limbs and trees twisted up by the storm. A log wagon was turned over and men were busy righting it. A dead ox lay nearby, half covered in fallen logs.

"Wonder if they even stopped working when the tornado come," Sunset said.

"They did, wasn't long," Uncle Riley said. "Not here at Camp Rupture. Hell, someone will gut and skin that ox there and eat him by nightfall. A man fell down, they might skin and eat him."

"That's Camp Rapture, Uncle Riley. Not Rupture."

"Not if you work here long it ain't. And I worked long enough to know I didn't want no more of it. I got a truss on to prove it."

"Sure wish I'd just shot Pete in the leg."

"Now that I ponder on it," Uncle Riley said, "I'm starting to agree with you, Miss Sunset."

2

As Sunset and Uncle Riley rode in, working men studied them, made note Sunset was wearing only a shirt. They put aside their work and began to move down the hill toward the wagon, like flies to molasses.

"What you doing with that beat-up white woman?" a man said to Uncle Riley.

"Just helping her," Uncle Riley said. Then to Sunset: "See, they gonna cut me or hang me."

"Take me to my mother-in-law's."

Uncle Riley looked at the men following the wagon.

"Oh, heavens," Uncle Riley said. "They look mean. It's that kind of mean only a dead nigger can make happy."

"I still got the gun. Maybe I can get five of them."

"There's more than five."

You could see screened-in sleeping porches on some of the houses, and on the porches were beds and the beds were there to take advantage of the night air and the screens were there to baffle the mosquitoes. The houses were painted industrial green and were jacked up on blocks or pilings. All around the houses chicken wire had been nailed and inside the wire, under the houses, chickens and geese pecked about. Most of the windows were black with soot from the power house and the grassless yards were sprinkled with sawdust from the mill.

Sunset's mother-in-law's house was classier than the rest. Had wooden shingles, electricity and fresh paint. Stood on treated pilings and there were no chickens under the house. They were confined to a large pen and chicken house out back, and they were fed in troughs and their water was in a big tub and it was changed daily. By the chicken house was a fenced-in lot and a shed containing a hog and piglets. The windows were fresh scrubbed and the yard had been raked clean of sawdust and there were marks in the dirt as if a giant hen had been scratching for worms.

The sleeping porch was large and not screened in, but framed by windows that could be cranked open. Sunset could see the potted plants her mother-in-law loved in big clay jars.

Parked in the yard was a black company truck with mud-caked tires and weathered wooden slats all around the bed. The sides of the truck were scraped from hard work and it was lightly coated in sawdust. On the side of it, with a finger, someone had written in dust: I'M DIRTY AS SIN.

As they neared the house, Uncle Riley turned the wagon so it came between the water pump and the house. He pulled alongside the front porch and the wide steps that led up to it. He yanked back on the wheel brake and loosely held the reins.

"You're gonna have to come around and help me down, Uncle Riley," Sunset said. "I help myself, I'll fall face first in the dirt and show my butt under this shirt."

"Oh, Miss Sunset, can't you wait for one of them white men?"

"All right."

Men, both white and black, gathered around the wagon. Sunset knew most of them, but she wasn't sure with her face like this they'd know her. Then she remembered her hair. No one around had hair like hers. Not as long and flame-red and thick as hers. And unlike most women, she always wore it down.

"What the hell's going on here?" one of the men said. It was

Sunset's father-in-law. He was big and looked like his son, Pete, only thinner of hair and bigger of belly.

His khaki shirt had wet swells beneath the arms and there were sweat frames around his collar and along his shirtfront. He cocked back his stained hat, said, "Goddamn, Sunset, is that you?"

"It's me, Mr. Jones."

"What in hell happened to you? And what are you doing with this nigger in his undershirt? He do this? Is that Pete's pistol?"

The black men in the crowd faded back carefully, using practiced methods of sidestepping and eye misdirection. In a matter of moments they had managed themselves to the rear of the swarm, hands in pockets, watching cautiously, ready to "yas suh" or bolt.

"I ain't got nothing on underneath this shirt and I'm weak, so help me down, but be careful."

Jones helped her down. Sunset said, "Uncle Riley here found me after the storm and helped me. I didn't have no clothes on, and he gave me his shirt."

"Well, I thank you for that, Uncle Riley," Jones said.

"You welcome, Mr. Jones. Just out gathering these here fishes, and along she come. I put my head down and gave her my shirt."

"That's exactly what he did," Sunset said, and leaned back against the wagon. "I can't hardly stand. I'm gonna need help up on the porch there."

Two men eagerly stepped from the crowd to give her a hand. Sunset thought they were holding her just a little too warmly. Their eyes were playing to the front of her shirt where she had misbuttoned it and she knew they were peeking at her breasts. She was too weary to worry about it. Besides those peeks, more men were seeing her freckled legs this day than had seen them when she was a little girl in short pants.

They helped her onto the porch as she used her hands to tug down the back of the shirt and not give a free show.

Jones followed her up the steps, took a look down the front of her shirt himself, said, "What you doing like this? Get hurt in the storm?"

"Something like that." Sunset turned and called to Uncle Riley. "Thank you for being such a gentleman, Uncle Riley."

"You welcome, Miss Sunset."

"I'll give you your shirt later. For reasons you can see, I got to hang on to it just now."

"Yes, ma'am. That's quite all right. You keep it you got a mind to. Reckon I better run along, get these fishes home before they go bad."

Riley let loose the wheel brake, clucked to the mules, and the crowd parted.

One of the men in the crowd, Don Walker, said to the man next to him, "You can bet that nigger enjoyed him a peek."

"Just hate it wasn't me," said the other, Bill Martin. "Even with her face all beat up like that, I'd take her."

"Hell, Bill, you'd take a hole in the dirt."

"Shit, I'd fuck a duck if it winked and bent over."

"I don't think you'd care if it winked or not."

In the Jones house, Sunset sat down in a cane chair next to the radio and watched shadows run down the hill and over the house like spilled oil.

Sunset said, "I shot him." She held up the gun. "With this gun. His gun. He had me on the floor hitting me. He tried to rape me. He'd raped me before. I couldn't have it no more."

When the truth of the matter sank in, Mrs. Jones, a tall,

handsome woman with mounded hair skunk-striped with gray, let out a noise so shrill and pitiful, Sunset could feel it in her bones. It made her flex her right foot so hard her shoe came off.

"You shot him?" Jones said. "You shot my boy?"

"Right upside the head."

"My God," he said.

"Didn't have no choice. He was raping me."

"Man can't rape his wife," Jones said.

"Sure seemed like rape to me," Sunset said.

Jones drew back his hand, and as he did, Sunset lifted the pistol. "I ain't gonna have no man beat on me again, I can help it."

"You're on a spree, that's what you are," Jones said. "You and that nigger. A spree."

"Uncle Riley don't have nothing to do with it. And if we were on a spree, you think we'd have come here? I didn't know no other place to go. I come for Karen."

"But why did you do it?" Jones said.

"Pete come home drunk. Guess one of his girlfriends over in Holiday, probably that whore Jimmie Jo French, didn't give him what he wanted. So he decided he wanted it from me. Even if I was second, or maybe third, choice. And he wanted it rough. He started beating on me, ripped off my clothes, and the storm come and blew the house away. Just took it out of there like it was made out of newspaper. I got hold of his gun and shot him. Walked off without no clothes on. Just these shoes and a curtain I found. Uncle Riley gave me his shirt."

"He was your husband, girl," Jones said.

"Sometimes."

Mrs. Jones had begun to shriek and run about the house like a chicken being pursued by a fox. She came to one wall, hit it with her palms, turned, ran to the other side, repeated the process.

17

"I didn't want to kill him and I didn't mean to. But I thought he might kill me."

"My own daughter-in-law. What have we done to you?"

"It's what your son done to me," Sunset said. But thought: I still remember your hand patting my bottom more than once when no one was looking.

"He was the constable," Jones said.

"Ain't no more," Sunset said. "Ain't nothing no more."

Jones pulled up a chair and sat down. It was as if a great sack filled with potatoes had been tossed onto the chair. He seemed to droop over the sides and shift all over.

Mrs. Jones had finally collapsed to the floor and was pulling her hair. "Pete. Pete. Pete," she said, as if he might answer. "Goddamn you, Sunset," Jones said. "A man's got urges."

"Where's Karen?" Sunset asked.

Mrs. Jones wailed and Mr. Jones sat in his chair. Neither responded. Sunset got up, put on her shoe, sat back down.

After a while, Mr. Jones said, "You know for sure he's dead?"

"He's dead, all right."

"Might still be alive."

"Not unless he's been resurrected."

Mrs. Jones let out another screech. This one shook the glass in the windows. She had begun to roll around on the floor.

"Where is he?" Mr. Jones asked.

"At what's left of our house with his pants down and his ass in the air."

Jones sat for a while, trying to swallow a lump in his throat. When he managed, he said, "Reckon I got to go over there and get him. You, missy, you're gonna pay for this. There's the law, and they're gonna make you pay."

"He was the law," Sunset said, "and he made me pay every day, and I hadn't even done nothing."

Jones got up and went out the door. Sunset sat and held the pistol in her lap. She looked at Mrs. Jones, who was lying on the floor heaving.

Slowly her mother-in-law put her feet under her and got up and walked over to Sunset. Sunset knew what was coming, but unlike with Mr. Jones, she didn't move. She figured she ought to take just a little for what she had done, and if she was going to take it, she'd take it from her mother-in-law, Marilyn Jones. The woman had always treated her good. She could take a slap.

But just one.

Mrs. Jones slapped Sunset with all her strength. So hard it knocked Sunset onto the floor and overturned the chair.

Sunset thought: Maybe I could have skipped that one after all. The slap struck her where Pete had hit her, and it burned like hell.

"You killed my boy," Marilyn said.

"I didn't mean for it to happen," Sunset said, then started to cry.

Slowly, she got up and righted the chair, pushed the shirt down over herself best she could, sat down again. She still had the revolver in her hand. She held on to it like a drowning man to a straw.

Marilyn stood over her and looked down, her hair loose now and hanging. She drew her hand back as if she might hit Sunset again.

"No," Sunset said.

Marilyn's face became less clouded. She studied Sunset for a long moment, opened her arms wide, said, "Come here, darling."

"Say what?" Sunset said.

"Come here."

Sunset studied her mother-in-law for a time, stood cautiously.

"It's all right," said Marilyn. "I ain't crazy as I was."

"About half that crazy could be too much."

"It's all right," Marilyn said, and took a step toward Sunset. They embraced. Sunset continued to hold the gun, just in case. She was hoping she wouldn't end up shooting the whole damn family. Maybe the chickens too.

"I lost a son," Marilyn said. "I ain't gonna lose no daughter, too."

"I didn't want to do it."

"I know."

"No. No, you don't," Sunset said.

"You might be surprised what I know, girlie."

3

The cyclone that tore up Sunset's house swirled on through the trees, carrying away her roof and goods, headed east, and was still kicking by early nightfall, tossing fish, frogs, and debris. It even threw a calf against a house and killed it.

The westbound train into Tyler caught the tail end of the storm, and the wind tossed fish against it and shook the boxcars and made them rattle like a toy train shaken by a mean child.

For a moment, it seemed as if the train might be sucked off the track, but shaking was the worst of it. The locomotive and its little boxes chugged on and so did the storm, which finally played out near the Louisiana border. The last of it was just a cool, damp wind for some hot people night-fishing on the banks of the Sabine River.

In one of the boxcars, Hillbilly sat with his guitar and his little tote bag and eyed the two fellas squatting across from him. They had climbed on when the train slowed in Tyler, and now as it clunked through the countryside and the storm was over, they began to eye him.

They pretended to ignore him at first, but he caught them sneaking glances. He hadn't liked them from the start. He had greeted them as they climbed into the car, and they hadn't said so much as eat shit or howdy.

They kicked a couple of sun perch out of the open doorway, shook the rain off themselves dog style, hunkered down like gargoyles opposite the open sliding door, and said nothing, just sneaked peeks.

Although Hillbilly looked younger than his thirty years, he had lived a full thirty. He had been around and seen much. He had played his guitar and sung in every dive in East Texas, Oklahoma and Louisiana. He had ridden trains all over the place, supped in hobo camps, boxed and wrestled for money at county fairs, where his wiry thinness and soft good looks had fooled many a local tough into thinking he was a pushover.

From experience, Hillbilly knew these fellas were studying him a little too intently. Like hungry dogs looking at a pork chop. One of them was short and stout and wore a wool cap. The other was taller, leaner, and hatless, with a thick growth of beard.

"You got the makings?" Hillbilly asked, even though he didn't smoke as a matter of course. But sometimes, you broke the ice, it could save you trouble. A cigarette could do that, break the ice.

The man with the cap shook his head, said, "You're a young'n, ain't you?"

"Not that young," Hillbilly said.

"You look young."

"Have any food?" Hillbilly asked.

"Just them fish in the doorway," said the bearded man. "You want that, have at it."

"I don't think so," Hillbilly said. "Ever seen that kind of thing before? Raining fish? I read about it. It was that cyclone. It sucked out a pond somewhere, throwed them fish all along here."

The men had no interest in the cyclone or the fish. The bearded man grinned at Hillbilly. Hillbilly had seen friendlier grins on alligators.

"You been on the road a while?" said the bearded man.

"A while."

"Gets lonely, don't it?" said the man with the cap.

"I'm not that lonely, really."

"We get lonely," said the bearded man. "Me and him just being together. We get all kinds of lonely. Man don't need to be lonely. Don't have to be."

"I'm not lonely at all," Hillbilly said.

The man with the cap said, "We can show you that you been lonely and didn't even know it."

"I'm fine. Really."

The man with the cap laughed. "It ain't really you we're worried about. It's us that are lonely."

"You got each other," Hillbilly said.

"Having each other all the time gets old," the bearded man said. "We want someone else to not be lonely with."

"God don't like that kind of talk. You boys ever hear about Sodom and Gomorrah?"

The bearded man hooted. "Who gives a damn about some Bible story? We get you bent over, you'll be happier than you think."

"Fellas, leave me alone."

That's when the one with the cap came up from his squatting position and sprang.

Hillbilly brought his guitar around hard, breaking it soundly over the capped man's head, knocking him back. Then the bearded one was on him. Hillbilly pushed him back with the palm of his hand, stuck the other hand in his pocket, pulled out his knife, flicked it open.

The one with the cap came in again, and Hillbilly stuck him under the short ribs. The knife went in as easy as poking a hole through a sheet of wet paper. The man dropped immediately. Went to his knees, tumbled on his side.

"Goddamn," said the bearded one, whacking Hillbilly in the eye. "You hurt Winston."

The bearded man grabbed Hillbilly in a bear hug and squeezed Hillbilly's hands to his sides. Hillbilly butted him in the nose and he let go. Hillbilly stabbed him in the groin and he stumbled back. Hillbilly's knife flashed again, high and wide.

The man held his throat, tried to say something, but couldn't. He sat down as if a chair had been pulled out from under him. He sat upright for a moment, then lay on his back slowly and tried to tuck his chin, as if this might seal the wound.

Hillbilly put his boot on the man's face and pushed with all his weight so the wound would bleed out. The man wiggled like a snake, but the wiggling didn't last.

"I told you to leave me the hell alone," Hillbilly said.

Hillbilly wiped his knife on the dead man's jacket, put it away, went over and looked at the one who had worn the cap. The cap had fallen off and lay on the boxcar floor.

Hillbilly picked up the cap and put it on, then he bent over the man. He was alive, but in the partial moonlight his dark eyes looked like creek pebbles under raging water.

"You done stabbed me," the man said. His voice sounded as if it were coming through a squeeze organ.

"You wasn't gonna give me a picnic lunch," Hillbilly said.

"That's my hat."

"Not anymore."

"We was just gonna get some loving. There ain't no fault in that."

"Unless you don't want it."

"I ain't gonna make it," the man said.

"You took it under the rib. I think I got your lung. You're right. You ain't gonna make it."

"You're a sonofabitch," the man said, and blood poured out of his mouth.

24

"You're right about that," Hillbilly said.

"Just a goddamned horse's ass."

"Right again. And I figure you ain't got but a few seconds to get used to the idea."

The man jerked and made a noise, then joined his pal in the long fall to wherever.

Hillbilly got up and looked at his guitar. It was junk now. And so was his way of making a living. Hillbilly tossed the busted guitar out the doorway, squatted and thought about things.

He could throw these bo's out, go into the next town, get off there. Then again, it might be best he got off when the train slowed in Lindale near the cannery. It was a pretty good jump because it didn't slow all the way, but he had done it before. You tucked and rolled and took your jump where the grass was thick, it was something you could do and not break your neck.

He did that, by the time they found these two, he'd be long gone.

Hillbilly glanced outside. It was black in the distance because of the woods, but the moonlight lay bright on the gravel along the tracks and made the stuff look like diamonds.

Hillbilly rummaged through their goods and found a potato, some salt and pepper in little boxes. He put these in his little bag and fastened it to his belt. He stood in the doorway for a long time, using one trembling hand to support himself on the frame of the boxcar, watched until he could see the Lindale lights.

Out there was Tin Can Alley. He had worked canning peas there, and he had worked picking the peas they canned. He had worked all along this railroad line, picking fruit, cotton, tomatoes, all kinds of jobs, and the only one he had liked was singing and playing that guitar. Now his guitar was broken, smashed over some amorous thug's head.

He looked back at the two. The one whose throat he had cut had a dark pool under his head. It looked like a flat black pillow there in the darkness. The other lay on his side with his hands pressed against his wound, eyes open, as if thinking about something important.

Hillbilly's mouth tasted sour with bile. He spat out of the boxcar, and when the train slowed coming into the Lindale yard, he took a deep breath, and jumped before it got there.

Wandering through the darkness, Hillbilly came to a wooded place. There was a little stream there, and in time he saw a flicker of light through the trees. He could smell smoke and he could smell food cooking.

He bent down and used his hand to cup up some water. He sat that way for a while, listening. There were voices coming from the light, and he decided to go to it. As he neared, he called out, "Yo, bo's."

A pause. Then: "Come on in. You got any fixings?"

Hillbilly moved into the light. Around a fire were three hobos. They had a can hung on a stick over the fire and were boiling some stew.

"I got a tater in my sack," Hillbilly said, and wished now he'd nabbed one of those fish in the doorway of the boxcar.

He came into the camp and took out the potato. The men around the fire stood up as he neared, just in case he might not be what he seemed.

"I put in some cooked beans a woman gave me," one of the hobos said. He was a little man with an old black fedora and clothes that had been patched so much the original clothing was no longer visible. He had been sitting on an old black jacket rolled up on the ground.

"I didn't have nothing to add but my best wishes," said a fat colored man wearing overalls. He was squatting by the fire.

"I had the can," the other man said. He looked pretty dressed up for a hobo. "I cleaned it in the creek there. It's a pretty fresh can, so it doesn't have rust in it."

Hillbilly gave the patched clothes man the potato and the man pulled out a pocketknife and went to cutting it up, skin and all, into the can of boiling water and beans.

"It'd taste pretty good we had some wild onions," said the colored man. "But I don't know we could find any in the dark."

"I got a little salt and pepper on me, too," Hillbilly said, and he removed the little bag he had tied to his belt and opened it again. He took out the little boxes of salt and pepper. "Give it a pinch of these here."

When the stew was cooked up, Hillbilly took his cup from the bag and the patched clothes man poured him up some. Then Patches poured some into a tin can the black man had, a metal plate the other man had, and he himself drank out of the cook can.

As they sat and ate, they talked about this and that, and then the important stuff. Where they could get handouts and who was an easy mark on up the road. Patches said, "There's this woman over near Tyler. She ain't got no man. She'll give you food if you'll come in the house and service her. I don't know she'd screw a nigger, though, Johnny Ray."

Johnny Ray shook his head. "I don't want me none of that. No trouble like that. No, sir."

"How does she look?" the dressed-up man asked.

"Look at her straight on, you might turn to stone," Patches said. "And her cunt hairs are all gray. Ain't so bad when you ain't had none in a long time. And then she's got that food. But don't kiss her. Her mouth tastes like sin."

"She looks like that, I wouldn't think of kissing her," said the well-dressed man. "Least, I don't believe I would. It's hard for me to know what I might do these days."

"What I need is work," Hillbilly said. "And I need a guitar. Mine got busted."

"You play guitar?" said Patches.

"That's why I need one," Hillbilly said. "I sing too. I don't have a guitar, I feel like half a man. I don't feel the half that's left is my good half neither."

"Hell, I play the spoons," said Patches.

"I got me a Jew's harp and a harmonica," said the colored man.

"I play them too, if that's all I got," Hillbilly said. "But I'm a guitar man."

"I can't play anything," said Well-Dressed. "Formerly I was a schoolteacher. Can you believe that? Now I don't know a thing I need to know. Goddamn Depression. Goddamn Hoover."

"You can listen," said Patches. "Me and Johnny Ray, we play good together. I get them spoons going, and he comes in on that Jew's harp or the harmonica, we get a lively tune playing. It would sound real good if you can sing. Me and Johnny Ray sound like two old frogs a-blowing."

"I can sing," Hillbilly said.

"Do you know 'Red River Valley'?" said Patches.

"You strike it up, and I'll come in singing."

Patches got out the spoons and went to it. Johnny Ray went to blowing his harmonica, and pretty soon Hillbilly began to sing.

He was good too, and his voice rang through the woods, and they played and sang tunes well into the night.

4

Pete's father and a colored man named Zack Washington brought Pete back. They went to Pete's house, or what was left of it, found Pete the way Sunset said they would. At first, in the early moonlight, Zack thought the man on the floor was colored, but as they neared, the black on him rose up and flew away with a furious buzz.

Pete had his pants down, his head on the floor, his ass to the wind. There was a strip of shit in the crack of his butt that had jumped out when Sunset shot him. Blood had run down his face, into his mouth, onto the floor, and had dried.

Zack held the lantern close to Pete's face and thought Pete's expression was one of mild surprise, as if he had just spooned up a bug in his breakfast mush. One eye seemed more surprised than the other.

Zack tugged him up, and when he did, the blood that had dried on Pete's face and the floor made a sound like someone tearing a piece of sandpaper in half.

They pulled Pete's pants up, rode with him propped on the truck seat between them, Mr. Jones holding Pete up, Zack driving, trying to keep his mind on the road, trying not to let the smell of feces and decaying flesh overwhelm him. Due to the heat, even on the short ride to Camp Rapture, even though the day was now cooler, Pete had turned choke-your-nose ripe, and after they had gone a little ways, ants that had gathered in Pete's clothing crawled out and got on Zack

29

and bit him on the wrists and hands and ankles.

Zack had not volunteered to get Pete's body, but Jones, who was called Captain by the colored workers because he was a main man at the mill, made him volunteer. Had he not gone, he knew he would have been out of work, looking to pick cotton for a fart and a song, hoeing between rows when he wasn't dragging a sack, so there wasn't a whole lot of saying no even considered.

Secretly, Zack was glad Pete was dead. Pete had pistol-whipped him once for not calling him Mister. Zack had referred to the constable as Pete, like the white men he knew.

"You done forgot your place, nigger," Pete said, and the pistol came out and the whipping commenced. It was a pretty brisk whipping, just a few blows, and Zack thought it was a good thing it wasn't the beating Pete had given Three-Fingered Jack. If it had been that bad, he would be pushing up grass and feeding the worms.

So Zack thought it was damn funny finding Mr. Pete the way he was, pants down, that silly look on his face, his crack full of mess, a bullet in his head, put there by his own gun, fired by a little redheaded woman.

Jones and Zack brought Pete home and made a cooling board by taking a door from the closet. They placed the door between two chairs and put Pete's body on it. Zack said a few kind words, then stepped out, without Mr. Jones so much as saying thank you or go shoot yourself.

If things weren't bad enough, Pete's daughter, Karen, arrived from having gone fishing with friends. Showed up shortly after Mr. Jones brought back the body, opened the door with a smile on her face and a lie on her lips. At fourteen, it wasn't the first lie she had told. She had picked up some fish after the storm to pretend she had caught them.

Instead of fishing with friends, she had been with a boy. Jerry Flynn. They had gone down by the creek to spoon, then the storm came up. They spent the time they had meant to spend kissing with their faces in the dirt, the storm howling all about them.

When the tornado passed, they started home immediately, in Karen's case to the Jones' house, where she had been visiting her grandparents.

When Karen came in the door the lie was lost. She saw her father stretched out on the cooling board. His hair was in his face, his tongue hanging out. His clothes were wet from the storm and his left eye was bulging from its socket like someone was inside his head pushing it out of his skull with his finger.

Karen dropped the fish, screamed, said, "Daddy, Daddy, Daddy."

Sunset, who had gotten some of her energy back and borrowed an oversized dress from her mother-in-law, came out of the back room when Karen screamed. She was still carrying the revolver. She took hold of Karen and dragged her out of there.

Marilyn wondered where Sunset and Karen had gone, but was too weak and too sad to find out. She hoped they were okay out there in the dark.

She knew only that her husband was happy about Sunset leaving, said he was going to get his shotgun and when he saw her next he was going to cut those long legs out from under her. And Marilyn knew he would too, and probably get away with it.

It was in that moment, sneaking in between her other thoughts, that Marilyn realized she had been worried to death about her granddaughter during the storm, but the worry had been tucked away when Sunset arrived wearing only a shirt, toting a gun, saying she'd killed Pete. Now she was thinking about Karen again, and she was thinking about Sunset too.

She thought about all this as she lay in bed, not able to sleep. She kept seeing things over and over in her mind, and the thing she saw the most was her son and the little hole in his head.

When they laid him out on the cooling board in the parlor, his head had turned and the flattened-out load from the bullet rolled out of his mouth and fell bloody on the floor.

She could still see it in her mind's eye, hear it as it snapped against the floor.

As she lay there, she realized another thing, and it pained her to think it, but she knew it was true, and she had known it for a long time.

Pete had it coming.

He was just like his father. For years now, Jones, which was what Marilyn called her husband, had considered his word gold, even if it was sometimes tin.

Pete was the same.

Jones had blacked her eye more than once—punched her all over, for that matter. Kicked her. Slapped her. And he had raped her. She had never thought of it as rape until now. She thought that was just his way, and the way of a husband.

But now she thought about what Sunset had said and what she had done and she knew it was not just the way of a husband, and if it was, it was a bad way.

She lay for a moment feeling the sweat on her lower back stick to the sheets, thought about how much better it was on the sleeping porch and wondered why they had not slept there tonight. She sat up in bed and looked at Jones. He had not bothered to take her tonight, but that was because of Pete. He didn't have any lead in his pencil because of it.

Tomorrow, she knew he would hit her. A way to take out

what happened to Pete on her. And he would find a way to make it her fault. He always said, "See what you made me do?"

Marilyn got up quietly, padded in her bare feet to the dresser drawer, pulled out a big Singer sewing machine needle, crept quietly into the parlor and looked at her boy lying there.

She had cleaned him up and put some of his father's clothes on him, had even managed to push his eye back in place and close his lids and cover the hole where the bullet had gone in with candle wax.

For a moment she stood looking at him. She reached out and pushed at his hair to make it look the way it did when it was combed. Then she went outside and looked under the porch. She found what she wanted. Her husband's fishing tackle box. She got some heavy fishing line out of the box and went back inside. She threaded the sewing machine needle in the dark by touch, went to the bedroom and very carefully removed the blanket from the bed, took to sewing the sheet to the mattress with Jones between them.

She was patient about it, silent and deliberate. When she finished, she had Jones sewed in tight with only his head exposed. She put the needle away, went outside and got the yard rake.

The rake had never been used except to scratch the ground to make it smooth, and now that she thought about that, it seemed silly. She raked the dirt sometimes to keep from going mad, listening to the whine of the saw, the sound of men and mules and clanking machinery, while anticipating her next beating.

Back in the bedroom she studied Jones for a while, then raising the rake, she brought it down hard on his head, trying to imagine she was standing in a watermelon patch busting a melon.

Jones came awake with the first whack, yelled, and she hit him again. His head turned toward her and she hit him once more, this time putting all her weight behind it. He tried to get up but the sewed sheet and mattress held him.

"You've hit me the last time," she said.

"You're crazy, woman."

"Been crazy till now."

She began beating him from head to toe. She beat him until she was too tired to beat him. She rested and he cussed, and she went at it again. Had she been stronger she would have killed him, but she wasn't that strong and she didn't spend enough time on the head. She beat at his big body, grunting with every blow, the sound of the strikes echoing through the house like a dusty rug being thrashed.

When she wore out the second time, she went out of there, and when she came back, she had her husband's double-barrel shotgun.

Jones' face was red. He was bleeding from his ears and nose and the sheet was spotted with blood.

"You ain't right, woman," he said. "You ain't right on account of Pete."

She pointed the shotgun at him. "I ought to just go on and shoot you."

There was something about seeing him over the barrel of the gun, the smell of gun oil in her nostrils, that made her want to pull the trigger.

"What's got into you?"

"I let you into me, and that gave us Pete. And I let you teach him how to treat women by letting you treat me way you did. Sunset killed him cause she had to."

"You can't mean that."

"She killed him for the reason I ought to done killed you. I ought to not let you treat me this way. Pete might not have been like he was, I hadn't let you hit on me."

She cocked back the hammers on the shotgun.

"Now don't do nothing you'll regret, Marilyn."

"I already got plenty regrets."

She went away, came back with a knife in one hand, the shotgun in the other.

"Now, honey, easy with that," Jones said.

"Don't call me honey. Don't never call me that."

She cut the sheet with one quick run of the knife, stepped back, flung the knife onto the floor and pointed the shotgun at him.

"Get up. Put your clothes on, take your shoes and socks with you. Don't come back 'cept to get the rest of your clothes. And don't make it tonight."

Jones sat on the edge of the bed. His body was marked with red striping and he was bleeding from numerous wounds. There was a bruise over his right eye that looked like a grease smear.

"You can't throw me out of my own house."

"I can shoot you all over it. I can do that. Shoot you here. Shoot you over there. I can handle guns. You know that."

"You wouldn't do that, hon—"

"Don't you dare say it. Put on your pants. Sight of you naked makes me sick."

Jones took a deep breath and gathered up his pants, stepped into them, pulled on his shirt. He started to put on his socks.

"Do what I told you. Take them socks and shoes with you. Don't stop for nothing else, or you'll stop forever."

"What about Pete?"

"He ain't going nowhere."

"The funeral."

"You'll hear about it. Come if you want. But don't never plan on coming back here."

"It's my house."

35

"It's as much my house as yours. I earned it, putting up with you. Besides, my daddy owned the mill, and now I own the mill, not you. I'm the one with money."

"You're just upset."

"I'm upset, all right. But I ain't just upset. I'm real upset."

"It'll pass."

"I don't think it will, Mr. Jones. I didn't know I had it wrong until today. Until Sunset killed Pete. I wanted to kill her right then, but it's you I want to kill now."

He looked at her as if he might see someone other than who he expected, but finally determined that it was indeed his wife.

He gathered up his socks and shoes.

"I tell you, you're gonna live to regret this."

"I ain't taking another whipping from you."

"A wife is obedient to her husband."

"I ain't your wife no more."

"In the eyes of God you are."

"Then he better turn his head." She put the shotgun to her shoulder, sighted down the barrels.

"Be careful. That gun's got a hair trigger."

Jones got up and left the room and she followed him.

"Don't stop at nothing," she said.

"I'm gonna look at Pete. You can shoot me if you want. But I'm gonna look at my son."

"Then look."

He pulled the dangling string, which turned on the overhead light, stopped by the cooling board, reached out and touched Pete's face. Before he went out the door he turned, said, "You and that little gal are gonna pay. James Wilson Jones does not forget."

"Then get on out while you got brains in your head to remember with."

"I'm gonna get ice over here. It's too warm for the body. I'll get ice sent over."

"That'll be okay. Now go. And don't you bring it. You get one of the fellas to bring it."

Jones gave her a look she had seen before. Right before a beating he was going to give her. But this time it wasn't going to happen. She felt strange. Good. Powerful. She had not felt this strong since she was a girl.

"Don't think to come back here," she said. "I'll be listening for you. And I won't say a word next time. I'll just shoot. And I want you to know I hate you. I hate everything about you, and have for some time. And today I hate you more than ever."

Jones went out and slammed the door.

Marilyn followed him out, yelled at him as he went down the steps and into the moonlight. "You leave that truck," she said. "I'm gonna need that truck."

He didn't look back at her, just kept walking.

Marilyn went out to the truck, got the keys out of the ignition, brought them inside the house with her.

They had seldom locked their doors here in the camp, but now Marilyn used the house key hanging on a nail beside the door.

As soon as she locked it, she remembered he had a key, so she put a chair under the knob. Tomorrow she'd have to find the camp locksmith, get the locks changed. She bolted all the windows down, locked up the back screen door, pulled the solid door to and put a chair under its knob as well.

She pulled the string on the light, dragged up a chair and sat in the darkness by Pete's body with the shotgun in her lap. She sat there and listened to june bugs beat against the window screen close to her. She could hear them beating even with the window closed. Now that the light was out, she wondered if they would soon stop. As long as she had lived in East Texas, she felt she should know the answer to that, but she couldn't seem to remember anything about june bugs at all.

They finally ceased. The house without the windows open grew warm. Sweat ran down Marilyn's face, into her nightclothes, made her underarms sticky. The house was quiet. In the back room she could hear the grandfather clock ticking.

She wondered where Sunset and Karen were. She hoped they were okay. Then it struck her.

She was hoping the woman who had killed her son was fine.

5

As the sun rose, pink and oozing through the woods like a leaky blood blister, Sunset discovered she too was bleeding. Not only from the wounds Pete had given her, but also from the fresh ones she'd gotten from her daughter, scratches and bites, additional damage from mosquitoes and ants. Sleeping on the ground had gotten dirt in the wounds and made them itch. Her side and stomach hurt, and she didn't even remember being hit there. Maybe had, maybe hadn't, might have just rolled on something, a root or rock.

She was sitting on the bank of Sawmill Creek, where she and Karen had spent the night beneath a big elm tree. She was sitting there feeling the morning sun, looking at her daughter, lying where she had finally cried herself to sleep, angry and confused, her hands clenched, her face squeezed up like a fist, damp leaves mashed against her cheeks and overalls.

Sunset turned away from Karen, studied the creek, watched as black button-sized bugs skirted over the water and some long-legged spider things ran over its surface as if imitating Jesus in a hurry.

The water was clay red from the storm, looked like blood, and it was flowing fast and loud along the new lines of the bank. The tornado had knocked all manner of stuff ass-over-heels, torn up trees, caused the old high line of the embankment to break up. When the warm wind blew, Sunset could smell fish rotting.

She tried to concentrate on the water and not think about Pete, but she couldn't do it. She repeated the events over and over in her mind, trying to find a place where she might have done something different. Kept thinking she'd wake up and it would be a bad dream. But that didn't happen. She was wide awake, sitting on the bank of Sawmill Creek sticky with sweat.

She lifted her hand to wipe her face, discovered she was still holding the gun. She had held it while she was telling her daughter what happened, held it while her daughter, in a moment of savage confusion, had hit her with her fists, clawed her with her nails, and bit her.

When Karen wore out, fell to the ground crying, Sunset tried to comfort her, tried to explain, but Karen put her hands over her ears and made a noise so she wouldn't have to hear it.

Finally, Karen fell asleep to hide from Sunset and the world, and Sunset lay down and slept a little, her finger off the trigger, but the gun still in her hand, the smell of the powder still in her nose, the sound of the shot still in her head.

She put the pistol in the pocket of her mother-in-law's loose housedress, and having it out of her hand, even if it was close, made her nervous.

She was suddenly glad she hadn't had it with her the day she fought Pete's girlfriend, Jimmie Jo French. She found out Pete was running around on her and blamed it on Jimmie Jo. Confronted her out front of the company store at Camp Rapture, went at her like a tiger. If she'd had the pistol with her then, the undertaker might have been wiping Jimmie Jo's ass and that wouldn't have been something she could have lived with, killing Jimmie Jo in a fit of jealousy.

She realized now Jimmie Jo was no more to blame than Pete. What she had been really angry about at the time was she had heard rumor Pete bought Jimmie Jo nice things. Clothes, even

40

jewelry. Pete never bought her anything. She thought for a while she might not be good in bed, and had done her all to fix the problem, thinking she'd make it so he'd like how he was getting it at home and get over Jimmie Jo, but that hadn't changed things. He stayed angry all the time, slapping her, punching her, forcing her legs apart while he rammed her like he was trying to poke a hole through a concrete wall, and if he liked it, she couldn't tell, it was just a thing he did, finishing up, getting off her like he was disgusted.

And he hadn't given up Jimmie Jo. Sometimes he came in smelling of her, not even bothering to clean the smell off before coming home, not caring if she knew, maybe happy she did. Sunset could never figure for what crime she was being punished.

Sunset wondered where Jimmie Jo was now. If she'd heard about Pete being killed, and how she felt about it. "Howdy."

Sunset looked up. A man was standing nearby. Sunset stood, felt like wires were being pulled inside of her and the wires had hooks and the hooks were hitched to her vitals.

She studied him. He didn't look like trouble. They never look like trouble, she thought. Pete hadn't looked like trouble when he started courting her when she was sixteen. He seemed fine enough and a good choice when they first married, until two weeks later, the night she had a cold and didn't want to bed him and he made her, and made her many times thereafter.

She put her hand in her pocket. She was glad she had the gun.

"You two hoboing?" the man said. "Don't see many women on the road."

Sunset said, "We're not on the road."

"That's good. You're a good bit away from the rails."

"So are you," she said.

41

"Guess I am."

The man wore a crumpled wool hat. It looked too big for him. He took it off and smiled at her. She noted he was nice-looking and maybe not as young as he first appeared. He had a little sack tied to his belt. Over one eye was a small black bruise.

"I'm looking for work. Some bo's told me there was a sawmill hiring."

"I don't know if they're hiring," Sunset said, "but you follow the creek west a ways, and you'll see it."

She started to say he would have to talk to her father-in-law, Mr. Jones, or the Captain, but she couldn't make the words come out. He wasn't her father-in-law now. She didn't have anyone but Karen and Karen hated her. Well, maybe she had Marilyn. The whole thing with Marilyn hitting her, then hugging her, had not quite registered yet.

"That girl," he said, "she ain't dead, is she? You didn't shoot her? I seen you put that gun in your pocket. You ain't gonna shoot me, are you?"

"That's my daughter. She's sleeping. We had a storm come through. Tore up our home."

"Reckon I caught the tail end of that one. I was in a boxcar at the time. Kind of scared me. Thought the damn thing was gonna turn over. You hunting? A pistol ain't the best for squirrels."

"No. I'm not hunting."

"Well, nice to meet you. If your daughter was awake I'd say nice to meet her. Storm bang you up like that?"

"It was a storm, all right."

"My name's Hillbilly."

"Mine's Sunset. Daughter's name is Karen."

"You sure got pretty hair. Your daughter's got pretty hair too, but it ain't the same as yours. Yours is fire, hers is a raven's wing."

"She got her daddy's hair," Sunset said.

"Reckon I'll go on now, see if I can get that job."

"You don't look like a sawmill hand."

"Ain't. Just need work. I'm a musician. I sing and play guitar."

"Where's your guitar?"

"Got broken. I'm trying to make enough to buy me one."

"Good luck."

"Thanks. See you around?"

Sunset thought a moment. She really wasn't sure about anything, but she said, "Yeah. I'll be around. See me again, hope I'll look better than I look now. I'm not normally this ugly."

"And I'm not normally this dirty. But I'm always this ugly."

She thought: False modesty. He knows he looks good.

Hillbilly tipped his hat. "Well, you take care now."

And away he went.

The sun grew large and yellow as the yolk of a fresh egg, turned the air hot as a gasoline fire. The heat stuck in the woods like glue, became gummy, and the gum got all over God and creation.

By ten in the morning every working man in the camp was exhausted, underarms dripping with sweat, crotches itching with it. Water barrels were sucked dry and the mules wanted to give it up. Even the oxen, normally steady as Job, were starting to wobble and froth.

That morning Jones had ice delivered to his house in washtubs, sent over a temporary basket coffin he borrowed from the camp store's owner. The basket coffin was put on the sitting room floor by Zack and another colored man named Hently, and they poured ice from the tubs into it. They removed Pete's clothes, and his smell filled the room. They placed him on the ice in the basket and put ice on top of him until the odor was quenched and he could not be seen, except for one finger that

43

extended from the chipped ice and pointed up, as if the corpse were about to make a suggestion.

Over at the mill houses, unlike usual, no one was talking about the heat.

"I don't think a woman ought to just be able to shoot a husband, she wants to," Bill Martin said. "Get that started, things in ever kind of way will get turned over and sat on. Hell, get so I tell my wife to get my breakfast ready, she'll want to pull out a gun."

"Working with you," said Don Walker, "makes me want to shoot you sometimes."

"You're a regular Fibber McGee. Except you ain't funny."

Bill and Don hooked their mules to a sled full of logs. Don called to the mules, Hank and Wank, and they started to pull the sled away. Don and Bill stood out to the side and Don held the long reins and they walked alongside the mules as they pulled.

"Haw, you sorry bastards," Don said to the mules, and the mules turned left.

Bill said, "You ought not talk to the boys like that."

"These boys are lazy if you let 'em be."

They met Hillbilly coming toward them. He smiled and waved a hand at them. Don pulled the mules to a halt.

"Excuse me," Hillbilly said, "but I'm looking for work."

"We ain't the ones to talk to," Bill said.

"Do you know who to talk to?"

"The Captain," Don said. "But now ain't a good time."

"When will be?"

"Ain't certain. His boy, Pete, got killed yesterday."

"Accident?"

"Not unless you call getting shot in the head an accident," Bill said. "Boy's wife shot him. Pete was the constable."

"Why'd she do it?"

"I hear he was beating on her."

"Can't say I blame her then," Hillbilly said. "I don't like a hand laid on me in anger."

"She was his wife," Bill said.

"Don't give him no call for that," Hillbilly said.

"What I been saying," Don said. "Been telling Bill just that."

"This woman shot him," Hillbilly said. "She wouldn't be a redhead, would she?"

"Hair don't get no redder than hers," Bill said. "How'd you know?"

"Just a guess," Hillbilly said. "Redheads are known for shooting husbands."

"I know a redhead that was known for other things," Bill said. "Talk about fire in the hole."

"All your goats got black or white or gray fur," Don said. "Ain't seen no redheaded ones, so you don't know nothing there."

"Keep telling you," Bill said, "you ought to get on radio you're so funny." Bill turned back to Hillbilly, said, "Good luck, young man. Maybe the Captain will talk to you. We did lose a man last week."

"Tree fell on him," Don said. "Me and Bill had bets on how long before that ignorant sonofabitch got a tree on him. He'd cut and kind of saunter away when the tree was coming down. He sauntered a little slow last time. Tree jumped back on him. They'll do that. Jump back. Drove that fella into the ground. Said the stuffing popped out of him like a Christmas turkey."

"You got to be quick working here," Bill said. "Not get no vines or limbs caught under your feet. I think that fella got some berry vines wrapped around his ankles. Get hired and don't mind your work, you'll be dead as him."

"Thanks for the advice, gentlemen," Hillbilly said. "If I was to talk to this Captain, where would I find him?"

"He ain't staying at his house no more," Bill said. "His wife done run him off and took sides with the daughter-in-law. He was in the mill house this morning, wearing the same old nasty clothes he had on yesterday. I don't know that he's really working. When you're one of the big men, you can coast, your boy's dead or not. You might have to talk to someone else about a job, though. There's others can hire.

"It's all a crying shame. Captain with his boy dead, his wife putting him out. He's a nice guy too. He loaned me considerable money I ain't paid back—"

"And don't intend to pay back," Don said.

"You don't know that," Bill said.

"You ain't paid me the dollar you owe me."

"I'm gonna. But I tell you, I owed his old lady, I don't know. She didn't want him to loan it to me. Said I was a bad risk."

"You are," Don said. "I want my dollar. I know that."

"She said that right in front of me. A bad risk. Tell you, with this Sunset killing her husband, and him a law too, we don't put an end to it, every woman in the camp and hereabouts is gonna feel they got the right to tell their men what-for over most anything they take a mind to. If it's loaning money or holding out with the hot wet kitty."

"Sunset," Hillbilly said. "That's what they call her?"

"On account of her long red hair," Don said. "Before Pete whacked on her, she was a pretty good looker. Now she looks like Three-Fingered Jack looked."

"Who?"

"Man took a beating from Pete," Bill said. "But he died from it. They called him that cause he had three fingers."

Hillbilly thought: No shit.

"This time it was Pete done the dying," Don said. "I ain't one

46

to feel sorry for him. Beating on a woman ain't right. Unless, of course, it's a whore. I had one take a couple dollars from me once, and when I got hold of her she got hers, that's what I'm trying to tell you. Her face looked like a speckled pup I got through whapping her."

"What about a place to live?" Hillbilly asked. He had looked the camp over. All of the houses seemed occupied and close enough together a man wanted to fuck his next-door neighbor's wife, all he had to do was hang his dick out the window, she hang her ass out of hers.

"There ain't really no places near. You can rent a tent from the camp store, make you a spot down the road a piece in the pines there. They ain't gonna cut them trees for a few years. Too damn small."

"Thanks again," Hillbilly said, and wandered toward the mill house.

Just before he got there, it occurred to him he had been curious but had forgotten to ask why this Pete had given Three-Fingered Jack a beating in the first place.

He thought too about the redhead by the creek, knew she was the one who shot this Pete.

It was odd to realize she and he were both killers.

Sunset lay back down after Hillbilly left. She did so with the intention of resting a moment, but surprised herself by falling asleep. She awoke from her nap with a hand stroking her cheek.

For a moment she thought it was Pete, in one of his rare sweet moods, but then she remembered it couldn't be Pete.

It was Karen.

"I didn't mean to say all them things, Mama."

Sunset managed to sit up. She had her hand in her dress pocket, had hold of the revolver. It was hard to open her hand

and let it go. She had slept with it in her fist, her finger out of the trigger guard, just holding it by the hilt as if it were a club. She had held it so long and hard her hand was cramping and for a long moment she couldn't extend her fingers.

"I just couldn't take the beating," Sunset said. "Wasn't the first one he give me, Karen. You just didn't know about it. He hit me so it wouldn't show. Except this time. He was a good daddy to you, but he wasn't no kind of husband to me."

"Why did he do it, Mama? What did you do to make him hit you?"

"What did I do? If I'd have done something, got crazy mad, started beating on him and he got crazy too, I could forgive that and understand. Maybe I could understand if something bad happened to him that was my fault, or he was sick and not thinking clear, but it wasn't nothing like that. Wasn't just him hitting out at me. He really went to work on me. Did it because he liked to do it."

Karen hung her head. "He didn't never hit me. You're the only one ever spanked me."

"He loved you. He adored you."

Sunset put her arm around her daughter's shoulders. Karen let it rest there.

"He always told me good night," Karen said. "He can't do that no more. We can't go fishing no more. And we always sang together. He taught me to sing. Said I was as good as Sara Carter."

"Better."

"You could have done something else. Didn't have to kill him. You could have just left him."

"I was going to, but I didn't know how to tell you. Wish I had told you. It's better than having to tell you what I told you last night. And I couldn't just go and leave when it was happening,

48

baby. Right then he wasn't letting me go nowhere. I was afraid he got through I wouldn't go nowhere again, ever. Look at my face, child."

Karen turned to look. Sunset noted, painfully, that Karen resembled her father.

"My nose is broken, my lips are busted up. Lucky I got all my teeth. Can barely see out of my left eye. Think your daddy loved me, Karen?"

Karen started to cry, laid her head against her mother. Sunset held her like that for a long time.

When Karen stopped crying, Sunset said, "Your daddy wasn't always bad to me. We had some good times. I loved him once. And I know he loved me. We met when I was sixteen and he was nineteen. That was too young. But we wanted one another and thought what we had was love, and it was, of a kind. But it was young love. We just wanted to play house, Karen. Thought being in bed together every night was love. Hear me? Keep that in mind you get all tied up with some boy and think you just can't live without him around you and in you."

"Mama, don't talk like that."

"That's the truth, and I got to talk that way now. We ain't got time for pretty words, just the truth. You save yourself from getting married till you're old enough to know who and what you want. That Jerry Flynn you're seeing. He's a good boy. But you're too young to think about marriage, and so's he."

"I ain't said nothing about marriage."

"No. But you could be thinking it. I thought it when I was your age. Got married and your daddy wasn't through with other women. He wouldn't never have been through with other women. I don't know any more to say. Wouldn't know what to say he died some other kind of way. But like this. There ain't no words . . . Do you hate me?"

Karen shook her head. "I don't know how I feel . . . What we gonna do now?"

"You could go to your grandma's. You could stay there till I could figure some things out."

"I don't want to go there by myself."

"You been there by yourself plenty."

"I know. But Daddy's there. Can't we just go home?"

"There ain't any home, Karen. It blowed away."

"Can't we just go there anyway?"

"If I can walk that far. I'm getting so stiff I can hardly move. Get there, all you're gonna find is the house is blowed away. There's just the floor."

"I want to go."

They walked out to the road, caught a ride with a man driving a rickety transport truck full of squawking chickens. The man, who had four teeth poorly arranged in his mouth, looked at Sunset when she climbed in next to him, Karen by the passenger door. He said, "You been in some kind of accident?"

"You could say that," Sunset said.

The man drove them most of the distance and let them out where they didn't have to walk too far, which suited Sunset fine.

When they got there it was noon and they were both hungry and had nothing to eat. As Sunset had said, there was only the floor left and a few items strewn about. The chicken house out back was gone, except for two posts with a tangle of net wire between them and a twist of feathers and meat where the storm had driven a chicken through it. The outhouse was gone too, leaving only the deep pit full of stinking waste. The yard was no longer littered with fish. There were a few left and they had dried up and shriveled in the sun and they stunk to high heaven. As for the rest of the fish, it was obvious what had happened to most of them. There were coon tracks in the dirt where they had come to feed. It looked like every coon in East Texas had attended a shindig there, dancing and leaping to cricket-leg music by the light of the moon.

In the not too distant trees they could see clothes and lumber and snarled limbs. There was a gap where trees had been knocked down by the tornado, and there was the overturned car wedged between two abused oak trees.

The walk had actually helped Sunset. She was moving more easily, feeling some oil in her joints, but she was tired and ready to rest. They sat on the flooring of the house and looked around.

Karen said, "I don't know what I expected. You told me it was all gone."

"Yeah, honey. Long gone."

"I'm so hungry."

"We can pick blackberries."

They went down by the creek where the berry vines grew thick and picked some blackberries and ate them as they went. The berries were warm and sweet and the vines were close to the ground. While they picked they were cautious to watch for snakes. After a while they went back to the flooring and sat on the edge of it and looked out at the day as the sun staggered past noon and began to tumble to the other side of the sky like a ball rolling downhill.

When Sunset felt strong again, they went and looked at the car. No doubt about it, it was ruined. Pete's files were strewn around it. Sunset began picking them up.

"These might be important to the next constable," she said.

Karen helped her. They tried putting the files back inside the wooden file cabinet, but it was too busted up. They gathered all the files, even those still in the cabinet, and put them in the car.

About two in the afternoon they went to sit on the flooring

of the house again. Karen sang, a little halfheartedly, but her voice when it was perking was really sharp, and Sunset thought: Yeah, she's good as Sara Carter, but with less nose in the notes.

After a while a truck came clattering down the little road in front of the house. Sunset looked up, saw the driver was her mother-in-law.

Karen broke and ran toward the truck, yelling, "Grandma."

Sunset said, "Watch you don't get run over."

The truck slowed and stopped. Karen jerked open the door, grabbed her grandma and hugged her.

Sunset walked over, said, "How'd you know we was here?"

"Where else was you gonna go? Don't you think you ought to come home?"

"I don't think Mr. Jones would like that."

"Honey, far as I'm concerned, there ain't no Mr. Jones no more."

6

When they arrived at Marilyn's house the body was in the basket and it was covered with a scrap quilt. Karen said, "I want to see him."

"I thought you didn't," Sunset said.

"I do now."

"You're sure?" Marilyn asked.

"No. But I want to see him."

"All right, baby," Marilyn said. "I fixed him best could be done. He ain't dressed now. But he's covered in ice. I'll show you his face."

Marilyn lifted the quilt and they took off the basket lid. Marilyn raked ice away from Pete's face. Sunset stared at the candle wax pushed into the bullet hole. Marilyn had added some rouge to Pete's cheeks and a touch of lipstick to his lips, powder to the rest of his face. This had been done before the ice, and the ice had turned it all to a mess. Sunset thought Pete looked like someone about to try out for the circus.

"It's kind of overdone," Marilyn said. "But he looked so pale. So blue around the lips. The ice messed it up. I didn't know at the time we were gonna put him on ice. I'll redo him before the funeral."

"Cover him," Karen said, and staggered off toward the sleeping porch. About the time she made it there, she began to cry.

Sunset started that way, but Marilyn caught her by the arm. "She needs to be let alone for a bit."

Sunset nodded.

Marilyn pushed ice over Pete's face, put the lid on the basket with Sunset's help. They covered the basket with the quilt.

Sunset swallowed, said, "Can you have me around? Knowing I done this?"

"Come on, girl. Let's go on the porch and sit."

They sat on the warm front steps and from there they could see the men and animals working at the mill. They could hear the saws whining, especially the Big Saw in the Big Saw House. The air was stuffed with the sappy smell of fresh-cut sawdust and the black smoke from the power house and the gray smoke from the drying kilns. The sunlight shining through smoke and sawdust made the air over the mill, and much of the camp, look green, but where the smoke was thin, some of the tin roofs caught the sun and threw it back to the sky in a silver flash that made Sunset squint.

She reminded herself that Mr. Jones was not far away, up there in the Big Saw House most likely, doing paperwork to the grinding sound of the saw. He did a lot of that these days, a lot less of the hard manual labor, a lot more of the firing and hiring and distribution of lumber. He had earned the right, she supposed.

She idly wondered if the man she had met by the creek had actually asked for a job. He may have been a hobo, but he didn't look like it. His clothes were not perfect, but she could tell right off he was a man who cared about his appearance, and he had a good one. She could tell too that he would only work hard work if he had to. He was not the kind of man who looked forward to a life holding a plow, stepping in mule mess, or working at a sawmill, for that matter.

There was something about that that appealed to her.

Then she thought: If I am such a good judge of character, then why did I marry Pete?

Marilyn said, "When I was a girl my great-granddaddy decided lumber was the future. He was born up North but moved to East Texas and went to work here doing farmwork. He looked around, saw this land was full of houses yet to be cut, and thought the thing to do was to start up a mill business. This was in about nineteen ten. He come here and took it over from a few loggers who cut trees and hauled them all the way to Nacogdoches. He hired them to work for him, instead of freelancing. He put in a real mill, and the mill took. It made money and he got rich. I own a big chunk of that mill, along with Jones, and Henry Shelby. You know all this."

"I do. Except I didn't know you owned part of the mill. I guess I should have, but I hadn't thought about it. I don't think about women owning much of anything. I just figured Jones owned all your share when he married you."

"Here's some more things you don't know. You don't know that my daddy liked Jones all right at first, but later not so much, so he made a contract that says if I ever decide, for whatever reason, to not want Jones to have any part of the mill, I can make that decision. Cause Henry married Daddy's sister, Henry gets his share no matter what."

"Are you saying you're going to fire Jones?" Sunset said.

"No. I even plan on letting him keep a large part of the mill. Less than before, but a large part. He's earned that."

Sunset nodded, not exactly sure where this was going, why Marilyn was telling her stuff she already knew, even why she was telling her stuff she didn't know. She could hardly look at her mother-in-law without feeling like she wanted to burst out crying.

"I met Jones when we come here from Arkansas, and I wasn't nothing but a girl and he wanted to marry. Wanted to get into a family had money. Mine had money cause of the mill. I

55

think I knew that then, that he wanted to marry me because of the money, but I didn't care. I thought Jones was a good man. But he wasn't. He beat me. Of course, you know what that's like, don't you? I wanted to make the marriage work. I was told a woman made the marriage work. That it didn't matter how many whores your husband laid with, if he beat you or cussed you, or whatever, you made it work, you made it work for the children.

"Pete, he growed up seeing his daddy talk to me a kind of way you wouldn't talk to a dog, and he seen his daddy 'correct' me, as Jones liked to call it."

"That's what Pete called it," Sunset said.

"I took it, because I was making my marriage work. What I was doing was teaching my son to be like his father. Now, his father has good points. He's a hard worker, and he never just laid back and lived off money that was mine cause of who I was. He liked the fact it got him a position in the mill. Position was everything to him. Big man. Big house. Big job. Wife that knows her place and a good strapping son that doesn't take anything from anybody. Jones had other good points. He treated Pete well. He got angry, he didn't take it out on Pete, he took it out on me. Jones was strong too, and when I was younger, I liked that. A strong man. Later, when he held me down and did what he wanted, I wasn't so proud of him being strong. I loved him once."

"I loved Pete once."

"I know you did. I saw the light in your eyes."

"He was good sometimes. He could be funny when he wasn't mad, and he had a fine voice. He was good to Karen, and she has a good voice too. He taught her to sing. But he had spells. Ways."

Marilyn nodded.

"I thought Pete wouldn't be like his daddy, but I was wrong. Another trait Jones has is he's hung like a horse. But I never really got to enjoy it. He just sort of jumped on me and did it, you know. If I'd have blinked, I'd have missed it."

Sunset blushed. She had never heard a woman discuss such things, and had certainly not expected it from her mother-in-law.

Well, she thought. In for a penny, in for a pound.

"Pete got that trait. The horse part. And the jump on you part. He didn't ever love me good but once. And I reckon that's the reason Karen was born from it. He wanted other babies, but I didn't never take again and didn't want to. With him it was like I was some kind of breeding stock."

"You not getting pregnant again shows God watches out for good folks."

Sunset thought: He was watching out for me, he wouldn't have let me marry that sonofabitch Pete Jones in the first place. And when he mounted me, God would surely have made it more fun.

She remembered that every time Pete finished, he made a little noise like a sick mouse trying to clear its throat. It came out when he finished. His hips died and the sick mouse went to work. A kind of cough followed by a soft choking sound, like maybe there were cobwebs down there. Then silence, and drool along her shoulder. She never did figure what that was about, the mouse sound, but it was constant and Sunset wondered if he did it with his whores and mistresses. Mount them, squirt, and make that little sick-mouse noise.

"Reckon you're wondering what I'm leading up to here," Marilyn said.

"I know Mr. Jones is gone," Sunset said. "I know that."

"Last night I had enough. That boy in there, he wouldn't be dead today had I not taken that hitting business from Jones without fighting back. Had I stood up for myself or took Pete and left, it wouldn't have happened.

"I didn't want my boy dead, Sunset, but I figure I'm to blame as much as Jones. I know you done what you had to do. Last night, I near done it to Jones. You hadn't done what you did, you might have got killed, and in time Jones might have killed me. I reckon he'd finally got too old to have the full fire in him, but he had enough to hurt me. Had days when hurting me made him feel better. He'd say I was off with some man, when he knew I wasn't and couldn't have been, cause I had been around all day. But reason had nothing to do with it.

"When I saw Pete in there, it all come to the surface, and I had had enough. I didn't care about making nothing work no more. I sewed Jones to the bed while he was sleeping and beat him with a yard rake."

"A rake?"

"That's right. Then I got Jones' shotgun and I sent him packing."

"What are you going to do now?"

"What are we both going to do now? I suppose we'll stay here together. I got money, dear. And I got me a resolve now. That's the word, ain't it?"

"I don't know."

"Yeah. That's what I got. A resolve. I haven't felt this good and strong in years."

"I can't live on your money, Marilyn, and won't."

"Don't be too high and mighty. What else you going to do?"

"I'll do something."

"It's best for Karen you live here. In time, you'll find another husband, or if you're lucky, maybe you won't."

"All men can't be that way."

"My experience is limited, and not good."

"I want to work, Marilyn. I want my own money for me and Karen, and I don't want to be dependent on a man. I been in that situation, and I didn't like it none."

"That ain't easy to do, dear. Not unless you're willing to accept my taking care of you until you can do better."

Sunset said, "I don't know if Karen will ever really forgive me."

"She ought to. I have. I don't like the fact my boy's lying in there dead, but I don't want to lose you and my granddaughter too. We're gonna do okay, Sunset. I promise. Know what?"

"What?"

"We need to go inside and let me work on that face of yours. I got some stuff will help take the bruising out and bring the swelling down. And I got some clothes might fit you better than those I gave you. I wasn't always so thick in the middle. Come on, dear."

Marilyn stood, smiled, held out her hand, and Sunset, after a brief pause, took it.

The funeral was on a little hill under a large oak. Pete was buried near the oak, next to the grave of Jones' mother and father, not far from the unmarked grave of a family hound that had traveled with them all the way from up North, then to Nacogdoches, and Camp Rapture, and finally, at the ripe old dog age of fifteen, had choked to death on a chicken bone at a family celebration.

The crowd was large. Many were there because they knew Pete, and many were there because it was the polite thing to do and there was not much else happening. They knew that afterward, at Marilyn's house, there would be lots of food brought by women from all over the camp.

Sunset didn't attend. Karen went to the funeral with her grandmother. Mr. Jones came, stood on the opposite side of the grave. He gave a good-soldier smile to his granddaughter, and she smiled at him. When he looked at his wife, the smile went away.

The preacher said good things about Pete and wished him to heaven, then the crowd walked away and two colored men, hired on for the day, threw dirt over the coffin.

There was a gathering at the Jones house. There was food and there was talk about Pete. About how brave he was. The times he did this or that. And there was the story of Three-Fingered Jack, of course. Finally the talk turned to crops and animals, the tornado, and the mill. Gradually that petered out, and everyone came by and spoke kindly to the family and left.

In the end, there was only Marilyn and Karen and Jones.

"There ain't no way we can get past this?" Jones asked.

"Karen," Marilyn said, "you run out so the adults can talk."

Karen hugged her grandfather, then, reluctantly, left.

"Can't believe you're doing me this way," Jones said, "after all these years being together, and our boy dead too."

"Should have done it years ago."

"I ought to slap your face, woman."

"Want your granddaughter to know how you treat me? She don't know that. I told her I just wasn't happy with you being around. But I didn't tell her the whole of it. Hit me now and hear me scream all over camp. I held it all them times before, but no more. You want that on the day we put our boy down?"

"I didn't never mean nothing by it."

"It meant something to me."

"You're letting that murderer stay here?"

"She did what she had to."

"How can you say such a thing?"

"Go, Jones."

Jones took his hat from the chair beside the door, where he always put it, placed it on his head and went out. Then he came back. He said, "This ain't over, you know. Not between me and Sunset, not between me and you."

He went away. She could hear his heavy boots pounding on the porch and down the steps. She stood at the screen door and watched him walk away. She was surprised to discover it hurt her to see him look so sad and small, his feet throwing up clouds of dust.

7

Henry Shelby and the camp elders came to see and talk to Jones late on a Friday afternoon, two weeks after Pete went into the ground. They thought it was past time to decide on a new constable for the camp and the surrounding area, so this meant a meeting was in order, and these meetings were always held at the Jones house, as it was the largest in the community, except for Henry Shelby's house, and Henry's wife didn't allow company because she drank.

Wasn't she didn't want folks there because they might see her drunk. She didn't want them because they might interrupt her drinking. Or she might have to put clothes on, being as she liked to drink naked, though she was prone to wearing one shoe from time to time. She once told Henry it made her feel closer to nature doing her drinking that way. Like maybe at birth everyone was squirted out with a birthday suit and a fifth of whisky, and one shoe.

Henry didn't like seeing his wife naked. She had been sweet when young, a lean-limbed woman with a peach between her legs. Now, when she sat, or when she stood for that matter, she looked like a pile of something, and the peach between her legs had become a rotten persimmon.

Still, he preferred her drunk. Kept her out of touch. Back when she was in touch, she always seemed on the verge of a hysterical fit or a case of the vapors. Always on him about some damn woman he was giving the eye, or about his own drinking, which was minimal to hers, or about his clothes, or how his hair had gone gray, as if he could help it, and did he have to carve the bunions off his feet with a pocketknife.

The alcohol had burned all that out of her.

She quit complaining.

She hadn't even complained when she heard her kin, Jones, had been shot by his wife. She was so far gone she just said, "Who?" Didn't attend the funeral. Stayed home naked and drunk, wearing that one shoe, scratching her back and no telling what else, with a stretched-out wire coat hanger.

Henry hoped his wife didn't have a lot of world time left. Hoped the time she did have she would stay drunk. Drinking all the time, he figured she was doing bad things to her liver. You can't live long with a bad liver. He'd always heard that, and he was counting on it. He had noticed a kind of yellow look to her complexion of late, and thought it might be due to some kind of jaundice from drinking. Then again, it could be from irregular bathing. The rolls of fat certainly held the odor, and sometimes when she moved, it was like shaking out a huge rug that had been wadded and mildewed.

But now the meeting was on Henry's mind. Not a pleasant matter, but more pleasant than thinking about his wife. He hadn't pushed the matter of the meeting before because of Jones. Didn't want to replace Pete too quick, as if he had never mattered. Not with Jones being a prominent person at the mill and in the camp, and his wife being someone who owned a large portion of the mill. That wouldn't be smart.

But now it was time, and Henry, along with the elders, decided to pursue the matter.

Jones was at his desk in the Big Saw House. His desk was not far from the saw, and Jones stuck cotton in his left ear, which faced the saw, to pacify the noise. At the end of the day, when the saw was turned off, it took an hour to stop hearing the grind of it.

When the elders came in, Jones turned his right ear toward them, listened carefully, nodded, went back to his paperwork. The elders, who had brought the proposition to him, this business about a new constable and how the camp needed to decide on someone and vote, stood for a while waiting for Jones to respond, until they realized he was no longer paying attention and had forgotten they were there.

Quietly, Henry and the others went out, shaking their heads.

Out of earshot, Henry said, "He's popped his top."

They hadn't been gone fifteen minutes when Jones finished up the last of his paperwork, some lumber orders for a town in Oklahoma, got up and wandered over to where the great circular saw was cutting pine with a loud buzz and a spray of sawdust and splinters.

Jones watched it whirl and cut for a long time. Watched as men loaded logs on the conveyor and the logs were split by the saw and they fell to each side and were moved along to be planed and prepared. He thought about Sunset, thought about Marilyn and Karen, but mostly he thought about Pete. It was on a day like this, hot and lazy, when the blood ran slow, that he had liked to take Pete fishing.

Jones wished Pete were alive so they could go fishing now. He would throw down everything if he could go fishing one more time with his son.

Jones was glad now that Sunset had shown no interest in him. He had hoped at some point she would let him into her pants. He thought his boy had made a mistake marrying Sunset, coming from the background she had, though he could understand why he would want to, way she looked, those long sleek legs, that fiery red hair, those fine, high titties. He thought maybe she would give it up for him the way she had for his son, but she didn't. Surprised him by taking her wedding vows seriously.

Now, all things considered, he was glad she had resisted him. He didn't like to think he might have taken pleasure from the pink little wound of a woman who killed his son.

In the last couple of days, he had gone from being sharp with grief to being dull with it. He felt like something small trapped in a corked bottle, a moth beating against the glass while the air was breathed up.

When a new pine log rolled onto the conveyor belt, Jones carefully removed the cotton from his left ear and climbed on top of the log and lay down on his back as if to nap, head toward the saw. He lay there and felt the hard bark through his shirt, listened to the saw whine. It made his eardrums throb, but he did nothing to protect them. He found he was pushing his head hard against the log, trying to see the blade by looking back, but he couldn't see it. He finally closed his eyes and the sound of the saw grew, became so loud he thought his eardrums would burst. He heard a man yell and heard men running toward him and he felt the log beneath him start to split as it went into the saw and he felt sawdust on his face and he knew he had won and that the great teeth of the saw would give him rest before the men could reach him.

By the time it was realized what he was doing, Jones was in the saw. The mew of the saw on skull and meat sounded different from the way it sounded when a log was cut, and unlike a log, it didn't cut smooth. The blade caught Jones' skull and whipped him around, snapping his neck. The lower part of his body swung into the blade. The saw teeth got hold of his khakis and snatched them off and wadded them up. The saw jammed, spraying Jones all over the Big Saw House. The saw screeched and wobbled and started to come loose, then someone who was thinking jumped for the switch and cut it off. When the saw died the air was so still it hurt the men's ears as much as the whine of the blade had.

Zack, who worked with a great hook on a long pole to feed the logs onto the conveyor belt, saw it happen. For years after, he said a man's sap sprayed even worse than a fresh pine log. He helped get what was left of Jones out of the saw with his hook and his bare hands. Later, he got the job of cleaning and re-oiling the saw. He found Jones' wedding ring caught up on one of the teeth. It was hooked there as if it had been placed carefully for safekeeping while Jones washed his hands or wiped his ass.

Zack thought about giving it to Mrs. Jones, then thought it might be better to take it into town and sell it. But if someone found out he sold the ring, it could go bad for him. So he put the ring in one of Jones' boots after removing what was left of ankle and foot. Interestingly enough, both boots were in good shape. No cuts or tears. Just bloody inside.

Later that night, at home, Zack thought about the beating Pete had given him and the way Jones had made him carry the body back. He thought about the ring again and wished he had kept it.

A week later, when Zack found a chunk of Jones, possibly a testicle, under a log fragment in the mill house, he kicked it around a while before using a stick to toss it out to the one-eyed stray cat that hung around the mill.

The cat took it in its mouth and ran away with it into the woods.

Marilyn got the news. She got Jones' boots, but not the clothes. The clothes were too much of a mess to return. She found the ring in the bottom of one of the bloody boots. She put the ring back in the boot, took it out back of the house, got down on her knees and buried it next to the chicken pen, crying as she did.

Sunset and Karen, standing amidst Marilyn's houseplants, watched her do this from the sleeping porch. The plants were tired-looking and slightly brown, needed watering. Sunset set it in her mind to water them and to clean up a dried dirt ring at her feet, the remains of a pot and plant now missing, probably dead and tossed.

"I can't believe it," Karen said. "Daddy, and now Grandpa. He couldn't live without her. She shouldn't have kicked him out."

"Maybe he couldn't live with himself," Sunset said.

"I think he loved her. I think he missed her."

"I think he missed having someone to hit."

Couple days after the funeral there was a camp meeting. As expected, it was held at the Jones house, though the church was briefly considered.

But as Willie Fixx, the preacher, veterinarian and part-time doctor, pointed out, "It's hot in there."

Henry Shelby called the meeting.

After a short day at the mill, six in the afternoon, they gathered there. All the men came directly from work and they stunk like dogs that had rolled in shit.

Sunset and Karen went around the house and opened windows, but it didn't help much. The air outside was stiff and heavy with humidity. It seemed to hold the stink in the room as if it were plugging the windows with its weight.

All of the men were white. Coloreds were not allowed at the meetings and had no say in the matter. Many of the men were shy a finger or two, and in some cases a thumb. The saws liked little sacrifices.

Sunset stood at the back of the room with Karen, watching.

She had on one of her mother-in-law's sundresses and she had a big black belt around her waist, and the revolver was conspicuously poking in the belt. She knew it was silly, but she never let that gun get too far away from her.

Sunset's head turned as Hillbilly came into the room. Someone had hired him, maybe her father-in-law, or Henry. When he came in he entered like a king. You almost expected someone to roll out a red carpet in front of him.

He stood at the back of the room opposite her and Karen, leaning against a wall, giving it a sweat stain. Even dirty and sweaty, with sawdust in his hair, his cap in his hand, she thought he looked pretty good. She tried to decide if he was twenty-five or a beautiful thirty-five.

Sunset watched the men idle about for a while, shaking hands, making sure to tell Marilyn how sorry they were about Mr. Jones.

Henry Shelby went up front. He had a way of walking that made you think of a man pinching something vital with his ass. He had on a black suit that smelled of naphtha. All of his suits smelled that way. His white shirt looked yellow in the overhead light. His black tie was wilted and fell over his chest like a strangled man's tongue.

Henry said, "Let's call this meeting to order."

The men sat.

Henry looked about, eyeing the camp elders. He said, "We're not going to bother with minutes or any fooferah, we're going to get right to it. Everyone knows why we're here. With Pete gone, it's time to elect a new constable. Things have got rowdy out in the community of late. Been a run on chicken stealing, for one. My chickens. And I want the hound that done it arrested."

A few men laughed.

Henry grinned, feeling like he had made a pretty good joke.

"Truth is," he said, "the community is growing. I think in a year or so, maybe less time than that, we're gonna come together with Holiday and make a real town. Holiday wants to expand, and they've found oil over there. Oil is bringing in money, just like the mill. And it's bringing in all kinds of lowlifes too. Gamblers, whores—"

A couple of men cheered.

"Very funny," Henry said, realizing a couple of them knew how well he knew the whores. "It's also bringing in grifters, thugs, you name it. Things are gonna get more out of hand, and instead of just having a constable here, a sheriff is gonna be needed eventually, and if Rapture and Holiday come together, there'll be just one law. Maybe a chief of police, some deputies. If it don't happen, we still need a constable around the community here. Now, I think it ought to be a young man, but not too young, and I think—"

"Henry," Marilyn said, "I think someone else might have ideas."

Henry turned, saw Marilyn sitting on a chair near the wall. "I'm sorry, Marilyn. You got someone in mind?"

"I do."

"Well, go on. Give us who you think."

"Sunset."

The room went silent.

"What do you mean, Sunset?" Henry said.

"I mean Sunset for constable."

Sunset said, "What?"

"That's right," Marilyn said. "You, dear."

"Me?" Sunset said. For a moment, she thought she might pee herself.

"Sunset helped Pete keep records. Knew all about who was who. Didn't you, Sunset?"

"Well, yeah . . . I kept some records. Some."

69

"You see," Marilyn said.

Henry didn't see. There were murmurs in the crowd. Henry said, "We know you're upset over all this, but—"

"She should take over the job until Pete's term is finished," Marilyn said. "You aren't forgetting he still had a year on his term?"

"But . . . he's dead," Henry said.

Marilyn's face reddened. "I'm fully aware of that, Henry. Fully. But he had a year. That means whoever you pick takes his place until the year's out. That's the way it was worked up in the Camp Rapture charter. Sunset here can take his place, at his community pay, and at the end of the year, she wants to run for the job, she can."

"But she's a woman," Henry said.

"She is at that," Marilyn said. "Ain't like a puppy. Don't have to turn her over to know what kind of thing she's got down there."

There were laughs in the crowd.

"Would you say Pete was tough?" Marilyn said.

"Yeah," Henry said.

"What about the rest of you?"

Bill, sitting in the front row with Don, said, "He sure beat the hell out of Three-Fingered Jack."

"He beat the hell out of a lot of people," said another man.

"He was tough as a nickel steak," Henry said. "We all know that."

"Tough," Marilyn said, "but Sunset killed him."

"Well, now," Henry said, "nothing's been said, but we was thinking we elected a new constable, maybe charges would be brought up on Sunset."

Henry looked out at the crowd, eyed a few elders, hoping for support. They murmured agreement.

"Sunset may be kin to me by marriage," Henry said, "but there's a number of us think this thing looks wrong, a woman killing her husband for being a husband. And look at her. Going around with a goddamn gun in her belt."

"So, you've heard the whole story?" Marilyn said.

"No. But the law should."

"The law was my son. And my son is dead."

"Then another law should hear the story. You don't just make a killer the law."

"Self-defense," Marilyn said.

"Marilyn," Henry said, "I'd think you'd be for the law looking into this. I don't understand your thinking. Pete and your old man dead, and Sunset living here in your house. And we don't even know the story she told is truth."

"She didn't beat herself up like that."

"She could have got hurt in the storm."

"Not like that."

"Man ought to be able to beat his wife, she needs it," one of the elders said.

"A man lays a hand on me, from this day forward," Marilyn said, "and I'll kill him."

"I'll second that," Sunset said.

This garnered a long moment of silence. A moth that had gotten trapped in the house beat around the ceiling, looking for a dark spot. This gave an excuse for a lot of men to look at the ceiling.

"I say we let Sunset do the job," came a voice from the rear of the room.

People turned to see who had spoken. It was Clyde Fox. He had removed his cloth cap and his black hair hung down, almost covered one of his eyes. He was big enough to go alligator hunting with stern language.

Henry felt his grasp on the meeting spinning out of control. He had come here feeling he had the situation by the balls, but now he was beginning to feel a grip tightening around his own scrotum.

"The storm didn't punch Sunset in the eye and mouth like that," Clyde said. "Reckon it's like the lady told it."

"That's right," Marilyn said. "And though it pains me to say it, my thinking is, ones deserve the sword get the sword. Even if it's my son. And there's this too. Sunset needs the job. She's got Karen to take care of. It would help her get back on her feet. We're a community first, aren't we?"

"It's a man's job," Henry said. "It ain't for nobody getting back on their feet. Job calls for a man."

"That could change," Marilyn said.

"It's not gonna change," Henry said. "We aren't running a goddamn charity here. This is a lumber mill community."

Marilyn nodded as if Henry had said something she agreed with. "You been thinking, I reckon, that maybe, if Holiday and Camp Rapture unite, you might have a shot at something like mayor, since Holiday's mayor run off. Am I right?"

"Well . . . it crossed my mind," Henry said. "I think I'm qualified. Your father gave me the position I have at the mill based on my qualifications."

"And marrying his sister," Bill said.

There was a laugh from the audience.

"Let this cross your mind," Marilyn said. "You think a woman getting on as constable in your camp would make you look bad, you ran for mayor, if the towns come together. Well, you ain't the boss of this place to begin with. Just so it's clear, I own most of the mill."

Henry swallowed hard. "Well . . . yes, ma'am . . . but . . ."

"But what?" Marilyn said. "Let me suggest strongly that

Sunset become constable. Pete had a couple men who helped him from time to time. Clyde being one. I say we let him help her. The other fella, I can't remember his name. But he moved off. But we can find another. She can finish out the term, then you can elect whoever you want."

"But a woman?"

"Woman's okay with me," Hillbilly said, pushing off from the wall. "I'm new here, and I know you don't know me, but why not? She doesn't do the job, get rid of her. That's fair enough, ain't it? Give her a month to get a handle on things, and give her some help. She can't do it, boot her out. Get you whoever. Hell, she's got her own damn gun."

Clyde said, "Sounds right to me."

"It's a tough job," Henry said. "She could get hurt. She'll have to deal with thugs and niggers and no telling what all."

"That's what the help's for," Clyde said. "Pay me and I'll help her. I ain't all that crazy about mill work. I still got all my fingers and arms, and I'd like to keep it that way. I been looking for a career, and I done said more than I usually say in a week."

"You take the job," Henry said to Clyde.

Clyde shook his head. "Nope. Rather work for the constable than be the constable."

Clyde glanced at Sunset. She smiled at him, and he sat down.

"I'll help too," Hillbilly said.

"We don't know you," Henry said.

"I don't know you either. I don't know this here community. But I'm willing to learn about it. I may not be here a long time, but I'll be here long enough to get her started."

"We'd have to pay you," Henry said.

"That's right," Hillbilly said. "I want the job because it's like this fella just said. Still got all my fingers and arms and I'd like to keep it that way."

73

"We haven't got that kind of money," Henry said. "There's only so much in the account for things like this. You'd make more at the mill."

"I'll take less on account of not having to be at the mill," Hillbilly said.

"We couldn't manage half of what you'd make at the mill."

"I'll help pay the first month for all of them," Marilyn said. "Out of my own pocket. After that, community fund takes over. Doesn't work out, we can get rid of her. Give her a month with Clyde and . . . what's your name, son?"

"Hillbilly. That's what I'm called, anyway."

"All right, Hillbilly. She works out, let her finish Pete's term. That's okay with you, isn't it, Henry? A month's trial."

Henry looked at Marilyn and his stomach turned sour. He could tell she didn't give a flying damn if it was all right with him or not. Jones had always been his buffer between Marilyn and himself. He knew she never liked him. After her daddy died, she got the idea that he had pocketed some of her father's money through fancy bookkeeping.

She was right. But she didn't know it for a fact and Jones hadn't believed it. But now with Jones gone, he knew his dick was in the wringer. And he knew her hand was on the wringer handle.

"We don't even know she wants the job," Henry said.

Marilyn turned her attention to Sunset, said, "Well, dear?"

Sunset was silent for a long moment. Then she said, "I'd like to give it a try."

There was a murmur in the crowd.

"We should put it to a vote," Henry said. "We only do things here at Camp Rapture the democratic way."

Marilyn smiled at Henry. "You're about as much a democrat as Genghis Khan."

There was laughter.

"Let's do it this way," Marilyn said. "Who here is against Sunset being constable? But first, I ought to make a little announcement. Depression or no Depression. I'm going to instate a nickel an hour raise across the board for everyone. Except Henry. He makes enough money."

Marilyn grinned at Henry.

Henry tried to grin back, but the inside of his mouth hung on his teeth and he couldn't make his lips do what he wanted. All he could think was Marilyn had never before had any say in the mill. She had never bothered to say anything. It was as if, with Jones' death, she had been given a dose of some kind of tonic. One thing he hated was a woman trying to grow balls. He wished now he had held the meeting in the church. Maybe she wouldn't have attended.

Then he thought: No, she's thought this one through. She wants Sunset for constable. People are going to laugh because I wasn't able to control this woman and her murdering daughter-in-law. If Holiday and Camp Rapture unite, no one is going to want to elect me to any position, not even street sweeper, not if I can't control these women.

"Marilyn," Henry said, "this isn't really a good idea, and you know it. Let's get serious."

"Oh, I'm serious," Marilyn said. "Show of hands for those who do not want Sunset as constable and a nickel raise. Stick them up there."

"When's that nickel an hour go into effect?" Bill Martin asked.

"As of next workday," Marilyn said.

"Gal's got my vote," Bill said.

There was a bit of foot shuffling. Some of the men looked off as if something exciting might be happening in a corner of the room, or somewhere near the ceiling.

75

A few hands went up, came down quickly, like they had merely been swatting at an annoying bug. Henry felt as if he had swallowed a bug.

"Good," Marilyn said. "Few against, so that means them that remain are for Sunset as constable. So, Sunset, you're the constable."

8

Clyde called her Constable Sunset, and the name stuck. Most men called her that around Camp Rapture as a joke, often said it within Sunset's hearing.

"There's ole Constable Sunset. Give her trouble, she'll make you put your nose in a circle in the corner."

"Or shoot you when you ain't looking and your pants is down."

The women weren't any nicer.

"She don't come from much, and she killed her husband, but look at her now. Thinks she's some kind of police. Ain't that precious?"

"She could put her hair up too. Looks like a floozy, all that red hair hanging down. I was her I'd dye it some more natural color."

After a few days of that, Sunset decided to move back home, such as it was, and to take her constable practice with her. She might have to see and deal with these people, but she didn't need to live right next to them.

Her mother-in-law made her a couple of skirts of khaki and tightened up a few men's shirts to go with them. Sunset wore Pete's star made of tin with the word CONSTABLE on it and a pair of lumberjack boots. She wore Pete's old gun holster too, and along with it, the .38 she had used to pop him.

She rode home in Clyde's rattling, wheezing pickup, along with Hillbilly. There was a hole in the floorboard where you could see the road go by.

Clyde sat on one side of her, Hillbilly on the other. Karen rode in the back of the pickup with supplies. Food. Incidentals. Some lumber, several large tarps, and a tent. This had been paid for by Marilyn, and Sunset made a note of the price, planning to pay her back soon as she could afford it.

As they bounced along the dusty road, Sunset noted that Clyde's clothes smelled of the sawmill. Clean, but with that faint aroma of sawdust and resin. The brim of his big black cowboy hat was curled up tight and the hat had a film of dust on it and the feather in the band was ragged, like a fish skeleton that had been picked clean by cats.

Hillbilly didn't have a drop of dust on him. He wore his cap at a jaunty angle. No feathers. Unlike Clyde, the collar on Hillbilly's shirt was well arranged and the shirt wasn't missing any buttons. He smelled like something sweet, and maybe even edible.

Clyde and Hillbilly helped Sunset remove Pete's file cabinet from the wrecked car and place it on the flooring that had been their house. Sunset took the loose files and put them on top of the damaged cabinet, determined to fix the cabinet and organize the files in the near future.

When they finished, Hillbilly said, "Reckon that ole car has gone its last mile."

"Clyde?" Sunset said. "Are we going to use your truck for our business?"

"Long as the gas is paid for and it don't fall apart. I got the engine held in with coat-hanger wire in places, so I don't want to hit any bumps too damn hard."

"I suppose we got what we got," Sunset said.

They used the lumber and canvas to put up a large tent over the flooring. It took them most of the day.

Inside, they marked off half the floor with a series of blankets and quilts hung from a rope that went from the front of the tent to the back and fastened to the tent poles. On one side of the tent was Sunset and Karen's living quarters, on the other, the constable's office.

Sunset's half had a mattress on the floor for her and Karen to sleep on, a washbasin, a couple of chairs, a table, four kerosene lamps, a stack of food and supplies, and a book on police work that had been Pete's. She had found it in the back of the file cabinet. It looked as if it had never been opened.

The office side consisted of the filing cabinet, four chairs and a long wooden table that had been donated by the sawmill. The top of it was pocked and marked from years of abuse, and on the edge of it someone had written: "Hannah Jenkins is a whore and she ain't no good at it."

First day they got the table, Sunset sandpapered the remark away and painted the table a dark green. The same green that was used to paint most of the houses in the camp, as well as the mill houses. It gave everything a kind of military look.

Clyde and Hillbilly repaired the wooden file cabinet and built a temporary outhouse of boards and the remaining piece of tarp.

"If a high wind don't come," Clyde said, "nobody will show their ass in the shitter. It comes a blow, all bets are off. Maybe tomorrow I can fix up a real outhouse and put some catalogues in there."

"He's got plenty of them," Hillbilly said. "Fact is, he's got more paper and catalogues and junk than the law allows. His house looks like it got blown away by that tornado come through here, and it all got put back willy-nilly in a pile by a flash flood."

"It's my pile," Clyde said.

That night, after Hillbilly and Clyde left, Sunset and Karen sat on their mattress on the home side of the tent. Karen still wasn't talkative. Sunset missed her old chatter. Karen went to bed early. Sunset read the one book she had on law enforcement.

Nothing in the book reminded her of anything Pete had done, besides wear a badge—the one she had on, in fact—and carry a gun. There wasn't a section on how to beat the hell out of people or how to cheat on your wife either. She got through about a quarter of the book before becoming bored.

She got a mirror and looked in it. Her face had lost most of the swelling, but her eyes were still black, and the left side of her lower lip looked like a tire with a heat bubble on it.

Sunset blew out the lamp and tried to sleep, but only dozed a bit. She dreamed off and on. Thought of her mother, who had been knocked up by the good Reverend Beck, the one who had inspired the log camp to call itself Camp Rapture. "Yeah," Sunset's mother used to say, "the Reverend Beck put more in me than the spirit of Jesus.

"Man will lie to you to get what he wants, kid. Even a man of God. Especially a man of God. Remember that, darling. Keep your legs crossed until you're about thirty if you can do it. You won't be able to, but work at it. And remember, it takes more than a poke to make you happy. Have him work that little button down there. You don't know what I mean, but I guarantee you, in time you'll find it."

Sunset hadn't understood the extent of the message then, except for the button part, which she had already discovered. By the time she understood the rest of it, she was too much in love with Pete to care about it. At least he married her after he knocked her up. That was something. It was better than her mother got.

Her mother had not only gotten knocked up and lost her man when Sunset was thirteen, she soon took up with a traveling shoe salesman who played the banjo, wandered away with him and his shoes, probably to the sound of a banjo breakdown, up and out of there, leaving a note that read: "Sorry, Sunset. I got to go. Mama loves you. I left you a good pair of shoes in there on the kitchen table. They shine up easy."

Sunset stayed with a farm couple for a couple of years, but they primarily wanted a farmhand. She wore out on that. Dug and picked up so many potatoes she had more dirt under her fingernails than a mole had in its fur. The man who owned the farm had also taken a liking to her. He never touched her, but she felt the way he was looking at her would lead to trouble. Anytime she was bent in the potato field, she had a sense that an arrow was pointed at her ass. But when she turned, instead of an arrow, it was the farmer's eyes.

She moved out. Or to be more precise, ran off. Got up in the middle of the night, threw what little she had in a canvas tote bag, and hit the road, way her mama had, but without the banjo and the shoe salesman.

Got a job in the cotton gin just outside of Holiday. Lived in the back of a dress shop for a month, sleeping on a pallet next to a widow woman and her three kids. Then she took up with Pete, who was tall and lean with coils of muscles knotting under his dark skin, shiny black hair, and a smile that made her heart melt like candle wax. One day he filled her belly with Karen.

She and Pete were married right away. He was twenty, and at that time working in the cotton gin. His beatings didn't start until after marriage. It must have been a Jones tradition. No beating your woman until the wedding vows were taken.

She lay there thinking about all this until she was as lonesome as an adolescent's first pubic hair.

She sighed, got out of bed, went outside barefoot and in her nightgown, strapping on her holster.

It wasn't a full moon, but it was pretty bright and the air was clean and a little cool. The night was full of fireflies. It looked as if all the stars had fallen to earth and were bouncing about.

As she stood there watching the fireflies circle her head, she heard a growl. She pulled the revolver and looked, saw a big black-and-white dog with one ear that stood up and one that hung down, squatting in the road, dropping a pile.

"Easy, boy," she said. "I'm not going to shoot you."

But the dog growled and ran away, leaving the aroma of fresh dog shit behind.

"My reputation gets around," Sunset said. She decided one of the first things she wanted was a box of ammunition. She felt safer with the gun than without it. She wanted enough bullets to shoot up the world.

She stood outside for a while, but the mosquitoes began to flock. She swatted a few of them, went inside, strapped down the tent flap, went to bed.

But she couldn't sleep. She thought about how she and Karen were just a few feet from where she had put the gun to Pete's head.

Boy, was he surprised.

The sonofabitch.

Still, having Karen here, near where her father had been shot, maybe that wasn't such a good idea. Wasn't really good mothering. Another place might have been better.

But where?

She couldn't stay with her mother-in-law. Forgiven or not, it just didn't feel right.

Sunset sat on the edge of the mattress, went over to the business side of the tent, seated herself at the table, pushed a pencil and a blank notebook around. Bored of that, she lit a lantern and carried it to the file cabinet, pulled up a chair for herself and one for the lantern.

There was a pile of loose files on top of the cabinet. She took the first folder and prepared to file it.

On the front was written: MURDERS.

Sunset turned up the wick on the lantern and opened the file.

There was a list of murders that had happened over the years Pete had been constable.

She thought it would be a good idea to familiarize herself with what had gone before. If she was going to play constable, she might as well know how to play.

One file said COLORED MURDERS.

She opened the file and read a bit. What it mostly amounted to was so-and-so shot so-and-so and so what?

Wasn't a lot of concern in there for the colored community. No intense sleuthing to find out who did what to whom.

There was one interesting situation that Pete had written about. A colored man named Zendo had found a buried clay jar with a baby in it while plowing his field. Scared he would be blamed for the baby's death, he moved the jar and its contents to the woods and left it there.

Since Zendo had the richest soil around, through heavy application of animal manures and leaves, his land had turned black as a raven in a coal mine. This dirt clung to the jar and was inside of it, along with the baby.

Pete tracked Zendo by using the dirt. He knew where the jar had come from, no matter where it had been found.

Pete finished his report with:

Talked to Zendo about the dead baby. Known Zendo for a while. Not a bad nigger. Don't believe he killed anyone. Probably some nigger gal had a kid she wasn't supposed to have, and it died, or she killed it, and buried it in Zendo's field because the ground is easy to work.

Can't tell if the baby was black or white cause it's all rotted up and ants have been at it. But I figure Zendo found it and didn't have nothing to do with it. He's a good enough nigger and I haven't never known him to steal

nothing or do nothing bad. He even works hard. I think he
hid it to keep from getting in trouble. I had it buried in the
colored graveyard on suspect of it being a nigger baby.

There was nothing else written. End of case. It was dated a
couple weeks earlier. It didn't mention who found the jar in the
woods, which seemed a bad bit of investigative work. Sunset
thought that sort of information might be more than a little
important.

She wondered too how Pete could see such a thing and not
even mention it to her. Then again, he didn't mention much of
anything to her if it didn't have to do with cooking his meals or
taking her clothes off. He spent the rest of his time being
constable or shacking up with other women, especially Jimmie Jo
French, the cheap slut.

Sunset looked through the other murder cases for a while,
grew tired, stashed the murder files, put out the lantern and went
to bed.

Next morning, sitting at the table with Clyde and Hillbilly, Sunset
had their first meeting. Clyde had let Hillbilly stay at his house
and had given him a lift.

Sunset noted that Hillbilly looked fresh, shaved, his hair
combed and oiled. It even looked that way after wearing a cap.

Clyde, on the other hand, looked as if he had rolled out of
bed, pulled on his pants and someone else's shirt. It was about a
size too small and one of the bottom buttons was unfastened. For
that matter, his pants were high-water, ending about two inches
above his socks and shoes. He still wore his hat, and his hair stuck
out from under it like porcupine quills. He needed a shave.

Clyde said, "You see that big old black-and-white dog out
there?"

"Saw him last night," Sunset said.

"Belonged to the Burton family. Old Man Burton moved off to look for some kind of work. Got too old for the sawmill. Had a relative up in Oklahoma said there was work. So he left the dog. Think they called him Ben. Ain't that something? Going off and leaving your dog cause you're moving. Like the dog don't get its feelings hurt."

"It's a dog," Hillbilly said.

"Yeah, but a dog's got feelings."

Clyde and Hillbilly argued this for a while.

Sunset said, "You know, this job ain't as exciting as I thought it might be."

"That's good," Hillbilly said. "Way I want it. I'm getting paid for sitting here, same as if I wasn't sitting here. I like it not exciting."

"I'm not complaining," Sunset said. "Just surprised. Pete was always gone doing something. Or doing someone. Now that I think about it, I think it was mostly the last part."

"Jimmie Jo French," Clyde said, then turned red. "Damn. I ain't got no sense."

"It's okay," Sunset said. "That's the truth, ain't it? I know it and everyone else knows it."

"I used to not talk so much," Clyde said.

"Fact is," Sunset said, "you was kind of known for that."

"Out at his house he didn't say no more than two words," Hillbilly said.

"Told you where the soap and such was," Clyde said.

"All right. Four words. I had to clean up out at the water pump, fight off mean chickens while I washed."

"They just don't know you," Clyde said.

"If we're gonna talk about baths and chickens," Sunset said, "this job is more boring than I thought."

"It'll take time to get into a routine," Clyde said. "You wouldn't think much goes on in Camp Rapture and round about. But it does. And you're supposed to help Sheriff Knowles over in Holiday if he needs it. Come Saturday night, it can get busy over there, with them honky-tonks and whorehouses and such."

"I'm supposed to help Sheriff Knowles?" Sunset said. "I thought we just arrested chicken thieves and asked drunks to shut up."

"Knowles don't usually need help," Clyde said. "Knows where the trouble is and who starts it. So it's not like he has to do any big detective work. Just sometimes there's more going on than he can handle. What with all them oil field people moving in. Did you know they got a picture show over there in Holiday now?"

"No shit?" Hillbilly said.

"No shit," Clyde said. "On bank night you can win money."

"Bank night?" Hillbilly said.

"Yeah. They got a contest. You can do a drawing. You win, you get cash money. Sometimes they don't give money, they give dishes."

"Can you sell the dishes back?"

"I don't know. I guess you might."

"I don't need dishes."

"First you got to win them."

Sunset listened to this exchange, said, "You know, I don't know about picture shows, or bank nights, or dishes, but I thought I was constable of Camp Rapture, not Holiday."

"You are," Clyde said. "But Knowles helps here, and you help there. How it's done."

"But I don't have jurisdiction there."

"Knowles don't have it here," Clyde said.

"Exactly," Sunset said.

"No one cares because most folks don't know about

jurisdiction," Clyde said. "Hell, they can't even spell it. Fact is, I can't spell it. Half the colored around here ain't never even heard the word. You got a badge. Sheriff Knowles has a badge. That's the sum of it. You're the law, Sunset."

"That's a relief," Sunset said, "but what if he does need me, and I end up with someone who's kind of rowdy, ain't for being arrested? What then?"

"Then we'll appeal to their human side," Clyde said, and pulled a slap jack out from under his shirt and struck the table with it. It sounded like a gunshot and made Sunset and Hillbilly jump.

"Damn, Clyde," Hillbilly said. "I near messed myself."

"This little buddy," Clyde said, shaking the slap jack, "is a real persuader. Make a woolly booger into a lamb, that's what it'll do. Make a bear pick you flowers."

Sunset looked at the slap jack. It was about a foot long, a folded piece of thick leather. It was flexible, but it had seasoned out hard.

"That don't work, you buffalo him," Clyde said.

"Buffalo him?" Sunset said.

"Means you take that pistol you got there, bring it up alongside his body so he can't see it, and clip him with a backward move, so's the barrel catches him below the ear where the jaw hinges. You do that, back to front, when he wakes up, his wife will be remarried and his kids will be grown."

"What if he's looking?" Sunset said.

"Then you tell him, 'Goddamnit, that woman's done got naked over there.' When he turns, you bring that pistol out and drop all hundred and so pounds you got on the back of his noggin. Hit him like you're trying to drive a nail. That won't do him any good, but it'll do you plenty. If there's more than one of us, and there ought to be, cause that's how you do police work, we all hit him from different directions."

87

"If that doesn't work?"

"Then we shoot him. The leg if you got time. If not, just pop him somewhere. Hell, you're the law."

"Guess we've covered arrest techniques," Sunset said.

"Some of them," Clyde said.

"Hillbilly," Sunset said, "you have a comment?"

"Not really. Well, I think I stepped in something. I'm going to go outside and clean off my boot. I'll clean up the floor here when I get done."

Hillbilly lifted his foot, looked at the bottom of his boot.

"Dog, I reckon."

"Suppose that makes you our tracker," Clyde said. "Way you recognized which kind of shit it is right off."

Hillbilly took off his boot and stood up.

"Before you go outside with that," Sunset said, "and believe me, I want you to, I want to thank you fellas. I don't know how much I know about this—well, I don't know anything. Not really. A thing picked up here and there from Pete. But I'm going to take it seriously and do the best I can."

"Wouldn't be here if I didn't think you were," Clyde said.

"How come you men did this?" she asked.

"I'm saving up for a guitar," Hillbilly said. "That's the truth and the long and the short of it. Other than not liking to work at that goddamn sawmill."

"I thought, hell, give the lady a chance," Clyde said. "Besides, I don't like working at the sawmill neither."

Clyde, with his own tools and Hillbilly's reluctant help, spent the morning building an outhouse out of lumber they found among the remains of the house. They had to climb a couple of trees to get at some of it.

Clyde seemed to have a real knack with tools, and Hillbilly

was an adequate board holder. He had attempted, at Clyde's request, to nail a board or two, but had only succeeded in getting the work crooked and hitting himself in the thumb with the hammer, causing Clyde to demote him to board holder.

Sunset, who watched this as she levered water from the pump, found Hillbilly kind of endearing, like a little boy. Another thing was, though hot and sweaty, Hillbilly still managed to appear sweet and clean.

Clyde, on the other hand, had taken on the appearance of a man dragged through a berry patch by a runaway mule. When he wasn't hammering and measuring and sawing, he was wiping back his wet black hair and scratching parts of his body that were best left to dark rooms and private attention.

About noon Karen got up, having spent all morning in bed. She got up complaining about how the outhouse construction, all the hammering and nailing, had woke her.

"It's darn near one o'clock," Sunset said. "Normally you'd be doing chores."

"Normally, I'd have a daddy," Karen said.

Sunset had nothing to say to that, and Karen turned pouty.

Two in the afternoon and the outhouse was finished. Clyde and Hillbilly found a tree to sit under, where they could enjoy the shade. Sunset brought them out sandwiches, sat down by Hillbilly with her own sandwich, and they ate. Karen stayed in the tent.

When they finished eating, Clyde said, "I think I'm going to be the first ass in that outhouse. I feel it coming."

"I don't need to hear that," Hillbilly said.

"It's just a natural process," Clyde said.

"Boys," Sunset said, "interesting as Clyde's outhouse habits are, I been thinking, and I believe it's time we start earning our pay."

9

Clyde knew Zendo and where he lived. Unlike many negroes, Zendo owned his own land and was not a sharecropper. He had worked in the sawmill for years, putting back every available dollar. Growing crops on the side while he sharecropped, feeding himself and selling the excess.

When he had the money, he bought at an inflated price, because he was a negro and in no position to quibble, a fine piece of bottomland near the creek, cleared a large chunk with an axe, a mule, and a strong back, and started growing vegetables. Used terracing and water channeling from the creek, staked tomatoes, fought bugs.

Fifteen years later, much to the dismay of many white farmers, his farm was the most productive in the county. People drove by just to look at it, lying there in its man-made black dirt, bordered at all four corners by massive compost piles contained within log structures.

Sunset and her deputy constables, and Karen, rattled out to Zendo's farm in Clyde's pickup. When they got there, they went by Zendo's house, which was in better condition than most houses in the area. The tar-paper roof was nailed down tight and there wasn't any cardboard in the windows.

They found Zendo's wife out in the yard. She was a big coffee-colored woman in a bright sack dress with a toddler clutching her leg. She had a pan of shelled corn in one hand and with the other she was tossing it to the chickens that gathered around her like servants before the queen.

Sunset got out of the truck and walked up to the lady, passing a small pig that was rolling in a damp depression in the yard, grunting, turning its head as if hoping for some sort of positive comment.

Nearby, a dog lay in the middle of a flower bed that had died out. The dog looked dead himself, but when Sunset walked up, his tail beat a few beats, then went still.

"Not a watchdog," Sunset said to Zendo's wife.

"Naw he ain't," the lady said. "I used to have a pig that would bite you, but we eating on him. Can I help you?"

"Yes, ma'am."

"How come you got that badge on? You some kind of farm inspector?"

"I'm the constable."

"Naw you ain't."

"Yes, I am."

"Really? You the constable? How'd that happen? Thought Mister Pete was the constable."

"No. I shot him."

"That's funny," the lady said. "You done shot him and took his badge. You funny, miss."

"Yeah, well, I really am the constable. And I really did shoot him. And he really is dead. And once again, I really am the constable."

"Oh," she said. "Well, no offense."

"Like to talk to your husband. Could you tell me where I might find him?"

"He ain't in any kind of trouble, is he?"

"Nothing like that."

Zendo's wife told her, with what Sunset thought was reluctance, that Zendo was still in the field.

On her way out to the truck she passed the hog and the dog again, but this time neither took note of her.

They drove to where the wife had indicated, got out of the truck and started walking toward where they could see Zendo having his dinner under a tree.

Two sleek, sweat-shiny mules stood nearby, still in plow harness, but the plow was no longer attached. The plow was leaning against the tree with Zendo. The mules had been hobbled and were mouthing grain from two flat pans.

The field Zendo had plowed, running the middles, cutting up weeds, was dark as sin, the rows straight enough to have been laid out with a ruler. The dark soil exploded with all manner of vegetables. Corn growing tall and green. Tied tomato vines twisted around wooden stakes, tomatoes dangled from them like little evening suns.

Zendo was biting into a biscuit when he saw a redheaded woman, a teenage girl, and two men walking toward him.

The woman looked roughed up, and his first thought was to run, just in case he was going to be blamed. Then he noted she was wearing a badge on her shirt. He considered this, but couldn't get a fix on it.

By this time, they were standing beneath the oak, looking down at him. He put the biscuit in his lunch bucket and stood up. It wasn't a long trip. He had a large head, broad shoulders, and a short body. If he mounted a Shetland pony, the pony would have to be cut off at the knees and placed in a ditch for Zendo's feet to touch the ground.

"Howdy, this hot day," he said, hanging his head, starting to shuffle his feet. "How is you folks? It sure is one of God's good days, now ain't it, even if it is hot."

"It's me," Clyde said. "You can cut the 'I sure is dumb' routine."

92

"Is that you, Mr. Clyde? I ain't seen you in a coon's age, if you'll pardon the joke. We got to do us some more fishing."

"I agree," Clyde said, stuck out his hand, and they shook. Hillbilly did the same, hesitantly. Zendo didn't offer to shake hands with either Sunset or Karen.

"Crops look great, Zendo," Clyde said.

"Bottomland," Zendo said. "And I treat it good. I run the creek water in it sometimes, does it with lots of cured manure and compost."

"Sure looks good," Clyde said. "Zendo, this is Sunset Jones. She's the constable in these parts now."

"Say she ain't," Zendo said.

"No. She is."

"Shut me up. Really? You the constable, miss?"

"I am."

"You're yanking on me."

"I tell you I'm not," Sunset said.

"I thought Mister Pete was the constable."

"He's dead," Sunset said.

"Oh, well, I'm sorry to hear that," Zendo said.

"He was my husband."

"Well, now, I'm sure sorry. How did he die, you don't mind me asking?"

"I shot him."

"Say you did?"

"That's what I'm saying."

"Dead."

"Yes."

Karen started back to the pickup.

"We'll be here just a little while," Sunset said to Karen's back.

Karen didn't answer, just kept walking.

"She's still sensitive about her father's death."

93

"I hear that," Zendo said. "Yes, ma'am. I understand. Mr. Pete was a good man."

"No, he wasn't," Sunset said. "He was a sonofabitch, and I'm glad I shot him."

"Say he was a sonofabitch?"

"That's what I'm saying. I bet you agree with me."

"Well, ma'am," Zendo said, "I ain't gonna argue with you none."

"We're here about dealings Pete had with you."

"Me and him didn't have no dealings."

"A body in a pottery jar," Sunset said.

"Oh, yeah. Was that. Said he wouldn't gonna make no big deal out of it."

"I read it in his files. Tell me about it. Tell me where the baby ended up, or if you have any idea whose it was."

Zendo told them pretty much what Sunset had read in the files. He found the body plowing, where someone had buried it in a large pottery jar, probably the night before. It was buried deep, but he was plowing deep, and the top of his middle buster broke the rim of the jar.

"I thought it might be one of them Injun pots. I've found a bunch of 'em. But it weren't. I looked in that pot and seen there was a tow sack stuffed in there. When I pulled that off the top, I seen a little baby about the size of a newborn kitten."

"Black or white?"

"Couldn't tell. It was all dirty, and there was some kind of stuff in there."

"Stuff?"

"Something sticky. It was on the edge of the pot and dirt had stuck to it. It was all over the baby. It was like someone had dipped the baby in it. I thought it was molasses."

94

"Was it molasses?" Sunset asked.

"I thought it was, but it had a smell to it, and I figure it was oil mixed in with the dirt."

"Car oil?"

"Maybe. I didn't know what to do with it. I feared it might be a white baby and white folks would think I killed it cause it was on my land, so I hid it in the woods."

"You buried it?" Sunset asked.

Zendo shook his head. "I ain't proud to say I didn't, but I didn't. Mr. Pete found the pot, knew the dirt on it was mine. Ain't no one around here got dirt this good. Not the way I treat it.

"Thought he was gonna think I done it for sure. But he didn't. Wasn't hard on me at all. Didn't even ask me if I knowed anything about it, just took and buried that poor thing over in the colored graveyard. Or said that's what he was gonna do."

"You know Pete found it himself?" Sunset asked.

"He just come to me about it. I reckoned he did. Suppose someone else could have found it, told him, and he figured out it come from my place."

"Where is the graveyard?" Sunset asked.

"Clyde here knows," Zendo said.

Clyde shook his head. "Not anymore. I used to. But I ain't been out in that neck of the woods in years. Since you and me hunted there last, and that's been—good grief, we was kids."

"Ain't that the truth," Zendo said. "You and me was the same tall then. Now you just like a tree, and me, I'm like a stump."

Zendo picked up a stick and drew a map in the dirt, made an X where the graveyard was, said, "Right there. Got to walk some to get to it. Can't go all the way there by car."

"Thanks," Sunset said. "You can finish your dinner."

Zendo said, "Guess Mr. Pete done hit the wrong person, didn't he?"

"On that day, yes," Sunset said.

They had to leave the truck on a clay road by a sweet gum and walk down through the trees to get to the cemetery. The air was heavy beneath the trees, and though the shade took away the direct heat of the sun, it was humid and the mosquitoes were thicker than tacks in a tar-paper shack.

Karen said, "Why would anyone put a graveyard down in the woods like this? Ain't they usually alongside the road?"

"Some white folks think it's a real laugh to mess with colored graveyards," Clyde said. "This way it ain't so easy to bother."

"Kind of hard to carry the bodies to the hole, ain't it?" Hillbilly said.

"Reckon it is," Clyde said, swatting a mosquito.

"Bugs are eating me up," Karen said.

"You can go back and wait in the truck if you want," Sunset said.

But Karen didn't go back. Finally the woods thinned and there was a trail.

"Didn't Zendo say turn left?" Sunset said.

"Way I remember it," Hillbilly said.

"Yeah," Clyde said. "That's how you go. It's coming back to me."

They walked along for a distance, and soon there was a large clearing that looked to have been worked with machetes, and just beyond that was a place of erected stones. There were oak trees in the cemetery with moss and vines growing up the sides, dripping off their limbs. There was one dogwood in the cemetery and some honeysuckle, and the aroma of the honeysuckle was strong and bees were buzzing the flowers on the tree.

Some of the graves ran right up to the trees, and you could see where roots had lifted the stones and made them sag. But it was a well-cared-for place and there were fresh flowers on many of the graves and voodoo beads and pieces of bright-colored glass on some of the others. There were even a few fruit jars with liquid in them.

"What's in them fruit jars?" Hillbilly asked.

"Home liquor sometimes," Clyde said. "They bring it out for the dead."

"That's silly," Hillbilly said, "and a waste of liquor."

Karen laughed at that.

Hillbilly grinned at Karen. "Me and Karen could drink that instead of it going to waste, couldn't we, kid?"

Karen laughed again.

Sunset said, "Karen don't drink."

"Course not," Hillbilly said. "Just making a joke."

Finally Sunset found a grave with a wooden cross over it. The cross was made of cheap lumber and two nails. Next to it were fragments of busted pottery. Written on the cross was: BABY.

"Pete did this," Sunset said. "I recognize the way he carved the B's into that cross. It's like his writing, way he makes his B's. He must have busted up the pot to get the baby out, or maybe it got busted later on by someone else."

"Daddy wasn't so bad," Karen said. "See how he done with the baby and all."

Hillbilly swatted a mosquito. "Long walk down here for nothing, you ask me."

"We could give the baby a name," Clyde said. "We could write it on the cross. We could call it something like Snooks."

"No, we couldn't," Sunset said. "And besides. We don't know if it was male or female."

97

"I still like Snooks," Clyde said. "It works either way. Girl or boy. You like Snooks, Hillbilly?"

"No," Hillbilly said.

"Hell, you got a name like Hillbilly," Clyde said. "What's wrong with Snooks?"

"Hillbilly's a nickname. And don't ask my real one, cause I don't tell it. What did we learn here, Sunset? What was this trip all about?"

"Don't rightly know," Sunset said. "Let's go back."

10

That night, before Sunset and Karen went to bed, it came a rain not too unlike the one that pissed on Noah's ark, but it didn't last long. Just wetted up the place, churned the creeks, made them rise, then moved on. The tent had been set up on top of the flooring of the old house, so they didn't get wet, but they could feel it against the floorboards, begging to come in.

The rain cooled off things, and when she and Karen lay down that night to sleep, it was comfortable and there were no mosquitoes.

Sunset lay in bed listening to the rain move south with a vengeance, thinking about the baby in the jar coated in oil, about how Pete had gone to the trouble to bury it and carve the word BABY on the cross.

It was a kind gesture.

And not like him at all. Especially if he thought the baby might be colored.

It was a side of Pete she hadn't known existed, and it was a side of him she wished she had known. It was also a side of him that confused her and of which she was suspicious.

Later on she heard the tent flap being thrown back. She sat up in bed and saw a man's shape standing there. He pushed the flap back farther and moonlight spilled in over him. It was Pete. Grave dirt was dropping off of his body and he looked mad enough to pee vinegar.

He pointed his finger at Sunset and opened his mouth to speak. Dirt fell out. Then he screamed.

Sunset sat up in bed.

She looked at the tent flap.

It was closed and tied. Outside she could hear crickets and frogs. The rain had passed. She had fallen asleep thinking she was awake.

Suddenly, once again, there was a scream.

It wasn't Pete. It was a panther, roaming the bottomland. They could scream like a woman. The sound of the panther had awakened her, not a dead Pete.

She looked over at Karen.

Still asleep. She gently pulled the covers up to Karen's neck.

"I love you," she said softly.

Lying down, she dozed uneasily, dreamed again. But she knew it was a dream this time, and it wasn't so bad. It was a dream about her putting the pistol to Pete's head, pulling the trigger, and in her dream the sound of the gun was sharp and sweet and it cut through her thoughts like a bright light and the light opened a gap somewhere down deep in the dark insides of her, and out of that gap came all the answers to questions long asked, and in that moment, that fine and wonderful moment, she knew things.

She came awake.

"Damn," she said. Thought: Almost had the answers. They were about to be revealed, all the goddamn perplexities of the universe, and I had to wake up.

The tent flap moved.

She reached over and pulled the gun from the holster where it lay on the floor and pointed it.

It was the black-and-white dog. It had stuck its head under the tent flap. It was soaking wet.

"Easy, boy," she said, but the dog bolted at the sound of her voice.

She put the gun away, lay there waiting to see if the dog would return, but it didn't.

Next morning, before daybreak, to the sound of birds singing loud in the trees and somewhere an agitated squirrel fussing, Karen got up along with Sunset. Karen started a fire in the woodstove and cooked a breakfast of eggs and toasted some bread on top of the burner for the both of them.

Sunset eyed all this suspiciously. It was the first time in days Karen had shown interest in doing anything.

Karen walked buckets of water from the water pump and heated them in a larger bucket on the stove and poured the hot water into a number ten washtub. By the time she had enough buckets to fill the tub, much of the water had cooled, but it was still warm enough for a bath with minted lye soap and special attention to her hair.

When Karen finished, Sunset went through the same ritual, washing her hair and combing it out. As Sunset dressed in her skirt and shirt, she saw that Karen was already dressed and had put her hair up in a kind of bun. She had on one of the few good dresses she owned, one her grandmother gave her before they had moved into the tent, and she had on her only good pair of shoes.

Sunset noted that Karen had even applied a bit of lipstick, not something she normally bothered with. She was also wearing perfume, and she had put on too much.

While Sunset was pulling on her boots and lacing them, Karen said, "Those boots aren't very feminine. They look like something someone ought to wear at the sawmill or to shovel horse mess."

"I'm a constable right now, not a New York fashion model."

"You ought to put your hair up," Karen said.

"I see you have. How come you're putting on the dog?"

"No reason. Just felt like it."

Sunset went to the dressing table they had rigged, held up a hand mirror. She thought: Maybe I could put my hair up.

Her face was no longer puffy and the bruises were starting to fade. She was beginning to look like herself, with a touch of raccoon styling.

About nine o'clock, Clyde's truck pulled up. Karen heard it, smoothed her dress, opened the tent flap.

Through the opening, Sunset could see Clyde climbing out of the truck, and on the other side, Hillbilly. She stood up, strapped on the holster and gun, stood in the opening.

A black car with white doors and a gold-and-black police insignia pulled up behind Clyde's truck. A man wearing a big white hat and khaki clothes, a gun and badge, got out of the car and walked over to Clyde and shook his hand, then Hillbilly's. He looked agitated. He spoke to Clyde.

Clyde said something, pointed toward the tent.

The man with the badge did a double take.

Clyde said something else. The man took off his hat, and with Clyde and Hillbilly trailing, he hustled over to the tent as Sunset stepped outside, Karen following.

"Miss," the man said, "I'm the deputy over at Holiday. Name's Morgan. I was sent here to get the constable for help. We heard Pete got killed by his wife, but I didn't know it was a woman took his place. I can take these here men with me—"

"I'm the constable. And I'm the wife . . . or was."

The deputy raised his eyebrows. "I'll be damned."

"Why do you need us?"

"Nigger's gone on a rampage. Killed the sheriff."

"Oh," Sunset said.

"Knowing that," Morgan said, "maybe you ought to stay here."

"What's the situation?" Sunset said. She had heard Pete say just those words.

"Well, I come over here cause me and Rooster are the only deputies, and this nigger, well, he done blowed the sheriff's head off and holed himself up in the picture show and won't come out."

"The picture show," Clyde said. "He didn't ruin it or nothing, did he?"

"I think he broke some of them giveaway dishes," Morgan said. "Some of the townsfolk wanted a piece of him, and the grocer brought out a gun and tried to go in there, and that nigger cut him off at the knee. I figure they'll be pulling that grocer around on a wheeled board now. Thing is, it's a nigger done it, and the town wants to lynch him. Sheriff didn't go in for that sort of thing, though I ain't really against a lynching when it's deserved. They're gonna want to rush the picture show, get that nigger and string him up and set him on fire, or burn down the picture show with him in it. Frankly, it's Rooster who's against it. He's got the nigger pinned in the show, and he's got them townsfolk pushing in on him, wanting him to get out of the way. He's between a rock and a hard place. I didn't know nothing else to do but to go to the nearest law for help. But I didn't count on no woman, and I ain't sure we ought not just let them have him."

"We'll follow in the truck," Sunset said. "Karen, you stay here. Clyde. Hillbilly. You got guns?"

"Not on us," Clyde said. "We got to go by my house."

"Reckon I gotta get back," Morgan said. "Wouldn't have come here it hadn't been so close, and you being the law and all. And well, Rooster sent me and he's head deputy. Still, I knew

Pete was dead, but I didn't know you was no woman."

"We'll be there," Sunset said. "You go on back and help Rooster."

"I'll do that," Morgan said, "but it gets too much out of hand, I'd rather it be that nigger than me. Gets that far, I'll hold the goddamn rope for them."

"You're a sworn officer of the law," Sunset said. "You'll do what you're supposed to do."

"Who the hell are you to talk to me that way?" Morgan said. "You're just a constable. Hell, you're just a woman. And wearing a skirt made out of some kind of man's pants."

"Let me put this where you can understand it, Morgan," Clyde said. "Give her any more mouth, and I'll hit you so hard, the mud flaps on your car will blow up. You hear me?"

Morgan's face muscles twitched. "You ain't got to say that. You and me have worked together before. That kind of talk ain't necessary. I just didn't know she was a woman."

"We'll see you in Holiday," Sunset said.

Clyde's place was on the way, off the main road, down a washed-out forest-lined path spotted with holes deep enough to lose a feed wagon.

They stopped there to get Hillbilly a shotgun and Clyde a pistol. At first, Sunset thought Clyde's weathered shack had been hit by the tornado, but the more she looked at it, the more she realized this was its common state.

The shingles had been flapped up, and some of them tossed around the yard. From the looks of them, way they were half buried in the dirt, they had been there for a long time. The chimney was held up by a board, and she could see inside the place through a gap between chimney and house. What she could see looked filthy and greasy and piled. Most of the windows had cardboard in place of glass. The yard was cluttered with pieces of wood and chunks of car parts and renegade chickens. A rooster charged at them with a business attitude, flapped his wings and pecked at one of Sunset's boots, then charged off, mission accomplished.

"That rooster was mine," Sunset said, "he'd be in the cooking pot tonight."

"That's George," Clyde said. "He's all right. He thinks he's protecting the hens."

Stepping over yard junk, fending off chickens, tiptoeing through a narrow garden path with bug-eaten vegetables, they moved cautiously over the creaking porch, avoiding gaps where the lumber had cracked.

The inside was cluttered with magazines and newspapers, car parts, broken dishes, cardboard boxes and apple crates full of who knows what. There were buckets arranged on the floor and on top of boxes and crates. Water was dripping from the roof into them.

Clyde wandered off to get the guns, threading his way through debris.

Hillbilly looked at Sunset, said, "Home, sweet home."

"Don't know what's sweet about it."

"He spilt some syrup over there by the stove, probably about, oh, I don't know, ten years ago would be my guess from the looks of it. But it's still sweet. I know, cause flies gather in it and get stuck. Want to see?"

"No thanks."

Clyde came back with a shotgun and a revolver. They looked much cleaner than anything else in the house.

"Is there anything you don't save?" Sunset said.

"Money," Clyde said. "I'm hungry. Had time I'd make me a little sandwich to take with me."

"Well, you don't have time," Sunset said, "but we could probably manage a little backfire through this place before we leave, and by the time you get back, things would be cleaned up real good."

"At least I know where everything is," Clyde said.

"No, he don't," Hillbilly said.

"I knew where these guns were," Clyde said, and gave the shotgun to Hillbilly. He handed him a fistful of shells as well.

"Where do you sleep?" Sunset asked Hillbilly.

"Not sure. Place never looks the same."

"You didn't ask where I sleep," Clyde said.

"This is your house. I figure you have a place. I was wondering about the houseguest."

As they climbed in the truck, Sunset said, "From now on, you boys need to be armed at all times. We can't be stopping off at Clyde's house for weapons when we need them."

"Just don't seem necessary most of the time," Clyde said, shifting gears. "This slap jack," he patted his shirt where it lay inside, "is usually enough."

"Well, you're full-time now, not part-time," Sunset said. "We're professionals and we got to act and look like professionals."

"Is that what we are?" Clyde said. "Professionals?"

Hillbilly patted Sunset's leg below the holster, said, "I see you're armed."

Sunset knew Hillbilly's pat on the leg and remark were unnecessary and an excuse to touch her thigh, but she couldn't bring herself to say anything against it.

She wished she could say, "Put your hand here, your mouth there, twist one of my legs behind my head and make me say calf rope," but instead she said, "I got the gun, but I don't have many bullets. Just what's in it."

"Things go well," Clyde said, "maybe you won't have to shoot any more people than you got shells. Some police officers, even in big cities, go a whole day without shooting anybody, including dogs with the hydrophobia. Hell, Pete didn't never shoot but one man, and I think he hit him by accident. Course, he sure beat a lot of them up, and Three-Fingered Jack died from a whupping, so maybe that evens out the score."

11

The road was muddy, the going slow. Ruts the tires fell into bounced them so hard Sunset thought her insides were going to jump out of her mouth.

Clyde said, "Hope all that wiring I've done to hold the engine don't give . . . hey, right over there, down that little road, there's an overhang. It ain't real high, but it hangs over part of Holiday. Gal jumped off it once, tried to kill herself, but all she did was hit where it widens and roll all the way down. Ended up lying up against the back side of the drugstore. She had stripped off naked to jump. Friend of mine was out back of the store letting water out, seen her roll down the hill. Said he'd just gone to church that morning for the first time in ten years, thought maybe it was a gift from God. It wasn't. She was mad as a hornet and cussing everything and everybody, including him. Said what he had out wasn't big enough to drain water, let alone use for anything else. She come out of it with some grass stains and some sticker burrs in her ass. My friend Lonnie never did go to church again. But it's good up there at night. Nice with all them lights shining up at you."

As they neared Holiday, alongside the road they saw oil wells poking up, and through gaps in the woods they could see more. The closer they came to the town the more wells they saw, some of them right in the city limits, even in the midst of town. There were so many they made a kind of metal forest.

"It ain't been no time that this here wasn't nothing but a

burg, now it's got ten thousand people," Clyde said. "Wildcatters, roughnecks, gamblers, thugs and whores. Oil makes people crazy, same way as gold— Damn. Ruts are near up to the axle. This ain't so much a street as a goddamn mud hole."

"See a hat on the ground," Hillbilly said, "most likely you'll find a man under it. Sitting on a horse."

A few mules and cars were slogging through the mud-rutted street, but for the most part traffic had stopped, and a crowd, whites and coloreds, had gathered near the new picture show. The white folks were in front, the coloreds lingered back a ways, lest they somehow be considered part of the problem. Folks hid themselves behind cars or poked their heads around the edges of buildings. A number of them were armed.

"I don't think you ought to drive up there," Sunset said.

"Don't know I can," Clyde said. "Go much farther, we might never get out of the mud. Be hard enough just to turn it around."

Clyde managed the truck onto a patch of solid ground, off the road, parked a pretty good distance away. They got out and walked along the wooden sidewalk opposite the picture show. Hillbilly was carrying the shotgun, and Clyde had the revolver in his hand, letting it dangle by his side.

The crowd turned to look at them.

"They're trying to figure that badge on your shirt," Hillbilly said. "Or in the case of the men, the hill on which it rests."

"Just keep walking," Sunset said.

They could see Morgan over there, and the other deputy. They were behind a parked truck. A dead mule lay halfway in the muddy street and halfway on the sidewalk. Its head was a mess and it had passed a pile of turds. They were still steaming.

"Shot the doodie out of him," Clyde said.

At the mouth of the picture show, they could see a door was partly open, and what was keeping it that way was a man's leg.

There was blood all around the door and a white hat was upside down on the sidewalk. Sunset concluded the body was the sheriff.

When they got even with the picture show there wasn't any way to get across other than to go through the mud.

"I can tote you if you want," Clyde said.

Sunset considered this, concluded the constable being carried across mud like a child wasn't the impression she wanted to make.

She said, "I'm the constable, I ought to act like one."

"You ain't the constable in this town," Hillbilly said.

"They asked for me, so I got to look the part."

"Who said the constable has to be muddy?" Clyde said.

Sunset hiked her dress to her thighs. Hillbilly grinned, said, "Damn. Reckon you're right. Walk across on your own."

As they crossed, she glanced repeatedly at the theater, but no one came out to take a shot at her. The sign on the theater said THE STRAND, and the marquee said "ANIMAL CRACKERS starring the Marx Brothers."

When they got to the other side, mud was caked on Sunset's calves. She hated to lower her skirt into the mud, but decided she wouldn't be as handy if she had to walk around holding it up. She also noted that men who had been worried about the man in the theater had stopped to pay attention to her. As had some women, who looked on, disapproving, from the sidelines.

At least, she thought, it takes them away from looking at my bruised face.

Driven up on the sidewalk was one of the city's two police cars. The other they had passed coming into town, parked behind a pickup where Morgan had left it.

Behind the car was Morgan and a badged man she assumed was Rooster. Rooster was long and lanky and wore a tall brown hat with a wide brim. His clothes hung on him like he was made of sticks, and his pants were stuffed into boots with big red eagles stitched on the toes. His ears looked as if they could flap and carry him away. His face was blushed all over, like he had just been scalded.

"He told me you was a woman," Rooster said.

"Was a woman when he saw me, still am now," Sunset said.

"I ain't complaining. Need all the help I can get."

"What happened?" Hillbilly said.

"Don't rightly know it all," Rooster said. "Lillian, she's the one takes the tickets, said this here colored fella, everyone calls him Smoky, come up to the window, said he wanted to buy a ticket. She wouldn't sell him one, of course."

"You got day features?" Clyde asked.

"Now and then," Rooster said. "With so many loafers around town now, they can bring in the day trade."

"Damn," Clyde said. "Going to a movie in the middle of the day. Ain't that something?"

"Forget the day features," Sunset said. "Go on. Tell it."

Rooster nodded. "Lillian told him this wasn't no colored theater. He said something about didn't it have a colored section, and she said no, and he went home and got a shotgun. She seen him coming and she ducked down in the ticket booth. He went inside and Lillian run for it. She come and got us. Smoky run everybody out of the show, and when we come over with the sheriff, and the sheriff went up there to talk to him, he got as far as the door, as you can see, and Smoky cut down on him."

"Sheriff knew Smoky," Morgan said. "Thought he'd be okay. I told him you can't tell nothing about a nigger. They can turn on you like a cottonmouth. I knew of one once got mad at his wife and cut his own throat with a butter knife. Had to saw through for about five minutes before it killed him. But he did it."

"Still," Rooster said, "I ain't never heard of nobody wanting to see a picture show that bad, have you?"

"Can't say I have," Sunset said. "But I guess now that picture show has a colored section."

"Reckon so."

"He might have really wanted to win them dishes," Clyde said.

"Thing is," Rooster said, "if Smoky ain't a big enough problem, couple times the crowd has threatened to burn down the picture show. I ain't been to the show yet. And neither have a lot of folks in this town, and we don't want to see it burned. And there's the colored fella. They want to lynch him. I reckon he's got it coming, but I'm the law, and the law is supposed to do these things—the arresting—not a bunch of thugs, and a judge and a jury are supposed to do the killing if he needs it. And he needs it."

"What about the grocer?" Sunset asked.

"Tried to go in there like a bad man, got his leg shot off. Didn't get as far as the sheriff. Wasn't six feet from the car here when Smoky poked that shotgun out and cut down on him. Told him not to try it, but did he listen? No. Ain't no one listens to me. He got toted off to the doctor over in Tyler. One we got here's all right if you got a cold. But don't get shot. Dumb bastard, going in like that. From now on he's gonna have to hop to work."

"What happened to the mule?" Hillbilly asked.

"Smoky took a second shot at the grocer, who was crawling behind the car here, mule got frightened from all the noise, broke from its owner, run up here and Smoky shot it."

"Why?"

"Beats me."

"What kind of shotgun he got?" Clyde asked. "A pump?"

"That's it," Rooster said.

"Damn," Clyde said.

"Is Smoky still there at the door?"

"Don't know. Don't want to go find out. Oh, hell. Here comes Phillip Macavee."

Sunset turned. A short man with a tall black hat and a belly that could have used a wheelbarrow under it was crossing the street, moving through the mud as if doing a high-step march. The crowd was getting braver as well. They moved out from behind cars and stood as if waiting for Macavee to give them the word to follow.

"Who's Macavee?" Sunset asked.

"Owns a well, thinks cause he's got money that makes his dick not stink—oh, sorry, miss."

"That's all right."

"Used to drive a pickup truck and gather up garbage. But he got lucky with a well. Been stirring everybody up. He's the main one says we ought to burn the place down. He's the one got the grocer worked up. The idea of a nigger hung up or on fire is just the sort of thing that would make him sleep good."

Just before Macavee reached them, Rooster said, "That nigger is gonna shoot anybody, wish he'd do it now, clip that Macavee one."

Macavee kept coming until he stood in front of Sunset.

He studied Sunset a moment, said, "Listen here, young lady. You ought to take that badge off. Ought to be home with some children, or some dolls. This ain't no place for play. Me and some of the boys think we ought to drive a car right up to the front door there, blazing away, and have some others come in the back. If we can't get close enough to shoot the nigger, we could toss some gasoline, get a fire going. Burn that picture show and that burr head both to the ground."

Sunset jerked the revolver out of the holster, and with a

motion quicker than she'd've thought she could muster, fanned the barrel alongside Macavee's body, over his shoulder, and back behind his jaw toward her.

It was a good blow. There was a meaty noise and Macavee's head jerked up and his hat leaped away. He seemed to focus on Sunset a second, then fell straight toward her.

Sunset moved just in time to let his face hit the mud. His forehead banged the edge of the board sidewalk.

There was a moment of silence.

Sunset looked at the crowd. There were a lot of open mouths. "Any of them decide they're coming for me," she said, "shoot above their heads first. Second time, shoot to wound."

"Is blowing off a leg considered a wound?" Clyde said.

"I'll be damned," Rooster said, looking at Macavee. "Wish to hell I'd thought of that. I just asked him to shut up."

Morgan flipped Macavee over. His forehead had a strip of blood where he had hit the board sidewalk and his face was coated in mud.

"I didn't kill him, did I?" Sunset said.

"Nope," Clyde said. "But he wakes up, you could tell him he's a waitress on a gambling boat and he'd believe it."

"I took your advice."

"You sure did. That's what Pete used to do."

The crowd, which had been following Macavee, moved back a step.

Sunset said, "Go on, folks. All Smoky would have to do is point and pull, and about half of you would be in the rest of you folks' pockets."

The crowed grumbled, backed up, found places behind cars or where they thought they were out of scattergun range.

Sunset put the revolver back in the holster, turned to Rooster, said, "Well, Smoky needs arresting."

"We done figured that," Morgan said. "Sheriff thought so too. But that didn't work out."

"Guess I'll have to go in and get him."

"You're kidding us, right?" Morgan said.

"I don't think so."

"You're here to help," Clyde said. "You ain't the one to do no arresting."

Sunset smiled at him, started around the front of the car, onto the sidewalk.

"Miss," Rooster said, "you ought not do that."

"You going in there to get him?" Sunset asked.

"No, I ain't," Rooster said.

"Morgan?"

"Ain't planning on it."

She looked at Clyde. "I think we're just about out of law enforcement. So that leaves it to me."

"And me," Clyde said.

"I guess I have to chime in on that, too," Hillbilly said. "But I want someone to note that I said I thought this was a damn bad idea."

"Noted," Sunset said.

"I want someone to note it ain't gonna get killed, so they'll remember I said it."

"Got you covered," Rooster said. "On the note part, and with a gun. But I ain't getting around in front of that car, and I advise you to step on back this way, ma'am."

"I'll do it," Clyde said.

"No, you won't," Sunset said. "Last time I looked, I was the boss. Give me that slap jack."

She unbuttoned the top two buttons on her shirt and took the slap jack from Clyde and slipped it inside her shirt so that it hung under her bra and under her left arm.

Sunset started walking toward the theater.

"Now's the time for me to tell you I ain't much of a shot," Rooster said.

Sunset paused. "Can any of you hit anything?"

"I couldn't hit an elephant in the ass with a two-by-four if I was standing behind him," Hillbilly said.

"I can," Clyde said.

"Then drape over the hood there, and keep a bead on the door."

Clyde leaned over the hood and pointed the pistol. "Don't walk in front of me," he said. "Sticks his head out, ain't asking questions. He gets popped. And watch it. You're about to step in mule shit."

Gun drawn, Sunset came to the open door and didn't find Smoky behind it. She stepped over the sheriff's body. Blood was on the floor and drying and it stuck to her shoes like gum. Nearby, a box of yellow giveaway dishes lay overturned and broken.

She made bloody tracks to the dark entrance, where she could hear movie voices. She stuck her head inside. It took a moment for her eyes to adjust, but pretty soon she could see Smoky's head. He was sitting in an aisle seat, the shotgun propped against his shoulder like a sentry.

Sunset didn't know how good a shot she was. She might hit him from where she was, but if she missed, well, there would be a blazing gun battle. She figured that happened, she would wind up on the bad end of the program. Already Smoky had one man dead, one man crippled, one mule harvested. A redheaded woman wearing a constable's badge wouldn't be much of a reach.

She put her gun away, said, "Smoky."

Smoky turned his head slowly, like it didn't matter. She

couldn't see his features, just a black face in shadows and screen flickers.

"My name is Sunset. I'm the constable over at Camp Rapture."

"That the sawmill place?" Smoky said.

"Yes."

"You're a woman."

"Everyone seems to notice."

"You sure you the sheriff?"

"Constable. Almost the same thing. I'm supposed to bring you out and they're going to arrest you. That's the way it has to be."

"They're gonna hang me. Cut my balls off first, make me suffer. I seen it done once. They even set the man on fire before they hanged him."

"I'm not going to let that happen."

"That's what you say."

"I got some men out there will help me see it don't happen."

"They gonna give me the 'lectric chair."

"You'll get a fair trial."

"Colored don't get fair trials."

"You killed a man, Smoky."

"Didn't have nothing against that sheriff. He was a good man. Just wanted to watch a picture show. Ain't never seen one. Ought to be able to watch a picture show. They could have a colored section. They could put a curtain up between us and them or something. Wouldn't have to see our faces."

"You don't go with me, do it my way, Smoky, you will be lynched."

"They'll kill me anyway. Nice and legal."

"Not with your pants down, cut up and tortured. Everyone seeing you humiliated. You want that?"

117

Smoky turned back to the movie. "I don't regret that ole grocer none. And I don't like mules either."

Sunset eased forward, slipped into the seat behind Smoky.

"You let me finish the picture show?" Smoky asked.

"I can arrange that."

"I'll keep the shotgun till then."

"I'll tell them outside," Sunset said.

"That ain't a real mustache, is it?"

"What?"

"Not you. That fella, in the movie, he ain't got a real mustache, does he?"

Sunset looked at the screen. "I think it's painted on."

"That's what I thought. That's supposed to be funny, ain't it?"

"I'll go out now, talk to them."

"I had to start that thing up there, what's it called, a camera?"

"Projector, I think."

"Had to do that so I could see it from the first. Figured it out. I was always good figuring stuff like that out. I could have worked here."

"I'll be going out now, Smoky."

"I rubbed my ass around in this seat real good, gave it a real dose of nigger butt, that's what I did. Don't tell them which seat. That way someone's got to sit in it."

"We'll keep it between me and you."

Sunset stood up slowly and walked out of the theater.

Rooster said, "Really think he's gonna let you take him when that picture's over? Whatever he's been drinking, you been drinking some of it too."

"Why don't we have you get him a little picnic lunch when you go back in," Morgan said. "Some chicken and light bread. Maybe some pie."

"Might not be a bad idea," Sunset said. "Hillbilly, go over to the cafe, see can you rustle up something already cooked. Tell them the law will pay for it. Have them sign a receipt or something."

Hillbilly started slogging across the mud.

"Which law is gonna pay for it?" Rooster asked.

"Your town, your bill," Sunset said.

"Can't believe you're gonna go back in there," Morgan said. "And with a goddamn picnic lunch."

"Beats a shoot-out," Sunset said.

"I'll go back in with you," Clyde said.

"I don't want to scare him, make him think I'm going back on my word."

"Why don't we show him an extra picture, maybe a cartoon," Morgan said. "Hell, woman, why don't you offer him a piece?"

Before Sunset could respond to that, Clyde hit Morgan on the jaw with his fist. Morgan did a kind of hop, twisted, fell face forward into the pile of mule dung, next to the dead mule's ass.

"He was building up to that," Clyde said, "and finally he got there."

"Give him about half a minute," Sunset said. "Then pull him out so he can breathe."

"People seen you do that," Rooster said. "They seen you hit an officer of the law, Clyde."

"Yeah," Clyde said. "Think they did. But since I'm kind of an officer of the law, maybe that evens it out."

Hillbilly came hustling across the mud with a plate covered with a red-and-white-check napkin.

"I had to get this off of a fella's plate. He didn't like it none. I didn't get nothing to drink. It's just chicken and biscuits."

"Let me have it," Sunset said, and started back inside.

"What happened to Morgan there?" Hillbilly asked.

"Fainted," Clyde said.

When Sunset disappeared into the theater, Rooster said, "I think Morgan has been in that mule shit for a whole minute or two now."

"Reckon you're right," Clyde said.

"We ought to turn him," Rooster said.

"I'm studying on it."

Inside, Sunset gave Smoky the chicken and biscuits. He took it and ate, watched the picture. She looked at the movie but couldn't hear it. Her ears wouldn't listen. All she could think about was Smoky and the shotgun. She quietly pulled the pistol and laid it in her lap, her hand on it.

When the movie was over Smoky set the plate on the floor in the aisle, stood up and gave Sunset the shotgun.

"It ain't loaded nohow," Smoky said. "Was, I'd have shot myself. I just had them shells I used. I shouldn't have shot the sheriff."

"Let's go on out, Smoky."

"I did get to see me a picture show."

"You did," Sunset said.

"Maybe I ought to shut the projector off."

"That's all right. Someone else will do it."

They went up the aisle, and when they got to the door, Smoky paused at the sheriff's body.

"Happened so fast," he said. "Brought the gun up and shot him. I didn't even think about it."

While they were pausing at the door, Sunset said, "Clyde. Hillbilly. Y'all come and help me."

With Smoky between Clyde and Hillbilly, they walked him to the police car where Rooster stood, pistol drawn. Morgan was up, sitting on the sidewalk. There was mule shit on his face.

Macavee was in the back of the police car, face caked with mud.

Smoky said, "They look like they come out of a minstrel show, their faces all darked up like that."

"We're taking Smoky with us," Sunset said.

"Okay by me," Rooster said.

Sunset reached inside her shirt, pulled out the slap jack, gave it to Clyde, said, "Okay, Smoky, start moving."

They plodded through the mud, past the grumbling white crowd and the quietly observing negroes.

"Them peckerwoods just gonna break me out of jail and kill me," Smoky said.

"You're not going to this jail," Sunset said.

They walked him to the truck, sat him in the truck bed with Clyde and his shotgun. Hillbilly drove them out of there with only the slightest grinding of gears.

Hillbilly said, "That was a brave thing you done."

"Maybe."

"Where we taking him?"

"Tyler."

Hillbilly reached over, touched Sunset's hand. "You are one brave woman," he said.

It was a good distance to Tyler, and by the time they got Smoky delivered to the jail, it was dark.

Clyde drove on the way back, not liking Hillbilly's motoring style. When they pulled into the yard, the truck lights shone on the big black-and-white dog standing near the water pump. It darted into the woods.

"Poor thing," Sunset said. "I'll put some food out."

"You'll have a dog you do," Clyde said.

"That's not so bad," Sunset said.

Hillbilly got out, held out his hand, helped Sunset down.

"Guess I'll see you tomorrow," Hillbilly said.

"Good night, Sunset," Clyde said.

"I'm not much of a law having to depend on a borrowed truck," she said. "What happens things go wrong at night?"

"Hope they don't," Clyde said. "Come on, Hillbilly. Let's go. I got to get some sleep. And you hold on to her hand too long, it's likely to come off."

"See you tomorrow," Hillbilly said again.

Clyde drove them away.

Sunset noticed the dog lying under a big oak, his head on his paws, looking at her.

"Come on, boy," she said. "Come on." But the dog didn't budge.

She walked toward him slowly, and he still didn't move. But when she was within ten feet of him, he jumped up and growled, then scampered into the woods.

Sunset sighed, stopped to study the stars she could see through the tall tops of the trees. Now that the rain had passed the sky was void of clouds and the stars stood out clear and bright as the eyes of a newborn. She could see shapes in the sky made by the stars and she tried to find the Big Dipper, but there were too many trees. She could only see a small pattern of stars and none of them seemed to be the Big Dipper, or the Little Dipper, for that matter.

Inside the tent, Karen was sleeping. Her breathing was loud and even. The dress she had put on that morning was draped over the back of a chair. She lay on the mattress with the covers pulled over her head, the lantern sitting on the floor, glowing with what kerosene was left.

Sunset hated to see the kerosene wasted when not needed. Too expensive. But she made a mental note not to say anything about it. Not unless it happened again.

She pulled off her shirt and skirt, tossed them on the chair with Karen's clothes. She had quit wearing slips and girdles, a real scandal in these parts. She thought as constable she might need to move fast, and too many undergarments hindered that. It was comfortable to sit on the edge of the mattress on the floor in her bra and panties.

Thinking about the day, she trembled, thought: Good Lord, woman, when did you get so bold? What if Smoky had had another shell for his shotgun and decided not to use it on himself? What then?

She blew out the lamp, climbed under the covers, tried to sleep, but sleep wouldn't come.

She lay there for a time, heard movement outside, around the tent. She suspected the dog.

She slipped on her skirt and blouse, picked up her pistol, eased to the opening, gently untied the flap. She took several deep breaths, then flipped the flap back and stepped barefoot into the night.

The dog wasn't there, but she did see a figure moving into the woods, quickly. A man. A very large man. She yelled, "Who is it?" but there was no answer, just the buzz of a mosquito in her ear.

Looking down, she saw an empty milk bottle next to the tent opening. Inside it was a rolled piece of paper.

Sunset studied the woods for a while, finally picked up the bottle, went inside, tied the flap shut. She went to the business side of the tent, behind the curtain of blankets and quilts, put the pistol on the table, lit the lamp there, shook the rolled paper from the bottle.

She spread the paper on the tabletop.

smokey my cuzin—got tole whad yew did—yew dun rite—yew wuz
rite by Smokey—he'z goner git whad he dun got fer hisself bud you
dun dun good by hem and i have you no i hep you any tym yew
needs it i is yers to cal on fer any kines of thangs—ther all kines of
thangs i no.

Bull

Bull. She had heard of Bull. If it was the same man, and surely it was. How many Bulls were there? His name was Bull Thomas, and he was a big black man that lived deep in the woods. Said to be well over six foot tall and over three foot wide, and when you found his footprints in the woods, the size boot he wore had to be at least a twenty-two. Because of that, it was said he made his own boots. She had even heard rumor that the boots were made out of a white man's ass. Guy wandered onto his property, and Bull shot him and made those boots.

Sunset smiled as she thought about that. Who had survived to tell this tale? Was it the white man? Wounded, his ass cut off, crawling out of the woods to tell the tale?

Story was, Bull's land was booby-trapped, and so was his house. He had set it up that way some years ago when Klan members decided he was too uppity. They had rode horseback through the dense woods out to his place to teach him a lesson. One of the horses got in a bear trap and had to be shot on the spot. One of the Knights of the White Carnation fell in a pit and broke his leg, and Bull shot another one in the arm.

The Klan decided that Bull was more than they wanted, and had since let bygones be bygones because Bull had put out the word if he ever saw them again he'd shoot to kill, that he wasn't impressed by their sheets, had sheets himself, but was smart enough to know they went on the bed, not over your head.

Bull was the only colored man Sunset knew of who could

talk that way to white men and get away with it. Partly because he stayed back in the deeper parts of the woods on his booby-trapped property, and partly because he wasn't frightened of much of anything and was willing to fight back, and partly because a lot of whites wanted to keep him happy and healthy because he was said to make the best whisky in these parts.

Sunset rolled the note up, shoved it back in the bottle. She found a flashlight, blew out the lantern, went to the other side of the tent and looked through her supplies. She found some hardened corn dodgers she had cooked up, took them outside and walked over to the oak where she had last seen the dog.

She put the corn dodgers on the ground, called for the dog. He didn't come and she didn't see or hear him. She gathered up the dodgers, went back and undressed, went to bed, the gun by her side.

It was a long time before she finally drifted off, dreaming about the poor baby, about Pete, and why he bothered to bury the child. She dreamed about the Marx Brothers movie, Smoky and the shotgun, the poor dead sheriff, the poor dead mule. Over and over, she could see herself pulling her pistol, really fast, fanning it against the back of Macavee's jaw, and him going down face first in the mud, then Morgan getting punched by Clyde, falling face forward in what that mule had left.

In her sleep she shivered a little, then chuckled.

Sunset rolled over in bed about daybreak and saw the dog was lying with his head just inside the tent flap. He had his paws under his chin and was watching her.

She slowly got out of bed.

The dog raised his head.

"Easy, boy," she said.

She inched toward him, her hand extended. As she neared, the dog backed out of the tent.

Sunset gathered up the corn dodgers from the night before, unfastened the flap, went outside. The dog was lying down again, paws under his chin.

Sunset held out her right hand with a corn dodger in it. She held the other dodgers in her left hand.

"It's okay," she said. "I know what it's like to lose family. Have em run off. Course, you ain't never shot any of yours, have you?"

The dog looked at her, turned his head from side to side, eased forward, grabbed the dodger, stepped back, gulped it down.

Sunset held out another dodger. The dog inched over and took it. This time he did not move away. She gave him another. And another. By the time she fed him the last corn dodger she was able to put out her hand and stroke his head.

"Want to be my dog? I ain't ever gonna run off and leave you. I promise."

The dog licked her hand.

When Karen awoke, Sunset was dressed and cooking breakfast. Pancakes. She had also poured some molasses syrup into a pan and was heating it on the stove.

The big dog was lying on the floor near Sunset's feet.

Sunset turned, saw Karen rise up, said, "Be easy. He's still a little skiddish."

"Will he bite?"

"Any dog will bite sometimes."

"Will he bite me?"

"Not if you're nice. Don't scare him."

"He don't look scared to me."

Sunset smiled. "Didn't have no butter. But the syrup is warm. It'll be on the table in a minute."

"Are we gonna keep him?"

"Yeah. I promised him. Reckon he's had enough promises broken."

"What's his name?"

"I think it's Ben. Think Clyde said Ben. I'm gonna call him Ben, anyway. Your daddy never would let me have a dog."

"I always wanted one too."

"He's a big old pretty thing, ain't he?"

Karen nodded, got up slowly, eased out of bed.

Sunset said, "Stick out your hand, easy like, and come toward him slowly."

Karen did that.

The dog stood up and licked her hand.

"He likes me," Karen said.

"There's a lot to like."

Karen bent down and hugged the dog. The dog licked her ear.

"Hello, Ben," Karen said.

"Wash your hands before you eat," Sunset said.

12

After about a week on the job, which was mostly sitting around Sunset's tent, delivering one foreclosure paper and making a drunk leave the Camp Rapture store after a fight, Clyde awoke in his broken-down bed thinking of Sunset. He had dreamed about her, and in the dream she was his, but the truth was he wasn't ever going to have her. Not with Hillbilly around.

He even had one dream where he killed Hillbilly by beating him to death with a chicken, then buried him in the yard, with the bird. He liked that dream almost as much as the one where Sunset loved him.

Clyde sat up on the edge of the bed and looked around the room. Newspapers, all manner of junk. Just a path from the bed to the door. And all the rest of the house the same way. Worse.

How did he think he could attract a woman when his house was a pile of shit. Hell, he was a pile of shit. You could stack shit any way you wanted, arrange it any way you wanted, but in the end, no matter how you worked it, a pile of shit was a pile of shit.

It never occurred to him to be any other way.

And then, when Sunset killed her husband, he felt the wind from a door being opened—a door he wanted to walk through. One that led to a room with him and Sunset. The possibility had not been there before, but now . . .

He wanted her. He wanted her to want him. And for the first time in years, he was worried about the way his house looked, the way he looked. And he was damn worried about Hillbilly. The sonofabitch could roll in dirt and come up looking good. He looked as if he had been created for the girls. All lean and handsome, thick hair, no nose, ear or back hair. Hell, his balls were probably smooth.

Clyde pulled on his pants, went through the newspaper path to the room where Hillbilly slept. It was a large room, but it seemed small, as all manner of junk was collected there. Clyde no longer knew what junk it was or why he kept it.

Hillbilly was asleep on a mattress on the floor. Nearby, a big pot was still full of water from the last rain that had leaked through the ceiling. Bugs had died in the pot. It looked real nasty. Clyde hadn't thought about it looking nasty before. But now he could see it. It was nasty.

"You might ought to go on and get up," Clyde said.

Hillbilly turned over slowly, blinked his eyes open. "Time already?"

"You go in today. Tell Sunset I got to take some time off, but I'll be back. I ain't quitting or nothing. And if she needs me bad, come get me. Take the truck."

After Hillbilly left, Clyde stood outside and studied the old worn-out house. Finally he went inside and dragged out a tarp he had saved. It was rotten in spots, but mostly sound, and he tied it between trees, moved some other items out of the house he thought he might need, like his guns, ammunition, pots and pans, lanterns, and such, tucked them under the tarp.

He spent half the day doing this, and pretty soon realized he was merely taking what was in the house outside, and therefore solving little to nothing.

He thought on it a while, put some of the items back in the house, came out and wet his finger by poking it in his mouth, held it up. There was no wind to speak of.

Back inside he got some matches, lit one to a pile of newspapers. The papers were so mildewed and stuck together, the fire went out. He got some kerosene and spread it throughout the house in a winding trail. On his way out the door he struck a match to it.

Outside, Clyde watched, hoping the wind wouldn't change and carry it to the woods. He was amazed at how fast the house caught. Pretty soon flames were licking out of the open door and broken windowpanes. He could hear things popping and crackling inside. All the printed news that was news for the last ten years was on its way to the gods, via a trail of smoke.

Fire licked up through the gaps in the roof and pretty soon the roof caught and the flames made a wavy hat and black smoke poured out of the holes in the roof and out of the fireplace. Glass in the windows popped to pieces. In less than an hour the house was consumed, except for the chimney, but with nothing to hold it up, it fell to the ground with a thunderous crash, tossing bricks in all directions. From the time of starting the fire to the time of flames licking at blackened lumber, broken glass and shattered bricks, about two hours passed.

After a while, Clyde took the shovel he had saved from under the tarp and went over and started stirring things with it, spreading the last of the fire out so it would die. He took water from the well and poured buckets of it on what he deemed trouble spots, places that might flare up again if left alone.

He had spared the chairs, placed them under the tarp, and now he picked one and sat and drank from something else he had spared. A bottle of whisky. It was cheap stuff and it tasted like it, all bite and no sugar. By late afternoon he decided it tasted pretty good and drank it all, fell asleep in his chair.

He did so with new plans in his head for a place to live. He would build a new house. One without newspapers and junk, mold and mildew, a leaky roof and a smell like chicken shit. This one would be fresh and it would be painted white and the roof would be fine, with a brand-new chimney made of red bricks and plaster.

He slept, wishing he could burn himself down and rebuild, maybe in Hillbilly's image.

Was there a blueprint for that?

The smoke had gone from black to white and from rolls to puffs, and pretty soon there wasn't even that, and by late afternoon, while Clyde slept, a soft rain came and stirred the ashes and made fresh smoke.

Lightning flashed and thunder crashed, but Clyde never knew it.

About the time Clyde was snoozing under the tarp and the rain was falling on what remained of his smoldering house, Zendo drove up in his pickup and parked in front of Sunset's tent.

He got out and went cautiously up to the tent. He didn't take hold of the flap. He stood a respectful distance away and called out.

"Miss Constable. Miss Jones."

Sunset and Hillbilly and Karen were sitting on the business side of the tent playing cards. They got up and went out. It was raining lightly.

Zendo had moved back to his truck, and was holding his hat in his hands, turning it like a steering wheel. The rain was running down his face and his clothes were damp with it.

"Zendo," Sunset said, "you look like you've seen a ghost."

"No, ma'am. I ain't seen no ghost. I seen something worse."

Karen, much to her dismay, was made to stay at the tent. Sunset and Hillbilly followed Zendo in Clyde's truck. Hillbilly drove.

They followed Zendo to the tree where they had first spoken, pulled up under it, parked and got out.

Zendo had unharnessed his mules, tied them to two separate trees near the oak to keep them from crossing up. His plow lay on its side, a middle buster attached to it.

Zendo came over, said, "I'll show you now."

He started walking, and they followed.

"I done decided to bust up a bit more of my land. Add a few rows here closer to the woods, to where I found that jar with the baby in it, and, well, my plow cut into it."

Zendo was pointing.

They looked down. There was a dark, round object sticking out of the ground and the top of it was covered in something stringy and oily. It had been cut open with the plow and it was dark inside where it had been cut, looked like old wet cork.

"Is that some kind of vegetable?" Hillbilly said.

"No sir, it ain't," Zendo said. "Come on around here."

They followed him. "Look down there now."

Sunset squatted, turned her head. The big turnip had an eye socket. It was full of black dirt. Below the eyes was a flap of nose and below that a lip, and part of it was gone, and what was left looked to have dried up like a worm on a hot stove. The lip was curled in such a way Sunset could see dirt-stained teeth.

"My God," she said.

"Is it a watermelon?" Hillbilly asked.

"No," Sunset said.

"Naw, it ain't no watermelon," Zendo said.

Hillbilly bent over, looked, said, "Nope. Not a watermelon."

It was long, slow, and careful work because pieces of it kept coming off, but when they dug the body up, they found it had been planted straight down, like a post.

The corpse was covered in something black and sticky. Zendo said, "That's just the way that baby was in the jar. All oily."

"Is that in your soil?" Hillbilly asked. "That oil?"

"Ain't no oil in this soil," Zendo said.

"No maggots," Sunset said. "So it may not have been here long."

"Reckon it's that oily stuff. It's kept the body from rotting outright. Or some of it. Maggots done eat what they gonna eat. Rest, they leave alone."

"Who'd think a maggot had taste buds," Hillbilly said.

"Way the weather is, hot as it is," Sunset said, "it still amazes me it ain't nothing but bones."

"There ain't no way figuring weather or what it'll do," Zendo said.

"Body ain't got no clothes on," Hillbilly said, "but I can't tell if it's a man or a woman."

"It's a woman," Zendo said.

"How do you know?" Hillbilly asked.

"Hip bones, way they spread," Zendo said. "She probably done had a baby."

"I wonder if she was white or black," Sunset said.

"She was white," Zendo said. "That stringy stuff on top of her head ain't colored hair."

Sunset took hold of the hair, rubbed it between thumb and forefinger. It was coated in oil, but it was fine and smooth.

"Probably right," Sunset said. "You got some kind of sheet or old blanket or something, Zendo? Something we could carry the body out with?"

"I can go up to the house and look," Zendo said.

"Would you?"

When Zendo drove off, Hillbilly said, "He sure is certain it's a white woman. I can't look at that hunk of rotten meat and tell

133

much of anything. But he knows it's a woman and he knows she's white."

"Think he would come and get us if he did it?" Sunset asked.

"Could be to throw us off."

"No," Sunset said. "He's as nervous and messed up about it as we are."

"Killers can feel bad about what they done . . . What do you think this oil business is about?"

Sunset shook her head. "I don't know. It's odd. And that baby was coated in oil. I don't get it. And why in the hell are they burying them here on Zendo's patch of land?"

"You're too innocent, Sunset."

"I don't think I'm near that innocent anymore," she said.

"Watch out for Zendo. I don't trust him."

"I think he's all right," Sunset said. "We take the body in, don't mention anything about Zendo or where we found it. Just say it's law business for now. Okay?"

"All right."

They waited about fifteen minutes before Zendo showed up with a ratty-looking patchwork quilt. "We had this for the dog to lie down on. I didn't want to use a new one. Will this be all right?"

"Sure," Sunset said. "She won't mind."

They managed the corpse onto the blanket, loaded it into the back of Clyde's pickup, drove it into Camp Rapture. They found Reverend Willie Fixx at his house eating a meal.

"Well, now," Willie said, holding the door open, his mouth shining with grease from his meal, his eyes roaming Sunset's body from head to toe and back again. "To what do I owe the pleasure, Miss Jones? You coming to be baptized? I don't believe you ever was, not even when you was a little girl. I got a robe you can wear, we can go down to the creek where it's deep and do it."

"I'm here on law business," Sunset said. "This is Deputy Constable Hillbilly."

"Hillbilly," Willie said. "I was trying to remember what I'd heard you called. I thought it was Bum."

"No," Hillbilly said. "That's my usual occupation."

"Law business, you say," Willie said.

"That's right," Sunset said. "You're the only one I knew to come to, since you fix dead bodies up for burying. Maybe I should have gone to the doctor. I wasn't sure."

"Body in the truck?"

Sunset nodded.

"Who is it?"

"Don't know," Sunset said. "Thought you might be able to help me there. Find out how she died, who she is."

"Body is pretty worn out," Hillbilly said. "Can't even tell if it's a man or woman or what color it is."

"Where did you find it?"

"I'd rather not say yet," Sunset said. "Law business again."

"I'm finishing up my dinner."

"We'll wait," Sunset said.

"Drive the body around back. You know where I mean?"

"I think so," Sunset said.

While Willie finished eating, Sunset and Hillbilly got in the truck and Hillbilly drove them around back. There was a low overhang porch there and a big pecan tree and lots of shade. They got out and stood between the car and the tree, and Sunset leaned against the tree. Hillbilly stood very close to her, and then, slowly, he eased his face toward her, and they kissed.

"I been wanting to do that," he said.

"And I been wanting you to," Sunset said. "But not here. Not now."

But she kissed him back.

"That'll have to hold us," she said.

"I suppose," Hillbilly said. "You're trembling."

"I believe I am."

About five minutes later Willie came out of the back, wiping his mouth with his sleeve. He looked in the truck bed at the blanket-covered corpse.

"Ripe-smelling," he said, as he pulled back the blanket. "Oh, yeah. That's a dead one. Don't know if it's white or a nigger?"

"No," Hillbilly said. "The body's coated in oil, which gives it a dark color. That and, well, the meat is so rotten."

"Let's see here. Well, it's a woman. You can tell by that pelvis flare."

Sunset looked at Hillbilly. Hillbilly shrugged.

"Let me see," said Willie as he climbed into the bed of the truck. "Eyes are gone, but looks to have a bit of hair still in place."

Willie took hold of the hair between thumb and forefinger. "Awful fine for a nigger. I'd say it's a white woman. Maybe I ought to say a little prayer over her, case it is a white woman."

"What if she's colored?" Sunset said.

"It won't hurt her none. Hell, say a prayer over a dog it don't hurt nothing, it's just when they're dead, they got no place to go. Haul her inside for me."

Hillbilly and Sunset took hold of opposite ends of the blanket and hauled the body out of the back of the truck, followed Willie inside. It was a small room and there were three wooden coffins against the wall, and there was a table and some instruments for embalming.

"Any way to figure who it is?" Sunset asked.

"No way I know. Thing to do is find if someone is missing. See if they fit the general description. I'll get a height measurement and such. But she needs to go in the ground pronto. She come out of the ground, didn't she? There's dirt mixed in with that oil, and it's spread all over."

"Yeah," Sunset said, "she came out of the ground."

"Might could figure better who it was I knew where you found her," Willie said. "Could even be someone I know."

"The country," Sunset said. "West of here, near the woods."

"The dirt mixed in this oil, the oil makes it dark, but it looks dark to begin with to me. Not all of it, just some. Her left side is dark dirt, the right side is a lighter kind of dirt. Ain't but one person got dirt like that around here. That nigger Zendo. I figure you found it at the edge of his plowed land, that would be the dark dirt on her left side, and the other dirt, that would be land unplowed. Hell, I figure he plowed her up—you figure Zendo did it?"

"I didn't agree with you," Sunset said. "I didn't say Zendo had a thing to do with it."

"Dirt like that, that's Zendo's signature. Everyone knows that nigger could drop an egg in the ground and grow a bush of chickens. It was found on his land, all right."

"Okay," Sunset said. "The body was found on Zendo's land, but you have to take my word for this. He had nothing to do with it."

"You know that for a fact?" Willie said.

"I'm going to say I do. I better not hear a word about this body being found on Zendo's land from anyone, because I'll know where the word came from."

Willie grinned. "You wouldn't threaten me, would you, little lady?"

"I will," Hillbilly said.

Willie studied Hillbilly for a long moment. "Never said I would tell. You're both being rude."

"I'm just a little frayed," Sunset said. "I've had a rough month."

"Suppose you have," Willie said. He extended his hand to Hillbilly. "No hard feelings."

He took Willie's hand and shook it. "None. But, still, don't say anything."

"Think that might have been a little excessive?" Sunset said.

They were riding along in the truck, heading back to Sunset's tent.

"I suppose," Hillbilly said. "Just didn't like the way he was talking."

"I can handle myself. You start handling things for me when I don't need for you to, don't ask you to, people will think I can't do what needs to be done."

"I just don't like that guy."

"I think the feeling was mutual. I don't think he liked me either."

"He liked you all right. I could tell the way he looked at you, especially when you didn't know he was looking."

"Was that the reason you were so hot under the collar?"

"I'm going to be damn honest, Sunset. I ain't the jealous kind."

"Oh," Sunset said.

When they arrived at Sunset's tent, they found Ben lying under a tree on his back with his paws in the air. He turned his head to look at them, but unlike before he didn't act frightened and he didn't dart away.

"You done spoiled him," Hillbilly said.

"I certainly hope so. He's had enough of the bad life. For that matter, so have I."

Inside the tent, Karen, fresh from a bath, well-dressed and groomed, sweet-smelling, greeted them.

"My," said Hillbilly, "aren't you the picture?"

And she was. She looked older than her years. Wore her black hair down, way her mother did, and her dark eyes looked as if they had been spit-shined.

"Just threw something on, really," Karen said.

Hillbilly grinned.

"Think I'm going to make some notes," Sunset said. "That's what Pete used to do. Seems like a good idea."

"What did you see?" Karen said.

"A dead body," Sunset said. "And that's all we know."

"I thought I might go for a walk," Karen said. "You want to walk, Hillbilly?"

"I'll walk with you," Hillbilly said. "I'm not taking any notes."

"Watch for snakes," Sunset said.

Inside she pulled out Pete's notes on the baby found at Zendo's. She thought about the body she had seen. Seemed obvious there was some kind of connection.

But what kind?

Who was the woman they had dug up today?

The baby. Whose baby was it? Was it black or white?

Did Zendo know more than he let on?

No. That didn't seem right. Zendo seemed honestly upset. Of course, it could be an act, but she didn't think so. Finding a body, reporting it like that might be a way to throw suspicion off yourself if you were white, but a colored man doing it—Didn't make sense. Not when colored were normally assumed guilty.

Nope. Zendo was truly trying to do the right thing.

Did the baby belong to the woman, and if so, why were the bodies found so far apart in time?

What was the oil about?

Why Zendo's field?

And why would anyone bury a body straight down, like a post?

Sunset tapped the pencil on the table, finally pulled paper in front of her and wrote down the day's events. She tried to remember everything said and done.

When she finished writing, she had the sinking feeling that she didn't have idea one where to go next with this investigation.

Investigation.

Damn, she thought. I'm investigating. I'm like a detective.

Hell. I am the law. Me. Sunset Jones. The law. Constable Sunset, you bet your ass.

But she still didn't know what to do.

13

When Clyde's drunk began to wear off, he awoke with a headache and the stinking smell of smoke in his nose. He looked at the ruins of his house. He didn't feel quite as happy about what he had done as before, but, on the other hand, he wasn't depressed either.

Well, no more than before he burned down his house.

Just thinking about Sunset and knowing he and she were about as likely as shooting a duck and having it hit the ground dressed and ready to be eaten.

He studied the smoldering ruins a while, then got up. When he did, it was like a shot went through his body and blew out the top of his head.

Whisky.

Bad idea, he thought. Bad idea.

Clyde sat for a while longer, and as the day grew cooler he grew restless and stronger and courageous enough to stand. He went to the well, cranked up a bucket of water and poured it over his head. He did this twice. He pulled up some more and drank from the bucket, poured the rest over his head.

He took out his pocket comb and combed his hair by feel and hoped he didn't look too ridiculous. He started walking down the path that led to the main road. He hadn't intended to do it, but all of a sudden he was walking, and at a brisk pace. As he walked, his head seemed to bob, as if it were about to come loose at the neck. The inside of his skull felt as if someone had held a rodeo there.

The day was so hot that by the time he reached the road his hair was already beginning to dry, and long before he reached his destination, the water that had spilled on his shirt and pants was dry as well.

It took him about two hours to get within reasonable distance of Sunset's place, and before he turned the corner that led to the last stretch of road that ran up to it, he saw Hillbilly come out of the woods, Karen beside him.

Hillbilly was smiling and Karen was laughing. Hillbilly stopped near the road and picked limbs and grass off the back of Karen's dress, and when he finished, Karen leaned over and kissed him on the cheek. He took her hand and held it, and finally she stretched away from him, letting her hand stay in his until she just had to let go. She turned, started back in the direction of the tent.

Hillbilly stood for a while, watching Karen retreat. Finally, when Karen was around the curve, he turned, unzipped his fly and began to pee.

Clyde, standing still at the edge of the road, partially concealed by bushes, hadn't been seen.

He waited a moment, and when Hillbilly fastened up his pants, Clyde stepped out of concealment, walked over to him.

"What in hell are you doing here?" Hillbilly said.

"Walking."

"I see that. Why?"

"I burned my house down."

"What?"

"Burned it down."

"How did that happen?"

"I set it on fire."

"You set it on fire?"

"That's right. You ain't got no place to come back to now,

142

Hillbilly. You're going to have to do otherwise. All I got now is a tarp and some of my stuff under it."

"Why in the world would you burn your house down?"

"I got tired of it. I seen Karen kissing you."

"What?"

"You heard me."

"Hey, just an innocent peck on the cheek."

"It looked more like a thank-you, if you know what I mean."

"Hell, girl's old enough to make her own decisions."

"Some slick talker like you, she's young enough to be thinking she's making decisions you're making for her."

"I said she was old enough and I could do what I wanted, but I didn't say anything happened. You're jumping to conclusions. Hell, man, you been drinking. You smell like a barroom floor."

"Sunset likes you."

"I know that."

"That's her daughter."

"I know that too."

"You ain't easy to reach, are you, Hillbilly?"

"I don't know what you mean."

"Ain't you got feelings?"

"Plenty of them."

"Just all of them are for you."

"It's that way with everyone, Clyde. Lot of people think they're generous, put others before them, but it ain't true. Not really. I'm just watching out for myself. That little girl wants to give me a peck on the cheek, or anything else, that's up to her. I want to let her, that's up to me."

"You think you're special, don't you, Hillbilly?"

"I think I got to do what I got to do, and that's all I think."

"Don't come back to my place tonight."

143

"No reason to. You burned it down. I'm going to go for a little walk. Tell Sunset I'll be back in a shake. While you're at it, ask her about the body we found today."

"Body?"

Hillbilly went to the road, started walking in the opposite direction of Sunset's tent. He paused, turned, said, "Hope you didn't burn your house down just to get rid of me. All you had to do was ask. Besides, even if you start fresh, which is what I figure you think you're doing, get a new hat and a close shave, it won't make any difference. She still won't be interested, friend. You'll still be you."

"You don't know nothing," Clyde said.

"Hell, I know that much."

Clyde arrived at Sunset's tent and Ben came up and smelled him. Clyde gave Ben a pat, went inside. Karen was sitting in a chair with a book in her lap. She was looking into space in a dreamy way. She didn't even notice Clyde until he spoke to her.

"Oh, hi, Clyde. Mama's on the other side."

Clyde went around the curtain, found Sunset at the table, writing furiously on a yellow pad. She looked at him when he came in, held up a wait-a-minute finger, and continued writing.

Clyde took a chair, watched her write. He liked watching her do most anything. Her hair was so red and long and smooth, flame-like, but much prettier in color than the fire that had licked his home to death. Her face was smooth and pink-cheeked and she had about the most beautiful nose and mouth he had ever seen. He really liked her mouth. Last night, in his dreams, her mouth had played a prominent part. He even liked the way her feet fit in her work boots; there was something so damn cute about those little feet in those work boots. And that thick gun belt. He shouldn't think of that as cute, but he did. If she had suddenly bent over and farted out "Old Man River" to the beat of her tapping feet, he knew he would have found that cute as well.

Cute. He had never even let the word run around in his mind before.

"You been building a fire, burning brush?" Sunset asked.

"Something like that. Hillbilly said he'd be back in a few shakes."

Clyde thought about what he had seen, realized he hadn't really seen anything. He thought he ought to say something anyway, but wasn't sure what to say. All he had seen was a kiss, and on the cheek.

"Oh, has Karen come back?" Sunset asked.

"Yeah. She's on the other side, sitting with a book. Hillbilly told me to ask about the body you found."

"I was just writing about it. Zendo found it."

"Another one?"

"Not a baby this time." And Sunset told him all about it.

When she finished, she said, "Hillbilly thinks Zendo might be involved."

"He ain't."

"That's what I thought."

"I've known Zendo all my life. I've known Hillbilly a few weeks. He ain't near the smart fella he thinks he is. I wanted to know something, I'd ask Zendo before I'd ask Hillbilly. Unless it was how to lay out under a tree."

"Hillbilly seems bright enough."

Clyde made a noise in his throat that sounded like someone who had just discovered he had been spoon-fed horse turds, but he decided not to carry on about Hillbilly any more. He thought he probably was making mountains out of molehills. When it came to Hillbilly, he wasn't the one to be asked an opinion.

"Was it a murder?" Clyde said.

"I think it was. Preacher Willie is looking at the body. It sure didn't bury itself in that field, but I can't tell how she died. Body is too worn away. Suppose she could have just died and someone decided to plant her out there like a tater, but I doubt it."

"Got any ideas for figuring out who done it?" Clyde asked.

"Not a one. I thought I'd write down what I know, look through Pete's files, see if that would help me."

"By finding something like it?"

"That's what I thought too, Clyde. Maybe there's been something like it before. Well, there has."

"The baby."

"Right. But maybe something else kind of like it. Where Pete knew who done it or had some idea."

"Wouldn't you have heard about it?"

"Pete didn't tell me anything. But the bottom line is I looked to see if there were any similar things happened, and I didn't find nothing.

"Thing I will say, Pete was pretty careful about writing down his constable business. There's a note on damn near everything. Most of them are brief, and he made them for him to know what he was talking about, so he could look back and remember. Some of this stuff, I don't really know what he's saying."

"You think a person can start over, Sunset?"

"Do what?"

"You know, change their lives. Maybe get something better for themselves."

"Well, you got this job for as long as it lasts. That beats the sawmill, don't it?"

"I mean really change? Change themselves."

"I hope so. Yeah. I think so. I swear, Clyde, you been around a hell of a fire. You're making my eyes water."

"What's that?"

"I said you smell like a campfire."

"I smell like it cause I burned my house down."

Sunset's mouth fell open. When she cranked it back up, she said, "My God. How did it happen?"

"I used a match."

"You did it?"

"Yep."

"On purpose?"

"Purposeful as I could."

"Where will Hillbilly stay?"

The question was like an arrow in his heart.

"I don't know. Not with me. Hell, I don't give a damn where he stays."

Sunset's face soured slightly. She said, "Are you having trouble with Hillbilly?"

"Just a little."

Ben barked, then Hillbilly appeared, pushing a hanging blanket aside. Sunset looked up at him. Clyde watched her face light up like a kerosene lamp in a dark, windowless house.

"Clyde burned his house down," Sunset said. "On purpose."

"Yeah," Hillbilly said. "I heard."

Karen slipped in beside Hillbilly. She said, "He did what?"

Sunset said what she had said before.

"Clyde," Karen said, "why would you do such a thing?"

"Starting over, honey," he said, "and burning out rats."

"That's funny," Karen said, and she smiled big. "You burned your whole house down to get rid of rats."

Clyde watched Sunset study Karen's smile, and thought, Yeah, that rat thing isn't that funny, is it? And that smile she's got, it's the first big one she's had since before her daddy died. I know it, honey, and you know it. And I think I know why, and though it's great she's happy, and I can tell you want to be happy for her, if I'm right, it's wrong why she's happy, cause she's just a kid, and Hillbilly, he's such a liar. You big beautiful redheaded gal, do you even suspect? Have you got any idea?

Course not. You're blind as Karen on account of that sonofabitch. Man, I can smell the heat coming off of you and her, coming off you for him. All hot and wet and willing, and here I am, wanting you, loving you, and you ain't even seeing me.

And maybe I'm the one who's full of it. Maybe he and Karen ain't got nothing going, except maybe he's like a daddy to her, and they were just walking in the dark part of the goddamn woods, and that's all there is to it, and maybe I'm jealous of you and Hillbilly, how you feel about him. Yeah, that could be it or part of it.

Hell. Of course it is.

14

The big truck rumbled along and now and then coughed black smoke. The hood rattled where it was tied down with a strand of baling wire and the body listed to one side where the shocks were wore out. It had big side boards and inside the bed were five men and three women and a kid, a boy about thirteen. The man driving was a red-faced guy with a cigar growing out of his teeth. He didn't have anyone sitting in the truck beside him, and wouldn't let anyone ride there, not even one of the wore-out women.

He had picked them all up earlier that day at the cotton gin in Holiday. Folks gathered there regularly looking for work, usually not finding it, and he knew he could pick up day labor by just showing up and promising a dollar a day to work his fields, which were way out of town, out in the low, damp lands between the trees.

Now that his crew was finished working, were hot and sweaty and worn out, he was supposed to take them on into Camp Rapture so they could look for work at the sawmill, and it was time to pay up.

He let out the clutch as he shifted to a lower speed to take a hill, didn't feed it any gas. The truck bunny-hopped and died. He pulled on the parking brake, got out, went around to the rear.

"I got some trouble," he said.

There was a slight groan from the folks in the truck, and one of them, wearing an old suit coat that was so damn thin you could almost see the green stripes on his shirt through it, sat up, took hold of the side boards and looked through them.

He was a big fellow, strong-looking, gone a little to fat. His hair had that look red hair gets when it goes gray.

"You just worked the clutch wrong," the man in the coat said.

"Well, it was that, but there's something wrong with it. I've had it happen before. I want everyone to get out and give me a push and maybe I can jump the clutch and start it."

"Get in and try it again. It'll catch."

"Naw, you'd think that, but it won't. It don't run right. I've had it happen before. Y'all get out now and push."

"When are we going to get paid?"

"When we get to Camp Rapture."

"Why don't we do it right now? I don't know why we got to go there to get paid. We want to go there to look for work. We don't have to go there to get paid. You can pay us right now."

"That sounds like a good idea," said another of the men.

"I hear you," said the driver, "but I want to get the truck going first. That's not much to ask. I got to go there to get the money."

"Why?" said the man in the suit coat.

"I don't, you don't get paid, cause that's where I got my money."

"A place like that got a bank?"

"No. But the store there, they keep some money for people. They ain't like a bank. They're better'n a bank. They hold it and you got to buy some things there for holding it, but they don't bust like a bank and they don't have interest, just something you got to buy now and then, something you'd buy anyway. Flour, maybe."

"They're not going to be open time we get there."

"I think they will, and if they ain't, I know the owner. It ain't a problem."

Slowly, everyone piled out. The red-faced man tongued his cigar to the other side of his mouth, said, "Now, y'all get at the back, and when I tell you, push. Stand kind of to the sides, so if it rolls back, it won't run over you."

"Let me give it a try," said the big man with the suit coat.

"I don't let no one drive my truck but me."

"Maybe you ought to," said the boy, "way you drive."

The boy was feisty-looking, with a shock of hay-colored hair hanging out from under his tweed cap.

"You ought not talk to your elders like that. You do again, and I'll backhand you."

"No you won't," said the man in the suit coat.

"Look here," said the red-faced man, "just help me get it going. We get into Camp Rapture and I can get you all paid."

"Let's just do it," said one of the women. She was tired and pregnant and had put in a full day. There was dust in her hair from the fields, and she had teeth missing. She looked as if at any moment she would dry up and blow away, leaving only her plump belly and the kid inside of it.

"All right," said the man in the suit coat.

They went to the rear of the truck, and the red-faced man got behind the wheel. He stuck his head out the window, said, "Get ready to push."

They split into two groups, four on one side, five on the other, near the rear, ready to push. The red-faced man said, "Y'all ready?"

"We're ready," said one of the men.

"Here we go," said the red-faced fellow. He started it up, worked the clutch and drove off a ways, began picking up speed.

"Hey! Hey!" yelled the boy, running after him. "Come back."

An arm stuck out the window and waved.

"Come back," the boy said again.

"I'll be damned," said the man in the suit coat. "I knew better than to let that happen."

"No you didn't," said one of the men.

Suit Coat looked at him. The man was thin and as tired and worn-out-looking as the pregnant woman, who was his wife.

"Goddamn it, we worked all day for nothing," said the boy.

"Reckon so," said Suit Coat, and they all started walking.

"Maybe we can catch him in Camp Rapture," said the pregnant woman. "Make him pay up."

"I catch him," said the thin man, "he'll lose more than his money. He'll lose some teeth, maybe some other parts of him."

"I doubt he's going to Camp Rapture," said another of the men. "That's just something he said."

"I guess we could go out to his field and look him up," said another man.

"It's a lot closer to Camp Rapture than his fields," said Suit Coat. "Figure I'll take the loss, just hope me and him cross paths."

"I'm kind of getting used to getting the shitty end of the stick," said the thin man. "I'm starting to kind of like it, think that's the way it's supposed to be."

"Don't say no more," said his wife. "Just don't mention it."

It was night, and cloudy and dark as the inside of an intestine when a car drove up in front of the tent. Hillbilly had walked off on his own and Clyde had walked back to the remains of his home. When Sunset heard the car, for some reason it struck her as an omen.

Ben growled furiously. Sunset, who was never far from her gun, though maybe not quite as welded to it as before, adjusted the holster on her hip, got up and went outside in time to see the lights of the car go dead. Ben ran up to the driver's side of the car barking. A man was sitting on the passenger side, but there was too much shadow for her to tell right off who it was.

Sunset called the dog a couple of times, and he surprised her by complying. He came and sat down beside her and went silent.

She remembered Pete had once said the scariest kind of dog is the one that stops barking and just goes to watching. She reached down and scratched Ben's head.

A man got out of the car, putting on his hat. He came around in front of the car, stepping lightly. He looked ready at any moment to jump up on the hood.

"Dog won't bite, will he?"

It was Preacher Willie.

"He don't bite me."

"I'll just talk from here."

"Go ahead."

Karen came out of the tent then. She still smelled sweet and her dark clothes and long black hair hung around her shoulders and blended with the night in such a way that she seemed to be little more than a white face floating in the void.

"It's that body you brought in," Preacher Willie said.

"Figured as much. Who you got with you?"

The man on the passenger side stuck his arm out the window, then his head. She still couldn't see him well. He said, "It's Henry, Sunset."

Sunset felt a sinking sensation. She had never really known Henry, but that day at the meeting, she had certainly seen where his thinking was. She also knew he was a man of power in Camp Rapture. His being there meant the preacher hadn't kept the discovery of the body quiet. She wasn't surprised. Hillbilly's little blowup had probably hurt his pride. And her, a woman in a position of power, asking him to be quiet probably hadn't helped either. And frankly, he was an asshole and might have done it anyway.

"Hello, Henry," Sunset said. "And, Willie, I see you did just what I told you not to do."

"I think I know why you didn't want to spread the news around," Willie said.

"That so."

"I know who it is."

"Tell me."

"She was wearing a necklace. You couldn't see it cause it had fallen inside of her, where she had rotted. And it was buried in her neck where it had gone to bad meat. It had her name on it."

"And?"

"Jimmie Jo French."

"My God. I knew her."

"Guess so. You knocked her around."

"I was upset about her and Pete."

"Her being dead would have made a difference for you and Pete, wouldn't it?" Henry said.

"Pete's dead too, so what difference would it make?"

"You might have thought of a difference then," Henry said.

"Then?"

"She's been dead a while. Most likely she's been soaking in oil, then she was buried. You do that, bury her in that field?"

"I was mad. Not crazy."

"Just talking here, Sunset."

"Sure you are."

"Mama," Karen said, "what are they talking about?"

"I'll explain later, hon," Sunset said, patting Karen on the arm.

"Jimmie Jo had a baby inside her," Willie said. "Baby had been cut out of her. Not in a doctor way. Someone slashed her open and jerked it out of her. I could tell that way she was cut."

"Jesus," Sunset said.

"Don't use the Lord's name in vain."

"I said Jesus, Willie. Not to hell with Jesus."

"Now that's enough."

"Keep talking, Willie. You come to me, so keep talking. You and Henry, say what you got to say."

Willie took a deep breath.

"What killed her was a thirty-eight slug in the back of her head. I dug it out."

"That gun you got," Henry said, "it's a thirty-eight, ain't it?"

"You saying I killed her?"

"I'm saying it could look like you did."

"Only if you wanted to say it, Henry. Why would I put her in oil?"

"To preserve her?"

"Why would I do that?"

"If you wanted to hide the body, get rid of it later."

"Ridiculous. I got rid of it once, why would I want to get rid of it twice. And there are lots of thirty-eights. I never had this one until after Pete's death."

"That's what you say," Henry said. "Ain't saying it ain't true, but I am saying it looks bad, Sunset. I don't know we can prove it, but I think I can make a pretty good case for it, and unless you want to go through a bunch of rigmarole, maybe get yourself in jail, maybe you should just turn in the job, let a man take it over."

"Someone you pick?"

"Someone the council picks."

"Hell," Sunset said. "You are the council."

"Mama would never do such a thing," Karen said.

"Think she'd shoot your pa?" Willie said. "Did you think that?"

Karen went silent.

"That's enough, Willie," Sunset said.

"Even if you didn't kill the woman," Henry said, "it all comes back to who's to say the business with Pete happened like

155

you claim. Law ain't even looked into it. You just killed him and took his job. And if you didn't kill Pete's girlfriend, it sure looks bad. And what happened to the baby? A vengeful woman might even go so far as to cut it out of a woman."

"And now you're cavorting with that Hillbilly fella," said Willie. "That don't look good neither. And I saw you kiss him, out the window, I seen it."

"Mama?" Karen said.

"It wasn't nothing," Sunset said.

"It looked like something to me," Willie said.

"That's enough. You've upset my daughter, and you're upsetting me, and it's just wind. You're just blowing wind."

Karen ran inside the tent, crying.

"Happy?" Sunset asked.

"No," Willie said. "Just saying it looks bad, that's all."

"I don't think that's what either of you are saying. And as for Hillbilly, he just works for me."

"I bet he does some work, all right," said Willie.

"Sure you're a preacher?" Sunset said.

"You know I am."

"Can preachers run from dogs? Are they fast?"

"What?"

"Ben. Get him."

Ben barked and leaped forward. Willie let out a yelp, turned and darted around the car, made it inside before the dog caught him, but in the rush, he lost his hat. Ben leaped on it, held it down with one paw and ripped at it with his teeth. It came apart like damp newspaper.

"That wasn't funny, Sunset," Willie said.

"It was for me," Sunset said.

"That was a good hat."

"Was," Sunset said. "I can give it back to you if you want it."

Ben darted around to the passenger side, began leaping up and down on his hind legs, snapping at the open window, tossing froth.

Henry rolled up the window. Ben bounced against the glass repeatedly, snapping, growling and biting the air. The glass grew wet with foam.

Willie started the car, stabbed the night with its lights, drove out of there at a high rate of speed.

"Bye now," Sunset said.

Ben ran after the car for a good distance before he turned around and came back, and Sunset took him into the tent and gave him water and food and petted him and kissed him on his hard old head.

When she finished that, she let him outside, turned her attention to Karen.

"You okay?" Sunset asked.

Karen was sitting on the mattress on the floor, her knees pulled up, clutching them with her arms. Even in the lantern light Sunset could see she was holding so tight her hands were turning white.

"Did you kill her, Mama?"

"What kind of question is that?"

"Did you kill her because of Daddy? Did you kill Daddy because of her?"

"I wouldn't do that. I didn't mean to kill your daddy. Not really. He was hurting me. Bad. And I reached for the gun."

"But you got over being hit. You're well. You'd have got just as well if you hadn't shot him."

"Unless he killed me."

"The baby. One in that colored graveyard. Is that my sister or brother?"

"Honey, we don't even know if the baby and the woman are

157

connected, and if they are, that don't mean it was your daddy's baby."

"They said she was Daddy's girlfriend. Isn't that what they were saying, and that you killed her on account of that? Was she really Daddy's girlfriend?"

"That's what they were saying. And yes, she was Daddy's girlfriend. One of many, honey."

"I thought Daddy loved you."

"So did I. Once."

"Do you like Hillbilly?"

"I like him. Yeah."

"You know what I mean."

"I don't know, baby. I don't know anything for sure right now."

"You kissed him?"

"I did."

Karen was quiet for a long moment. Finally she said, "Why were those men so mean?"

"Henry wants me out of this job so he can put in who he wants. I don't know why he's so determined, other than I'm a woman and he doesn't like the idea. And he doesn't like your grandma much. She has more power at the mill than him. She could fire him, she took a mind to, and she might take one, now that your grandpa is gone. I think Henry wants to run for some kind of office. Thinks Holiday and Camp Rapture are going to unite into one town."

"Are they?"

"I don't know. Probably. I don't know why he's so sweated up over me."

Karen rolled over on the mattress and lay down, without letting go of her knees. She lay in bed like that and cried so hard Sunset thought she might come apart.

Sunset moved to the mattress, sat down, reached out slowly and touched Karen's hair, began stroking it.

Karen didn't resist.

After a while, giving out a loud wail, Karen turned to Sunset and climbed into her lap like a child and clung to her neck.

Sunset held her, kissed her, and a half hour later Karen fell asleep in her arms.

When Karen was asleep, Sunset maneuvered her onto the mattress, covered her, returned to the business side of the tent to put away what she had been writing.

Sadness squatted down on her like a tired elephant. She sat down at the table and put her head in her hands and thought about what Henry and Preacher Willie had said.

Maybe she should just turn in the badge. That would make things easier. She hadn't killed Jimmie Jo, but Henry and Willie sure wanted to make it look that way, and they wanted to make it look like she killed the baby too, cut it out of its mother's belly for meanness.

How ridiculous.

They can have their damn badge, she thought. They can have their damn job. And I'll . . .

I'll what?

I won't have any money.

Then people will feel certain I did it.

And even if Henry and Willie don't tell—and that was unlikely—they'll have their way.

No. I'm sticking.

I'm sticking and I'm going to find out who killed that woman and the baby, which has to be the baby in the colored graveyard. She hadn't told Willie about that. Only she, Karen, Hillbilly and Clyde knew. Provided they hadn't told anyone.

They want this job, they'll have to take it from me, and I won't give it up without a fight.

15

After being abandoned by their "boss," the five men, three women and the young boy trudged along until the sun withered into a thin red line seen faintly through the trees. Then night fell and entwined moonlight through the limbs of the forest in the manner of fine gossamer, finally turned dark and dropped shadows. The moon glowed cool white in the crow-black heavens along with the sharp white points of the stars. Then came a wad of dark clouds, blowing in fast but hanging overhead. There was very little light then, except for that which crept through the gaps in the overcast.

Most of the group decided to camp beside the road, but the man with the suit coat and the boy kept walking toward Camp Rapture.

The trees held the day's heat like an armpit in a seersucker suit. With the now limited moonlight it was difficult to see far ahead. They walked where the trees didn't stop them, and this kept them on the road. Crickets chirped all around them, and down where the creek cut through the trees they could hear a bullfrog making a noise that made the hairs on the back of the neck stand up.

"Sounds like he's got a busted horn," the boy said.

"Them big ones always sound like that," the man said. "You'd think after hearing that, you seen the one done it, he'd be ten feet tall. What's your name?"

"Everybody calls me Goose, but that ain't my real name."

"Do you mind being called Goose?"

"It's better than my real name and what they call my brother."

"What's he called?"

"Dump."

"Dump? Why's that?"

"I don't rightly know. Well, I think it was because he was always messing his pants. He was doing that until he was eleven years old. He was older than me by a year."

"Was?"

"He got something and died. Polio, I think. My mama and daddy had nine kids, and I decided I could do all right on my own. Give them others, my sisters, a better chance."

"Some of them sisters had to be older than you."

"Yeah. But they ain't got the adventure in them like me."

"You never did tell me why they call you Goose."

"Cause I run like one."

"What's your real name?"

"Draighton."

"I don't know that's so bad."

"I like Goose better."

"All right, Goose."

"What's your name?"

"Lee."

"Ain't that coat hot?"

"It is. I hang on to it because I got to have something when winter comes. I can take it off when I work, put it over me at night. It ain't so bad to wear just walking, not if you're used to it."

"All I got is these here clothes and this cap. My shoes got holes in the bottom. I had to stuff them with cardboard."

"I got mine fixed the same way, son."

"I got a stick of peppermint I stole from a store. It's kind of busted up on account of it's in my front pocket, but I could split it up with you, you want."

"All right."

The boy dug the peppermint out of his pocket. It was busted up good, but he collected the pieces and split them up, poured part of them into the man's hand.

The man put the pieces in his mouth all at once. They had bits of lint and dirt on them, but he was so hungry he thought of the lint and dirt as spice. The last meal he had eaten was two days ago and it was a boiled shoe that he and some bo's fixed alongside the tracks. There was a tater cut up in the mix, but he didn't get any of it, and the shoe, though cut up and boiled soft enough to eat, still had the taste of shoe dye about it, and it made him throw up later.

Right now, he was so hungry his stomach felt like his throat was cut.

"What you gonna do in Camp Rapture?" he asked the boy.

"Try and get a job just like you."

"Boy your age shouldn't have to work. Chores maybe, but not a man's work."

"That's what I keep saying, but it don't seem to matter none. I've done every kind of work there is, except one that makes big money. I can plow, I can tote, I can paint and I can pick. I worked in a carnival some until the boss bent me over a wagon wheel and stuck his thing up my butt."

"Sorry."

"It hurt some, but least he got shit on his dick. Later on I set fire to the little wagon he was in, and he got caught on fire, but the carnies put him out. I run off then, before he got to feeling better and figured out I done it. He had this one pinhead worked there that was real mean when he wanted her to be. She'd jump on you and just whale with both hands fast as she could go, and she could go fast all right. I figured he'd sic her on me. He'd done it to others."

"You have been around."

"You name it, if it's hard to do and hurts the back, I can do it."

"Wait till you're my age."

"How old are you?"

"I'm in my fifties. We'll leave it at that. Clouds are parting. Moon's coming out."

They walked on for a ways, then Lee reached out and stopped the boy. "Look there."

A huge black snake crawled across the road with a whipping motion, its head held up.

"Goddamn," the boy said. "That one's longer than Satan's dick."

"You really ought not talk like that."

"I like you, but you ain't my daddy."

"You're right."

"Was that a water moccasin?"

"I think it was just a big old chicken snake. They don't hurt nothing. Less it's chickens, eggs, or rats. I don't mind the rats, but you can sure get put out with them if they get in your chicken house and you was wanting eggs for breakfast."

When they were certain the snake was deep in the woods, they continued walking.

"Chicken snake poisonous?" Goose asked.

"Naw. But they still give me the creeps. I reckon they're God's creatures just like us, but I see one, and there's a hoe handy, I'll take to it and chop off its head, poisonous or not."

"Reckon old snake was lucky you didn't have a hoe tonight."

"That's right. One time when I was a kid a coachwhip snake

163

chased me around my house a bunch of times, and when I went inside to hide, it rose up and looked in the window."

"Naw."

"It did. Window wasn't high off the ground, but it scared me bad. Mama got the hoe and chopped off its head. Later, I learned a coachwhip will chase you, but if you stop, it'll stop, and you can chase it. You stop chasing, it'll turn and come after you. They're kind of playing. I think it was looking through that window for me to come out and play some more. Wanted me to take a turn chasing it. And my mama went out there and chopped off its head. Always made me feel kind of guilty."

"You look kind of like a preacher."

"Don't confuse me with one. Though I have done some preaching in my time."

"Just to make money, work the rubes? Do some of that healing stuff?"

"No, son. I meant it and I didn't heal nothing, cause ain't nobody can heal but the Lord God hisself."

"Why ain't you still preaching?"

"Sort of fell off the wagon. I could still hear the call but I couldn't tell no more what the Lord was calling. I felt like a man going deaf. Still good enough ears to hear the sound, but not enough hearing to understand it."

"What was it knocked you off the wagon? Booze? Gambling? Pussy?"

"I know I'm not your daddy, but you really are too young to talk like that."

"I don't know no other way to talk. As for booze, gambling and pussy, I've had me some of all three, so I guess I can talk about it, and I can tell you straight out that I like pussy the best. Which was it with you?"

"All of them. Including some you didn't name. Fact is, I ain't

164

just here for a job. I've come here to set some things I done here right as they can be set. Gonna try and give a lady an apology, if she's here and willing to take it."

"And if she ain't willing to take it?"

"I wouldn't blame her."

"What if she isn't in Camp Rapture?"

"I try not to think about that. It makes me feel bad to think that, so I don't think about it, and won't, unless she ain't here. Then I got to start up with a new set of worries."

"It happen a long time ago?"

"Yeah."

"So let it go. My pappy always said, you already done something, ain't no use noodling on it. It ain't gonna get better if you do."

"He may be right. But I'm not doing it just for her. Doing it for me."

"Hell, I don't feel guilty about nothing I've done."

"Maybe it's because you haven't done anything really bad."

"I stole that peppermint. I've stole other stuff."

"That's bad, but it could be worse."

"It wasn't so bad you didn't eat that peppermint."

"I was hungry."

"Why I stole it and about four others. That was just the last one left. Got a cigarette, Lee?"

"No. Don't smoke. And you're too young to smoke."

"There you go with that young stuff again," Goose said. "What about a chaw, or some snuff?"

"Same answer," Lee said.

After an hour or so, Lee and Goose discovered they were farther from Camp Rapture than they thought and that it looked unlikely they would make it before morning.

This was all surmise on their part, as neither had any exact idea how far it was. Lee had been there before, but it was many years past, and much had changed since then.

Goose said, "I'm so damn tired, I think I'm gonna fall over."

"Me too," Lee said. "I can tell by the hang of the stars there. Look right there through them trees—"

"I see em."

"I can tell by where they're hanging it's getting pretty late on, and I'm as tuckered out as a tick in a tar bucket."

"Me too. But I can go on a bit if you can."

They walked on a little ways more until they decided they just couldn't take it anymore.

"Ain't like when we get to Camp Rapture they're gonna be waiting on us with open arms and a hot meal," Goose said. "Reckon dirt out here is good as dirt around there. Won't be the first time I've laid in dirt."

"You're right," Lee said. "Let's cash it in."

They veered off the road, into the woods, looking for a place to lie down. Just a few yards off the road they found where leaves were mounded up under a tree, and in that moment that pile looked like a featherbed. Then Lee saw that the tree, a massive oak, had a large low limb that had been split, possibly by lightning. It was wide enough to hold a body and split deep enough to serve as a kind of natural hammock. Lee put leaves in the limb and said, "Now you got you a bed, Goose."

"Not me. I can take care of myself. I don't need no help to lay down somewhere. Besides, I don't climb no trees I don't have to. I don't climb nothing I don't have to."

"Isn't more than five feet off the ground," Lee said.

"Still, ain't for me."

"You ain't much of a boy, not wanting to climb trees."

"It ain't the climbing worries me. It's the falling."

166

Lee took the limb and Goose lay down on the leaves. "These leaves piled up like this, my daddy used to tell me that there was ape-men did it at night. Piled them up, I mean."

"You think they did?"

"I don't know. I guess not. It was a good story."

"What were your people like, Goose?"

"Just like other people, I reckon. Poor. But they was poor before the Depression. My mama was part Cherokee, and my papa was half Choctaw. When the dust come I left so they wouldn't be in such a bad way with all us kids. I went down here to East Texas, and they carried on out to California."

"Why didn't you go with them?"

"Didn't want to go no place where the weather stays the same. Can't stand it when summer drags on. I like it when I don't know it's going to rain or storm, be clear or hot. Course, I liked it better before I didn't have a roof to get under and some regular food. Maybe I'd have been better to have gone out there to California, now that I noodle on it."

"I been. It's nothing special. Just more of the same, only with a steady climate and oranges. Like you, Goose, I don't like it steady all the time. Changeable weather teaches a man how to be changeable hisself. He can move with events. You can't learn character when everything is smooth."

"Maybe I don't need no character. Maybe what I need is three meals a day and a bed and some kind of something over my head so I don't get rained on."

"Could be, Goose."

Pretty soon Lee heard Goose snoring, and was surprised that now he couldn't sleep. His mind was racing, and Goose's snoring wasn't helping.

He lay there and looked up into the limbs of the tree. At first it was just dark up there, but in time his eyes adjusted and he could make out limbs, and finally, through gaps he could see a few stars.

He felt an old urge. The one he had when he was preaching. The urge to reach out with his thoughts to God, who surely must lie behind that veil of night and stars, and maybe wasn't as mean as he seemed to act. Sometimes he thought God was just mean to him.

Maybe he deserved it.

He didn't know what he deserved anymore, and didn't reckon it mattered. Deserving had nothing to do with it.

There once was a time when he had felt close to God, had thought himself God's servant.

But that was many sins ago.

He lay there and looked and thought and finally the sky lightened, and finally he closed his eyes.

16

Marilyn drove out to Sunset's tent early the next morning. Found her and Clyde there. Clyde was sitting out front in a wooden folding chair drinking coffee. Sunset was feeding Ben from a big metal pan, some bread soaked in grease and yesterday's gravy. Beside the food pan was a larger pan full of water.

Marilyn pulled the truck up close to the tent. The dog turned to look at her.

"He gonna bite me?" Marilyn asked through the open truck window.

"He minds pretty good," Sunset said. "But I'll come over and walk you to the tent."

"That's all right, we can talk while we ride," Marilyn said. "Get in. Howdy, Clyde."

Clyde lifted his coffee cup.

"Don't look you're hurting yourself none," Marilyn said.

"I don't know. I think I might have strained a little bit a while ago. The elbow, you know, when I was lifting my cup."

Sunset gave Ben a pat, climbed in the truck beside Marilyn. Marilyn cranked up and drove off.

Marilyn said, "Where's that other one?"

"Hillbilly? I don't know. He was supposed to come in, but he ain't done it so far. We keep pretty loose hours. We ain't exactly solving a bunch of crimes, but still, he was supposed to have been in. Clyde took his truck home last night, and Hillbilly had to walk to wherever he's going. He ain't staying with Clyde no more. I think they ain't getting along for some reason, and then Clyde burned his own house down."

"What?"

"Burned it down. It was his way of cleaning it, or so he said. That's one crime we solved. Who burned down Clyde's house. He did it. Now he's got to sleep under a tarp."

"You know why they ain't getting along, don't you?"

"No."

"You. I don't know nothing about it, and I can tell you why. They both like you."

"Maybe."

"You're breaking hearts, and don't even know it, Sunset. Understand you got some real crimes, though."

"So, Willie's been to talk to you," Sunset said.

"Henry."

"I can't figure which one of them is the ass end of the snake, and which is the teeth," Sunset said, "but they're just one long snake far as I'm concerned."

"They told me what they think."

"They can think all kinds of things."

"I think they're gonna try to have you removed at the next camp meeting. They may even try to bring charges against you, about killing Pete, Jimmie Jo, and killing and burying that baby in the colored graveyard."

"Why in hell would I go on a killing spree? All of a sudden I go out and kill Jimmie Jo and her baby and then shoot Pete. Why would I do that?"

"Jealousy. It answers a lot."

"I wasn't that jealous, and I wasn't that mad. I ain't resigning. I didn't kill that woman, and I'm trying to find out who killed her. It just takes time. Hell, I'm a constable, not a detective, and I'm learning the job. Even Pete had to learn the job."

"I heard how you handled that situation in Holiday. Sounded like you done good."

"I think so."

"Fella got lynched anyhow."

"Do what?"

"A crowd broke in and got him out of jail and cut his things off and set him on fire. They even took pictures. They were selling them over at the general store as postcards."

"That's horrible. I didn't do no good at all."

"You brought a murderer to justice."

"No, I brought a murderer to a lynching, which was what they were trying to do in Holiday. They done to him just what he said they'd do to him. It's like I didn't do nothing but put off what was gonna happen."

"They were gonna kill him anyway. Had it coming."

"Maybe so. But not burned to death with postcard pictures made of it. Jesus Christ. The law would have at least been quick and there wouldn't have been no pictures to sell—I guess it's quick. Damn."

"They say it was the law there let them have him."

"I hope that ain't true."

"Sorry, Sunset."

"Me too. More than sorry. Hell, maybe they're right. I ain't much of a constable. I've had a dead baby and dead woman and I don't have a clue who done it or why, and the one thing I thought I done pretty good worked out just like it would have if I'd stayed at the house. And now there's folks think I did the crimes I'm supposed to be solving, and when Henry and Willie get through, more folks will know."

They drove along for a bit in silence. Marilyn broke it with: "I'm gonna do what I can to keep you constable. But I can't make no promises. It was one thing when it was thought you killed someone beating on you, and there was a nickel raise, but if Henry adds this to it, convinces folks you might have killed Jimmie Jo, and a baby, or at least talks them into believing you ain't doing enough to solve it . . ."

"When's the meeting?"

"Couple of weeks. Thursday, noonish. And it's just gonna be the camp bigwigs, not the whole camp."

"I'll be there."

"You might not want to do that," Marilyn said. "It could turn ugly as the ass end of a bulldog."

"I know."

"Got any idea at all who done this, or why?"

Sunset shook her head. "None. But there's some things that have occurred to me, and I'm gonna try and run that around in my head a little more today, then go and do something about it."

"Darling, sure would be good if you could figure this out before that meeting."

"Frankly, that ain't likely. But I'll work on it. And Marilyn . . ."

"What, hon?"

"Things like they are, you've done right by me. I really am sorry about Pete."

"I ain't gonna lie to you, Sunset. Some mornings I wake up and I want to kill you. I know better, but I want to kill you, and I can't understand why Pete's gone or why you done it. Then a few minutes later, I know exactly why you done it. But I still don't like it. I also miss Jones. I wouldn't have taken him back or nothing, but I miss him sometimes."

"I hurt about it a lot," Sunset said. "I ain't proud of it, but I thought he was gonna kill me. I ain't never gonna put up with that kind of thing again."

"Thing is, you and me, we got to stick together. We got to

make sure things are good for Karen. Where is Karen?"

"Sleeping."

"This late?"

"Yep, she's a regular Rip Van Winkle. Kind of got into prettying herself up. Guess she's getting to be a woman."

"For that little boy she was seeing?"

"She's kind of forgotten him. Think she's got a crush on Hillbilly."

"Better watch that."

"He knows she's a kid. It's one-sided. She just walks around moon-eyed a lot."

"You don't know him well enough to know that, know if he'd turn it two-sided."

"I think I do."

"But you'll watch it?"

"Sure."

"Another thing. That girl you found, she was shot with a thirty-eight."

"So I've heard. Damn, how'd you know that?"

"They done spread the word, honey. That gun, it could be Pete's, and he could have done it, I suppose. I don't like saying it, but he beat on you, he could have shot her if he found out she was carrying his baby and he didn't want it. Could have been that way, and if you don't know who did it, a case could be made. Hell, Jones has a thirty-eight in that glove compartment right there in front of you. Lots of people got thirty-eights."

"I'm surprised you'd suggest that Pete done it."

"Not because I like the idea, or know he did it, but it could save you some time, till you found out who. It might be the answer they need at the town meeting."

"And if I don't find out who did it? If it ain't Pete?"

"Reckon he can take the blame good as any."

Sunset saw Marilyn blink, then a tear squeezed out of her eye. She had a very fine face but the way the sun was shining on it the wrinkles were more visible, like little plowed lines, and her hair had come loose in places and dangled on her cheeks and forehead. Sunset thought it made her look like some of those Greek statues she had seen in books, thought of the story she had read about Helen of Troy, thought Marilyn might look as Helen would have looked at sixty. Still beautiful. Sort of face an artist would want to carve in granite.

When Marilyn wiped the tear away with the back of her hand, Sunset said, "We don't need to talk about it no more."

Marilyn nodded. "Let's ride a little. Something I want to show you."

They threw up a lot of dust on sandy back roads and came to a small house with a big porch, and sitting in a rocking chair on the porch was Bill Martin. He had a pair of crutches beside him.

Next to the house was an old blue truck speckled with rust, and a black Ford that wasn't too old and looked in pretty good shape.

"What happened to him?" Sunset asked as they pulled into the yard.

"A tree kicked back on him. Got out of the way mostly, but it hit him some. He's sprained up. Heard about it from Don Walker. Ain't much goes on at the mill that Walker and Martin don't blab about. They know everyone and everything."

Marilyn killed the engine, said, "Fact is, I think he's probably faking some to get a few days off work. He likes money, but he don't like working for it."

"Why are we here?"

"He borrowed some money from Jones. Thinks with Jones dead maybe I don't know about it. Or so I figure. I heard about this extra car he's got, and I got an idea."

They got out of the truck and walked up to the porch. When they did, a dog that had been asleep under it, embarrassed he had been snuck up on, leaped awake and banged his head on the porch, started barking.

"Shut up!" Bill said. The dog, to show who was boss, barked a couple more times, went silent, lay back down in the soft sand beneath the steps. Sunset could see his beady eyes watching them as they walked up to the porch steps and stopped. The dog was a big black-and-white hound with cut-up floppy ears, souvenirs of past coon hunts.

"Good morning, Mrs. Jones, and Constable Sunset," Bill said.

Sunset thought when he mentioned her name he sounded a little snide, but she let it pass, as it was really too early to just shoot him, and it wouldn't look good, shooting a man on crutches.

"Good morning, Bill," Marilyn said.

The door opened and three heads appeared. Children. Ranging from age nine to twelve, Sunset thought. The way their heads poked around the screen it looked as if they were stacked on top of one another, two girls, and at the bottom the youngest, a boy with a face like a rat, eyes like goat berries. Sunset figured none of them had ever seen the inside of a schoolhouse, such as it was. Camp Rapture's schooling only went to the ninth grade. You wanted any more after that, you had to go over to Holiday, where it went up to the eleventh. Most didn't bother after learning to read and write and cipher. Beyond there was just fieldwork or maybe store work, or for the damn lucky, barber college over in Tyler.

Sunset wasn't even sure that when summer ended Karen would go back to school. She did, she'd have to go to Holiday, and she wasn't sure how she'd manage it.

175

"Y'all get on back in there in the house," Bill said. "Adults are talking out here. Get on, now."

The heads disappeared as if a hole had opened up and they had fallen down it. The door slammed.

"Damn kids," Bill said. "Can't get no goddamn rest around here. Wife just had to have three of them, and then she up and died."

"Pretty ungrateful," Sunset said.

Bill gave her a look, and it was a look Sunset recognized as one of confusion. He was trying to decide if Sunset was poking fun or commiserating.

"I'll get right to it," Marilyn said. "You borrowed some money from my husband. It's past due."

The flesh on Bill's face nearly fell off the bone.

"I ain't forgot, Mrs. Jones. Not for a minute. Soon as I can get back to work, I'll try and get that paid off."

"How'd you come by the car?" Marilyn said.

"I traded an old syrup mill and the cooking goods for it. It didn't run when I got it, but I've fixed on it."

"It runs now?"

"Yes."

"Well, I heard you had a car and a truck, and I think we can make a trade. What you owe Jones for the car. You'll still have the truck to get around in and do work around here."

"That's a good car," Bill said.

"I wouldn't want a bad one."

"I need that car."

"You got a truck."

"I like the car."

"You owe me money."

"Yes, ma'am. I reckon I do." Bill studied on the situation for a while. "I could give you the truck and owe you some."

"You've owed me for a long time, Bill. When you needed it, we helped you out. It did help you out, didn't it?"

"Sure. It helped. I had to have help when the wife died."

"So?"

"Well . . . I had to have it."

"And we gave it to you."

"Jones gave it to me. You didn't want him to."

"And with good reason. You still owe him. But the debts owed him are now owed me."

"Things ain't been good for me."

"I understand your circumstances, but you still got a debt due, and me and Jones went a long time without mentioning it. This car will cover it, and I'll call it square. I didn't want to call it square, the car wouldn't be enough. It would be the car and then some."

Sunset could see it pained Bill more than the pain in his foot to lose that car.

"I voted for Sunset for constable when you wanted me to."

"You voted for a nickel an hour raise," Marilyn said.

"Ain't there another way?" he said.

"You can pay the money you owe me instead of the car."

"Damn," Bill said.

"Did you think I forgot about you owing the money?"

Bill grinned. "Kind of hoped you had."

Marilyn shook her head. "Nope."

"I could still pay it out."

"It's past time for that. You can pay me half of it now, or you can give me the car. That's as good a deal as it gets."

"I ain't got even a quarter of it. Times are hard. You're giving me the Jesse James."

"No, I'm giving you a chance to pay your debt, and actually come out ahead."

"What if I don't?"

"That's why I brought the constable. I have the papers you signed for the debt in my car."

"You don't know if I paid Jones any."

"I know the contract you signed said there would be a receipt for every payment you made. I haven't got any receipts. Want to show me yours?"

"You'd have me arrested?"

"I would."

"Oh, hell," Bill said, as if he were being magnanimous. "Take the damn car."

When Bill crutched the keys out to them, along with the title, which he signed over, Marilyn handed the keys to Sunset.

"It's yours," Marilyn said.

"You didn't tell me the car was for her."

"Didn't need to," Marilyn said.

"Are you sure, Marilyn?" Sunset said. "I mean, it's a good car."

"It sure is," Bill said.

"That's why I want you to have it," Marilyn said. "You need it. You can't be depending on someone else all the time. What if Clyde quit?"

"I don't know what to say."

"Say thanks."

"Thanks, Marilyn."

"I don't want her to have it," Bill said.

"Why's that?" Marilyn said.

"Well, I know she's constable, but she ain't really."

"Yes, I am," Sunset said. "Really. And if you hadn't paid your debt to Mrs. Jones, I'd have arrested you."

Bill looked as if he could eat glass.

"It really bothers you a woman has this job, doesn't it?" Sunset said.

Bill crutched back to his porch and his rocking chair. When he settled into it he began to rock furiously, as if he might rock himself off the porch and on out of East Texas, a place where women became the law and hoodwinked him out of cars for money owed.

"Good enough," Marilyn said. "You drive it home, Sunset. Tell Karen I'm going to come get her soon, take her to the picture show over in Holiday."

"Sunset's done been there," Bill said from the porch. "That's where she saved that nigger."

"You'll be happy to know he was lynched," Sunset said.

"Already heard. And you'd have saved a lot of trouble if you'd done let them go ahead and do it while he was in Holiday. I reckon he ate some meals over in Tyler. He wasn't worth that, even if he only got bread and water."

"I'd shut up if I were you," Sunset said. "Don't forget you're talking to the law."

"I ain't talking law business. I'm just talking. Y'all go on, now. You got what you wanted."

Bill rose from the rocker, stood tall on his crutches, worked his way into the house, let the door bang.

Sunset had learned to drive when she was a kid working on the farm, before she got the sniff on what her male foster parent had in mind for her. Then she ran off and didn't drive much after that. She drove for Pete once in a while, but not often, just when he really needed something done. He didn't like to see a woman drive, especially his woman, and the idea that she could drive, that she might drive away, was not a comfort to him. He liked her handy, as he liked to say, which meant under his roof and under

179

his thumb, trapped like a rat in a shoe box, no air holes.

So as she drove, the window down, the wind blowing her red hair as if fanning a blaze, she felt a kind of glory rise up in her. The flesh on her neck and cheeks flared as if bellows were beneath her skin, pumping up heat from coals she thought dead, and her skin seemed to lick at the air, and the taste of it was sweet, and she felt strong, her bones suddenly of iron, and along she drove, the dust rising up, some of it coming through the window, making her cough, sticking to the sweat on her face, but she didn't mind. Didn't mind at all, because there was a fine fire in her and it made her comfortably warm even in the not so comfortable East Texas heat, and out the window she saw the world no longer in the dusty whites and grays of the road, but in the bright greens of the pines and the cedars of the forest and the blues of the sky and the bouquets of Indian paintbrushes and bluebonnets and buttercups and sunflowers and all manner of wildflowers that fled out of the woods and stopped at the edge of the road as if on parade, saw all this as the roar of the car startled bright bursts of birds when she made curves too fast, and in that good moment she felt as if she was the queen of all she surveyed.

Sunset drove the black Ford to her tent, and when Clyde, who was still sitting in a chair out front, saw her, he stood up, walked out to the car to greet her.

"You steal it?" Clyde said through the open driver's window.

"No, I let a drunk man feel my tittie for it."

Clyde gave her a shocked look, and she laughed, told him how she had come by the car, telling it while she sat with her hands on the wheel, her head against the seat, turned slightly so she could speak to Clyde, doing it that way so she could feel her car.

"Hell, you can fire me now you got a ride."

Sunset climbed out of the car and closed the door. "Don't be silly, Clyde. I couldn't do without you. You're my right-hand man. And speaking of my left-hand man, where is he?"

Karen came out of the tent. Her hair was combed and she looked way too neat and clean for just getting up. She said, "Whose car?"

"Ours. Courtesy of your grandma."

"Really?"

"Really."

"Oh, heavens," Karen said. "Our very own car."

Karen came over to look at the car and Sunset went to the water pump and washed the dust off of her sweaty face. She pulled her hair back to do it, and when she turned her head to let the water run over her face, she saw Clyde looking at her, and the way he looked, it was so sweet, and she thought, Oh, hell, don't fall for me, Clyde, because I can't do it, and then she turned her head the other way to wash that side of her face, and she saw Hillbilly coming down the road, walking in that cool, collected way he had, and she thought it odd he seemed free of sweat and dust, and the way the sun hit his cap, it looked like some kind of dark halo.

In that moment, a heat like she had felt driving the car, maybe even hotter, rose up in her, but it wasn't just her face this time, it was her loins as well.

"Hi, Hillbilly," Karen said.

"Hi, darlin'," he said.

17

Lee, dreaming he was Tarzan asleep in a tree with Jane in his arms, awoke to the sound of a moan.

For a moment, upon realizing he was not Tarzan, he was confused, had no idea where he was, and when he looked above and saw the limbs of the tree, he decided maybe he was in fact Tarzan, and that the moan belonged to Jane. Since no Jane was present and he was fully dressed, he determined it was not a moan of ecstasy or even a moan connected to backache, but it was a moan, perhaps from falling from the tree, because trees, for all their romance, really weren't that good to sleep in unless you were a monkey.

Then he came full awake. He was in a tree, but not in Africa, and below him lay Goose.

He rolled over and looked down. Goose was sitting up with his back against the tree. Goose said, "Goddamn it. I done been snakebit."

"What?"

"Snakebit. Copperhead."

"You sure?"

"Course I'm sure. Woke up when it bit me. It weren't no chicken snake. I know them copperhead sonsabitches are poison. I know that much. Saw it crawl in the leaves there. Got me on the hand. It was a little one. Don't hurt much."

"Where exactly did the snake go?"

"Well, he didn't tell me where he was planning on finishing

out," Goose said. "But in them leaves, over there."

Goose pointed.

Lee dropped down from his limb and looked around and found a heavy stick.

"He done bit me," Goose said. "I ain't gonna get better cause you hit him with a stick."

Lee tossed the stick down. "You're right. We got to get you to a doctor. Can you walk?"

"Bit me on the hand, not the leg."

"Thing to do is to walk slow and careful, not hurry. Poison gets het up and runs right through you that way."

"Am I gonna be okay?"

"Sure. But we got to get you to a doctor."

They went out on the road and started walking. It was good and morning now, already starting to turn hot. Lee hoped Camp Rapture was not too far away, and that a doctor was there, and that they wouldn't be too late. He looked about, hoping to remember the place better, get some idea of where they were, but he might as well have been in Romania.

As they walked, Goose said, "Hand's starting to hurt like fire now, and get heavy."

Lee looked at the boy's hand. It was swollen up huge and turning dark.

"Put it inside your shirt. Unbutton a couple buttons. Put it in there Napoleon style, so you don't let it dangle by your side."

"Oh, Jesus. It hurts."

"I know, son. Just keep going."

They went a ways, then Goose fell to his knees. "My head's all whirly. I'm hotter in the head than a jacked-off mad dog."

"It'll be all right."

Goose hit face forward in the dust.

Lee picked him up and carried him in his arms. This was

hard work and he didn't get too far before he had to put the boy down. He picked him up again, but this time he threw him over his shoulder. This was hard, but not as hard as carrying him in his arms. He went twice as far this time, stopped, and with great difficulty, shifted the boy to his other shoulder.

Goose wasn't talking anymore. He wasn't making a sound. He felt hot to the touch. Nonetheless, Lee talked to him. "We're gonna make it, son. Can't be that damn far. I been here before, long time ago, and it don't seem it's that far."

But they walked on and the road kept stretching. Lee wanted to stop, lie down. He was exhausted with the weight and the heat, but he kept plodding. He thought: I'm damn glad Goose ain't a fat boy or I'd go straight down and never get up. But then, if he was a fat boy, he probably wouldn't run like a goose and the name Goose wouldn't fit him. They'd call him Pig, something like that.

His legs grew heavy and his arms grew tired, but he tried to focus on the road ahead, thinking that around each far ahead curve he would see Camp Rapture. He wondered what Camp Rapture was like now. When he left it, it had just become a camp and it had the name all fresh and new and it wasn't much to see. Goddamn. How long ago was that? Thirty? Thirty-three years? He couldn't really remember. He was in his early twenties then. He was in his early fifties now. No. What was he thinking? Time had slipped by him. He was fifty-four. Was that early or middle fifties? Oh, Christ, this boy is heavy. And it's hot, so goddamn hot, and the boy is hot. So hot.

Lee stumbled, went down. The boy slipped off his shoulder and struck the road.

"Jesus, son, I'm sorry," Lee said. But the boy was unaware of the fall or the fact that he was being spoken to.

With the effort of Atlas lifting the world, Lee managed the boy up again, switching this time to holding one leg and one arm and slinging the boy across his back. This was better for a while, but soon his arm ached and his leg ached and he thought: I must lay down a while. But no. Can't do that. Every second counts. He glanced at the boy's hand, which was now dangling. It was black and large and didn't look like a hand at all. It looked like some kind of creature.

"We'll make it, Goose," he said, and wondered if they would or even if the boy was still alive. As he plodded on, he relaxed, tried to feel the boy breathing, and could. Could feel the slight and strained movement of the boy's body as his lungs labored.

"For God sakes, Jesus," Lee said. "I know I done some wrong. But don't take it out on this boy. Help me help him."

Jesus didn't reach out of the heavens to offer a hand.

God didn't provide a chariot or a doctor.

The Holy Ghost didn't cheer him on.

Lee pushed on, stumbled, went to a knee, got up, kept going, said to God and Jesus and the Holy Ghost, "You sonsofbitches. All three of you."

Then he heard the sound.

He turned, almost falling as he did.

Coming down the road was a truck with side boards. Lee stepped to the center of the road. The truck swerved and pulled to the left side of the road, something clattered in the truck bed as it came to a stop. A woman was driving. She looked about his age. Nice looking with a gray stripe down the center of her hair. She had eyes like icy blue fire. She reached over and rolled down the window.

"What's wrong?" she said.

"Boy got snakebit."

"Poisonous snake?"

"His hand is swole up big as my head. He said it was a copperhead."

185

"Get in."

Lee got in, laying the boy across his legs. He removed the boy's tight-fitting cap and wiped his hair out of his eyes, used the cap to wipe the sweat from his face. He laid the bitten hand across the boy's chest. The hand was black and very huge. It looked as if it were tapped lightly it might explode. Lee rolled up the boy's sleeves. There were runs of red and blue lines going up his snakebit arm.

"See how it's done him," Lee said.

Marilyn glanced at the boy's arm and hand, started onto the road.

"Thought I could get him to Camp Rupture, to a doctor, he'd have a chance," Lee said.

"He's got a better chance we go see Aunt Cary. She's a midwife, but she knows about snakebites and all manner of things a doctor don't. Guess she's a kind of a doctor herself."

"Hope you're right."

"She's closer."

"Camp Rapture ain't as close as I remember it."

"When do you remember it? How long ago?"

He told her.

"There used to be a straighter road to it," she said, "but it kept getting washed out from the creek, so they reworked it. This one winds a mite, but it don't get flooded as much."

"You sure about this Aunt Cary?"

"Done a lot of people good," Marilyn said. "Seen her do all manner of things. Seen her come into Camp Rapture once and deliver a baby by cutting the mother's belly open. Baby lived, and so did the mother. Aunt Cary sewed her up with fishing line and she got all right. Something like that, or something like this, I trust her more than a doctor. Besides, she's closer, and this boy needs whatever he's gonna get right now."

They took a turn off of the main road, down a narrow trail. The truck bumped and thumped along, the junk in the bed clattered. Lee looked over his shoulder through the back window. Saw posthole diggers and a shovel and axe leaping about back there.

He wished they would bounce out. The noise was giving him a headache.

At first Marilyn drove fast, but the trail was too bad for that kind of driving, so she slowed.

"He's breathing funny," Lee said.

"Snakebite affects the lungs," Marilyn said. "All kinds of things, but the lungs is one thing. Get so you can't breathe, then it pumps poisons to the heart."

The woods grew denser. There were long vines hanging from dark twisty trees with thorns. They bounced along a path even more narrow than the one they had been on and pulled into a clearing where an old house set. The house was small and the porch sagged. The yard was littered with wagon parts, plows, a chopping block with an axe in it, and assorted chicken feathers.

Marilyn parked near the porch, got out, called to the house: "Aunt Cary. You in there? It's Marilyn Jones. You in there? Got us an emergency."

The door opened and Uncle Riley came out on the porch, followed by his son, Tommy.

"That's her husband, Uncle Riley," Marilyn said. "And that's their son, Tommy."

Lee noted that Uncle Riley looked younger than he was, hardly like an uncle. He was a big, powerful man with a shaved head. He was wearing too short pants and a too tight, stained white T-shirt. The boy was barefoot, wearing overalls. His hair was long and the kinks went up in the air like springs that had sprung.

"How are you, Miss Marilyn?" Uncle Riley said. "Can I help you?"

"We got a boy snakebit, Uncle Riley. Copperhead. He's swole up good. We need Aunt Cary."

"She out gathering some roots. Tommy, go find her, tell her get back here quick as she can."

Tommy darted back into the house and out the back. They heard the back screen door slam as he went, snappy as a rifle shot.

"Let's get him on in here," Uncle Riley said.

Lee and Uncle Riley carried Goose into the one bedroom and laid him on the bed. Uncle Riley put a pillow under Goose's head and looked at the hand.

Lee looked around. There were a number of shelves and on the shelves were jars and sacks, and in the jars he could see roots and what looked like dirt and some colorful powders and in one jar he saw several water moccasin heads floating in a liquid the color of urine. Some of the jars with snake heads had streaks of red in them like sticky runs of blood.

Uncle Riley bent over Goose, looked at the hand. "He was bit good."

"Said it was a small snake," Lee said.

"If it was a young'n, them's the worst kind. They all hot with sap."

The back door slammed, and a moment later a very pretty, slightly heavy woman with reddish skin and little black freckles on her cheeks entered the room. She had a red-and-black-checkered rag tied around her head. She didn't pay any attention to Lee or Marilyn, but bent directly over the boy, looked at his hand, poked it with her finger.

"Tommy," she said, "go in there and get me the little sharp knife. One I use on them pears. Bring it here with some of my medicine and a glass."

Tommy left, came back momentarily with a glass, a pocketknife, and a jug.

Aunt Cary laid the glass and knife on the edge of the bed and used her fine white teeth to pull the cork from the jug. She poured a bit of what was in the jug into the glass.

"This here is some of Mr. Bull's best," she said.

Lee could smell that it was white lightning. Aunt Cary took a swig from the glass, poured a little more into the glass, set it on the floor and knelt down by it. She opened the pocketknife, dipped it into the booze and drank what was in the glass after she did. She sat on the side of the bed and took hold of the boy's hand and poked the wound with the knife. She didn't cut across or make slashes, just poked straight into the bite marks. Dark pus squirted out. She picked up the jug, splashed some of its contents onto the punctures.

"Get me my stone," she said.

Tommy scrambled away, came back carrying a white knotty stone that filled his fist. Aunt Cary took it, pressed it against the wound.

Lee watched as the stone darkened.

"Is it sucking out the poison?" he said.

"It is."

"That's a rock?"

"I call it a milk stone. Tommy, go pull the milk jug up from the well."

Tommy darted away. While he was gone, the stone became darker yet.

"I don't know it's really a stone," she said, "but it sucks that poison out all right."

Tommy came back with the damp milk jug. It had been hung down the well on a rope and the jug and the milk were cool. Aunt Cary poured the glass half full of milk. She set the glass on the floor, said, "Look at this."

She dropped the stone in the milk and the milk turned dark as a thundercloud.

"Comes out best in milk. I done it in water some, but it don't work as good. Seems to get sucked out by that milk."

When the glass was so dark with poison and pus you couldn't see the rock, Cary gave the glass to Tommy, said, "Pour that out and don't get it on your hands. Bring it back to me. Mind you don't pour it near the vegetable garden, you hear me?"

"Yes, ma'am."

Once again, Tommy disappeared. He came back with the glass empty of milk and full of stone. The stone looked larger, like a sponge that had swollen, but now it was as white as in the beginning.

Aunt Cary poured white lightning into the glass, shook it gently, plucked out the stone and put it back on the bite. It filled with poison again.

Aunt Cary pulled a Bible off a shelf, flipped it open, rapidly found what she wanted. She read a couple verses aloud. When she finished, she said, "Them's healing verses."

"I recognize them," Lee said. He reached out and touched the boy's head. It was sweaty and hot, but not as hot as before.

"I'm gonna fix him up something to drink now," Aunt Cary said. "It'll cut that fever down some."

"Will he be all right?" Marilyn asked.

"That's up to the Lord," Aunt Cary said. "But I think he will. Yes, ma'am. I think he will."

Lee noted another surprising thing. The swelling in Goose's hand had gone down and it was no longer black. It had turned a light blue and the lines that had been running up his arm had lost length. The punctures were oozing blood now, not poison.

"Riley," Aunt Cary said to her husband, "reach there behind the stove, see if you can find some cobwebs."

Uncle Riley went to the cookstove, looked behind it, scooped up a batch as if he were gathering the strands of a weave. He brought them back and Aunt Cary wadded them up and pushed them on the punctures. They turned dark red and clotted up.

"Stops the blood from runnin'," Aunt Cary said. "I don't never clean behind the stove. Don't never know when you'll need the webs."

Lee reached out and touched Goose's hand gently.

"I'll be damned," Lee said. "Fever's near gone."

"Cause the poison is out of him," Aunt Cary said. "And we'll all be damned, we don't change our ways."

18

A little later that day, Henry, already feeling slaphappy from having found out something that would make Sunset look like a killer, got another bit of news that was like fine egg-white icing on a double-layer chocolate cake, even if in retrospect, he had been forced to spread the icing a bit himself.

He had gone to work, and bored of it, sitting in his office with nothing really to do, decided to get out of there, drive over to Holiday and look up a little honey he knew who would do the dirty deed for five dollars and two bits. It was an odd price, but it was her price, and she was worth every bit of it. Blond and buxom with enough ass for two, but tight and nice just the same, prone to heat rash pimples on her inner thigh.

Driving over, passing the drugstore, he noted, as always, the apartment above it. It was a curious place. Painted bright red with only two little windows facing the street, looking like square eyes in a heatstroked face. At the back of the place were a lot of windows. They looked out at a wall of dirt and grass that was part of a huge wooded overlook that hung above the drugstore and the apartment. Up there lived John McBride. Henry did business with McBride, but when he wasn't doing business with him, he tried not to think about him. He wasn't the kind of guy you wanted to think about you didn't have to. He had come from Houston by way of Chicago, at Henry's request, and sometimes he wished he had never taken that step, because McBride, he was a guy started out working for you, then after a time, you got the feeling you were working for him, that you couldn't get rid of him. He was suddenly all over your business and a part of it. Then you wished you didn't know him, even if he could be handy about some things, because he seemed to have come from a place much more South than Houston, or Mexico, for that matter. Way South.

And with him came the other one. The black one. The one who said little and talked as if he were speaking to someone unseen standing just to your left and behind you. Yeah. The black one. Looked like a big beetle in his hat and Prince Albert coat. McBride's bad shadow.

Henry didn't like to think about that one at all. Didn't even like to think his name for fear it might bring him around. If McBride was from far South, the other one, he came from deeper down than that.

Henry turned his attention back to the whore he had come to see, but when he arrived on Dodge Street, he was disappointed to find she had an appointment elsewhere.

It looked liked the beginning of a bad day. Henry wasn't interested in going back to the mill, and he wasn't really all that interested in going home to watch his wife drink, but it struck him that he had a little black book hidden in a panel inside his desk drawer at home, and in that book were the addresses and a few numbers of whores with telephones or some connection to someone who had a phone. They were women he had not used but knew about, had been given their information by associates. He had not really planned to use them because of already having the blond honey he liked, but that hadn't worked out, and he still had the urge to clean out his pipes, and now, disappointed, he wanted to see if there was someone else he might contact, so he drove home on a mission for that little black book.

As he went in the house, Henry didn't call out for his wife.

That was never profitable, as she might appear at any moment, a big stack of flesh, looking like heaped-up mashed potatoes moving about on their own accord, topped by hair as greasy as a leaky oil filter.

As he entered the house, he saw, sticking up over the sofa, a fat white foot. He eased over there, called his wife's name, but she didn't answer.

He peeked over the couch. She was naked, as usual, and her other leg was on the couch and turned awkward, and he had a bird's-eye view of the thing that made her a woman and not mashed potatoes, and the sight of it, like some kind of hair-lined wound, made him jump.

Then he noticed the rest of her wasn't looking too good either. Her breasts, thick with fat, had fallen back to cover her face—mercifully, he thought—and the fat that made up the rest of her flowed over the couch and floor in heaps.

He called her name a couple of times.

No answer. He went around and took a look. Not much to see. He started to reach out and move one of her breasts so he could see her face, but the thought of it gave him a shiver. He hadn't touched one of those things in years, and he wasn't excited about starting now.

He went to the fireplace, got a poker, used it to lift the breast up, held it there for a moment, like some kind of vicious animal he had shot but feared might still be alive. Under her tit was an arm, bent across her face, and in her fist was a glass and the open end of the glass was pressed against her face.

And then he got it.

She had been standing on the other side of the couch, and in her usual drunken stupor she had thrown her head back to toss down a drink, and the movement had caused her to go over backwards. She had fallen over the couch, gaining momentum when her breasts hit her in the face like sacks of flour, then the rest of her got going and she hit the floor hard.

Or maybe she had a heart attack.

It didn't matter. She was dead.

Or was she?

She had fooled him before. To the point where he thought he might talk to McBride about some business, but he didn't want to push his luck, not with the mayor gone and McBride the reason and hired by him.

Henry looked at his wife carefully. There was vomit all around her mouth and on the floor, and her mouth was wide open, the glass halfway in it.

Henry lowered her breast with the poker, then used it to jab her in the side a couple of times, just to make sure. He gave her pretty good pokes, but she didn't get up or move or make any noise.

He laughed. He hadn't expected to laugh. It just came out of nowhere, like a summer storm. He started and couldn't stop. He jigged around in a circle.

Lately he had begun to doubt the existence of God, but now he knew he was wrong. Not only was there a God, but the sonofabitch was on his side.

He put the poker back, found a glass and her bottle on the fireplace, poured himself a strong shot of whisky, drank it, drank another. It had no effect on him.

He was giddier than whisky could make him. He couldn't have been happier than if a fairy godmother had granted him six more inches on his dick.

In the bedroom he got a quilt, brought it back and tossed it over her.

She moaned.

It wasn't much, but it was a noise.

Henry stopped, listened, looked. Hoped he had heard nothing more than the growling of his own stomach, an unexpected passing of gas. But no, she was moaning again.

Henry went over, lifted up the quilt. Her eyes fluttered weakly, closed. Her hand with the glass still in it flapped away from her mouth and slapped against the floor.

He had been wrong about God.

He bent down and pulled the quilt back over her face, then he took hold of the quilt and pressed it down so that it fit tight over her nose, and he leaned forward, so that he was putting all his weight on her, and weak as she was, she didn't struggle much. Her foot sticking over the couch waved a few times like a flag of surrender, then went still.

Henry kept pressing. He used his free hand to take out his pocket watch and flip it open. He looked at it and kept the pressure on with his other hand, adding his knee to the side of her head as he pressed. He watched the hands on his watch carefully. Her rolls of fat jiggled, but she didn't get up and didn't lift a hand to struggle, just jiggled.

After a moment even the fat had ceased to move, and checking his watch, he saw that he had been holding the quilt over her nose for about four minutes.

Tired, he let go and stood up. Finally, he bent over and lifted the quilt. She looked dead. He got the poker again and prodded her a few more times with it, this time harder than before, but against the quilt so as not to leave marks.

This time God was on his side, even if he had had to help.

He poured another drink, sipped it slowly, then went to get Willie. He could have called, he and Willie had phones, but this was a message he wanted to deliver in person. He hadn't felt this giddy since he was twelve and got a .22 for his birthday and shot his neighbor's cat out of a tree.

As he drove over he wondered if Willie had a box big enough for the old bitch. She had to be about the size of a goddamn bear. It would take a bunch of men to haul her out. Maybe even a well-fed ox.

Okay. Not an ox. But he had visions of an ox at the door, long chains fastened to it, then to her foot, and the ox being driven forward with brutal swipes of a whip, pulling her old dead fat ass over the couch and out the door.

Then he thought: Maybe I should dress her first?

No. Too much trouble.

What clothes would he bury her in?

Well, he could cut a hole in a quilt, pull that over her head. That was an option.

Thing was, not to look too happy. It might all double back on him he looked too happy. They might think he, instead of bright and shining fortune, had done her in.

And, of course, he had.

As he drove along, he decided things were good. First the stuff on Sunset, now his wife, dead by drink and gravity and the clutch of his hand.

God love fermentation.

God love Isaac Newton.

God love the muscles in his hand.

Without realizing it, he began to sing.

19

The woods were stuffy with heat and dense with mosquitoes and the sunlight was split by trees. The light hit the cross on the grave and made a shadow and speckled out on the leaf-covered mound on the ground.

Clyde and Hillbilly leaned on their shovels and looked to Sunset for instructions. Hillbilly and Clyde weren't talking to each other any more than they had to.

Sunset noted that though Hillbilly was not drunk, he had buzzed himself this morning with the hair of the dog, and it made her mad. He had a job and she was his boss and she thought she ought to say something, but decided to let it go.

She wasn't sure why she let it go, but she had some idea. And she didn't like that idea. That wasn't the way to do things. If it had been Clyde she would have said something to him. But it wouldn't be Clyde. Clyde would show up ready to go and on time. That's the way Clyde did things.

And today, this morning, she actually decided there was something to do. Thought of it shortly after she drove the car home.

"Y'all just gonna lean on them things?" Sunset said.

"You ain't got a shovel," Hillbilly said.

"I'm the boss, so I'll just fight mosquitoes."

"I don't get it," Clyde said. "What we doing this for? I don't want to look at no dead babies. Besides, won't be nothing left but a bone or two if there's that. And what's it gonna prove anyhow?"

Sunset slapped at a mosquito, turned it into a little dark wad on her cheek. "I got to know there's a baby here."

"Zendo saw it," Clyde said.

"I know," Sunset said. "I believe him. But I want to see if the baby ended up here."

"Why wouldn't it?" Hillbilly said.

"I don't know," Sunset said. "I guess it would. But what I'm wondering is why was Jimmie Jo and the baby killed?"

"Pete could have done it," Clyde said. "Got pissed off at the woman over most anything, and done it, just the way he might have done it to you, you hadn't killed him first."

"That's been considered," Sunset said. "He was mean and capable of killing, but I don't think he'd have done it like this. He would have just raped her and shot her in the head and been done with it."

"Someone did shoot her in the head," Clyde said. "And with Pete's caliber of gun. One you're wearing. Way I see it, you just solved who killed who, and that's what I'd tell that damn council. Pete got mad at his girlfriend, killed her and her baby, and if he was drunk enough to rape and kill that woman, like he might have done you, I think he was drunk enough to cut a baby out of her. After he done it, he got drunk or drunker and got to thinking on it, took it out on you and damn near killed you. End of story. Let's go to the house. It's too damn hot to dig."

"Lots of people got a thirty-eight," Sunset said. "Course, I wouldn't have thought Pete would hit me when we married. I wouldn't have thought he could give anyone a beating like he gave Three-Fingered Jack."

"What was that all about, anyway?" Hillbilly said. "It must have been some beating. I hear about it all the time."

"Pete was fighting over Jimmie Jo," Sunset said, "so I ain't partial to the memory. And he done it in front of me. He seen

199

Jack, told him to leave Jimmie Jo alone, with me standing right there, then started in on him. Pete didn't care I knew he was pulling her panties down. He cared Jack wanted to. I figure Jimmie Jo told him about Jack, to get something started. She was like that. It might have been Jack didn't have nothing to do with her and she was disappointed he didn't want it."

"I'm starting to wish I'd seen that fight," Hillbilly said.

"Other thing I'm thinking," Sunset said, "is Pete may have known she was carrying his baby, and that's what made him so mad at Jack."

"You're saying he was in love with her?" Clyde said. "Not just catting around?"

"I think he gave me a beating over knowing she was dead. He wanted her and couldn't have her, so he took it out on me. He loved her, not me."

"Well, he didn't have no taste," Clyde said. "And I still think he killed her. He might have done it because the baby wasn't his. You think about that? It might not have nothing to do with love. He could have beat Jack up because he was jealous all right, but not because he was so in love. Just didn't want some other man pawing over what he thought was his. It's something to consider, ain't it?"

"It is," Sunset said.

"That's how it could have been," Clyde said. "Could have made him mad enough to cut the baby out of her, hide her and the baby out there by Zendo's field. Zendo found the baby, so Pete come and looked it over and didn't try to blame it on Zendo, not because he was nice but because maybe he felt a little guilty about it and didn't want to nail someone he knew didn't do it. So he took and buried the baby, hoping the woman wouldn't be found."

"That's another thing I don't get," Sunset said. "He killed her, why did he bury the baby here and leave her in the field?"

"Maybe he wanted her found for some reason," Clyde said.

"Didn't mind her being found, but maybe didn't want folks to know he'd rip a baby out of her."

"That was figured out pretty quick by Willie," Sunset said.

"He might not have known it could be figured that easy," Clyde said. "I ain't got that part figured out. But he could have done it, then got killed, and now all his bad work is showing up. Damn, that sounds pretty smart for me."

"Maybe," Sunset said. "Guess I don't want to believe it was Pete. Don't want it to be that. He's still Karen's father. And it just shows my judgment in men was worse than I thought."

Clyde looked at Hillbilly, said, "A woman can make some bad judgments in men."

"Let's dig," Sunset said.

"Still don't see the point," Hillbilly said. "There's a baby, so what? Still won't know any more than you did, baby or not."

"Humor me," Sunset said.

They dug deep before they found a little wooden box. Sunset said, "I think we ought to crack it open."

"Don't feel right about this, Sunset," Clyde said. "Dead baby and all, disturbing its eternal rest."

"Because it's eternal," Hillbilly said, "you aren't disturbing anything."

Sunset took the shovel from Clyde, stuck the point of the shovel between lid and container, levered the lid off.

There was an object wrapped in a small blanket that had become damp and dark and was starting to rot. Sunset reached down, unwrapped a small, dark, leathery-looking skull.

"It's a baby all right," Hillbilly said.

"Poor little Snooks," Clyde said.

Sunset touched the skull. "Oil on it is what preserved it," she said. "Darkened it and made it leathery."

"Is it a colored?" Hillbilly asked.

"I don't know," Sunset said. "I don't think anyone could know now."

Sunset peeled aside the blanket. The rest of the body was small and wiry-looking and a lot of it was rotted away. Clyde said, "Guess the head got the main dose of oil."

"Yeah," Sunset said.

"What's that?" Hillbilly said.

Sunset rewrapped the baby and looked at what Hillbilly saw. It was a metal box. It nearly filled the casket and there had been some kind of cloth over it, but the cloth had almost rotted away and was the texture of an old spiderweb.

When the baby was wrapped again, Sunset gently lifted it and placed it on the ground and pulled the long rectangular box out of the casket. "It's padlocked," she said.

"Stand back," Hillbilly said, and when Sunset moved away he struck the lock with the point of the shovel and there was a spark and the lock snapped open.

Sunset opened the box. Inside was an oilskin bundle wrapped in rotten twine. She snapped the twine and took out what was in the wrapping.

A ledger.

Sunset opened it. The pages had maps drawn on them and bits of arithmetic worked out in the margins, and there were a couple of pages folded up inside the ledger. She opened one of them and looked at it. It was a page with a land description on it. The other was more of the same.

"Looks like a surveyor's map," Hillbilly said. "See that stamp on it. It was registered in Holiday. My guess is it's supposed to be there, in the courthouse."

"I don't reckon Pete put this here for nothing," Clyde said. "Still, that's pretty awful, hiding it that way with poor Snooks, for whatever reason."

"Why don't we try and figure on it where there aren't so many skeeters?" Hillbilly said.

"All right," Sunset said. She folded up the papers, put them back in the ledger, laid it on the ground, put the baby back in the box and they reburied it.

"Clyde," she said. "You're religious some. Say a prayer over it. I haven't got a damn thing to say to God, if there is one."

Clyde studied Sunset for a moment, said a few words. Sunset returned the ledger to the strongbox and let Hillbilly carry it back to the truck for her.

She sat between Clyde and Hillbilly and Clyde drove. While they drove Hillbilly played a harmonica, and he was good at it.

"I thought you was a guitar man?" Sunset said.

He stopped playing. "Am. But what I got is this harmonica. I got a Jew's harp too, but I'm not too good at it."

"I can agree with that," Clyde said. "I've heard him play."

"Clyde," Hillbilly said, "you wouldn't know good music if it stuck its finger up your ass."

"Maybe it ain't good the way you play it."

"Boys," Sunset said. "What about a guitar, Hillbilly?"

"Got to get some money first. Thought we got paid for this."

"End of the month, I think."

"I've done a lot of work along the road I didn't get paid for," Hillbilly said. "Lot of people kind of faded when it was time to put the money down."

"There's nowhere for them to fade," Sunset said. "Marilyn is good for it."

"I got to buy a little lumber and start building on a house," Clyde said. "It comes winter, my young ass is gonna be pretty damn frosty I don't get a roof and walls . . . Sunset, what do you think all this stuff with the book and the baby means?"

"I'll have to study on it," Sunset said.

20

Lee and Marilyn sat on the edge of Uncle Riley's porch, sweated, dangled their feet and drank lemonade Aunt Cary had made. Aunt Cary had gone back to the woods to gather roots and such, and Uncle Riley was plucking a chicken in the backyard while Tommy climbed a tree.

"Reckon he's gonna be all right now," Marilyn said.

"I think so. Glad you came along."

"Me too. You looking for work?"

"I am."

"The mill's pretty full, and there ain't much else in Camp Rapture. You might try Holiday. They're hiring a lot over there because of the oil business. It's booming."

"Heard tell of it. But I got some things to do in Camp Rapture first."

"Is it a secret?"

"Guess not, though I don't know I want to scream it from the rooftops. Haven't really talked to anyone about it before 'cept God, and he didn't seem interested. You interested?"

"I asked, didn't I?"

"All right. Long time ago, when I was a young man, twenty or so, I got the calling. Lord come to me one morning and I knew I had to preach."

"I've always wondered. How does the Lord come to a preacher? Did you see him?"

"No. And it wasn't no burning bush neither. My family tried

to settle some land in Oklahoma, but it didn't work out. There was some Indians felt it was their land, and I reckon it was. Government had cut it all up and given it to white folks wanted to settle, but these Indians, four or five of them, they thought it was theirs."

"You mean, like they were on the warpath?"

"Not like no cowboy movie. These were civilized Indians. Had suit coats and hats and forty-fives. But they was less civilized when they killed my mom and pa. Murdered them in our home and left me there with the bodies. I don't know why they didn't kill me, but they didn't. One of them put a pistol right to my forehead, and cocked it, but he didn't pull on me. He just looked at me for a minute, then he and the bunch of them run off. For a few days I wished they'd killed me, but after a while I was glad they didn't, cause I set out to hunt them down."

"How old were you?"

"Fourteen. This was in ninety-four or so."

"Did you hunt them down?"

"Law got one of them, and he was hung. I got after two myself. Chased them all the way into Kansas. They split up there and I settled on one of them. Laid for him outside a whorehouse in Leavenworth, and when he come out, I jumped on him from behind and cut his throat."

"Jesus."

"Yeah. Pretty horrible. But it didn't faze me then. I went on the lookout for the other one, finally found him, and shot him in the back. Hid up in a tree where I knew he'd ride by, and when he did I used a rifle I'd stole, and shot him. You know I learned later a colored man was hung for that rifle I stole. I didn't know about it until years later, but he was hung cause it was thought he done it, even though they didn't find the rifle. He rode through same place I had not long after I'd come by. Imagine that, hanging a man for stealing a rifle. And on top of that, he didn't steal it. I had a mind, once I found out about it, to say something, but I didn't, because I figured I might get hung myself, and my telling the truth wasn't going to bring that man back.

"Anyway, after I killed the second man, I figured on finding the other ones, and I was lying out in a field somewhere in Kansas, in the open, at night, trying to sleep, looking up at the stars, and the vengeance went out of me. Felt like the Lord reached down and got hold of my heart and pulled the blackness out of it and filled me up with a light. Decided I was gonna be a preacher right then. Ended up in Camp Rapture about 1900."

"My God. You're the Reverend."

"Not anymore. Name's Lee Beck. But, yeah, I was the Reverend then. And I came to what you now call Camp Rapture, and I done some good. I done some baptizing and civilizing. And then, like David, I lost my way. I took advantage of a young woman. Her name was Bunny Ann."

"I knew her."

"You did?"

"Yes. Not well. But I knew her."

"I had my way with her and run off. I don't know if she's married now, or around, or what, and I don't want to disturb her life. I just want to come and apologize to her. Set things right."

"What about your daughter?"

"What's that?"

"You didn't know she got pregnant, had a daughter?"

Lee's shoulders sagged under his coat.

"A daughter. She had a daughter?"

"Your daughter, if Bunny told it right. She gave her your last name. And you want to know something else?"

"I'm not sure."

"She's my daughter-in-law."

"My God."

"It gets a mite more complicated."

"Before you tell me, what about Bunny Ann? Is she still here?"

"No. She run off with a shoe salesman."

"A shoe salesman?"

"Yeah."

"Well, I guess I should have took her with me. Or not run off. Just wasn't ready to settle down and I'd had my way with her, and me a Reverend, and I guess I thought I ought to run, like I could actually hide out from God."

"I will say this. A shoe salesman, in my book, is a lot lower than a preacher."

"Guess that's some comfort. How are things more complicated?"

"Has to do with my son, and what happened to him. Your daughter's husband. She's called Sunset, by the way, though her mama named her Carrie Lynn."

"What happened?"

Marilyn told him. She told him about Pete and what Sunset had done, told him about her husband and how he had rode on a log into the saw, all of it.

When she finished, Lee said, "I've set off a chain reaction. I've made all kinds of things happen, and none of them good. It's a thing you don't count on when you're young, how you can do something and have it turn into all kinds of things. My God, how is Carrie Lynn—Sunset?"

"She's all right."

"After what she done? What about you? How are you taking it?"

"She had to do it."

"I believe that. But Pete was your son. Surely—"

"Like I told her, I got my moments. Moments when I hate her. But they're moments. And another thing, you have a granddaughter."

"Jesus."

"Name's Karen. She's hurting right now, as you can guess. I was you, I'd quit chasing Bunny Ann. She's made her life and moved on, and maybe got some shoes out of the deal. She had as much to do with creating that girl as you. You ran out on her and Bunny ran out on Sunset, and now you got this daughter and granddaughter. Could be that's where you ought to put your time. With them two."

"I feel like I been poleaxed."

"I can imagine. After you was a Reverend, where did you go?"

"I had all kinds of jobs, all over the country. Finally, I felt the need to come back here and see Bunny Ann. Now, I don't know I want to find her anymore. It's like you said. I got a better place to put my time. If they'll have me. Do you think they will?"

"I can't answer that for you, Lee."

They sat in silence after that, drinking lemonade, and would have continued in silence if Goose hadn't called out from inside the house.

"I got to go see to him," Lee said.

In the bedroom he found the boy trying to sit up.

"Here, let me help you."

Lee folded a pillow over and let Goose rest his head on it.

"I don't feel so good," Goose said.

"Feel a lot worse if we hadn't got some help."

"Where are we?"

Lee told him about Marilyn, about Aunt Cary, Uncle Riley and Tommy.

"This here is their own bed they done put you in," Lee said.

"Colored folks?"

"You ain't going to get funny about that, are you?"

"I ain't got nothing against colored. I ain't got nothing against nobody. 'Cept maybe that snake. Lee?"

"Yeah."

"I'm gonna get well?"

"Looks like it."

The boy looked at his bandaged hand.

"Case I don't, I ought to tell you something, especially since you're a preacher."

"I ain't a preacher no more. I been a Pinkerton Man too, and a lot of other things, but no one thinks to call me those. Just Preacher. And I ain't one. God done long gone from me. And you're gonna be all right. You don't need to confess nothing to me."

"I ain't never had no pussy, Lee. I lied about that. I just wanted to sound big."

"That's all right."

"I want some, but I ain't never had none."

"You'll have your chance someday. I think we ought to talk about something else, and if I was you, I'd drop that line of talk and thinking until I was about sixteen or so, then I'd wait until I got married."

"Did you?"

"No."

"Hard to wait, ain't it? And you got to do it with a bad girl you ain't gonna marry."

"Don't believe that. Ain't no girl or woman any badder than you make them. I ain't your daddy, and I ain't no preacher, but trust me, lead the good life. Things you do, they set off a line of events that can be good or bad. I was just telling Marilyn that."

"The woman picked us up?"

"Yeah."

"Is she pretty?"

"She's old as me. But yeah, I think she's pretty."

"You ain't had none while I was sleeping, have you?"

Lee lightly slapped Goose's head. "You can stop that talk. Lay down and shut up. I'll see what we're gonna do next."

"You ain't gonna leave, are you?"

"No. I ain't gonna leave you."

"Like you said, you ain't kin. You don't owe me nothing. You don't have to stay."

"Ain't got nothing better to do for the moment. Reckon I'll keep up with you for a while. You rest now. Aunt Cary and Uncle Riley are gonna fry some chicken in a bit. You can eat, can't you?"

"Like an old wolf."

21

The freedom of the car was exhilarating, and because of it, as well as because it seemed a commonsense plan—and if it had not been she would have convinced herself it was—Sunset decided to drive to Holiday the next morning, take a look over at the courthouse, see if she could figure out something about the maps in the grave.

She had looked over the ledger, and decided it wasn't connected. The ledger had notes from cases, and not many of them, as it was pretty new, and she figured Pete had just stuck the maps in it, then buried it all together, maybe to help protect the maps. Yeah, that was it, she was pretty sure.

Thing to do was go to Holiday, look at the courthouse, see what was there. And she planned to take Hillbilly with her, send Clyde out to look at the land next to Zendo's, talk to Zendo, see if he knew anything about who owned that stretch. She knew she was doing it too because she wanted to be alone with Hillbilly, and that irked her. She was letting her loins make decisions for her. It was always said that men thought with the little head and not the big head, but something other than her head was certainly doing some of her thinking, and she didn't like it, but couldn't resist it. In fact, thought of it made her a little light-headed.

As for Karen, she would drive her over to Camp Rapture first thing in the morning to spend the day with Marilyn. Marilyn would like that, and she thought Karen would too, and maybe they'd go to Holiday, see a picture show.

Hell. She might see a picture show herself. Or go to the Oil Festival that was being held in honor of what oil had done for Holiday. Which was turn a nice peaceful burg into a mud hole full of thugs and noise and tall metal derricks and too many people rubbing shoulders and no telling what all else against one another.

The whole idea of having a car made Sunset feel as powerful as the gun made her feel. Only better. Free. Was that how men felt all the time?

Or most of them, anyway?

And she had two men who wanted her.

Clyde. Who she didn't want.

And Hillbilly. Who she sure as hell did want.

But it was great to be wanted after being locked away so much of the time in the house, and when she was wanted by Pete, it was as a punching bag. Punching with his fists. Punching with his penis. No love there and no true want of the sort she cared about.

Things were maybe not wonderful, but they were better than they were when Pete was alive.

If it wasn't for what it did to Karen, what she was having to deal with, she'd maybe consider shooting a husband every day. It had certainly opened some doors.

Sunset was thinking about all this as she fed Ben out by the big oak beside the road in the near darkness. There was still light but it was fading fast and the light that was there held dust motes in strands so that they looked like tresses of fine blond hair hanging amidst the trees.

Sunset took in a deep breath and savored the taste of the air.

Karen was inside the tent, reading a book. Clyde had relented and given Hillbilly a ride somewhere, then probably gone home to his burned-down house to lie under his tarp.

Sunset was enjoying this time. Just her and the dog. Even

being away from Hillbilly and thinking about being with him was in this moment better than being with him. She could let her imagination work overtime.

"Howdy," said a voice.

Sunset wheeled, dropping the pan in front of Ben, and began pulling her gun from its holster.

Before she could pull it clean, a hand went over hers, a hand larger than both of hers put together, multiplied by two, and with that movement, quicker than sight, the gun was out of her grasp and a colored man with an explosion of head hair and a heavy beard, a man no wider than a log wagon and no taller than a pine, was standing in front of her, holding the gun in the palm of his hand.

Ben wheeled, growling.

"Easy, boy," the big man said.

Ben stopped growling, whimpered, pushed up against the man's leg like a cat.

"You ain't got no cause to worry," said the colored man. "I ain't here to hurt you. I come to talk."

"Bull?"

"That's right."

He gave her back her gun. She looked down at Ben. "Some watchdog."

"Dogs like me," Bull said. "'Specially since I been coming up nights making friends with him. Dog is loyal 'less he likes to eat rabbit entrails. Then he only loyal long as it takes to get him used to eatin' some every night."

"So that's what's been wrong with his appetite."

"Me and him are friends now," Bull said, leaning over to pet Ben on the head. "But he's a good dog. And a good watchdog for you. I hadn't had a good heart, he'd have known, and rabbit guts wouldn't have got him to be friends. Not all dogs know that.

Some like rabbit guts no matter who gives them out, but this one ain't that way."

"And how do you know?"

"Cause my heart, like his, is good and true."

"My God. You're the biggest man I've ever seen."

"My brother was bigger when we was kids. I think he'd have grown to be bigger if he'd growed up, but he got drowned, swimming in the Sabine. I'm seven foot, just so you know. I don't know what I weigh, but you wouldn't want me to fall on you."

"Why have you been making friends with my dog?"

"I been leading him out in the woods a piece. Didn't want to just come up and have him go at me and didn't want to frighten you none."

"Too late for that. You frightened me plenty."

"You done good by Smoky."

"I got your note."

"My talking is a lot better than my writing. I never got no learning or spelling, except what I picked up, so I got to guess at things. Wasn't even sure I told you what I wanted to tell you— Smoky and me, for a long time, we was like brothers. Then he got a little tetched. He wasn't bad tetched, but he was tetched. You doing what you did, it ain't often any whitey does a thing for me or mine, but you did, and I appreciate it. Because of it, I come to tell you something."

"All right."

"Brought a jug of shine. It's on the other side of the tree there, where I been waiting. You up for any?"

"Ain't never drank any."

"Can be powerful bad for you, don't treat it right. But treat it right, it'll treat you right."

"Let me get some glasses."

*

When Sunset went in the tent, Karen was by the flap.

"Who is that, Mama?"

"A friend."

"A colored friend?"

"He's colored and he seems friendly."

"Are you sure it's safe? He looks like a giant."

"He is."

"He might hurt you."

"He took my gun away from me and gave it back, so I don't reckon he's got plans to hurt me. Bring out a couple chairs so we can sit a spell, and you come on back in the tent."

"I'm scared with that big man around."

"There's a shotgun right there, courtesy of Clyde. You can sit with it if you like."

Sunset got the glasses and Karen carried two chairs out. Bull was leaning against the oak, holding a small white jug.

"How do you do?" Bull said to Karen.

"I'm fine," Karen said, and hustled back to the tent.

"She think the big nigger is gonna rape and slaughter y'all, set fire to the tent and eat the dog?"

"Something like that."

They sat in the chairs and Bull poured them each a little dose of his poison. The dog lay down between them.

Sunset sipped.

"Oh, Jesus," she said. "It's like drinking coal oil on fire."

"But with a sweet smooth aftertaste," Bull said.

Sunset laughed, held the glass and didn't sip. Bull, on the other hand, pulled deeply. When he brought the glass down, he said, "There's all sorts of talk cause you helped Smoky, and it's white people talk."

"It's just talk."

"Some of it's Klan talk."

"I know half the people in the Klan."

"They talking about correcting you."

"How do you know?"

"Colored people can be almost like they invisible. Workers, maids, laundry women. They hear things, and it all gets back to Bull."

"Why do they tell you?"

"Don't know. Maybe because I ain't afraid of no white man. Actually, I am, there's enough of them, but they don't know that."

Bull grinned at her. Sunset thought his grin looked a little like a bear baring its teeth.

"Tell you true, missy, ain't got much use for white folks. Hate them cause they hate me, and I didn't reckon there was one good one among you."

"Can I suppose I'm a good one?"

Bull grinned. "You can. And maybe, if you're good, there's two good ones. Even three. I won't figure to think there might be four."

"There's really a lot of us."

"I'm not here cause I'm wanting to suck on whitey's tit, and I don't mean yours. I'm here cause I owe you cause of what you done. You may have done it cause of the law, but you done it. That's something. Go on. Have another sip. It'll lighten your load."

Sunset took another sip. It was as if a blazing mothball were flowing down her throat.

"Wow," she said.

"I get told all kind of things," Bull said. "Cause I'm the man supplies the drink for the colored folks, and they like to drink, and talk, and drink helps them talk . . . whatever the reason, it's a fact. So I'm telling you, watch yourself. There's people don't like you cause you're a woman, same way they don't like me cause I'm colored. It ain't got no rhyme or reason. You and me, we got our place and we ain't staying in it, and there's plenty don't like that. They like things where, and in a way, they can count on them. Colored does this, woman does this. We ain't doing it, and it ain't going down well. Way they may come for you, cause I think they will, is the Klan. Maybe not. But maybe so. You see someone in a sheet you shoot their sheeted head off. I tell you one thing, them sheets make good targets."

"Did you really have them come for you?"

"I did."

"What happened?"

"Didn't work out for them. Like I said, them sheets make good targets. Just don't shoot too high. Might think that pointed cap ought to have their head in it, but it don't. Not unless you're aiming kind of low into it."

Sunset had to think about that a moment, then she got it.

"You're quick, Bull."

"More ways than one. What I know, though, is I die, my body gets found, I don't know any colored will care enough to do anything with it, which is okay, but I fear peckerwoods might get me. Old boy over in Sacul. They hung him and cut him up and sold his bones for keepsakes. Come and get your nigger bones, two cents. I die, I'd like someone to just burn me up, leave nothing but ashes."

"That business with Smoky," Sunset said. "The thing you're giving me credit for. It didn't work out too well. You know that?"

Bull nodded.

"That wouldn't be your fault, gal. You done what you could. You got more brains than your husband, and I'm glad you killed him."

"Did Pete ever bother you?"

"Just once."

"I suppose that didn't work out well for him."

"No. It didn't. I sort of relieved him of the same gun I just took from you and slapped him a bit and sent him home. I figured he wouldn't mention much about it, having a nigger take his gun, give him a slapping, empty out the bullets, and give it back to him."

"What did he come see you about?"

"You're drinking it."

"Heavens. I'm breaking the law, drinking illegal-made whisky."

Bull grinned. He had a lot of fine white teeth. "Now I got something on you.

"He wanted to see I paid him to run my business. A little cut of the pie. But I ain't really all that big on business partners. Especially white constables."

"I'm a white constable."

"So you is. Another thing. Always thought white women, small like they was in the ass and such, not powerful in the face, with them little old skinny noses and that funky hair, was ugly. But you don't look bad for a white woman."

"I don't know if that's a compliment or not."

"It'll have to do."

"Would you like to eat? I was about to fix dinner."

"You don't want to seem too cozy with a nigger. Got enough folks mad at you. Killing Pete. Being a woman constable, then helping out Smoky. But I'll be watching for you some. I ain't got nothing else to do but dangle at home. It's not like I get to go to too many church socials."

"Do you want to?"

"Not really. My days, girl, are numbered. Starting to get rheumatiz. Slowing down. Them whites that hate me, they gonna

218

get me in time. I know that. So I ain't afraid. Once you know you're done for, you ain't afraid no more. Well, a little. But what's gonna happen is gonna happen . . . I'll check on you now and then. Something comes up where I can pay back what you done for Smoky, I will."

"What I did was get him to Tyler to be lynched."

"You tried. Listen here now. Need me, hang a strip of white cloth on the other side of that oak there. I'll see it. Maybe not right away, but soon. And I'll come. You know, it's kind of good to be out of them deep woods a bit. I forget the real color of the sky, seeing only bits of it through the trees, and some of it looking green cause of the sun on the leaves. Kind of tired of staying back there in them woods, pretending to be a booger bear."

"Got a feeling you might be a booger bear, Bull."

Bull smiled, corked the jug, reached down and gave the dog a pat. "I'll be gone now."

Bull rose, walked behind the oak, and when Sunset stood to see him off he wasn't there. He had blended into the brush and trees. Once she thought she heard him moving through the undergrowth, but when she looked there was nothing. Then the last strands of light were gone and there was darkness, falling like a curtain. The wind picked up and brought the damp dirt smell of the creek to her nostrils, a night bird called, a fistful of crickets started up as if they had just punched the clock, and within moments a few lightning bugs appeared.

Sunset took another sip of the shine and shivered. She poured the rest on the ground. Ben came over and sniffed the shine in the dirt, jerked his head back and went away.

"Good dog," Sunset said. "Believe me, you don't want to drink that. Pickle something in it maybe, but drink it, uh-uh."

22

Next morning, much against Karen's will, Sunset drove her to Marilyn's. Karen sat in the passenger seat, stiff, arms crossed, a look on her face that made Sunset think of someone being forced to eat tacks.

"Thought you'd want to see your grandma," Sunset said.

Karen shifted in the car seat, but didn't uncross her arms.

"I wanted to go to the Oil Festival."

"Who says you can't? Ask Grandma. She'll take you."

"Hillbilly told me about it," Karen said.

"He told me too," Sunset said. "That's how I knew."

"He said he'd take me."

Sunset let that sink in, said, "He didn't mean like a date, dear. He meant you could go with us."

"Well, I'm not going with you, am I?"

"Grandma wants to see you. You can go with her. Besides, you're thinking the wrong things about Hillbilly. He likes you. But not in that way."

"How would you know?"

"I know."

"Because you like him. Because you kissed him."

"All right. You got me. I like him."

"Well, I like him more."

Sunset decided not to get into who liked who more. She said, "He's too old for you, dear, and that's the end of it."

"You're just jealous."

"I am not jealous."

"You think he can't like me because I'm young."

"He can like you, but not that way. And that's the end of it, Karen. You're going to your grandma's, and you can go with her or you can sit at her house. That's up to you."

"Do you like him better than Daddy?"

"I just like him. Nothing more."

"You didn't answer me about Daddy."

"I loved your daddy when I loved him, and I still love things about him, certain memories, but he made me not love him. Beatings tend to make you feel a lot less warm toward someone, dear."

Karen made a snorting sound. "You liked killing him."

"No. I didn't."

"That didn't sound real convincing."

"I've explained it as best I know how. And I've explained to you how it's going to be with Hillbilly and you."

"You think you know everything."

"I do not. I know I don't know everything. If there's one thing I know, it's that I don't know everything, and in fact, don't know much."

"You sure don't. You don't know nothing. You don't know a thing."

"That's enough out of you, young lady."

"You going to hit me, like you say Daddy hit you?"

"No. But I'd like to. I'd like to a lot. And I don't just say your daddy hit me. He did. I didn't get the way you saw me by beating myself up. You know he hit me, baby. You knew it before I killed him, didn't you?"

"No."

"Yes, you did."

Karen leaned back in the seat and glared out the window.

They rode the rest of the way to Camp Rapture in silence, and when Sunset pulled up in Marilyn's yard, Karen got out of the car, slammed the door, ran up on the porch and inside.

Sunset sat for a moment, considered trying to talk to her, but thought: No. There's no end to trying to explain what can't be explained.

She turned the car around, was about to leave, when she saw Marilyn in her wing mirror. Sunset opened her car door, Marilyn came up and leaned in.

"Karen seems a little huffy," Marilyn said.

"Young girl blues," Sunset said.

"Well, she'll get over it. I'm going to fix her a good breakfast, see if she wants to go over to Holiday, go to a movie or something."

"They're having a thing they call the Oil Festival. Supposed to have music and such. I'm going to be over there today myself. On business."

Marilyn smiled.

"Here's something might make business better." Marilyn handed her three envelopes. "It's a payday for you and your boys."

"Early, isn't it?"

"It is. But you can only go so long without money."

"Thanks."

"You're welcome. Do your business, but take a little time for yourself. Reckon you've earned it."

By the time Sunset reached her tent, Hillbilly and Clyde had arrived. Hillbilly was camping down by the creek about two miles away, walking distance, but Sunset had talked Clyde into picking him up on his way in the night before.

Clyde hadn't liked the idea, but she had convinced him. She

only had to look him in the eyes, smile and flirt a little. She felt about as tall as an amputated flea after doing it, but she'd done it anyway and thought she might do it again it worked so well.

Sunset got out of the car, said, "Howdy, boys."

They greeted her, and Ben came over for a pat on the head. She looked up and noted Clyde was a mess of hair seeping out from under his hat, sleeves half rolled, pants sagging, a growth of beard that made his face look dirty.

Hillbilly, even if he was living by the creek, looked as if his clothes had been pressed. His hair was combed and he was clean-shaved and alert-looking. No drinking this morning.

Clyde, on the other hand, looked as if he were coming off a bender, though she had a feeling he wasn't. That it was just the way he felt. Maybe he was regretting burning down his house.

As they strolled over, she started to tell them about Bull, but decided not to. She wasn't sure why. Seeing Bull was a lot like when she was a girl of eleven in the woods picking berries and she'd come upon a small black bear rooting against a hickory nut tree. When she walked up, it stopped rooting and turned to look at her, rising up on its hind legs. They stared at each other for a minute. Then the bear settled down on all fours and walked directly toward her.

She froze.

The bear came within inches, extended its nose, and smelled her, and she smelled the bear, and it was an earthy smell like dirt, dung and urine. Maybe to the bear, she smelled as bad as it did to her.

When its nostrils were full of her, the bear sauntered past her and disappeared into the woods.

It was an amazing moment, and she never told anyone.

Not that she had many people to tell. Her mother was still around then, but she spent most of her time drunk and shacked up, so she wouldn't have told her anyway because it wouldn't have meant anything to her. She'd have thought: So you seen a bear, no big thing.

Fact was, she wouldn't have told anyone had there been anyone to tell.

It was her special moment and she clung to it.

Meeting Bull was the same way. Least for now. And she was going to keep it to herself. Way he had appeared and disappeared more expertly than the bear. And she could still taste that awful whisky on the back of her throat, a peppered fire of broken glass and greasy sins.

"What we're gonna do today is split up," she said. "Hillbilly, you're gonna go with me. Clyde, I want you to go out to Zendo's. See if you can find out anything about that land that connects to his, where the body was found."

"Why?" Clyde said.

"Maybe there's some kind of connection. Me and Hillbilly are going to check at the courthouse. See if those papers we found mean anything. Find out why they aren't in the courthouse and if they're supposed to be there."

"I'll be through by noon," Clyde said. "Before. Why don't we all ride over to Zendo's, then Holiday?"

"I think we can cover more time and ground this way," Sunset said.

"Oh, I think some time can be made all right," Clyde said.

"That's enough, Clyde," Sunset said. "You work for me, and this is a job of work, and if you don't want to do it, then you don't have to. I'm asking you to do something needs to be done."

"That's not all you're asking."

"She's the boss," Hillbilly said. "That's what you told me."

"Quit being foolish," Sunset said. "Both of you. That's enough. Now listen up. I got some good news. We got paid early."

She passed out the envelopes. Hillbilly peeked in the envelope. "Well, it's money."

"No one promised you'd be rich," Sunset said.

Clyde took his envelope, folded it and put it in his back pocket, and without a word, got in his truck and drove off.

"Think he's going to do what you asked?" Hillbilly said.

"I do. I'll get the maps, and we can set out."

"While we're over there, might as well hang around a bit, see a picture show, maybe go to the Oil Festival."

"This is work, Hillbilly."

"I know. But we could, you know?"

"I suppose."

He grinned at her. "You haven't forgotten our kiss, have you?"

"How could I?"

"Where's Karen?"

"At her grandma's."

"Thought she was going to come with us. I told her about the festival."

"You had plans all along to go, didn't you?" Sunset said.

"Didn't you?"

Sunset hoped she wasn't the blushing sort.

"Now I know why she isn't here," Hillbilly said.

"Awful sure of yourself, aren't you?"

"Sure of what I want, if I'm not sure of anything else."

"Karen's got a little crush on you. She's acting a little too old for her age."

"Is she?"

"Yes, she is. And that's why she isn't here."

"That the only reason?"

"I'll get the maps."

*

225

The town was flying colorful streamers from derricks and rooftops and there was a big white banner stretched across Main Street that read in big blue letters OIL FESTIVAL, HOLIDAY, TEXAS. The streets were thick with people, cars, wagons, mules and horses. It reminded Sunset of ants crawling over a carcass.

Main Street had dried out after all the rain, but the drying had left deep ruts and rifts. On one side of the street, water had washed dirt up on the wooden sidewalks that had turned to mud and hardened. In some of the street's deeper holes gravel had been tossed and had sunk in already, doing little to nothing toward repair.

Sunset bumped the car along, and they bounced past the picture show. There was a line at the box office going around the corner and partially into the street. Sunset looked to see what was showing, saw it was still the Marx Brothers movie. Memory of that brought back thoughts of sitting in a chair behind Smoky, waiting on him to finish so she could bring him out and carry him over to Tyler, only to have him lynched.

Maybe she didn't want to see a moving picture today after all.

She drove over to the sheriff's office, parked in front next to a sign that said NO PARKING. There was one large oak that grew by the sheriff's office and there were ten colored men sitting on the ground, their backs against it. Sunset noted there was a chain around the tree, and all the men had on cuffs and these were attached to the chain. A tall man with black hair sticking out from under his hat, wearing a badge, toting a shotgun, was parading up and down in front of the tree in a nervous kind of way.

They went inside, Hillbilly carrying the tin box with the maps and papers.

Rooster was sitting behind his desk. His hat was on the desk in front of him and he had his hands on either side of the brim as if holding it down. His body was all sharp angles and thin pink flesh. The hair on his head was almost as red as Sunset's hair, and it stood up toward the top and middle of his head like a rooster comb. Sunset thought: Now I get why he's called Rooster.

He looked up at them, said, "Whole town is nuts. Ain't a thing you can get done or keep from being done. It's a mess."

"Suppose money is being made," Hillbilly said.

"Reckon so. That's why they come up with this Oil Festival in the first place. Money. Wasn't bad enough we got everyone trying to get in the picture show, now we got people from all over come in to hear music and see fireworks."

"What's with all them fellas chained to the tree?" Hillbilly said.

"Run out of room in the jail. Drunks mostly. And the white men in there don't want to be jailed up with colored."

"Nothing more impressive than a picky criminal," Sunset said. "Where's your partner?"

"He up and quit after Clyde hit him. I'm sheriff now. You know, one of his teeth finally come out from that smack. One in the back."

"He don't need that one," Hillbilly said.

"I was just admiring the badge," Sunset said. "How's it feel to be sheriff?"

"Ain't so sure I like it or want it. It was better when I was a deputy and had someone tell me what to do. You ain't here on some kind of business, are you?"

"Maybe," Sunset said.

"Maybe?"

Hillbilly put the box on the sheriff's desk and opened it. He took out the maps and the papers. Rooster looked at them, said, "These look like papers supposed to be in the courthouse."

"What we thought," Sunset said.

"These are land papers," Rooster said. "Survey papers. How did you come by them?"

"Found them," Sunset said.

"Found them?"

Sunset nodded.

"Any idea about this stuff?" Sunset said.

The sheriff studied the papers for a while, shook his head. "Just what I told you. You'd need to go over to the courthouse to find out more."

"What we planned," Sunset said, "but I thought I'd make a courtesy call. Then we thought we'd stick around for the Oil Festival."

"On business?"

"With our badges off," Sunset said.

"Oh. Well. Okay. Me, I'm just gonna sit in here and wait till someone gets killed or something and someone comes to get me. I ain't getting out there. It's too damn busy."

A man built like a stump wearing a white Stetson came out of the back. He had a badge pinned to his shirt.

Rooster said, "Oh, this here is my deputy, Plug. He just hired on."

"Howdy, Plug," Sunset said.

"Damn, you are one fine-looking woman," Plug said.

"Thanks," Sunset said.

"I got another deputy too. Tootie. He ain't here right now."

"We're parked in the place says no parking out front," Sunset said.

"That's all right," Rooster said. "That's the business spot."

"It's a black Ford," Sunset said.

"Lot of black Fords," Rooster said.

"Should I make a note to put in the window?"

"Naw. We'll figure it out."

Sunset and Hillbilly went out, the box under Hillbilly's arm. They left their car in front of the sheriff's office, walked over to the courthouse, threading their way through people, many who stared at Sunset with her badge and gun as if she might be playing dress up and was part of the festival's hijinks.

"What are you supposed to be?" a man said, grabbing her shoulder.

"A constable," she said.

"Well, you look right cute. You don't work out of Dodge Street, do you?"

"No."

"Sorry, then," and he went away.

"Dodge Street?" Sunset said.

"It's where the whorehouses are," Hillbilly said.

Sunset jerked her head toward the retreating man. "Well, that sonofabitch," she said.

Hillbilly laughed.

"How do you know about Dodge Street?" she said.

"Word gets around," Hillbilly said.

The courthouse was set in the middle of Main Street. The street forked around it and gathered together again on the other side. The building was made of smooth pink stone. It had long wide steps in front of its long wide doors, and it was the only large and only pretty construction in town, one of the few made of stone. All the windows on the street sides were scabbed in spots with dried mud.

In spite of the heat outside, it was cool in the courthouse, and when Sunset put her hand against the edge of the stone doorway, it too was cool, like a dead body. There were only the sounds of their heels as they made their way to a wide stone desk that curved around an attractive woman wearing a black pinned-on hat.

When she looked up she saw Sunset, but quickly shifted her gaze to Hillbilly. Hillbilly smiled, and Sunset could see the woman swallow, and she had an idea how she felt in her stomach because she felt that way herself the first time she saw him.

Sunset explained her purpose, law business, but didn't go into detail.

The badge and Hillbilly's looks did it. The woman walked them down a long corridor, and on either side of the corridor were laced-up boxes. As the lady walked, her hams shifted beneath her black dress in a way that made Sunset think she might be trying to throw her ass out of her clothes.

Sunset noted Hillbilly was watching this with appreciation, and she gave him an elbow. He gave her a grin.

"Everything you want is in these rows, and there are some tables and chairs in the back. You can look at whatever, but you can't take anything. You don't plan to put anything in that box, do you?"

"We got some law business in the box," Sunset said. "I'm not going to put anything else in it."

"All right, then. You are the law. But I had to ask. That's my job."

The woman went down the corridor, and Hillbilly watched her go. So did Sunset. It was an impressive departure that warranted the music of a marching band, certainly plenty of bass drum.

At the table in the rear, Sunset opened the tin box and took out the two maps. At the top of each was a letter and a number. One read "L-1999." The other read "L-2000."

Sunset used the pad and pencil on the table, wrote the numbers down, put the maps back in the box. They went down the corridor looking until they came to a row low down containing boxes with those numbers written on them. They each took a box to the table. There were strings attached to a clasp, and these held down a cardboard flap. They removed the strings and opened a box and poured the contents on the table.

Inside were maps that looked like the maps they had.

Almost.

They were marked up different. Hillbilly said, "I can't make head or tails of this."

"It's the same maps."

"I know that. But so what?"

"It must mean something, or why else would Pete have put them in the grave. Wait a minute. Same maps, but they're marked different. See this. It doesn't quite match. The land is cut up different by this red line."

"Maybe the reason there are two maps is someone bought a piece of the land, cutting it up."

"Could be."

Sunset opened the other box and studied the papers inside. There were numbers written on the papers too. She studied these and studied what else was in the cardboard box, similar papers.

"This is giving me a headache," Hillbilly said.

"Look here. These numbers are the same on the maps, they're cut up different on the courthouse maps, but the names of ownership are the same."

"Where are you seeing that?"

Sunset showed Hillbilly some papers she had gotten out of the cardboard box. "The names are Zendo Williams for one piece of property, and for the other a list of names: Jim Montgomery—he's the mayor of Holiday. Or was till he disappeared. Well, I'll be damned. Henry Shelby."

"From the mill?"

"One and the same. John McBride. I don't know him."

"What's it mean?"

"I don't know."

"You said the mayor disappeared. To where?"

"No one knows. Some think he ran off with a woman. It's anybody's guess." Sunset frowned. "Now my head is starting to hurt."

Sunset studied the maps, studied the dates on the papers that declared ownership.

"They charged Zendo more an acre than was paid for this other land, which is right next to him. See?"

"So?"

"They charged him more because he's colored."

"That happens," Hillbilly said.

"It shouldn't."

"World is full of shouldn'ts, dear. Most of the time what goes on is what folks can get away with. That's my rule of thumb."

"Something else. Zendo's land shows two hundred and seventy-five acres. That's how it's drawn out on the map from the grave. But on this other map, it shows a piece of Zendo's land being part of the land owned by Henry, the mayor and this McBride fella."

"Maybe Zendo sold it to them."

"Maybe. But the dates on all the papers are the same. Looks to me, Pete had the originals in the grave, and these are the replacements, and they've slightly altered Zendo's land."

"Wouldn't he notice?"

"Buy a chunk that big, someone else wants it, white men, they could have had it surveyed the way they want. That way, Zendo wouldn't know they shaved off what looks like twenty-five acres. It's all trees along the border there, or mostly, so he could get fooled. He's pretty much got to take their word for things anyway. They robbed him with some little red flags and a marker on a piece of paper, and he probably doesn't even know it."

"So this whole map thing is about stealing some nigger's land."

"Looks that way—Hillbilly, don't call Zendo that. 'Colored' is polite."

"Whatever you like. But I still don't see why your husband was hiding this in a dead baby's grave."

"Me either."

Sunset folded up the maps from the cardboard boxes and put them in the tin box.

"You lied," Hillbilly said.

"Law business. I'm not going to bother to explain to Miss Pendulum. I don't want any more folks knowing about this than need to know. Whatever it means."

"You are a sneaky one."

"And pretty too. Plug says so."

"Plug is right."

Sunset laced the cardboard containers up, put them back in place, and left, Hillbilly carrying the metal box from the grave.

23

When Clyde got out to Zendo's place, most of his anger had gone away. He could see why Sunset would prefer Hillbilly to him in the looks department, but she wasn't considering his worth. Course, he had a burned-down house and an about-to-fall-apart pickup and was living under a tarp, but inside he was as good as anybody and better than most. He had plenty of goddamn worth. He was certain of that. Or pretty certain. Certain enough.

He drove with the windows down so that the wind blew away some of his stink. The night before he had slept under the tarp on a pallet on the ground, and during the night he had rolled off of it and gotten filthy, and when morning came, he wasn't up to washing off in cold well water and didn't have time to heat it, and if he had, all the bathtub he had was a number ten tub. Sometimes, he got in that tub, he had a hard time getting out, big as he was. It was like that damn tub stuck to his ass. The larger tub, the long one he kept on the back porch, he'd forgotten to save in the fire. It had melted.

That aside, one thing was certain, he wasn't going to win any points with Sunset if he didn't bathe.

When he got to Zendo's field, Zendo was in a row, plowing. It was a narrow row between corn high as an elephant's eye and green as fresh grass. Zendo was using only one mule. He was plowing in the opposite direction, so Clyde leaned against the tree where Zendo ate his lunch and waited until he came to the end of the row and started back around another.

As he came, Clyde saw Zendo raise a hand in greeting, and keep plowing. Clyde waited for the long run to end, and when Zendo pulled the mule out of the field and tied the lines to the plow, Clyde came forward and shook his hand.

"How you doing, Clyde?"

"Hanging low and to the left."

"Least you hanging. Get out there, plow a few rows of this business, them doodads will suck up."

"No plowing for me," Clyde said. "I had that job once and the mules run off. I was working for Old Man Fitzsimmons, and he wasn't none too happy. I spent the day chasing mules and didn't get no real plowing done. He fired me."

Zendo chuckled. "Well, now, you come all the way out here to tell me about chasing mules?"

"Nope."

"Didn't think so."

"Constable sent me. Who owns the land next to you, Zendo?"

"I don't rightly know. Ain't never seen anyone over there, but I heard trucks along the road back there. Well, I did see Mr. Pete there a couple times, riding along."

"How'd you see him?"

"Now, don't tell on me, Clyde, but there's a little pond over there, and I thought I'd try some fishing. It's fed from a creek, so I thought it might be ripe with fishes. Wasn't. But I was down there fishing when I heard a car and seen it was Mr. Pete."

"There's a road there?"

"That's what I'm saying."

"Is that where you took the baby's body?"

"I'm ashamed to say it was."

"Hey, I was in your shoes, knowing how white people can be, I might have done the same."

"You're white."

"Partly. Part of me is Indian. And lot of me is contrary. Can you show me where you put the baby? It might be important. I'm not sure why, but it might be, and Sunset—the constable—wants me to look around."

Zendo took Clyde for a walk through the woods. It was a long walk and it was so warm, breathing was like sucking in cotton balls. It was some time before they came to the pond Zendo told him about. It wasn't very large, and you could see where the creek fell into it. The pond water was dark and scummed over and no vegetation grew in it and growth was thin around it.

"Can't believe you thought anything was in that hole. A snake maybe."

"I was just hoping."

They went around the pond, through some brush, came out through a split in the trees. A narrow road twisted between the pines, curved into them again, ran out of sight.

"I put the pot with the baby in it right here," Zendo said. "Figured maybe Mr. Pete would see it. Or someone. Didn't think about it being tracked back to me. Clyde, you think maybe we could go back? I ain't never been no farther than this, and shouldn't have been that far. Could be a white man's property."

"You're with me."

"I am, but you're different. Some other white man see me over here, might think I'm getting too big for my britches. Besides, I got lots of plowing to do, and that ole mule only stand so long before it wants to try and get loose of that tree I tied it to."

"I understand. I'm going to look around."

Zendo walked away, and Clyde strolled down the road. He hadn't gone far when the trees disappeared and there was just a stretch of land where sickly saw grass and a lot of pathetic yellow weeds grew.

Clyde saw sunlight gleaming off something on the ground, walked over there, found the saw grass was mushy beneath his feet. He thought at first it was water running under his shoes, but it was too dark for water, even stagnant water.

He bent over, stuck his fingers in the stuff, rubbed them smoothly together. He smelled his fingers, knew then what was under him.

Moving forward a bit, the ground became softer and the grass disappeared. Seeping up through the ground was something dark and slimy-looking and the sunlight striking it made it look blue. Dead dragonflies and frogs and even a bird were in the seep and they were slicked over with it.

Oil.

In that moment, Clyde knew why the pond behind him was so filthy and dead-looking. The water was mixed with oil.

"Goddamn," Clyde said.

He walked wide of the seep, careful not to step in any deep place. He strolled around and studied the oil seep from all sides. It was fairly wide, and if it was finding its way to the surface like this, then there was a lot of it down deep.

He had seen an oil well go off in Holiday, and it had been something. The earth rumbled like it was coming apart. Men put their hands over their ears or stuffed them with mud. Oil exploded out of the ground, through the derrick, sprayed high and wide in one black rush, tossing hot drops all around. It took them a long time to tap it, and that well was still pumping. A place like this, it could do that. Down below was enough oil to make a man filthy rich with just one carbon-black ejaculation.

Clyde thought of the baby and how it was dark with oil, thought about what Sunset had said about the body of Jimmie Jo, how it too was oiled down.

Clyde took off his hat, wiped his face with it, was about to leave when he saw a flash of light through the trees. The light held, so he started walking toward it.

Pretty soon he was in the trees, and after that he came to a clearing in their center. In the clearing was a house. It wasn't a large house, but it was a good one. It had been built simply and had a tin roof and Clyde could see a bit of tar paper poking out under the tin.

The flash he had seen was sunlight hitting the roof. A good distance to the side, in the trees, he could see an outhouse. It too had a tin roof with projecting tar paper.

There wasn't any porch on the house, and the door was close to the ground, but there were rocks under the door, and all around the edge of the house. Since this wasn't a rocky area, they'd have to have been hauled in. It had been tedious work. Someone had cared about this little house and wanted it to be good and sound.

Clyde called out, "Hello, the house."

No one answered and he didn't hear anyone stirring.

Clyde touched the door, and it swung open. He checked and found the lock wasn't broken, just unlocked.

Inside it was musty and hot, but the place, though simple, was nice. It was one big room with a cookstove, bed, table, a few chairs, a cedar chest. There were some nice curtains and on the table was a pretty fancy kerosene lamp with a big brass shield for throwing light. There were shelves with dishes on them and a half-full bottle of hooch.

Clyde found some matches on the table next to the lamp, and lit it. The room filled with light. There wasn't really anything special to see. He opened the cedar chest. It was full of women's clothes, some of them a little on the garish side. He recognized one of the dresses. He'd seen Jimmie Jo wear it.

Clyde closed the chest, put out the lamp, and started back to

Zendo's property. When he got there, Zendo offered him water from a wooden barrel. Clyde took the dipper and drank. He didn't say anything to Zendo about what he had found. He wasn't sure what to make of it, and he thought he ought to discuss it with Sunset before anyone else.

He drove into Camp Rapture, went by the general store and bought a soft drink. Driving out, he saw a funeral going on up on the hill. A massive tool crate was being lowered by mules, rope, pulley and tripod, into a hole big enough to bury a baby hippo. He recognized Henry up there, next to the hole, along with Willie Fixx, the preacher. There was a colored man working the mules and two other coloreds standing on either side of the hole, managing the lowering of the box.

Clyde recognized the colored man in control of the mules as Zack Washington. He didn't know the other two. No one else was there. He wouldn't have known it was a funeral if it hadn't been for Fixx's pickup with the black cloth over the side boards.

He wasn't sure whose funeral it was, but he figured it was someone had to do with Henry. Considering it was a crate and not a coffin going down, he made the jump to Henry's wife. It was rumored she'd gotten strange and fat, scary and pickled, and now Clyde figured she had gotten dead.

Goose was sitting in a rocking chair on the shack's weathered porch. He had a plate of fried chicken balanced on his lap. He was eating a piece of it greedily and greasily. A yellow cat was sitting on the ground near the porch watching Goose eat and the cat had a look that made you think seeing Goose eat that chicken was tearing its heart out.

Lee was in the yard with Uncle Riley, placing sawed logs on a chopping block for Uncle Riley to split with an axe. Uncle Riley was in his undershirt and it was covered in dark bursts of sweat.

When he swung the axe it came down hard and he gave out a grunt and the wood went in half and grasshoppers jumped. The yard seemed full of them.

"I ain't never seen so many grasshoppers around," Uncle Riley said.

"I have," Lee said, "but it was more than this, thousand times more. They come out of the sky like a buzzing cloud and ate every damn green thing there was, including shirts."

"For real?"

"If it was green, they went at it. It was the dust bowl, and them bugs was starving like everyone else."

"Now that's a story."

"It's true."

"I wouldn't think a bug knew one color from another."

"I'm just telling what I seen."

After a few more pieces were chopped, Uncle Riley said, "That's enough. We got stove wood for supper, breakfast and tomorrow noon, and besides, my back hurts."

"I can chop some," Lee said.

"Naw. That'll hold us."

Uncle Riley slammed the axe into the chopping block, took a bandanna out of his back pocket, used it to wipe sweat from his face and the back of his neck. He looked where Goose was eating.

"Boy's healing up good."

"Yes, he is. Thanks to you and Aunt Cary."

"She knows her business."

"I've never seen anything like it. Tell you another thing, way he's been fed here, I think it's the most food he's had in a week. I appreciate it."

"He is a scrawny thing. You his daddy?"

Lee shook his head. "He told me a story about his family and him going off on his own so things would be easier at home, but

I think they abandoned him somewhere. I don't think he could go home if he wanted to. Me and him, we worked together at a farm, got cheated out of our money, and we were on the road together, then he got snakebit and Marilyn came along. We ended up here. Thank goodness."

"You better leave him here another day or two."

"I like the idea of him staying, because he needs to. Me, I don't want to impose on you."

"You ain't imposing. You the first man I've had to play checkers with in a long time."

"You just like me because you beat me every game."

"That helps."

"Naw. I reckon I gotta move on. I have someone to see, some things to fix, much as they're fixable. I ain't going real far, though, and I'll be back. In the meantime, you should move Goose out of your bed and put him on a pallet. Giving up your bed to him like that was real Christian of you."

"When he heals up, what about him?" Uncle Riley said.

Lee looked at Goose. He was ravenously finishing off his last piece of chicken.

"I don't know," Lee said. He was thinking he'd told the boy he wasn't going to go off, and now he was planning to do just that. He always meant to stay, but he always ran. Maybe where he went the boy had to come too. Maybe that was the way to be from now on. Not leaving people you cared about.

As they were talking, Marilyn's truck, still rattling the junk in the bed, pulled up. When she got out, Lee took note that she looked very nice and fresh and was wearing a bright green dress with white trim.

Uncle Riley and Lee greeted her.

"I come by to see how Goose is doing," she said, "but I see he's doing pretty good."

From the porch, Goose raised a hand in greeting.

"That's real nice of you, Marilyn," Lee said.

"I had another reason. I was going to give you a ride. You said you were going to see Sunset."

"Well, that's good of you. I'd like that. But truth to tell, I thought I'd leave out tomorrow. I feel like I ought to spend another day here with Goose, and besides, I got to beat Riley in some more checkers."

"He ain't won a game yet," Uncle Riley said. "But you could join us for dinner, Goose ain't ate all the fried chicken yet."

Marilyn smiled. "I think I will."

24

Sunset and Hillbilly put the box with the maps in the trunk of the car along with Sunset's gun and holster, and when they came out from behind it, they noted more colored men and one colored woman had been added to the trotline around the oak. Plug was outside now, under the tree, and he was giving the prisoners drinks of water from a wooden pail with a long metal dipper. The new deputy that had been there before was still there, cradling the shotgun in his arms, looking out at the street, watching women pass.

She and Hillbilly went about town, bumping into people, finally making it to the bank to cash the checks Marilyn had given them.

They went to the cafe and ate steaks and drank coffee and walked back and behind the courthouse where there was a fair going on and the street was closed off with blue and yellow sawhorses. There was a band playing, strong on fiddle and banjo and female voices. Hillbilly talked them into letting him sing, borrowed a guitar that lay idle against a chair, and went at it.

And Sunset couldn't believe it, because he was just as good as he thought he was, his voice sometimes deep as the bottom of an old Dutch oven, sometimes sharp as the prick of a pin, blending well with the sweet voices of the women. He sang about love and he sang about loss and he sang about sundown and the rise of the moon. Sunset felt his voice slide into her and bang around on the inside of her skin. He sang three numbers, gave the guitar back to the band to the sound of much clapping and cheering, and with what Sunset thought was a bit of reluctance, came down from the riser smiling.

Sunset took off her badge, put it in the snap pocket of her shirt. "You're good," she said.

"I know," he said.

They found a place where they could throw baseballs at bottles and Sunset hit one of them and Hillbilly hit four. Sunset won a free toss, which she missed, and Hillbilly won a little brown teddy bear with red button eyes, which he gave to her. They guessed a fat man's weight, and when the fat man got on the scale, they were both wrong. They had pink cotton candy and drank root beer out of paper cups and had some greasy sausage on a stick and shared a bag of popcorn and shelled some hot peanuts. They tossed hoops at sticks stuck up in the ground, and this time Sunset was better than Hillbilly. She got her hoops on four sticks and won another bear, a big blue one with a white belly. She and Hillbilly walked around carrying the bears, stomachs churning with their lunch, the cotton candy, the root beer and the heat. Sunset laughed and made fun of the bear Hillbilly had won and said it was too short to be much of a bear, and he told her how her bear would eat too much, and pretty soon they were laughing and poking one another and walking close together. Their hands found each other and their fingers entwined. Night fell and it was cooler and they walked back to the car holding hands and Hillbilly said, "We'll miss the fireworks," and Sunset said, "I suppose we will," and she drove them out of there, drove them on up to the place Clyde had told them about.

Sunset didn't say a word, just drove off the road, down the narrow trail Clyde had pointed out, going slow because it was rough, and Hillbilly, he didn't say anything either, and the trail wound up amongst the dark trees and finally it widened and they came upon the overlook.

Sunset parked close to the edge, killed the lights and engine. Through the windshield, as Clyde had said, they could see out and down, though not too far down, and they could view the whole of Holiday lit up like Christmas because of the festival. The lights were so pretty it made you want to jump down and get them. Even the oil derricks had been festooned with lights, and the lights on the derricks seemed to float high up above the others like gigantic fireflies.

With the windows down it was crisp and comfortable and the music drifted up from the town and an echoing voice sang "Take a Whiff on Me," or at least that's what Sunset thought it was, but she couldn't really hear it that well. Without saying a word Hillbilly slid next to her.

She turned her face to his, and when their lips met she felt a lot less cool than before, but it was a good heat, and it came from deep down and spread over her like a soft blanket on a dark fall morning, and pretty soon her hands and his hands began to probe and the view was forgotten.

In the front seat, legs parted, she took him in and he went to work on her; it was a moment as fine as any she'd ever had, and when it ended, it didn't end, but started up immediately again, and they changed positions, and moved every which way two people could move, and when she was near this time she felt as if all the bright hopes of the world were rising up inside of her, then the top of her head blew off, and down in the town below the fireworks were set off, and they burst high in the sky and brightened the windshield, and she laughed and couldn't stop laughing for a long, long time, then Hillbilly made a sound she liked and pulled out and she felt a hot wet spray, then he collapsed on top of her, heavy and warm and smooth to touch, his breath and hers going fast, their chests rising, gradually slowing, finally calm, and for a considerable time neither of them spoke nor wanted to.

25

Morning after the Oil Festival, when Rooster pulled up at the sheriff's office, Main Street was a sun-bright mud hole full of debris, piles of dung (human and animal), and three passed-out drunks, one of them a fat, pale woman without drawers, her skirt over her head. Rooster started walking up the street, paused long enough to reach over and pull the woman's skirt down without looking directly at her.

The coloreds who had been picked up for drunk and disorderly were still on the trotline around the oak tree, sleeping. Plug had fallen asleep guarding them, his back against the sheriff's office, his shotgun across his lap. His helper, Tootie, who had half the brains Plug had and was ashamed of that half, was nearby, asleep in the grass. Rooster figured he was as drunk as those on the trotline.

Rooster decided not to wake them. Wasn't like the men on the trotline were going anywhere, and he didn't want to stir Plug or Tootie, especially that asshole Tootie. He didn't want their company, not with what he had to do, who he had to see above the drugstore. About noon he'd let all the drunks go home, anyway.

He looked up the street where he had to go, thought, Sheriff Knowles wouldn't have let him get into this kind of business.

"Rooster, you're a good man," Sheriff Knowles used to say. "You just need some direction."

But Sheriff Knowles was gone now, and the only direction

he was going now was up the street to see that man. And he didn't want to see him. Ought to arrest him. But wouldn't. Couldn't. Didn't have the guts. And he was in too deep.

Above the drugstore the whole top floor was an apartment. Rooster hated when he had to go up there, taking the wobbly stairs.

Inside, during the day, the dark curtains were pulled back from the many tall windows at the back, but it was never lit up good. Way the great overhang was, behind and above the drugstore, with all the pines and oaks at the top, it blocked a lot of sunlight and there were no electric lights in the entrance room, just a couple of lanterns and they were seldom lit, so there were always shadows. There was an unnecessary wooden divider halfway down the middle of the big room and it split so you could go right or left. The divider didn't go to the ceiling, and if you were tall enough you could see over it. Rooster had never gone to the right, near the windows and the light, only left, along the dark hall where the floorboards made a sound like ice cracking and led into the dim rooms beyond where McBride liked to stay. Then there were the other rooms behind those, the ones he hadn't been in. But he had seen the Beetle Man come from back there, and he didn't like the Beetle Man. He called him that because of the long coat he wore and the little black bowler. Somehow, in his mind, they made him look like a big bug.

Rooster went up the stairs, adjusted his gun belt, squared his shoulders, knocked on the door.

There was a long pause, then the door was opened by a woman wearing only black silk hose and a red garter at the top of one of them. The rest of her was bare. She had one hand over her crotch like that hid something. Her breasts flopped and her blond hair was pulled up and pinned back and there were loose strands of it falling all over her face, as if the sun were running over her head. Her nose had a little white scar along the side of it.

Rooster took off his hat and held it, almost in reverence at what was before him. It sure beat having the Beetle Man answer the door.

"Come on in, sugar," she said, moved her hand away from what it hid, like having made the effort was enough.

He had seen her before (though he was seeing a part of her now he hadn't seen), but he didn't know her name. When the blonde turned away, leading, her naked ass moved from side to side like a couple of happy babies rolling about.

They went left of the wall, where a row of decorative silver platters hung. He looked and saw himself in one of the platters, squashed and twisted by the silver and the light. They went alongside the polished bar, into a room full of couches and a bed, and in the center, a table with a white tablecloth on which sat a silver coffeepot, silver cups and plates. Above the table was an electric light on a string. The bulb was dusty and the light was poor. A ceiling fan cranked the air around and the air smelled of garlic and tobacco, a whiff of sulphur from struck matches.

McBride was lying on the couch directly across the way and the smoke from his cigar filled that side of the room and hung above him in a blue-black cloud. He was wearing a gray as ash silk robe. It was half open. The hair on his chest and forearms was gray and his mustache was too black. Rooster figured him for sixty, even if he looked a tough fifty.

He had on the stupid wig he wore when he was in the apartment. A big black thing that didn't go with his Irish red skin. When McBride went out he wore a black bowler hat without the wig, and the hat fit tight, worn that way to battle the wind and hide his head, which Rooster assumed was bald or near it.

"Rooster," McBride said, and stood.

The robe fell wide open and Rooster saw more of McBride

than he wanted to see. McBride went over to the table, sat down in one of the chairs. As he sat, his wig shifted, and Rooster tried not to look. It was hard to figure where to look. High you had the hair, low you had, well, you had all of McBride.

"Sit, Rooster. Have a cup of coffee?"

Rooster sat. "Suppose," he said.

"Good," McBride said. "Hey, bitch, get us some coffee."

"I ain't no maid," said the blonde.

"Fresh. And don't make me ask again."

The blonde went away. McBride smiled at Rooster from under his mustache.

"Sometimes you have to slap them a bit, high and low, but they come around, that's for sure. What do you think of that ass?"

Rooster felt himself turning red. All he could say was, "It's nice."

McBride laughed.

"Nice. That's some first-rate pokadope. Whatcha got? It's early for me, and I was busy, as you can see. I don't think you came over here to drink a cup of coffee."

"No, sir."

"Oil Festival go well?"

"I suppose."

"Good. And your business here is?"

"The constable over at Camp Rapture."

"How could a constable concern me—wait a minute. Ain't it Pete's bitch? Yeah. Heard about that. She's the one when that old fart of a sheriff got killed, came over and pulled that nigger out while you stood around with your thumb up your ass. Hit Macavee with her gun, didn't she?"

"Yes, sir."

"How is old Macavee?"

"He left town."

McBride grinned. "Gal sounds like some kind of punkin. Hear she's good-looking too. That right?"

"I suppose."

"You suppose. Is she, or isn't she? She look as good as the tail I got here?"

"She wears more clothes."

McBride guffawed.

"Reckon she does."

"She come by the office the other day with one of her deputy constables," Rooster said. "They call him Hillbilly. Anyway, she showed me something. It was land maps. Maps of a colored fella's land. Zendo. Only it was the maps before they was sliced up. You know what I mean."

McBride leaned forward, put his elbows on the table, which caused his massive hairy forearms to flex.

"How did she come by them?"

"They got to be the ones Pete and that whore Jimmie Jo had. I don't know how she got them."

"The maps Pete stole? The ones you told me about."

Rooster nodded.

"You told Henry?"

"You told me anything like this came up, I should come to you first."

"You did right, Sheriff. And I'll tell Henry, not you. You look nervous, Rooster. I hate a nervous man. Makes me think they're trying to sneak around and put a finger up my ass."

"Sorry, Mr. McBride," Rooster said, and looked up as the blonde came back into the room. She had let down her hair and put on some clothes and had a fresh pot of coffee and a ceramic cup. She poured some into McBride's silver cup, then set the ceramic cup in front of Rooster and poured his coffee.

"You want to feel her a little, go ahead. She's on my tab, ain't you, honey?"

"I'm okay," Rooster said.

McBride laughed. "You're anything but okay. Go on out of here, kid, you're making Rooster sweat."

Rooster tried not to watch her go.

"You'd like to have that swing on your front porch, wouldn't you, Rooster?" When Rooster didn't answer, McBride said, "Did you get the maps back?"

"They didn't offer to give them back."

McBride shifted, uncrossed his legs, put both feet under the table.

"You didn't ask for them?"

"I wasn't sure what to say."

"Cause it was a good-looking woman had them? Am I right?"

Rooster drank from his cup, almost sloshing the coffee. He said, "Something like that."

"So, what did they do?"

"I told them to go to the courthouse."

"You told them to go to the courthouse? Now, that's dumb, Rooster. That means you gave them a chance to put things together."

"Yes, sir."

"The maps don't mean nothing without you put them one to the other. Not smart, Rooster. They go to the courthouse, look at records, they're gonna see what's been changed. That was Pete and his whore's game, pulling the records as a threat, gonna tell some big law unless they were dealt in, and not in a little way, like you, but in a big way. Big as me. Big as Henry. Nope. That old dog ain't gonna hunt. That's why I was called in, to fix things. And I did. All you had to do was say, 'Those maps are city property. Don't know how they come into your possession, but I'll need to put them in their proper place, and I want to thank you for bringing them by.' Wouldn't that have been simple, Rooster?"

"It would have. Knew it soon as they left."

"Then it was too late, wasn't it, Rooster?"

"Yes, sir."

"Things been going good here. Earned my money here and there, but I haven't had to do much. I got people to do it for me, and I like that. I've moved up in the world. I think it and it gets done, but not by me. I don't like to do what I don't have to do, bother with a thing I don't have to. And now you make me bother. The woman . . . What's her name?"

"Sunset."

"Now that's a snapper of a name. That a nickname?"

"She's got red hair. I don't know her real name."

"Ain't nothing nicer than to peel one down and see that red hair fanned out between her legs. Shakes her hips, it's like a red flag waving at a bull. But that's not our concern here, is it? Now, we got a bump in the road and you've run us over it. Know what happens when you hit a bump, Rooster?"

Rooster shook his head.

"A bump can knock shit out of the back of your wagon. Knock shit all over the goddamn place. Hear me, now?"

Rooster nodded.

McBride reached under his ugly wig and scratched his head.

"Shit gets knocked out, then I got to go in and do more work than needs to be done, and mind you, I don't dislike the work, but I don't like to undo what don't need undoing or fix what shouldn't have to be fixed. You following me here, Rooster?"

"Yes, sir."

McBride sucked deeply on his cigar and let the smoke come out of his nose. "Can we maybe give this bitch some money for the maps? She go for that?"

"I don't think so. She seems pretty sure of herself, like maybe she wants to do some good."

"A do-gooder. They can be trouble. Like Christians or teetotalers, they can latch on to a thing like a goddamn bulldog and not let go, even if it ain't good for them. I hate do-gooders. Give me a lawman or a politician any day, and I can work with them. Even a preacher can be worked around, but the true Christian or do-gooder, they're hard to figure."

"Maybe Hillbilly will come around," Rooster said. "He was a deputy constable, but he's quit. He's in town now. He knows her and what she knows, might know where the map is."

"I don't know from Hillbilly. You're trying to pass your job to someone else, Rooster. I don't like that."

"No, sir."

"This goes South, me and Henry, we could lose a lot of oil money. Do some prison time I don't want to do. I ain't never done time and I've done plenty things might have given it to me. I don't intend to take a dose of bad time now. What you're gonna do, Rooster, is you're gonna go see this woman. Say you got curious, went to look at the records, saw they didn't match, think someone is trying to cheat that nigger . . . What's his name?"

"Zendo."

"Zorro out of his land."

"Zendo."

"Tell her that. Appeal to that do-gooder nature. She'll probably turn around and give you the maps, thinking you're gonna take care of things. She doesn't give you the maps, then we got a problem. There's lots of people you can have a problem with, Rooster, and it'll work out. You don't want no problem with me. Comprende?"

"Yes, sir."

"I don't mind a little graft, a little reach out, but I like a man knows his part. Not like Pete, who wanted to take me and Henry big. That I don't like. You wouldn't do that, try that, would you, Rooster?"

"No, sir."

"Good. Now we're done. Except for a little last something."

McBride rose, his robe flopping open. Rooster looked at his coffee cup on the table. McBride went into the other room and came back promptly. He had a fistful of bills in his hand. He came over and stood by Rooster. He was so close, his penis was almost rubbing Rooster's elbow. He said, "Hold out your hand, Rooster."

Rooster turned in the chair, held out his hand and McBride put a hundred-dollar bill in it. He put a second hundred. Then a third. He folded up the other four and put them in the pocket of his robe. "I'm paying you for coming to me like you're supposed to. But I'm not giving you all I would have given you, because you screwed up, Rooster. Get the maps, amigo."

McBride closed Rooster's hand up with the bills in it, squeezed so hard Rooster tumbled out of the chair and rose up on his knees. McBride's penis hung in his face.

"Kiss it, Rooster."

"No."

"Sure. You kiss it."

McBride squeezed Rooster's hand harder and there was a cracking sound. Rooster leaned forward and kissed the head of McBride's penis.

McBride let go, stepped back. Rooster, red as flame, stood up.

"Weren't no call for that," Rooster said. "You shouldn't have done that."

"Hell, Rooster, kissing my dick just sweetened up your day."

*

255

When Rooster was gone, McBride called out to the blonde. She came in and he took her to the couch. When he was finished, she said, "I don't know why I bother to put anything on."

"I didn't ask you to dress," McBride said. "You go on, now. Go home."

"I didn't mean to make you mad. It's just Two is making me nervous."

"He's up?"

"Yeah. I don't want to stay back there with him. I didn't mean to make you mad."

"You didn't make me mad, I'm just sick of you. Go on now while I'm in the right mood about it."

She went in the other room and put on her clothes. When she came out, McBride was stretched out on the couch.

She looked at him but didn't speak.

When she was gone, he got up, locked the door behind her, had some coffee, fastened up his robe, went to the kitchen. He had just eaten, but he wanted to cook, and he figured he cooked what he wanted the right way, it would take a while. He put on his apron. It was a big one with short frilly sleeves and a bit of lace around the bottom and on the sides. He got down some pans and lit the kerosene stove and put a pot of water on to boil for spaghetti. He took a clove of garlic, tore it apart in his hands, placed the pieces on a cutting board, used a mallet to smash it. He did the job so well none of the garlic got away from him, but it made his eyes water.

He heard a noise, turned. In the doorway, standing in the shadows, was Two, wearing his long black Prince Albert coat. Way it fell around him, with the split tails, it made him look like a giant beetle, all black and thick and silent, with blazing green eyes. A nigger with those eyes and that Prince Albert coat. It didn't seem right, but there he was.

McBride said, "I'm gonna have some food cooking. It'll take a while, but I can make extra. You want I should fix you some?"

"We are not hungry," said Two, and he went out.

26

Night before all the business with Rooster and McBride, Sunset drove home high on Hillbilly's loving. She dropped Hillbilly at the campsite where he was staying, which was about two miles down the road from her tent. It was a simple place that he had built of sticks and such, had draped old shirts over to make a kind of hut. When she asked him where he got the shirts, he said Clyde had given them to him. When she asked him how they were getting along, he changed the subject. She parted from him with what she thought was the softest, sweetest kiss she had ever tasted.

She wanted to take Hillbilly home with her, but feared Marilyn might arrive the next morning with Karen, and that wouldn't look too good, especially not with Karen pining for Hillbilly like a bitch dog in heat. Still, she thought maybe they could look into someplace better for him to stay. It would be nice if he had his own place and she could go there.

When she arrived home, Ben came out to meet her. She saw Clyde's truck was parked by the big oak. She could see a boot on the dashboard. She opened the trunk, gathered up the box with the maps and things in it, went over to the truck. The windows were down, so she leaned in on the passenger's side. Clyde was stretched out, that one foot on the dash. There was enough moonlight so she could see his face, and with his hair hanging in it, his eyes closed, snoring softly, he reminded her of a big boy. He really was sweet-looking, handsome really, just rough around the edges.

She went inside the tent with Ben at her heels, put the box on the table on the work side, tried to think about it, but all she could think about was Hillbilly, the way it had been up there on the overlook, the soft good-night kiss.

Then she thought: How dumb can I get, mooning around like a child, and I'm thought to have committed murder, not only on Jimmie Jo and her poor baby, but on Pete too. She figured Henry was making sure it was played out that way, that she had murdered Jimmie Jo because Pete was seeing her, and that, in turn, she had murdered Pete because of it and called it self-defense.

Worse yet, her daughter had a crush on the man she had just bedded in the front seat of her car. Clyde was out front in his pickup like a jilted teenager waiting for her to come home, and on top of all that, she had discovered some kind of plan to rob Zendo of his land, and she didn't know what to do about it.

And there was something else. Something that kept working in the back of her mind. Something she could feel but couldn't see or take hold of.

She thought she wanted coffee, but decided that wouldn't be good. Not this late, and she felt too lazy to make it. She thought she might want a shot of whisky, even Bull's moonshine, but she didn't have any of that, and knew if she did she'd regret it pretty quick. She settled for going out to the pump and working the lever to fill a glass of water. Ben followed her out, and she pumped the pump so that some water went into the pan she kept under it for Ben. It was cold water and sweet and she stood out by the pump and drank it and used one hand to rub Ben's head while he drank from the pan.

She heard the truck door open.

Clyde came out a little wobbly, said, "Howdy."

"Howdy."

"I was waiting on you."

"I see that."

"You're pretty late."

"How would you know? You been asleep."

"It was late when I went to sleep. I heard the pump handle."

"Sorry."

"All right."

"You learn anything out at Zendo's?"

Clyde got the two chairs they left outside the tent and brought them over by the water pump. They sat and Clyde said, "I learned that land next to Zendo has oil on it."

"Now some things are coming together," Sunset said.

"Maybe you got some things I don't know about. Only thing coming together on me is my ass cheeks from all the sweat I put out today."

"Nothing I want to hear about more than your sticky ass," Sunset said, "but, how about you tell me what you learned?"

"There's a little house on the land too. Nobody lives there, but I went inside and found a dress I've seen Jimmie Jo wear. It was the kind of dress you seen on her once, you don't never forget it."

"Don't remind me."

"There's a big oil pool not far from the house, and the grass is all dead around there, and the oil is seeping up from the ground. It's even run into a pond over there. I figure the place is worth a fortune."

"Can I suppose that's the oil Jimmie Jo was soaked in?" Sunset said.

"Fits. Someone shot her, put her in it to send a kind of message, her and the baby, I think."

"I think Jimmie Jo and Pete knew about the oil and were trying to run some kind of scam or something. I don't know what, but something."

"Why do you say that?"

"The maps. And me and Hillbilly found some other things at the courthouse. Come inside."

In the tent, at the table, by lantern light, Clyde looked at what was in the box—the original maps and the ones Sunset had stolen.

"So some white men are trying to take Zendo's land because it has oil on it," Clyde said.

"Yes, and him being colored, they can do it easy."

"Maybe Zendo sold them the land."

"I don't think so. But I'm not going to ask Zendo. Right now, less Zendo knows, better off he is."

"Why ain't they started drilling?"

"Just haven't had time, I guess. It takes some work to get it all together. Maybe they need seed money."

Clyde pondered that, said, "Maybe— I know the names on that paper, except for McBride. You know him?"

Sunset shook her head.

Clyde slid down in his chair. "You been all business tonight, Sunset?"

"No."

Clyde nodded. "Go to the festival?"

"I did."

"With Hillbilly?"

"I did."

"You like him?"

"I do."

"Anything else go on besides the festival?"

"Nothing that's your business. You ought to be ashamed, asking a lady that kind of thing."

"Karen at Marilyn's, ain't she?"

"Yeah."

261

"You didn't bring him back with you, so maybe it didn't go so well."

"It went well enough," Sunset said. "And it ain't none of your business."

"You look kind of light on your feet."

"I'm not on my feet."

"It's a saying. You know, like you're on a cloud."

"Don't think too far ahead, Clyde. I think I'll go to bed now, and you can go to hell."

"Okay with you I skip hell and just sleep in the truck here? I ain't really got nothing better back at my place. A tarp and skeeters."

"Got mosquitoes here."

"I ain't been bit once tonight."

"Suit yourself, Clyde."

"Good night, Sunset."

"Good night, Clyde, and it still ain't none of your business."

When Karen awoke the next morning, for a moment she didn't know where she was, then remembered she was in bed in her grandmother's spare bedroom. In the moment of awakening, she recalled the movie she had seen the day before in Holiday, her grandmother at her side, and it was a good memory, because the movie had been funny (her first movie), but it wasn't a memory she had long to relish.

She sat up quickly, swung her legs over the side, and wearing only her slip, leaped out of bed, sprinted through the house, across the screened-in porch. She made it through the screen door and down the steps in time to spill vomit on the ground. It just kept coming, and she thought after a while she was going to throw her stomach up through her mouth, but finally she stopped heaving.

She sat down heavily on the porch step. The inside of her mouth tasted like someone had put peed-on mildewed socks in there, tamped them down with a shitty stick. The awful stench of the sawmill didn't help any, and the color of the sky, yellow-green, was the color of the steaming vomit soaking into the ground.

She thought maybe she had a cold, or flu, but she didn't feel bad all the time. Just in the mornings. Queasy. Like her insides were being boiled in hell's kitchen. Then she would explode, get rid of it. Usually after lying down for five or ten minutes, she was good as new. It had been that way for several days now, and her appetite had at first been dull, then suddenly ravenous. She found herself craving fried and peppered pig skins, which she hadn't had since she was a child. That and mustard. She hadn't found any pig skins, but last night she'd made herself a mustard sandwich, thick with the stuff, on two slices of bread, and when she finished it, she ate another, and even now, after vomiting, the smell of mustard in the puke, she was craving it again.

She held her head in her hands until it quit trying to spin around, was about to get up, go back in the house, when Marilyn came out on the porch and sat down beside her.

"You okay?"

"Yeah."

"What's wrong?"

"I threw up."

"I heard that."

"I didn't mean to wake you."

"Oh, girl, I been up for hours. I was in the kitchen. Maybe you should take some tonic."

"I'm all right now."

"Something you ate?"

"Probably . . . I don't know . . . Grandma . . . Can you get pregnant . . . doing it the first time. I thought the first time didn't take."

"Oh, God. You didn't?"

Karen turned to look at Marilyn, her face looking as if someone had sucked all the juice out with a straw.

"I did."

"Hillbilly?"

Karen nodded. "How'd you know?"

"Figured immaculate conception was out. You been sick mornings, besides this one?"

"Couple, three days now. Mama didn't even notice."

"She's got a few things on her mind these days. I don't suppose you told her?"

Karen shook her head.

"I'm such a tramp."

"No. No. You're just a girl. He's a grown man. He knew how to play you. Some men, they don't care about anything but the feeling they get."

"I liked it too."

"Well, least you got that out of it, and you don't always get that."

"I love him so much."

"You're in love with love, baby, not him. He's a man thinks he's a playboy. I knew soon as I saw him. And I think that's good of me. I don't know I pick men so good, and even if Pete was my son and your father, I don't know Sunset picked so good either, or is picking good now."

"What am I gonna do? I can't tell Mama."

"You have to tell her."

"Then what?"

"Have the baby, or get Aunt Cary to take care of it."

"Take care of it?"

"Get rid of it before it's born."

"I couldn't do that."

"Then you'll have it. And you'll raise it."

"Won't nothing ever be the same again."

"No. But you can live with change. Me and your mama can live through what we're living through, you can live through what's gonna happen to you. And we can help you."

"I did a bad thing."

"I've done a bad thing or two in my time, honey. Some things I don't even talk about. Sometimes, you get like a fever, and it just happens. All kinds of things can happen, and then you got to live with regrets. Some are easier to live with than others."

"I can tell you things I can't tell Mama."

"That's what grandmas are for. Hell, girl. You ain't done so bad. Just followed the path all us animals want to follow. At your age, girl goes into heat, it don't take a lot of persuading. Unlike a dog, we people stay in heat, and it's at its hottest when we're young. Get some pretty fella like Hillbilly saying the right things, it's easy to do something you ought not. Ain't a thing wrong with loving, girl, it's who you love and what they want from you that matters."

"He said I was pretty."

"He didn't lie. You got your father's coloring, your mother's bones. Did he tell you he'd marry you?"

"No. I thought about all that, and he didn't ever make me any kind of promise. Just told me good things about myself, and he touched me, and when he did, I felt like I had to have him."

"Like you wanted to be burned up by him."

"That's right. How'd you know?"

Marilyn laughed. "I haven't always been this old. I ain't been that hot in a time, but I know what it feels like. You keep a memory for it."

265

"Grandma, I feel like I been put in a sack and shook up and throwed out."

Marilyn took Karen in her arms and held her. "Relax now. We'll figure this out."

"You gonna tell Mama? She likes him, you know. I heard Willie say she kissed him."

"I know she likes him. I don't like that she does. And yeah, you got to tell her."

"I don't know how."

"I'll help you."

That morning Sunset drove over to see Hillbilly in his camp, but the little hut he had built of limbs and leaves and old shirts wasn't there anymore, and neither was he. It was as if he had been plucked up and toted off by the wind. She got out and looked around and found where he had dragged the little hut apart and thrown the pieces of it up into the woods. There was a kind of savage finality to the way it looked.

She drove home.

Back at the tent, Clyde and Ben were out front. Clyde had made coffee and was sitting in one of the chairs by the water pump, drinking a cup. Ben was sitting beside him, Clyde's arm around his neck. When she drove up, Clyde went inside and came out with a cup of the same for her. They sat in the chairs and she sipped the coffee.

After a while, Clyde said, "Hillbilly coming in to work?"

"I don't know."

"Wasn't at his spot, was he?"

"No."

"Could have just moved it, found a better place."

"You don't think that, do you?"

"Nope."

"You hope he's gone on, don't you?"

"Yep. And nope."

"What's that mean?"

"I hope he's gone. But I don't want him to lie to you and make you sad."

Without looking at him, Sunset put her hand on his arm.

Clyde swallowed. He made himself relax so he could feel the warmth and weight of her hand through his shirt sleeve. He took a deep breath. She was wearing a bit of perfume, just enough to sweeten the air around her.

It wasn't much, that hand on his arm, but it was something, a tidbit he could enjoy. Like a blind hog finding an acorn, it wasn't filling, but it fed the appetite.

27

After his talk with McBride, Rooster went to his office, trembling, his hand aching. It wasn't broken. McBride's strong grip had shifted bones and now they were shifted back, but it was sore.

Rooster thought about what McBride made him do, felt sick about it, felt about two inches tall if he could wear stilts and stand on a stump. There wasn't any need for McBride to do that. He had done it just because he could, the wig-headed sonofabitch.

Rooster got a wash pan, filled it with water, used a thick bar of soap to wash his lips, rubbed with it until they were near raw and the soap taste was in his mouth; he thought he'd gag from it, but determined it was a taste better than the one he was remembering.

After the soap, he took off his hat and put his face down in the pan of water and held it there for as long as he could hold his breath. When he came up, snorting, grabbing for a towel, he didn't feel one bit cleaner.

He marched out on the office steps, looked up the street, stared at the red apartment over the drugstore, felt like he should go in and get the shotgun, trot back over to see McBride. He'd make him suck on the barrel, that's what he would do. Should have bit the bastard's dick off, that's what he ought to have done, tore it out by the roots with his teeth. What a coward he was, doing what he did. Should have let McBride break his hand before he did what he did.

He thought about the shotgun some more, but didn't think he could do it, and if he tried, he might end up with it up his ass, McBride working the pump action, pulling the trigger till it didn't work anymore. It was easy to be tough out here on the steps of his office in the sunlight, but up there in that stuffy room with the little bit of light and all the shadows and McBride in his ugly black wig, that was another thing. And there was the Beetle Man, too.

Rooster thought about getting one of Sheriff Knowles' cigars from the desk drawer, smoking that, to kind of purify himself, clean out his mouth with smoke, but the more he thought about the big fat cigars Sheriff Knowles had smoked, the less he liked that idea.

He walked around the edge of the office and looked to see the colored men still on their line, sleeping, and Plug and Tootie still sleeping as well. The dew had settled on them and Rooster could see it lay damp on Plug's hat and the knees of his pants. Rooster was so angry, he thought he might take it out on them for sleeping, then he thought better of it. He didn't want them up.

Rooster observed a fistful of grasshoppers hanging on the edge of the building, and to quench his anger, he used his hand to smash a couple of them, wiped the waste on the edge of the bricks with a quick scraping motion.

He went back around front and stood on the steps again. He was wiping at his mouth with the back of his clean hand, when a blue car came down the street, veered around the passed-out fat woman, paused with the motor humming. The passenger door opened and Hillbilly got out with a blanket bound up and tied over his shoulder. Rooster strained to see who was driving. It was some man he had seen around town, but didn't know. The car drove on past the office in the direction of the courthouse.

Hillbilly stopped in the road for a minute, studied the fat woman lying there with the precision of a marine biologist studying a beached whale, then came walking toward Rooster. As Hillbilly passed him on the walk, he nodded.

Rooster said, "I thought you was constablin'."

"Sometimes," Hillbilly said. "Today I didn't want to. I don't know I'm gonna want to again. I'm actually a singer and picker. Did some singing last night, and I know that's what I got to do. Got some pay, so I hitched in to look for a guitar to buy. You don't know of any?"

Rooster shook his head.

"Your mouth's all red. You got some kind of hives?"

"No. I do know this, though. That gal, Sunset, who I figure you like . . . you do like her, don't you?"

"Well enough and in certain ways," Hillbilly said.

"She's in for some hell, friend. There's a way maybe you can help her."

When Rooster finished saying this, he felt stunned. It had just leaped from his mouth like a frog.

"I try to mind my own business," Hillbilly said.

Rooster gave him a quizzical look. "You are the law."

"Ain't so sure I want to be any kind of law anymore. I never felt I fit good being the law. Ain't you the law? This has something to do with the law, you're the law. I'm retired."

"I like that redhead," Rooster said.

"Hell, any man likes that redhead," Hillbilly said.

"That's not what I mean. She's got heart. She's got more courage than I got. And she's gonna need it."

"How's that?"

"McBride."

"John McBride?"

"How'd you know?"

"Seen his name on a paper at the courthouse."

Rooster nodded. He saw the fat woman lying in the street move, start to get up. She managed to roll over and get a knee under her.

"I think you're a man that'll play angles," Rooster said. "I'm not sure Sunset is a woman that'll do that."

"What does that mean, I'm a man will play angles? What are you getting at, Rooster?"

"I think you can help her and maybe make some good money quick like."

"Where does it come from, this quick money?"

"Me."

"Tell you what, buddy. I got better things to do with my morning than play at riddles."

"Henry Shelby over at the mill in Camp Rapture—"

"I know who he is."

"—he come up with this idea, you see. He was hunting on land belonged to this colored, Zendo, and he found oil. Zendo don't even know it's his land. Or if he thought it was his land, Shelby fixed that. Day after he found the oil, he went and asked Zendo if he'd sell, telling him he wanted it for the lumber company, and Zendo said no, he didn't want to sell, and Shelby asked him how big his land was, and Zendo didn't know. Just bought him a patch and farms part of what he knows is his patch. A colored, he don't ask a lot of questions when he gets something around here, even if he pays near double for it. Glad to have what he knows to be his, even if he has more and don't know it. Course, he don't know about the oil. That might change his thinking. Surveyors hadn't even bothered to come and stake out the land he bought. Just drew it up on paper, and you got to really study them papers to know what they're about. And Zendo, if he's like a lot of the coloreds around here, he don't even read. So, Henry Shelby, he says, 'Tell you what, I'll pay to have your land surveyed so you'll know exactly what's yours, cause since I can't buy your land, I can buy land next to you.' That's no big thing to Zendo, a free survey, cause now he'll know exactly what he owns."

"And the land got cut up different than it was supposed to be," Hillbilly said. "Yeah, me and Sunset sort of got that part."

They watched as the woman from the street came stumbling by. Rooster thought she looked like one of the women from Dodge Street. She was lurching in that direction. When she passed them and was far enough away, Rooster continued.

"They cut Zendo a bigger piece than he thought he owned, to make him happy about things. But they kept the rest of it, a big chunk, the oil land. Shelby, to make this work, had to have the mayor in on it. He knew him pretty good, see."

"I thought I heard he run off, or something," Hillbilly said.

Rooster nodded. "Or something. Mayor and Henry were card-playing and whore-running buddies. Shelby tells him what he knows, cause he needs the mayor to mess with the papers at the courthouse. Make it official. So he has to cut him in. Then this McBride shows up, and the mayor, he isn't around anymore. I reckon Henry wasn't that big a buddy of the mayor after all."

"Ain't it kind of scary you knowing what you know?"

"They needed me, they cut me in. I don't get a piece of the oil, just get paid, by them. McBride mostly, but I know it comes from Henry. Now I'm in deep. And I'm scared. I don't want to do nothing really bad, and I'm figuring that's what they're gonna want. Something bad. Sometime soon."

"You're trying to keep those maps secret, might not hurt you put a better guard on things at the courthouse," Hillbilly said. "You're gonna be a thief or help out thieves, figure you ought to be smarter."

"They never thought anyone would think to look, Pete dead and all. And if they did look, so what? The original papers were gone. Then Sunset comes up with them. I should have asked for them. She'd have given them to me, wouldn't be no problem."

"Why didn't you ask?"

Rooster shook his head. "I don't never make good choices. I got to get them papers back. For her. And for me. I thought maybe you could do it, for her. It's worth a hundred dollars."

"That's a lot of money right now."

Rooster nodded.

"But you still haven't laid it all out for me," Hillbilly said.

"What you need to know is this: Get the papers back and she won't get hurt, cause there's someone will hurt her for those papers."

"McBride?"

"Yeah, McBride. He may not do it himself, but it'll get done. Get the papers, the maps, she's got nothing, maybe there's no problem."

"Just make up some new maps."

"The old ones show up, that'll make a mess."

"Tell you what," Hillbilly said. "Hundred dollars sounds good, but that part about you being scared and the mayor missing, that don't sound good. Thing best for me to do is to forget we talked and stay away from Sunset. I've had my moment there, and it was a good one, but I'm moving on."

"Maybe you're a lot smarter than I thought."

"Comes to watching out for me, I'm plenty smart."

"What about Sunset?"

"Haven't a thing against her. She's a woman can make a man happy. I just don't want to be that happy, having the same woman around all the time. It's not the way I am. I got to have bigger stakes than any hundred dollars. My rules for me is take the path

273

where there ain't nothing in it, and if there is, go around. See you, Rooster."

Hillbilly went down the street. Rooster watched him for a while, then a shadow fled over Main Street.

Rooster glanced up.

At first he thought it was a flock of birds. But they were close down and he could hear the buzz of their wings.

Insects. A large swarm of them. They turned suddenly as one, darted to the top of the overhang behind the red apartment, disappeared into the woods.

It was the day of the town meeting. Sunset thought about it all morning. She also thought about Hillbilly. She sent Clyde to search for him. It wasn't a thing Clyde wanted to do, but she knew he'd do it, knew she had that power over him, and felt like an ass because of it. But not enough of an ass not to do it.

Walking toward her car, Sunset noticed there was a lot of space between the limbs of the trees, letting in more sunlight than usual, and for a moment this confused her. Then she realized it was because lately it had been so hot and dry the trees were thirsty. Their limbs sagged, the leaves shriveled, turned brown and let loose, crunched beneath her feet like crackers.

She was thinking about the meeting when Marilyn's pickup rumbled into the yard and parked. Inside Sunset saw not only Marilyn and Karen, but sitting next to the passenger window, a big, somewhat handsome older man. In the truck bed was a young boy.

When they got out, the man, wearing a worn-out suit coat, lingered by the truck, and the boy stayed in the truck bed. Karen came up to her mother, reached down to pet Ben, who was sitting beside Sunset in a manner of defense.

"Is Hillbilly here?" Karen asked, and her voice broke when she spoke.

"No," Sunset said.

"Where is he?"

"I'm not sure. Who's that?"

"I don't know. We picked them up at Uncle Riley's house. I heard the boy got snakebit. That boy keeps looking at me, Mama. He makes me nervous."

"Why don't they come on up?"

"They're afraid of Ben."

"Take Ben in the tent with you. Make him lay down."

"Can I talk to you later?"

"Sure. Put Ben up."

"Come on, Ben."

Ben and Karen disappeared into the tent. Marilyn stopped at the water pump to pump water and wash her face. She looked up at Sunset, beads of water rolling off of her. "That's Lee. The boy is called Goose."

"Who are they?"

"The man is someone you ought to meet."

"Yeah?"

"Lee," Marilyn said, "come on over."

Lee came over and nodded. He said, "Hello, Sunset."

"You know me?" Sunset said.

"No. But I'd like to."

Sunset looked to Marilyn for help. Marilyn walked off toward the great oak by the road. Goose wandered over to the outhouse and went inside.

"I don't know you, then?" Sunset said.

Lee shook his head. "No. But we have a connection. I'm your father."

Sunset and Lee both stood silent for a long time, then Sunset, very quickly, slapped Lee, slapped him so hard he actually went to one knee.

275

Slowly Lee rose, a hand to his reddened face.

"You sonofabitch," she said.

"You hit hard for someone so little."

"Sonofabitch."

"Without a doubt," he said. "If it means anything, I didn't know you existed."

Karen and Ben stuck their heads out of the tent. Goose came out of the outhouse in time to see Lee rising to his feet. He said, "Lee, you all right?"

"I'm fine. Just stay back."

"Go on back in the tent," Sunset said to Karen.

"But Mama . . ."

"Just once, just goddamn once, do what I tell you."

Karen's head darted back inside, followed by Ben's.

"Just had your way with my mother and took off?" Sunset said. "That was it, huh?"

He nodded. "Yes, that's what I did. But I didn't know about you, not until Marilyn told me."

Sunset tossed a look at Marilyn.

Marilyn, standing by the oak, shrugged.

"After all these years you show up, and it's supposed to matter to me?" Sunset said.

"It doesn't have to matter. I understand why it might not matter. But I didn't know about you, Sunset. I was young. Your mother was young. We made a mistake. Hell, I made a mistake. I seduced her, and me a preacher . . . back then anyway. Not now."

"What do you want from me?"

"A few minutes."

"You don't owe him anything," Marilyn said from the safety of the oak, "but it might be worth hearing."

"You ran off," Sunset said. "My mother ran off. Though at

276

least she cared for me for a while and left me a nice pair of shoes. Long worn out, I might add. And now you show up. I've been beat and raped and I've shot my husband, found his girlfriend dead and dug up her baby, and now I got you. What the hell did you do, old man, put a curse on the entire family?"

"In a way, I have. That's why I'm here. Was that my granddaughter?"

"I assume you're referring to the girl with the black hair, not the dog?"

Lee sighed. "I know when I'm whipped. But listen to this, and nothing else. I want to know you. I don't even know you and I love you—"

"Bull."

"I know how it sounds."

"You couldn't."

"But I do. You're my own flesh and blood. Only flesh and blood I got—you and Karen, not the dog. And I love you because I think God brought me back here to make amends, to do right by you. To love you without condition."

"That's nice of you. And if God's so smart, why did he let you run off in the first place? Answer me that."

"It was me run off, not God."

"Yeah. Well, I'm not that fond of either one of you."

"Sunset," Marilyn said, "when we're young, we're foolish. You and me, we should know something about that. Being foolish over certain men. Foolish in other ways."

"I've been fooled by one man, and bad, and I don't want to be fooled by another. Even if it's my father."

"We always get fooled," Marilyn said. "Anybody can fool anybody, and for all kinds of reasons."

Sunset studied Marilyn. Marilyn walked away. Sunset turned back to Lee, said, "Hell, I have your eyes."

"Yes, you do," Lee said. "And my hair. But you look like your mother."

"I'm not a drunk, though."

"She wasn't a drunk when I knew her. She was young, like me, fresh and had hopes. Maybe I doused them."

"Kids made fun of my hair when I was little. Better dead than red on the head, that kind of thing. Never got to go to school much. Never had much of anyone to help me do anything."

"You seem to have turned out all right. And a constable. With a gun."

"I wasn't elected. Not really."

"How many women do what you're doing?"

"I don't know of any—what's your name again?"

"Lee. Last name Beck, same as yours. But I wish you'd call me Daddy."

Lee and Sunset went for a drive. She drove where he suggested, trying to put it together, trying to decide how she felt and how she ought to feel.

She stopped where he said stop, near the creek, up beyond the sawmill at Camp Rapture. They got out and walked around, Lee going first this way, then that way, finally stopping at a spot on the edge of the creek.

"It wasn't all washed away then. Used to be a piece stuck out over the creek here. Had some small trees on it. And it was private under them trees. Bushes and grass were grown up around it. There was red bugs, though. Plenty of them."

"Storm took that piece of land away not long back. A storm I damn well remember. I shot my husband during it. I knew the place you're talking about well. Used to come here to play."

He smiled at her. "Did you?"

"I did."

"You were conceived here, Sunset. Well, almost. You were conceived on that piece of land got washed away."

"You and Mama . . . here?"

He nodded. "May not seem romantic to you, but it was to us. Came here often, and one time it was more than just holding hands. There was just that one time. I never knew that it took, so to speak. We used to lie here together and hear the water running below, and sleep in the heat of the day when we thought we wouldn't be missed. You see, your mother, like you, was pretty much on her own. No family to speak of."

"She might have been all right then. Later, she drank."

"Let's walk."

Sunset and Lee strolled along the creek. Lee said, "It's too late for me to find her. I know that now. But I've found a daughter, and that could be enough. That and a granddaughter. If you'll let it be enough."

"What about that boy? He a son of yours?"

"No. He's a boy I met on the road. Got snakebit and your mother-in-law gave us a ride to Uncle Riley's place. His wife saved him. He's mostly well from it."

"Karen says he stares at her."

"Karen's pretty, and Goose, well, he's a little over-developed. Or would like to be. He ain't no real trouble, though."

They were sitting now, on the edge of the creek, feet hanging over the bank.

Lee leaned back, looked at the sky, took in the trees, seemed to absorb it all through his skin.

"Marilyn—does she like you?" Sunset asked.

"Not the way you're thinking. I guess it could be that way if we worked at it. I don't know. She seems nice. But there's a ghost in her smile."

"What's that mean?"

"She's got her own burdens."

"Reckon so," Sunset said.

There was a smile on Lee's face when he said, "I believe in God, Sunset, but to me, he's not the God you were talking about, the one you don't trust. And I don't know he's a he. Don't know God's anything. Not anymore. I don't think God has to do with trust or lack of trust. Nothing we pray for or want. God just is. It all come to me in just this minute, sitting here on the bank, looking up at things, the sky so blue, the trees so green—"

"They look brown to me."

"Yeah. You're right. They're dry. But you see the point?"

"No."

"Way I was taught to believe, way I believed, it was all too simple, and in a way too complex. I see that now. I've had like a flash of light, a kind of understanding. There's a pattern under the false patterns we build. A connection between everything. A gathering of parts that all snap together like some penny puzzle. We sit here along this creek in the hot sun with the bugs buzzing around, water running below our feet, the sky blue, the trees . . . brown, and if we're still, if we lay back, we'll feel the Earth turning. The Earth and you, everyone else on this big old ball of dirt, all of us together, a union of parts and thoughts and purpose, spinning around and around, each and the other part of the same."

Sunset studied him, said, "Yeah. Me and them and it. Except for all of those assholes who hate me and want to see me go to jail for killing Pete, who was trying to kill me. Those assholes who want to say I killed a whore named Jimmie Jo, and now her baby. You bet I'm in union with all of them, spinning here on this ball of dirt. In union with all of them except those assholes who hate coloreds and lynch them, even after they're supposed to get a fair trial. In union with everyone, except my daughter, who I don't know how to deal with. Except for this man I thought I loved, who may have done me like you done Mama. Yeah, me and this world and this universe, we're all just one big union."

"Okay. We'll cut those particular folks out of my moment of revelation."

"You're so full of it."

"I am."

"Are you conning me?" Sunset said. "You conned Mama. Are you conning me?"

"My conning days are over."

"That's just what a con man would say."

"You're right."

"I been conned by one man, maybe two now, I'm thinking, and I don't want to be conned by my own father. I had one more worry and one less friend, I'd be Job."

"You can depend on me. Promise you that. I'm not going anywhere. I'll be around. I'm going to make my stand here. Going to get to know you, and Karen. If you'll let me. And Sunset, maybe I'm not the one to tell you, and maybe I shouldn't know before you, but Marilyn, she told me. I'm not sure why, but she did."

"Told you what?"

"Karen's pregnant."

"Oh, God. When could she have?"

"It's worse."

"How can it be worse?"

"Marilyn says the father is someone you know well, not a boy around here, a man. Guess the one you're saying may have conned you, and I got to say probably did."

"Hillbilly?"

"That's the one."

Sunset studied Lee for a lie. He smiled at her. A small smile, one that said, I'm friendly. Please don't slap me.

"All right," she said. "Now the worst has come."

"You'll handle it."

"I'm not so sure."

"Bad as it is, you'll do fine. And this Hillbilly, you don't worry about him. He's not worth it. We'll do okay by Karen, the baby. You'll see."

Sunset shook her head. "You're sure grabbing lots of problems and you haven't known me but about an hour."

"You seem to pack a lot into every minute."

"Ain't that the truth."

"I owe you a lot of hours, Sunset. I just didn't know it. Now I do. You going to let me do something about it? Be a father?"

"Is it too early to hug?"

"Probably. But we can try it anyway."

They hugged, and she thought it would be touch and move away. Polite. But she found herself clutching him hard. Then she was crying and he was patting her back, saying, "Easy, baby. It's okay. Daddy's here." She let out a single wail, like a wounded coyote, loud enough to startle birds into flight.

28

In search of Hillbilly, Clyde drove into Holiday, cruised the streets, saw him through a plate-glass window at the cafe, parked and went in.

Hillbilly sat at a table by himself drinking coffee, a saucer with a fork and pie crumbs on it at his elbow. He looked up as Clyde came in, stood over the table.

"Clyde," Hillbilly said.

"Sonofabitch."

"Damn, man. We're in a public place."

"Step outside, Mr. Song Bird. We won't be public then."

"We'll be on the street, moron. That's public too."

"Yeah. Well, at least the furniture won't get broken."

Hillbilly sighed. "What's the matter with you?"

Clyde looked around. Patrons were starting to stare. He sat down at the table, put his elbows on it, leaned forward, said, "Sunset didn't tell me, just sent me to look for you, but I know what happened."

"And what was that?"

"You charmed her. You gave her some line of bull—"

"I don't do that."

"Not with your mouth, but with your eyes, your ways. You got her to give herself to you because she thinks she loves you, and you probably did the same to her daughter. And now, you don't show. What you doing in town, Hillbilly?"

"I quit."

"Quit cause you got what you wanted."

"A paycheck, Clyde. I got a paycheck. Now I can buy a guitar."

"And you got them. Sunset and Karen."

"She didn't tell you that, I can bet that, so how would you know?"

"I can tell way she's acting."

"You're jealous."

"You're right. You didn't even tell her you quit. How come?"

"I was going to send word. Maybe drop by. Look, I got a place now." Hillbilly gave the address. "Come see me when you cool down."

"You sorry bastard. If a man could sell you for what you think you're worth, he'd be a rich man."

"I didn't lie to anyone. I got what I wanted, but they wanted it too."

"Sunset thought there was more to you than there is. Karen ain't nothing but a little girl."

"There's an old saying, Clyde. Goes, If they're old enough to bleed, they're old enough to breed."

"Step outside. Come on. Step outside."

"You're twice my size."

"And I'm gonna give you twice the beating."

Hillbilly sighed. He drank the last of his coffee, stood up, took coins out of his pocket, put them on the table.

They went outside. Hillbilly said, "I don't want to make an ugly scene. Let's go around back."

"You don't want to make a scene, all right. You like lying and doing your business in the dark."

They went around back of the cafe. Clyde said, "You want a little bit at a time, or all at once?"

"Any way you want to dole it out will have to do."

Clyde came at him then, kind of roared as he did, and he felt powerful as a bull, mad as a rabid dog, and Hillbilly wasn't there. It was like the ground opened up and the sonofabitch was gone, because the next thing was Clyde found himself floundering at the air, felt a battering ram fall out of the sky and hit him in the ribs. By the time he realized Hillbilly had dodged and hit him with a left hook, it was too late, because now, behind it was a kick to the balls, and when he bent over, Hillbilly leaped in the air and brought his elbow down on the back of his head, hard and sharp enough to make stars leap to sight, then he was on the ground, face down, and Hillbilly was kicking him, the eye, the ribs, the arm, then the little bastard grabbed his hair, pulled his head back, and Clyde felt cold steel on his throat.

"I can cut your throat quicker than you can say that's sharp, or I can let you go with just opening your mouth, putting it down on that rock in front of you. You get to choose."

"You little—"

Hillbilly cut him. Not deep, but a little. All Clyde felt at first was pressure, then a sting, something wet running down his chest and inside his shirt.

"Next time, all the way across. No in-betweens. This is it. You get to choose. Cut throat. Mouth on the rock. Which is it? Answer."

"The rock."

"Put your mouth on it."

Clyde did, and it tasted of dirt and there was a kind of copper taste in the back of his mouth to boot.

Hillbilly's knife went away, and with all the force he could muster, he stamped down on the back of Clyde's head, and Clyde's teeth bit into the rock.

There was another kick, to the side of the head, and another, and Clyde went out.

When Clyde came to, Hillbilly was gone, and so was a piece of one of his front teeth. He stood up and felt the tooth and cussed. He couldn't believe how easily he had gotten his ass whipped. Here he was, coming in like a knight on a charger, and the dragon, a miniature one at that, had whipped his ass, and handily.

He hurt all over, his neck was bleeding where the knife had cut him, and he was spitting blood. He limped out to his truck, started back to Sunset's place. As he drove, he could hardly work the clutch, he ached so bad, and his vision was blurry, his eyes filled with tears. He felt like the biggest old donkey ass in creation.

Rooster left town about the time Clyde arrived, drove on out with the intention of seeing Sunset, lying to her, ready to try and get the maps back. But just before he came to her place, not really knowing he was going to do it, he veered onto a little hunting trail that went left. He bumped over it, stirred up a burst of quail, drove until there wasn't anything to drive on, came to a thin line of thirsty trees growing on a long red-clay hill.

He parked and looked in the mirror. Under his hat was a thin, long-nosed, ghost face. He didn't like that face, not only because it was ugly, but because it had all the character of a frog. He looked at the hill and the line of trees, thought the hill was most likely an old Indian mound. It had the looks of one. Back home in Mineola, he had plowed into them and found pots and arrowheads and bones.

He got out and leaned against the car, thinking, listening. He heard a train way off, its lonesome whistle calling, and he knew up beyond that line of trees was the track.

Rooster took off his gun belt, reached through the open window, laid it on the car seat, removed his badge, put it there too. He went walking up the rise, through the trees, came to a spread of gravel, then the tracks, glinting blue-black in the hot sun. He could hear the train rumbling toward him in the distance. He stuck his foot out, rested it on the rail. He could feel the train inside his shoe.

As it made the curve, it would slow, Rooster knew that, because not far up was a water fill, and it would stop there. That's where hobos jumped on the train. He looked around in case he might see a hobo, but there were none.

Rooster squinted his eyes, looked down the track, saw the train coughing along, growing bigger as it came. He stepped back into the line of trees, and when the train was making the curve, it slowed considerably, almost to a crawl, and he began running. He frightened a couple of doves in the bush as he ran, and they scattered skyward, startling him, but he kept running, and he made the train, got on it with one leap, edged his way between the boxcars and rode there, jiggling with his feet on the boxcar connection. At the water stop he thought maybe he could slip down, find a car open, or open one himself. Then he could ride inside, lay back and travel right on out of this life. Ride until he wanted to get off. No set place to go. Just ride till he couldn't take it anymore.

He thought about Sunset, her not knowing, not expecting what was coming, and he figured Plug and Tootie, they'd go along easy with whatever McBride wanted, same as him. Briefly, he considered jumping off, going back to warn her. But no. He didn't even have the guts for that. He felt as if McBride would know he was running away, that somehow he would sense it, come looking for him, or most likely, send Two. He didn't want to be near Holiday or Camp Rapture, or East Texas for that matter, when McBride found out he was gone. Louisiana might be too damn close. A guy like that, he could hold a grudge for most anything.

Rooster watched the trees speed by, saw the ground rise up on either side of the train, momentarily throwing shadow over him, then the hills were gone again and there was a speckle of pines, a scattering of houses. He took a deep breath. When he let it out again, he said, "Good luck, redhead."

The train blew its whistle, rolled around the bend with a rumble and a squeak, then ducked out of sight, taking Rooster with it.

When Clyde drove up into the yard he sat behind the wheel of the truck, not wanting to get out. He noted Sunset's car was gone, and he was glad of it.

A stocky man and Marilyn were sitting in chairs out front, shelling some peas Marilyn had brought with her. They were shelling them into sacks. A boy was sitting on the hood of Marilyn's truck eyeing Karen, who was sitting beneath the oak shelling peas into a shallow pan. Clyde tried to figure who the hell the man and the boy were, but they seemed to fit, so he didn't get out and ask. He never wanted to get out.

The stocky man saw him, got up and came over.

He stuck a hand through the window. "Lee Beck. Marilyn says you're Clyde."

Clyde shook the hand briefly, said, "I'm what's left of him."

"What happened to you?"

"I got beat up."

"I can see that."

Marilyn, Karen, and the boy came over.

"Clyde," Karen said, "are you okay?"

"My pride is beat up the most," Clyde said. "Well, actually, I think me and my pride got about an equal beating. I got a chipped tooth too."

"Who did it?" Karen asked.

"That's the worst part," Clyde said, opening the truck door, getting out, feeling woozy. "That goddamned pretty boy. Hillbilly."

Karen burst out crying and ran into the tent.

"I didn't know she cared," Clyde said.

"I think it's Hillbilly she cares about," Marilyn said.

"Well, she need not worry about him. He's as perky as a goddamn guinea hen. Though he might have bruised a knuckle or two. Damn, I thought I was a tough sonofabitch, but he was something. I hope she doesn't think I hurt him."

"Karen just recently found out Hillbilly's a turd," Marilyn said. "She's carrying his baby."

"Damn," Clyde said.

"Thanks, Grandma," Karen said from the concealment of the tent. "Thanks a lot."

"People are gonna know soon enough, dear. And this here is family and friends."

"Feared as much," Clyde said. "Thought it might be, but I didn't say nothing cause I didn't want to do no guesswork. I should have, though."

"You're talking about me," Karen said. "I'm here, you know."

"You want to get in on this," Marilyn said, "come out of the tent."

"You don't fret none, baby," Goose said. "I'll take care of you."

"You don't even know me," Karen said, and this time she poked her head out. "I don't even know your name."

"Goose," said the boy. "And I know all of you I need to

289

know. You're the prettiest thing I ever seen."

Karen made a sound that was unfriendly, pulled her head back inside.

Lee said, "Goose, that's my granddaughter you're talking to."

"And I don't mean nothing but respect," Goose said.

"Where's Sunset?" Clyde asked.

"She went to the town meeting," Marilyn said. "They're talking about removing her."

"Ain't this the perfect day?" Clyde said.

29

Marilyn hadn't offered her house for the meeting this time, so it was held at the church. Marilyn said she'd go with Sunset, thought she could wield some power, but Sunset asked her not to. She wanted to go alone, had some things to say.

Sunset got out of the car, shifted her holster until it was comfortable, stood in the shadow of the leaning church cross for a time, watched a crow on one end of it drop its load onto the church roof. She took a deep breath of sawmill stench, went inside the church.

It was stuffy in there, and Henry Shelby and the town elders were sitting in a pew at the front. A stout man wearing a bowler hat and a nice gray suit was up front leaning on the preacher's podium, looking bored. She had never seen him before. He was maybe sixty, almost good-looking. Still solid, had a thick mustache and was red-skinned and robust. His hands were draped over the top of the podium and they looked like two huge white spiders resting. When he lifted his head and looked at her, she felt as if she had been dual stabbed all the way through to the back of her head. And when his eyes moved, she felt those stabs in the groin.

As she came in, the men in the pews turned their heads and looked at her, watched her carefully as she walked down the aisle.

"We didn't think you'd come," Henry said. "We thought you'd send your mother-in-law to talk for you."

When she was standing at the pew, Sunset said, "Henry. You and me, we need to talk. Alone."

"There's nothing to be said, Sunset," Henry said. "This is a formality. We're removing you."

"We need to talk alone."

"You said that."

"I want to talk to you about some land with oil on it. A big pool of oil."

Henry just looked at her.

"This land has a house on it, and the oil on the land is the same that was on Jimmie Jo."

The big man behind the podium laughed.

The elders looked at Henry. Henry's face had lost its color.

"All right," Henry said. "Maybe me and her should talk alone. It's important, I'll let you know."

The elders looked at one another. One said, "Henry, this isn't the way we do things—"

"It is today. Y'all wait outside for a while. Go over to the store, get something to drink." He dug in his wallet, gave one of the men a few bills. "It's on me."

"What about him?" Sunset said, nodding toward the man leaning on the podium.

"He don't want a Coke. He doesn't go."

"Henry," said one of the elders, "are you sure?"

"I'm sure."

They were slow about it, but the elders got up and went out. McBride came out from behind the podium, sat in the same pew with Henry, crossed his legs, leaned back as if waiting for someone to serve lunch.

Henry studied Sunset, said, "This had better be good."

"I think you already know it's good. But not for you."

"This sounds like some kind of blackmail."

"Maybe."

"It didn't work for Pete and Jimmie Jo, it ain't gonna work for you."

She tried to figure what Henry was talking about, sort of got it. Pete and Jimmie Jo had tried to outflank Henry and this guy, but it hadn't worked.

Another thing hit her. If they were stealing Zendo's land, there were probably others. Plenty of blacks who couldn't read, or could and wouldn't say anything for fear of sticking to tar and feathers, dangling at the end of a rope, becoming a gasoline-soaked torch for white sheets to dance by.

"Me and Pete are different," Sunset said.

"I can tell that," Henry said. "Any man can tell that."

"Hear, hear," McBride said.

"You're different, all right," Henry said. "You're different from other women. You're a looker, Sunset. And you're a tramp. Pete married you because you're a tramp. Then he found himself a bigger and a better tramp."

"You don't know anything about me," Sunset said.

"I know a tramp when I see one."

"And I know a thief when I see one."

"You're a tramp pretending to be a man, going around with a gun on your hip. Does that gun make you feel like you got something you don't got? You know, a Johnson?"

"Henry, my guess is, even with me not having a Johnson, mine's bigger than yours."

McBride laughed again. Henry looked at him, then back at Sunset. "Get on with it."

"Sure you want this fella to know what I'm going to say? Not that I care. It'll all come out soon enough."

"He knows lots of things already. You say what you got to say, little lady. And I use the term lady loosely."

293

"Most of it don't need to be said. You're cheating Zendo out of his land, you and the mayor were, before he went off—he didn't go off, did he?"

"He's not here," Henry said.

Sunset looked at McBride. "That's why you brought this guy in, isn't it? To get rid of the mayor? Strong-arm people. Keep you out of it."

"I didn't say that."

"Mayor's probably in some hole somewhere, like Jimmie Jo and her baby." Sunset studied McBride. "But you know about that, don't you?"

"I don't put people in holes," McBride said. "I don't like digging. And I don't like babies hurt."

"Who is this guy, anyway?" Sunset asked Henry.

"McBride," McBride said.

"He's an associate," Henry said. "From Chicago. I knew him through a fella."

"Weren't there enough thugs around here?"

"Listen here, Sunset," Henry said. "I don't like you. But I tell you what, I'll cut you in for what Pete was gonna get, you hadn't shot him."

"What was Jimmie Jo's share? A dose of oil and a thirty-eight slug in the back of the head?"

"A thirty-eight slug?" McBride said.

Sunset worked up a fierce gaze. "The baby was cut out. That's as low as it gets. That your work, McBride?"

"I didn't know she had one in the oven," McBride said. "That's a bad break for the kid, that being done. I didn't know about the kid."

Sunset thought McBride looked surprisingly sincere.

"Don't say so much," Henry said to McBride.

"Nothing's been said that matters," McBride said.

Henry looked at Sunset, said, "No one really cares about a nigger's land, Sunset. Not really. We could cut you in for a share of it. Hell, you're such a nigger lover, you can give Zendo part of your share, all of it. The truth is, a nigger ain't got the sense to run a piece of oil land, and don't deserve the money."

"But you do?"

"Oh, yeah."

"How much does he get?"

"I'm a full partner," McBride said.

"Did you start that way?" Sunset said. "You a full partner from the start? Bet not. Bet you got the mayor's share. Where is the mayor, McBride?"

McBride grinned at her. "All I know, he gave up his job when he disappeared. I think Henry here is going to be running for that position."

"That's right," Henry said. "They got the town council filling in until the emergency election, next month. Then I'll run. I think I've got a good chance."

"Not if the council knows about this."

"Frankly, you're just a fly on the end of my dick, Sunset. A third of the council is Klan, and I don't know any of the others got much love for niggers."

"Thing is," Sunset said, "bet they'll all want their little share, though, won't they? That'll split up your prize considerable, won't it?"

Sunset was fishing, but she could tell from the look on Henry's face he had thought about that, and didn't like the idea. McBride looked like he had before. A happy green-eyed guy. A guy used to things turning out his way.

"Rooster in on this?" Sunset asked.

"He was," McBride said. "But he left town today."

"Way the mayor did?"

"Rooster seems to have caught a train," McBride said. "Sheriff's car was found out by the tracks just before we come here."

"Listen here, girlie," Henry said. "Let me lay it out even clearer. I won't remove you from office. You play constable, run around with your gun and badge until the term runs out, then you give it up. Do that, I'll give you a cut of the oil money. A good cut. There's a little house on that land Pete built for his whore. Think about that. He built her a house and was going to make her rich on that oil money, and you, you weren't going to get a thing out of the deal. That was part of his little blackmail scheme. A house, a piece of land, a slice of the oil money. He was gonna shake you loose, honey, and keep the whore. I'll give you the deal he wanted, one I wasn't going to give him or Jimmie Jo. How's that? Better than living in that tent, ain't it?"

"I wouldn't trust you as far as two grown men could throw you," Sunset said. "And by the way, did it occur to you, I tell Marilyn what you've done, you'll be out at the sawmill?"

Henry pursed his lips, shook his head and grinned.

"Well, Marilyn is looking for an excuse, now that she drove her old man to suicide and she's got the purse strings. I've known her a long time. I think Jones kept her in line. I think she's got a conniving streak herself. Tell that old sow to let 'er rip. I've put back money, and I'm going to make new money, and I got a little inheritance from the wife, her having a piece of the sawmill and all. Thing for you to worry about is not how to get me but how to not get got yourself."

"Gonna send your white-sheeted monkeys? I ain't scared of them. One of them puts a foot on my property, comes near me or mine, I'll arrest him. And if I can't arrest him, I'll bloody up his sheet."

McBride made with his chuckle, the one that made Sunset's ass clench and her skin crawl.

"Something needs to be taken care of, I like to have people knows how," McBride said. "Or do it myself, I got to. Not a bunch of crackers playing dress up, passing signs and symbols between themselves.

"Now, sweetie, you don't know me. But I'll tell you this. I think the Bible will back me up. A woman, she's got a function. And it's important. That's how a man stays satisfied, how babies come into the world and pickles get canned. But a slut wearing a badge, talking to men like she's a man, that ain't one of her functions. Me, I'm a business partner with Mr. Shelby here. And I'll get my share. I don't give a hot turd in a hog's ass about councils and mayors and maps and who knows what. You hear? You don't want to rile me. You don't want to even make me a little irritated. You might want to stroke my weary brow, you know what's good for you, lay back, let me take some tension out of you, cause I can do that. Thing that's getting you by now, this minute, is you're cute. That's gonna get you through this meeting today. It ain't good for another day. Hear me?"

"Think you're scaring me?" Sunset said, feeling very scared, letting her hand rest on the butt of her gun, because McBride, he'd shifted in the pew and his coat had fallen back and she could see there was one big pistol hanging from a holster under his arm. She knew he knew she could see it, meant for her to. He shifted again, let the coat close. She kept her hand on her gun, casual, but ready, determined not to show how scared she was, keeping a calm smile on her face, holding her legs stiff so her knees wouldn't knock.

Then she saw something behind the closed curtain at the back, where the choir gathered and the curtain was pulled open when they sang. Feet sticking out from under the curtain. She said, "Who's back there?"

"Believe me," McBride said, "you don't want to know."

"Tell him to step out."

McBride grinned. "All right. Two."

Two stepped out. He was partially hidden in shadow, but there was light from the door, and it gave enough she could see him. At first he looked short, but Sunset realized he was over six feet and thick and built like an oak. He was black as wet licorice and the whites of his eyes were very white. He smiled. His gums were dark. Blue gums, they called colored people like that. He wore a bowler hat like McBride, but it fit lower. He had on regular clothes but his jacket was black and silky and had long tails. There was something about him that made her skin try and turn itself inside out.

"What's he supposed to be?" Sunset said.

"He's a big nigger," McBride said.

"Why's he here?"

"I told you," McBride said. "You don't want to know."

Sunset studied McBride, said, "You got your ugly little hat screwed on too tight. Don't you know it ought to come off in church? Or will your head come off with it?"

McBride's face collapsed like a sail without wind, and Sunset realized she had hit home. The hat? No. His head? That was it—sonofabitch was bald. And vain about it. She gave him a slow smile. McBride's features remained the same; the sail had not regained the wind.

"You're in my jurisdiction now, Henry," Sunset said. "You and your thug and your thug's thug, or whatever he is. All of you."

"But you're not the law in Holiday," Henry said. "The map's not your concern, and as the law is sort of under my jurisdiction over there, well, I suppose I'm the law."

"Zendo's land is under my jurisdiction," Sunset said. "You boys say your prayers and leave. I don't want to find you here within the hour. I do, I'll arrest you."

"For what?" Henry said.

"For being ugly in church."

Now was the time for an exit, Sunset thought, while she was one up.

Sunset started down the aisle, for the open door.

Henry called out to her. "Have we got a deal, you and me?"

She kept walking.

Outside she held out her hands and looked at them. They were shaking.

Henry said, "Think she'll go with us? Take the deal?"

"Not that one. I hope she doesn't. Me and her, we need to get close, and I like a reason to be mad."

"I think she'll take the deal. She's tough now, but she'll think about it. She'll take it."

"She'll pass."

Henry looked up, studied Two.

"Did you have to bring the shine with you? Bring him here?"

"He does what he wants."

"I don't get it. I hired you, but you brought this guy down."

"It cost you a train ticket. Get over it. He had to ride back with the niggers. It wasn't no easy thing for him."

"He is a nigger."

"Two ain't got the same way of thinking niggers got around here."

"What's that mean?"

"It means he ain't no shine boy."

"Why's he stand around like that? In the shadows. He gives me the willies."

McBride grinned. "He likes it dark. He thinks he's some kind of shadow. Come here, Two."

Two came over, stood in front of the pew, his hands

299

dangling by his sides. Up close Henry took note of Two's blazing green eyes.

"Two," McBride said, "show him your head. Tell Henry what happened."

Two took off his bowler. At the top of his forehead, the hair, which was cut short elsewhere, was gone and there was a scar, a horseshoe shape. It was deep and purple and had ridges.

"Jesus," Henry said. "A mule kicked you?"

"God gave me this," said Two, and his voice had a kind of gush to it, like a shovel slipping into fresh mud. "I was struck by a bolt of God's lightning, and God made me Two. Made me hungry."

"He got kicked in the head, right?" Henry asked McBride.

"He just told you what happened."

"God have a mule?"

"He's a piece of work, ain't he?"

"How'd you come by him?"

"That's a long story."

"What's he mean there's two of him?"

"That's why he's called Two. Used to just be Cecil, but that ain't good enough no more. Now he's Two. There's him, then there's the other one, but they're both inside of him. He's so goddamn special has to be two of him. Am I right, Two?"

Two nodded.

"Sometimes they got to talk to one another, figure things out. Ain't that right, Two?"

"This is giving me the crawls, McBride. We got to have him around?"

"He's good in a spot. I been in some places where me and him had to ride high, and we did."

"He does what you say?"

"Only if he wants to. Most of the time, he wants to. We got a connection."

"Is he dangerous?"

"Of course he's dangerous."

Henry studied Two, standing there, still as a board, a smile on his face, the green eyes looking down like the eyes of some kind of feral animal. The same kind of eyes McBride had, only more so.

"Took the urge, he'd bite your face off, Henry. Eat it. Niggers got that cannibal thing in them, you know."

Henry snapped a glance at McBride, and McBride laughed.

"Don't worry. He ain't gonna eat you. Not just yet. Will you, Two?"

"I think not," Two said.

"He don't talk like a nigger."

"Two was educated, weren't you, Two?"

Two nodded.

"He learned things some white men never get to learn, but Two, he got to. He can do higher mathematics, Henry. He can read any goddamn book ever written without moving his lips, and he's read a lot of them. Ain't that right, Two? He's got a pretty special life. Here he is, half nigger, half white, black as the goddamn ace of spades, and his father and his nigger mother, they took care of him, treated him good, like a white man. And the father, a white man, he went off and left his other son, a white boy, to his mother, a white mother, and the mother left the son to the nuns. But the boy, he come out of it. He was tough. Made his way. He's done all right. But he didn't get no education. Didn't get a thing he didn't scratch in the dirt for. And Cecil here—Two—he got it all given to him like that black skin of his was white as snow. God smote him for being an uppity nigger, didn't he, Two? That's the real reason you got smote."

"He gave me powers."

"See, Two figures it different. Thinks God blessed him. He won't accept a horse kicked him, knocked his brain around. That ain't the story is it, Two?"

"God struck me with a thunderbolt, gave me powers."

"What do you have to do in return, Two?" McBride said. "What do you have to do to put a smile on God's face?"

"Suck souls."

"Suck souls?" Henry said.

"Yeah. Ain't that some shit? Likes to put his mouth over the face of a dying man or woman, and suck. He'll do it if they're fresh dead, too. They don't have to be on the boat, they can done be off and on the other side, and old Two, he goes to sucking."

"You're pulling my dick?"

"Nope. He sucks souls. Or thinks he does."

"I do," Two said.

"You seen him do it?"

"I have. He helped me with that gal, he sucked her face, helped me hold her down in the oil, and then he sucked her face. Got oil all over him. It's horseshit, though, ain't it, Two? You're not sucking any souls. You're just sucking, right?"

"You know the truth, brother," Two said. "You know I tell the truth and that I am here to assist you so that my need, God's need for souls, can be satisfied."

"Wait a minute," Henry said, just getting it. "Is he . . . your half brother? A nigger?"

"You trying to make a point, Henry?"

"No . . . No. I've seen some nigger gals I'd have done, got the chance. It could happen. Could happen to any man, diddling a nigger. There's half-white children all over East Texas. It don't mean a thing outside of getting your wick dipped."

"My daddy lived with Two's mother. Lived with her like he

302

was proud. Must have caught hell for it, but he done it anyway. I guess that's what they call love, whatever it is. Figure when that nigger died, Two's mother, that's what drove Daddy to drink. He loved that nigger in a way he didn't love my mother, and her white."

Two made a sound in his throat like someone tasting something good and sweet. McBride looked up at him.

"Go back to your place," McBride said.

Two grinned at him and sat in the pew next to McBride.

"See," McBride said, "he don't always do what I ask."

30

Sunset drove away, her mind on McBride, those eyes of his, the way he moved, as if he might suddenly turn into something liquid and molten, flow over her and burn her to death. And the one called Two. Jesus. Two gave her the jumps.

Hillbilly, she thought of him too, what he had done to Karen. Hell, what he had done to her. The lying silver-tongued sonofabitch. She had given him everything and showed him everywhere, and he had played her like a fish on the line, landed her, gutted her, devoured her, gone on his way, ready to cast again.

Goddamn that Hillbilly.

It was all her fault, dealing with and trusting Hillbilly.

Her knack for picking men had not changed. It was the same. She could still pick them. As long as they were bad.

And now she had a father. After all these years, a father, and maybe, just maybe, he was okay. Still, she had to keep her guard up. Her luck, he'd probably leave one morning with her car packed full of her belongings, maybe take Ben too.

She drove by the cutoff to her tent, went on toward Holiday. Drove to the spot where Hillbilly had enjoyed her, parked there, looked out over the town, down on the blood-red apartment and the drugstore, the courthouse, looked across to the sheriff's office, all the places of business, Main Street dotted with people and automobiles, animals and wagons, the oil wells sticking up. In the day, without the lights, it wasn't so pretty. She heard a man say once that at night, with the light just right, any whore that wasn't big as a house could look pretty, but in the light of the day, a whore was a whore and looked that way. Holiday was a whore.

She took the pistol from its holster, checked it for loads. It had five. She put in another. Six now. She spun the cylinder. Sat for a while. Backed the car around, drove on into town.

She went along the streets slow, hoping to see him, but no sign. She stopped, went into the cafe. No Hillbilly. She tried a number of other spots but didn't find him. People on the street, they saw her face, they stepped aside.

Walked all over, but didn't find him. Finally, she felt weak, as if she were recovering from some kind of disease. The Hillbilly disease. The fever was breaking.

She knew then she couldn't find him. Must not find him. Couldn't let that happen. Not right now. Not the way she felt. Not with six loads in her gun. She did, she'd do what she wanted to do, and she couldn't do that. She was the law. She had Karen to take care of. That old abandoned dog, Ben, who she'd promised not to leave. She had to watch after him. And now she had her father, and there was that silly kid too, the one they called Goose. He probably came with the package. Maybe he had a goddamn dog somewhere, with three or four pups perhaps, a sister with a cat.

No. She couldn't do what she wanted. She had to do something, but shooting Hillbilly in the head wasn't it, fine as the thought seemed right then. She'd be crucified. Not only because she'd be guilty as homemade sin, but because, as Henry said, so many hated her. An uppity woman. Almost as bad as an uppity nigger. No. Worse. She was not only a woman and uppity, she was a nigger lover, way they saw it. A woman with a badge and a gun, her husband dead by her hand. She ought to be bent over a stove, cooking, her dress hiked up with a husband entering her from behind while she used one foot to turn a butter churn, the other to rock a cradle.

She walked back to her car like she was stomping ants, drove away.

The day was falling off now, getting toward afternoon. The horizon looked as if it had been slashed with a razor.

When she reached home, Marilyn was out to one side of the property with posthole diggers, digging away. Clyde's truck was gone. She didn't see anyone else.

She walked up to Marilyn.

"Where is everybody?"

"I nearly messed myself, dear, way you came up."

"Sorry."

"Karen is in the tent. Goose borrowed a shotgun, went squirrel hunting. Lee and Clyde said they were going into Holiday on business."

"What business?"

"They just said business."

"Probably a beer."

"Maybe," Marilyn said. "Hillbilly, he beat hell out of Clyde."

"Hillbilly?"

"Whipped him like a galley slave."

"I can't believe it."

"Believe it. He looked any worse you'd have to bury him. I think Lee went with him to cheer him up."

Sunset nodded, said, "What are you doing?"

Marilyn smiled at her. "Digging a hole."

"What for?"

"A clothesline. Karen said you hang clothes over bushes."

"That's right."

"It'll be easier with a clothesline."

"I was going to dig holes and cut posts myself. Just haven't gotten around to it. I hate shoveling. I hate chopping too. Come to think of it, I hate work."

"Posthole diggers are better than a shovel. I can work these all day. Easier to dig a hole straight down, and deep, and you can widen it with the diggers pretty quick. A woman can handle these good. It's kind of fun, good for you, out here in the fresh air. And from the looks of your face, maybe I ought to loan you my posthole diggers."

"Henry won't be with the sawmill much longer."

"How's that?"

Sunset told her all she knew. It came out first like a hole in the dike, a trickle, then more, till finally the dike collapsed and it flooded out.

When it was over, Sunset said, "I'm not going to cry. I've cried too much. All I'm doing lately is crying. I'm the constable. I'm not supposed to cry."

"Who says?"

"I say. Except I am going to cry."

Marilyn slammed the posthole diggers in the dirt so that they stood up, then she hugged Sunset, and Sunset cried. The gray sky had gone black and now it was night and the stars were slipping out as if being squeezed from a bag, and Sunset, she was crying.

"Hell," Sunset said, "I ain't supposed to cry. I'm the constable. I cried on my daddy just a bit back, and I don't even know him. I cry all the goddamn time."

"I hope it's not because Henry's quitting."

Sunset guffawed. "No."

"I was going to let him go anyway, soon as I looked the books over good. Figure he's been stealing for years. Jones wouldn't believe me when I said it, and that's why Henry hates me. He knows I know. He knows too, deep down, I'm pretty vengeful. I can put up with a lot, like Jones, but when I've had enough, I let loose. Jones found that out."

Sunset wiped her tears away with the back of her arm.

Marilyn said, "Pete come to me sometimes and cried."

"Really? What about?"

"I don't know. Really don't. He'd come see me, I'd fix him something to eat, then he'd tear up."

"All the time?"

"Now and then. But he cried about something. Cried on my shoulder like when he was little, and it was nice. He seemed like my boy then, not like the man he'd become, a man like his father."

"I wonder if he was crying about me? Not being like he wanted, however that was."

"I don't know."

"He could have cried for me. Just once. I would have liked it, same as you."

Sunset took a deep breath, steeled herself for what she had to say next. "Daddy told me Karen is pregnant. You told him."

"I should have told you. But when I found out Lee was your father, thought maybe he was the one to do it. Are you mad?"

"No."

"Come on, dear. Let's you and me go in, see what we can find for supper. I'll finish this another time. And maybe you can talk easy to Karen. She needs support right now, like you did when you was ripe with her."

"She ain't all that ripe. She could get rid of it, she took a mind to."

"I don't think that's the way she'll go."

"All right," Sunset said. "It's her choice, and whatever choice she makes, I'm here for her."

"We both are."

308

31

Hillbilly lay with his back propped against the headboard, smoking a rolled cigarette. He had one hand on the sleeping whore's ass, was thinking about waking her again. She was supposed to cost, but so far she hadn't. He had smooth-tongued her, not only in the ass, but in the ear, told her how she deserved better than the life she had, how she was pretty, and she was, except for the scar where someone had hooked a knife in her nose and cut her. But the rest of her made the scar look small. When she got naked, the scar seemed like nothing at all.

He had a lantern lit on the little table by the window, and it gave just enough light. He liked a little light when he was having sex, not just to see the woman, but so she could see him. He knew women liked to see him, way he looked. He glanced across the room, saw the guitar he had bought. It was propped in the corner. It sure beat the harmonica and the Jew's harp. They were all right to carry a tune, but not much for making real music. A guitar, that was the instrument.

Hillbilly felt a pang of regret, remembered the colored man who had owned the harmonica, the Jew's harp, the hobos with him. It wasn't a thing he was proud of, cutting their throats while they slept, but he needed stuff. The harmonica and the Jew's harp, what little money they had, a few odds and ends he wanted. Way he saw it, he did what he had to do. It was easier to cut them all while they slept.

He'd tried to rob one, made a tussle of it, he'd have had a fight, and though he was handy in a fight, he didn't want to fight three. He learned long ago the easy way was the best way.

The hobos had been good to him, shared their food and music, but he did what he did because that was the way of the world.

Sunset had been good to him too. And one night, out on the overhang, she had been real good to him. He had hoped to carry that on longer, get the real juice out of the deal, but he couldn't resist the daughter. He knew that would come down on him eventually, poking her.

Maybe it was time to move on, forget hanging around Holiday. Go to the next town, work some honky-tonks. Made enough money, he could live a better life. Not just more goods, but a better life. Less lying and cheating, and killing. Maybe he could do that. For a little bit, he thought he could do it with Sunset. But there was the daughter, sweet and ripe and ready to go. Seemed every time he found what he wanted, there was always something nice on the other side of the fence, and he had to reach for it.

He put his cigarette in the saucer beside the bed, rubbed the whore's butt. She woke up and turned over. She grinned at him in the lantern light. "You're a mighty, mighty man, Hillbilly."

"I'm glad you seen that."

"I don't think you mean to pay me, do you?"

"Ain't got no money to pay with. Spent it all renting this place for the week, buying a guitar. Wasn't that song I sang payment enough? Hell, Jimmy Rodgers couldn't have done no better."

The whore laughed. "A song don't pay nothing I got to pay, but it was nice. And I don't know Jimmy Rodgers could do better or not. I ain't had Jimmy Rodgers."

"I can sing a song for another round."

"Baby, you don't need to. Come here."

Clyde said, pointing the flashlight on the number painted at the top of the stairs, "This here is the place. This is the address he give me."

Lee nodded.

It wasn't high up there, a short run of stairs on the outside of the building, and you were there. They could see light through the window. Below the window was an alley, some garbage cans.

"He's tougher than you think," Clyde said. "He whupped my ass like I was standing still and about half retarded. I'd done about as good against him if I'd went in there with a blindfold on, my dick fastened to a chain and anvil."

"What you do," Lee said, "is you stay where you are, and I'll go up."

"Didn't say I was afraid, just saying he's mean as a boar hog with turpentine on his balls. He ain't no big man, and he beat me like I was a cripple. You got to know, this guy is the devil, he wants to be."

"I know you're not afraid, just want you to stay here."

"I got a slap jack, you want it."

"No, you keep it."

"Take the flashlight, then. It's a heavy one."

"No. You keep that too. I can see all right."

"Heavy ain't got nothing to do with seeing. I was talking about scrambling his brains with it."

"I know, but you keep it."

"We ought to go up together. Together, we got a chance. You don't understand, this fella, he knows how to fight. He's got some moves."

"I got one or two myself."

"I think he's got three or four. Maybe five."

Lee grinned at Clyde. "I'll be careful. What I want you to do, is stand down here, that slap jack ready. See that window, you stand under it. But not directly under it. You'll get a signal of sorts. It comes, you lay down on Hillbilly's head."

"With me down here, him up there? I better go up."

"No. You stay."

"Watch your teeth."

Lee went up the stairs. They were solid and didn't creak much. When he got to the door at the top, he stood back on the landing, took a deep breath, kicked the door with all his might. The lock sprang and the door swung open and slapped back against the wall.

Lantern light lay across the bed, and when Lee stepped into the room, Hillbilly, or the man he hoped was Hillbilly, sat up in bed, the sheet falling away from him. He had come out from between a woman's wishboned legs, his manhood poking up like a tent peg.

Lee said, "You Hillbilly?"

"What of it? Who the hell are you? What the hell you think you're doing?"

"Why I'm the angel of the Lord."

"You're fucked up, is what you're gonna be."

"I got a daughter named Sunset. A granddaughter named Karen. I think you know them."

For a moment Hillbilly was quiet, then he said, "Yeah. I know them. Real well."

"That's what I thought. Well, I'm here to beat your sorry ass."

"There's plenty tried," Hillbilly said, rolling out of bed, his tent peg turning into a limp little hose.

"I think you're a little too proud, son. I'm going to take some pride out of you. By the handfuls."

"Old man, I'm warning you. You don't know what you're stepping into. You look way past it."

Lee went for him. The whore screamed.

Hillbilly moved. He really moved. It was so fast he hardly seemed to move. One moment he was in front of Lee, the next he was gone.

Hillbilly knew he was fast, damn fast, knew too he had the old man, and when he slid to the side, twisted to come around and hit the old man in the back of the head, he was already grinning.

But the old man wasn't there. The old man leaned, and Hillbilly's fist went past and the old man snapped out a right and hit Hillbilly and took the grin away. It was a good shot. A damn good shot. Hillbilly hadn't felt one like that in a long time. But he took it. Took it good. He was still standing.

He ducked, went for the old man's knees, but the old man did a kind of backward hop, the grab missed, and the next thing Hillbilly knew, the old man had a forearm under his neck, had latched on like a dog tick in a hound's ear, and now the old man was falling onto his back, bringing his leg up between Hillbilly's bare legs, kicking him in the plums, carrying him over.

Hillbilly hit the floor on his back, so hard the lamp on the table jumped. He twisted around and came up, tried to come back on the old man, but the old man rolled to his feet and was facing him. Then Hillbilly felt the delayed pain in his balls, like someone had put them in a vise and tightened the crank. He bent forward, sick.

The old man came at him then, and it was fast. Real fast. As fast as Hillbilly thought he was. Faster. And the old man brought with him friends from hell. A left and a right. Followed it with a left hook that shook the inside of Hillbilly's mouth and something came loose in there, then the old man had him by the waist, was lifting him up, rushing him backwards to the window, slamming him through it.

The whore bellowed throughout the whole thing, but she screamed loudest when Hillbilly went through the window, glass flying, blood drops spraying.

"You killed him," the blonde yelled.

"Well, I was trying," Lee said.

Clyde heard the racket, thought, I better go up, and was about to, when out the busted window came Hillbilly, hair, dick and balls flapping in the wind. It was a damn good drop, and Hillbilly hit hard. Still, the sonofabitch was trying to get up.

Clyde thought: Well, I guess that's the goddamn signal.

Clyde went over there, and Hillbilly, spotted with glass cuts, his mouth dripping blood, on his hands and knees, looked up.

"You," Hillbilly said.

"Howdy," Clyde said, and swung the slap jack as hard as he could. The first blow caught Hillbilly on the side of the face, and he dropped, tried to rise again. The second blow caught him on the back of the head, and Clyde laughed as he delivered it. This time Hillbilly went down, stayed there.

Clyde turned, saw Lee coming down the stairs. He looked fine, his hair a little ruffled, his suit coat twisted. He was carrying a guitar. There was a woman at the top of the stairs wearing a sheet, cussing and yelling. Some lights in the downstairs apartment went on.

Lee walked over to where Hillbilly lay face down, studied him a moment, put the base of the guitar on the ground, rested one hand on the neck, leaned on it like it was a crutch. With his other hand he unfastened his pants, got out his Johnson, let piss fly. He wetted up Hillbilly's head and the side of his face real good.

He said, "Here's a message from the big dog."

Hillbilly stirred, raised his head slightly.

"Sonofabitch," Hillbilly said.

"Here's a good-night tune," Lee said, took the guitar by the neck and swung it. It was a beautiful swing. It whistled in the night, and when it struck Hillbilly, it made a sound like a rifle shot, then there was a ping and a sad throb of strings.

Hillbilly was down again, not out, just lying there, fragments of guitar all around, strings wobbling in the air like insect antennae. He got to his knees, cocked his ass in the air, as if ready to take it from the rear, froze there, not able to move, blacked out.

Lee put a foot on him and pushed and Hillbilly rolled over on his side and didn't move. Lee fastened his pants, took Clyde by the elbow, said, "Let's go. I need a drink. I don't drink nothing alcohol, but a big bracer of cold milk will do me."

Goose and Karen were out behind the oak, sitting on the ground with a pan of water and some knives, a kerosene lamp on the ground. Goose was skinning and gutting the four squirrels he had shot. Karen put them in the pan of water and used her hands to rub any loose hair off of them.

"Four squirrel, four shots," Goose said.

"You were using a shotgun."

"They weren't sitting on the end of it."

"Did you know them and rats is kin?" Karen said.

"Naw, they ain't."

"They are. They're like in the same family or something."

"They don't look like rats—well, maybe they do a bit.

315

Suppose they could be kinfolks. I got kinfolks might be rats, the way they look, so I guess any family can have rats in it."

"Maybe we ought not think on that too much."

"Sounds like a good idea to me. I ain't much on thinking I'm eating a rat's cousin."

"All four of them are nice and fat," Karen said.

"I love squirrel. Ain't had one in ages."

"Well, you shot them, so you get the first pick of the meat."

"How do you like them fixed?"

"Fried. Squirrel and dumplings. I like them all kind of ways."

"Me too . . . you sure are pretty."

Karen smiled at him.

"You sure are blunt."

"Just think you ought to tell a girl something like that."

"You're pretty young, aren't you, Goose?"

"You're young too."

"I ain't as young as you."

"Well, I ain't so young I don't know a pretty girl when I see one. A girl like you, you was my girl, I'd take care of you. Anything you needed or wanted, I'd get it."

"How about a million dollars?"

"It might take some time, but I'd get it. I'd rob somebody I had to."

"That's not what a girl wants to hear. Least it ain't what I want to hear."

"What do you want to hear? I'll say it."

"That ain't the way either, Goose. Like that, it don't have no meaning."

"I can't say nothing right, can I?"

"Not much."

"I still think you're pretty."

"Thanks."

"That was my baby in you, I wouldn't run off. I'd make sure it had a home."

Karen teared up. Goose said, "I didn't mean to mention that. I didn't mean to make you sad."

"That's how it is, ain't it? Got myself knocked up, didn't I? Listened to Hillbilly. Told me I was pretty, just like you did. Told me lots of things. I ought to known he was just talking. Just wanted under my dress. I'm just a chippie."

"Naw, you ain't. You just got tricked, that's all. Anyone can get tricked."

Ben came up, sat down, tried to look polite. Goose gave him the squirrel innards to eat.

"You finished, Goose?"

"Got them all done."

"Why don't we take them to the tent and I'll fry them. You can help me."

"I'm for that."

When Lee and Clyde drove up, got out of the pickup, Sunset came out of the tent wiping her face with a napkin, wiping away the grease left from the squirrel she had been eating. She watched as Lee and Clyde came toward the tent. They looked happy.

"You two fellas look like you just ate the canary," she said.

"Naw," Clyde said, "but we busted his ass. He tried to fly like a canary, but the ground got in the way."

"Yeah," Lee said. "He was lucky the ground stopped his fall."

Clyde let out a hoot.

Sunset studied them for a long moment, thought maybe they were drunk after all.

Lee said, "I don't know how you'll feel about it, Sunset.

Maybe it wasn't the thing to do. Childish, perhaps, but we went to see Hillbilly."

"Had a come-to-Jesus meeting with him," Clyde said. "Well, Lee here, he was the preacher, I was just in the amen corner."

"You both jumped on him?"

"Not exactly," Clyde said. "Not that I'd have cared if we had, and had some help. I wouldn't have felt bad the army helped us."

"Tell me."

"We went over where Hillbilly told me he was," Clyde said, "and he was with some whore, and your daddy went up there and beat Hillbilly's ass like he was nailed to the floor, threw him out a window. I hit him with the slap jack then. Twice."

Sunset brought her hand to her mouth. "Did it . . . hurt him?"

"Hell, yeah," Clyde said. "He didn't bounce worth a damn. You hit a guy with a slap jack, it's gonna hurt. But that slap jack, it wasn't nothing to what he got upstairs, way he came out that window, butt naked."

"Is he . . . dead?"

"Naw," Clyde said. "Wasn't that big a fall. But he ain't pretty no more. I don't know it's permanent, but he looks like he went through some kind of grater and got put back together by a drunk."

"I'm sorry, Sunset," Lee said. "I know you had feelings for him."

"Should have seen it when Lee hit that sonofabitch with his new guitar," Clyde said. "That was an ace moment, that's what I'm trying to tell you."

Sunset slowly smiled. "Wish I had been there to see it."

"Especially that part when he come naked out that window," Clyde said, "flapping his arms. Fallen from five feet higher, they'd be digging his ass out of the ground with some kind of machinery."

Sunset laughed, got between them, put her arms around them, "You boys ought to be arrested, but hell, that ain't my jurisdiction, now is it?"

"No, it ain't," Clyde said.

"There you are," Sunset said. "I'm gonna have to let it go. Come on inside. We got fried squirrel to eat."

32

Back in bed, upstairs, the whore nursed him, but Hillbilly didn't like it none, because she had seen him get his ass beat. And handily. And by an old man. And he wasn't looking so good right now. When he checked himself in the mirror, he saw a guy he didn't know. Guy with glass cuts all over him, like some kind of pox, a broken nose, fat lips, swollen right eye and a cheek that looked like something a chipmunk ought to have, all stuffed up with nuts. But it was just a swelling where a back tooth had come out. His balls weren't peachy either. All black from being kicked, like rotten plums about to drop off. The fall made him hurt all over. His knees were banged and so were his elbows. He couldn't believe he hadn't broken something. He felt a little shook up inside, like something big and fast had run through him, gut to gill.

The blonde pulled a glass sliver out of his penis with her fingernails, put it on a handkerchief on the end table by the bed.

"You can go," Hillbilly said, as she placed a damp cloth on his business, making him wince.

"Honey, you sure?"

"Yeah. I want you to."

"That fall was bad. You could be broke up inside. Maybe you ought not be alone."

"No. You can go."

"You gonna come see me?"

"Sure."

"It won't cost you nothing. You didn't finish, you know."

"I know. You go on, now."

She got up, put on her clothes. When she was at the door, she said, "I'm sorry about your guitar."

"Okay."

"You still got the harmonica."

Hillbilly snatched the damp rag off his crotch and threw it at her. "I said get out."

The rag struck her on the shoulder. She opened the door and went out quickly.

Hillbilly lay there and thought about what he would do next. Besides move slowly.

Then it came to him. Rooster had given him an idea. It wasn't the one Rooster had, the one he wanted him to do, it was another.

He thought about the red apartment over the drugstore, where McBride stayed. He had to go over there, talk to the man, see was there a place for him in this operation McBride and Henry had going.

One thing he prided himself on was he took the easy path on everything, unless it had to do with getting even. The easy path wasn't necessary then. He'd crawl over sharp rocks and kiss a mule's shitty ass to get back at someone did him wrong, especially some old man made him look and feel foolish in front of a goddamn whore.

He thought he'd get up right then, get dressed, go over and see McBride, but his body thought different.

It said: Lay down, boy. You ain't doing so good.

Hillbilly listened. Let his body have its way. But his mind raced, and his mind had ideas, and his mind was mean.

After they finished eating, and the ass whipping Lee had given Hillbilly was told another time, and everyone was sitting around inside the tent drinking coffee, Sunset slipped outside with a strip of white cloth she had torn from an old towel. She tied it to a limb on the back of the big oak tree.

Ben trotted up, watched her tie it. When she finished, she knelt down and gave him a pat.

All she could do now was see if Bull showed.

She hoped he would.

She needed him.

And she was pretty sure Zendo, though he didn't know it, needed him as well.

33

Couple of days went by and the white strip hung from the oak limb and the weather turned deadly hot and the trees sagged as if the sky were leaning its weight on them. Grasshoppers were everywhere, nibbling at what greenery they could find.

Walking about was like trudging through invisible bread dough and breathing was like sucking up dried leaves. At night, Sunset came out and sat by the oak. Clyde had taken to sleeping in his truck in the yard, and Lee was sleeping on the business side of the tent, with Goose, and she and Karen were sharing the other side.

But when everyone was sleeping, Sunset went out, found Ben, pulled a chair next to the oak, waited for Bull to show up. Sat there petting the dog until he tired of that business and lay down at her feet.

After a couple of nights, she was starting to have doubts Bull would show. He didn't really owe her anything, and what goodwill he felt for her may have passed. He might never come this way again, never even know a rag was hanging.

She thought about Hillbilly, remembered how he had touched her and cooed to her and made her feel. She thought about Karen, what he must have said to her to have his way. Maybe he said the same things to Karen he said to her. Though, now that she thought about it, she couldn't remember him making her a promise at all. Not with words, anyway, but his hands and lips and eyes spoke volumes, and those were all lies.

She was glad her daddy had kicked his ass.

And yet she hoped he wasn't hurt bad.

Hoped his looks weren't spoiled.

She didn't like him, but didn't like to think of him messed up, ruined. The kind of beauty he had ought not be ruined. Fact was, it shouldn't age, never change one teeny bit.

And what about Henry and McBride and the one called Two? What of them? What should she do?

She was thinking on this when Lee came out holding a cup of coffee in either hand. She looked up as he came over. "I thought you were asleep."

"You think I'm asleep every night when you come out here. Besides, Goose snores." He handed her a cup of coffee. "Thought you might want this."

She smiled at him. "Sure."

Lee had her hold both cups while he dragged the other chair over, sat down, took a cup and sipped it.

"Daddy, I'm in kind of a mess. I ain't sure what to do about things."

"You saying you want to tell me?"

"Yes."

And she did. Told him all of it, about Zendo and Zendo's land, about Henry Shelby and McBride and Two, about her talk with them in the church. And for the first time she told someone about Bull, about the rag she had tied to the oak.

She ended saying, "I think maybe they'll take it out on Zendo. I decided just now I'm going to have Clyde go there, maybe be a lookout, in case they send someone around. Have him go over there with a shotgun. And then there's Bull. He said he'd help."

"People say lots of things."

"Believe me, I know."

"I've said some things myself, but there's not a thing I say now I don't mean. Do you believe that?"

"I'm trying. I want to believe. But that's the story of my life, believing the wrong people."

"All right then, for what it's worth. You can look at this two ways. It ain't really your problem. You didn't cheat Zendo. It's not your fault someone might want him killed. You could just warn him, move on, let it go.

"Course, if he's out of the way, a little nifty work with a pen, that land could end up theirs. With him alive, they could do it anyway, but he might could make enough of a stink to prove it's his. So either way, you're taking a chance with his life."

"I want answers, not choices."

"I might have been able to give you some years ago, during my preacher days, cause I thought I knew everything. What I do know is you got to have a kind of center, Sunset. You follow me? You got to work out of that center, and you don't let that center shift. You may fail it, but you don't let it shift."

"All right, that's all well and good. But what do I do? I thought about telling Zendo, but I've been afraid to tell him. Thought that might be worse for him. He might say or do something he shouldn't."

Lee sipped coffee slowly, said, "In other words, you're not treating him like a man. You're treating him like a slave that needs tending, and you're his massa."

"I didn't say that."

"I'm saying how it seems to me."

"People here, a lot of them, they see it that way. That a colored ain't supposed to make too many decisions. I try and treat Zendo like he's not colored, and he thinks he can make some choices like everyone else, I could get him killed."

"You could treat him like a man, go to him, tell him the

truth, say, hey, I don't know what I can do for you. There's just me, and Clyde, and my run-down old man, and these guys, they're professionals and serious. Cheating and killing, that's what they do. So you're on your own. Then you've warned him. It's up to him to take care of himself. You could do that."

"And my center wouldn't have shifted?"

"You have to decide that. I can't tell you that. You got to feel you've done the right thing, what you could."

"Or?"

"You do the job you signed on for. Most of the time this job isn't anything much, but sometimes it might be. And when it is, do you decide then to not do it because it's hard? Could be you're not up to it, and if you're not, that's no shame, that's just the way it is. But if you're up to it and not willing, that's a whole different thing."

"How do you know you're up to it?"

"You don't. But you got to want to be up to it."

"And if I decide I want to be?"

"Plan. And count me in."

"Howdy."

Sunset and Lee jumped.

Ben sat up, looked embarrassed, like, man, I'm the goddamn dog here, and I didn't hear this fella, didn't see him.

Standing behind them, one hand on the back of Sunset's chair, was Bull. The air seemed charged with electricity, and it was full of an earthy smell that bit at their nostrils.

"Don't you ever come up normal?" Sunset said.

"I don't know normal," Bull said.

"Daddy, this is Bull."

"Hello, Bull," Lee said. "You damn near made me load my pants."

Bull grinned, gestured at the white strip hanging from the limb. "See you done hung the rag out. Need me?"

"I do," Sunset said.

"What way?"

"Zendo, a colored fella. He needs a protector."

"You mean the farmer?" Bull asked.

"Yeah. You know him?"

"Know who he is. Everyone knows who he is, cause of the way he farms, way his soil is, like it's magic or something. He can grow big old tomatoes in the hottest of weather, corn higher than two of me. He's the best there is. He's got a name for it."

"That's right," Sunset said. "Even while we're talking, it could have already happened, someone getting to him, hurting him and his family."

"Why would anyone do that?" Bull asked.

Sunset explained. When she finished, Bull went over and sat down with his back against the oak, considering. After a moment he said, "So you waited on me for this? Ain't there plenty of white men around? Your daddy looks ready enough. Little long in the tooth, like me, but them's the ones you got to watch, ain't that right, dad?"

"That's right," Lee said.

"You kind of waited a while to decide maybe Zendo needs help, didn't you?" Bull said.

"I don't think I really knew what I wanted until tonight," Sunset said. "I don't think he was in any real trouble till just lately, after I talked with Henry and McBride. But even then, I didn't really know what to do. Then tonight, I talked to Daddy, and well, he said some things, and it come together. I think. And frankly, this watching Zendo, I think you're better able to do it than me, or Clyde or Dad."

"Say you do?" Bull said.

"Don't you?" Sunset said.

"Maybe. But I do this. Zendo wants the help. You got to do something else. You got to stop these men want his land. Ain't that your law job?"

"It is."

"It would please me big to see a colored make big money, and that oil could do it."

"And it could make him a target," Lee said. "You can't spend money in the grave."

"Yeah, well, there's that," Bull said. "White folks can't hardly stand a nigger if he's gonna have money, especially if he might get more than them."

"We'll cross that bridge when we come to it," Sunset said.

"Lady," Bull said, "you can trust me to do what you want, but I got to trust you to do what I'm saying. You got to go after them bad men and take them down. Arrest them, whatever it is needs doing, you got to do it."

"All right," Sunset said.

"You got a gun, Bull?" Lee said. "Cause I figure you might need it."

Bull pulled up his shirt. A little pistol was in his waistband. "This just for close up. Leaning against a gum tree in the woods there, got me a pump ten-gauge. Thought maybe you'd take better to me I didn't stroll in with it in my hand."

"Ten-gauge will do," Lee said.

"You're telling me," Bull said.

"Sunset, is there anyone else you can go to for help?" Lee said. "More the merrier, something like this."

"Problem is," Sunset said, "I don't know who's in Henry's pocket, and who isn't. Don't know all who's Klan. I could take a chance here and there, but I'm thinking more people know about this, bigger we might make the problem. I could be lining up people I think are on my side, and they could be on Henry's."

Lee nodded. "That sounds right."

"What about you, girl?" Bull said. "Your family? You think on that?"

"All the time. I thought about sending Karen to her grandmother's, but that would just put Marilyn into it too. Wouldn't be any safer. Goose, course he don't know. Guess he ought to, so he'll have a choice to leave or stay. And Clyde, he knows everything, except he don't know about you."

"That him over there with his foot on the dash of that truck?" Bull asked, pointing to Clyde's old battered truck in the drive.

"That's him," Sunset said.

"All right, then," Bull said, "I know what needs to be. I'm gonna see Zendo, talk to him."

"When?" Sunset asked.

"Figure since I don't sleep much nohow, I'll go over there now, stay near till morning, watching. Zendo comes out tomorrow for work, I'll talk to him."

"Is Zendo's place close by?" Lee asked.

"No," Bull said. "But I can go through the woods, cut down on some distance."

"Better yet, I can drive you there, drop you off near the place," Lee said. "That is, if Sunset will loan me her car, and you'll show me the way."

After Bull recovered his ten-gauge and Lee drove off with him, Sunset walked by the truck where Clyde lay, peeked in. A flashlight shone in her face. She flinched, put her hand to her eyes.

"Sorry," Clyde said sitting up, turning off the light.

"I thought you were asleep," Sunset said.

329

"No. Just lying here. Listening to you and Lee and Bull talk."

"That's eavesdropping."

"It wasn't on purpose. I was sleeping here."

Sunset opened the truck door and slid in beside him as he sat up behind the steering wheel.

"You got a place of your own," she said.

"Sort of. If you count burned-up lumber."

"You saw Bull?"

"I rose up for a peek. He's large."

"I'll say."

"Do you think you can trust him?"

"He came to me. He told me to put a strip of cloth on that tree when I needed him, and he came. So, yeah. Clyde?"

"Yeah."

"I been pretty stupid—about Hillbilly, I mean."

"I agree."

"Sometimes, well . . . you can have something beautiful right in front of you, not see it because you're looking around it, trying to see something else."

"You're not talking about me, are you?"

"I am."

"Listen, Sunset . . . if I thought you meant that . . . I mean, I know you don't mean it . . . that way. But if you meant something good by it. Anything. It would make me happy. But I don't want pity."

"Don't make me mad, Clyde. I'll borrow that slap jack of yours and hit you with it. I'm an idiot. That's all I'm saying. I'm not proposing or anything. I'm not saying I'm in love. But I'm saying I was an idiot and you tried to tell me. You're a good friend."

"Again," Clyde said, "I got to agree with you."

"Be all right if I give you a kiss?"

"Just friendly, you mean?"

"Sure."

Sunset leaned over and kissed Clyde on the cheek.

"That kiss wasn't pity, was it?" Clyde asked.

"Don't be silly, Clyde. There's nothing to pity about you."

"You're not just saying that?"

"I'm not. It was what it was."

"Whatever it was, it was good enough. Good night," Clyde said.

34

Next morning, when Zendo got his mules out of the shed out back of his house, fed them, dressed them in harness and took them to the field, he found Bull sitting under his oak where he stopped for lunch every day. He had seen Bull only a few times before, but now, up close, he was frightened by him. He was huge and his hair was wild and he had a kind of dead look in his eye, way a fish does when it's laid out of water too long.

Zendo had been leading the mules with their lines, ready to hook them to the plow he had left in the field, but when he saw Bull he stopped by calling "Whoa" to the mules.

"You Zendo?" Bull asked.

Zendo nodded.

"How you doing, Mr. Bull?" Zendo said, walking around from behind the mules, standing to the side of one, holding the long lines.

"Oh, I'm making it. Ain't no reason to complain, I reckon, as it don't change much if I do."

"Well, me too, I reckon."

"Naw," Bull said, "you ain't doing so good."

Zendo felt a sensation akin to someone suddenly poking a stick up his ass. If there was one thing he didn't want, it was having the legendary Bull Stackerlee mad at him. It amazed him Bull even knew who he was.

"How's that, Mr. Bull?" Zendo said, surprised at how high his voice sounded.

"Well, now, let me say on that different," Bull said, standing up from the tree. "In one way, you doing so good the angels would sing, and you don't even know it, and in another, you got your dick in a wringer and whitey, he's got his hand on the crank."

"That's quite some difference, one from the other," Zendo said.

"It is," Bull said. "You want the good news first, or you want the shit?"

Zendo, as confused as if he had awakened in another town and found himself naked, said, "Well, Mr. Bull, I think it would be best to get the bad news out of the way, then have the sugar."

Hillbilly half filled a cup with water from a pitcher, held the cup under his balls, and by spreading his legs and bending his knees, lowered them into it. It helped ease the pain a mite. He stood like that, as if riding an invisible horse, his left hand holding the cup of water and his balls, and with his other hand, he drank directly from a bottle of whisky.

Last night he had been drunk, and he awakened this morning feeling terrible, had to have enough of the hair of the dog to take the edge off the buzz, but he wasn't drunk now and he wasn't going to get drunk today. What he was going to do was get dressed, go over to see this McBride fella.

It took him a while to scrape his life into a heap, but he finally got dressed and went out. It was a hot day and the sky, though blue, looked heavy, as if it might fall and crush him. There were a few strands of clouds, like strips of cotton torn from a blue mattress, stretched out across the sky.

The street was full of dust and grasshoppers. Hillbilly had never seen that many on a street before. In a field maybe, but not like this, leaping all over and in the middle of town.

333

Hillbilly, walking slightly bowlegged, grasshoppers jumping about as he went, waddled to Main Street, over to the red apartment above the drugstore. It took him a while to get there, and when he went up the stairs it was sheer pain. He hurt everywhere, but the small of his back, from the fall, and his balls, from the kick, were the worst. Every step, those two places felt as if they were being struck with an iron rod.

When he reached the landing he knocked on the door, and after a while it was answered by the blond whore he had had with him when Sunset's old man broke in.

"Well," he said, "you get around."

She looked at him for a long moment, said, "I am a whore, you know."

"Oh, I know," Hillbilly said.

"How are you?"

"Never better."

"You looking for me?"

"I wouldn't have known where to look. And no. I wasn't."

"Why are you here?"

"At least that's a question I don't have to ask you, is it?"

"No," she said, "I suppose not. I still owe you a finish."

"Sure," Hillbilly said. "McBride, he in?"

She nodded. "Go now, and I'll tell him you were a salesman."

"Why would I do that?"

"I got some ideas about what you want to do," she said. "I don't know all of it, but I know enough from hearing things here, know what happened to you, and I can put some of it together. Like maybe you want to get back at that woman constable, her father, through these men. But these people, they're bad, Hillbilly."

"You do pick up a lot of information."

"I get around."

"I bet you do," he said. "But, darling, I'm bad too."

"Not really."

"Oh, yeah," Hillbilly said. "Really."

She took a deep breath, let it out.

"You answer the door along with selling ass?" he asked.

"I do pretty much what I'm told to do."

"I'm telling you, get the man."

"You aren't paying me. I do it for money, Hillbilly. You, you haven't given me a dime."

"But I gave you a good time."

"You and everyone else. I thought, you and me . . ."

Hillbilly grinned. "Every woman I know thinks that."

The blonde's face got tough. She said, "Wait here."

It was a great patch of land and once it had been covered in trees, but they had long since been cut, gone to the mill, except for three. The three were two oaks and a sweet gum, and the oaks were at the front of the house, and the sweet gum was to one side. The house was two-story and it had a porch around the bottom that went all the way around, and it had the same on the second floor. It was painted white as hope and the grass that had been planted had been cut close to the ground by enough negroes with push mowers to form a tribe. Dry as it was, the short grass was well watered and pretty green.

Sunset noted that it was more of a house than Marilyn had and she owned a chunk of the mill. But here Henry's house was, bold as a tick on a patrician's ass, not caring if the look of it made you wonder where the money came from.

Sunset, Clyde with her, parked her car in front of the place, sat and looked.

Clyde said, "That bottom porch is big enough to live on."

Sunset got out of the car and went across the lawn, Clyde

hustling to catch up. They went up to the door and she knocked. The door was opened by a big fat colored woman with a bandanna on her head and enough pattern in her floor-length dress to confuse and make you dizzy. There was a noise inside, a kind of snapping sound. It came and went, but it was pretty steady.

"Yes, ma'am, what you be wanting?" the colored woman said.

"Henry," Sunset said. "I want to see Henry."

"I go ask him."

"No," Sunset said. "That's all right. We'll just come in."

"I got to have you invited," the maid said. "I just got this job."

"It may not be a job long," Sunset said. "Sorry."

"She's the constable," Clyde said.

The maid studied the badge on Sunset's shirt. "She sure is. I ain't gonna be stopping no law."

The maid stepped aside and Sunset and Clyde went in.

"Where is he?" Sunset said. The maid pointed, and at the same time Sunset saw him. He was in front of a large fireplace mantel, a couch between them and himself, taking ceramic knickknacks off of the mantel, throwing them down as hard as he could. He had hold of a pink cat when they came up. He threw it down and smashed it and its pieces mixed with the stuff already there.

Henry looked up as they came into view.

"Hate these things," he said. "Wife had them all over."

"Nice way to treasure her memory," Clyde said, "smashing her knickknacks."

Henry smirked. "What you want, girl? Think over what I told you the other day?"

"I did."

"I take it, him here, you decided not to go with what I suggested."

336

Sunset nodded.

"That's your choice, girl. Now, thanks for coming to tell me. Leave."

"We're leaving all right," Sunset said. "Leaving with you."

Henry's mouth opened slightly. "You ain't gonna arrest me?"

"I am."

"What for?"

"All the things you told me the other day."

"I didn't tell you nothing. I was just talking. It's just my word against yours."

"I'm the law. You shouldn't have told the law."

Henry's face looked as if he had just been given a mouthful of alum.

"Thought I could talk to you," he said, "reason with you. I said some things that were tough, but I thought you'd listen. Thought you were smart."

"Guess you were wrong," Sunset said. "Clyde. Bring him along. He resists, knock the hell out of him."

Clyde went over, said, "Resist, Henry. Make me a happy man."

As they went out the door, Clyde holding Henry by the arm, the maid said to Henry, "Want me to sweep up that mess you made back there?"

Henry didn't answer.

"You gonna pay me?"

He still didn't answer.

"Then you gonna clean it up yourself, that's what you're gonna do. I ain't got nothing against them knackers."

". . . and I can be of help," Hillbilly said, finishing off a kind of diatribe, and when he said it, he tried not to let his voice crack, hoped he wasn't sweating too bad. It was hot in the apartment, but he was sweating more than the man in front of him, McBride. McBride was sitting in a chair that he had drawn up right in front of Hillbilly, whom he had asked to sit on a low couch by the wall.

Hillbilly sat there with his hands in his lap, for once not thinking about how bad he hurt, because this McBride, his eyes made Hillbilly queasy, and he was wearing a funny wig and a goddamn apron. A frilly thing that went from chest to knees, had red splatters on it. But he didn't look sissy and it didn't seem funny. Not this fella.

Maybe he was just getting soft, getting his ass whipped like that by an old man, and it was making him less confident about everything and everybody. He hadn't had an ass whipping since he was a boy and his daddy beat him with a razor strop, beat him unconscious a couple of times. But since leaving home he hadn't lost a fight, and now he had lost one to an old man, and here was another old man, and he was scared of him. More scared of him than of Sunset's father. This fella, something had fallen away from him that ought to be there, that was for damn sure. You could see it in his eyes.

That wasn't bad enough, there was the big nigger too, and he was called Two, and he had been talking to himself, asking questions like someone was with him, not questions directed at him or McBride, but questions in the air, questions he answered himself. And now, goddamn it, the big nigger was sitting on the couch beside him, and he had one hand on Hillbilly's knee, and Hillbilly, he couldn't figure that, didn't know what that was about, but the hand lay there like a big black crab, heavy and warm and firm as a log grapple.

The blonde had been made to leave the room, and he wished she was there, wished he had been nicer to her. He needed a friendly face right now. These fellas, he found it hard to charm them. Men were like that a lot of the time, saw through him, maybe not all the way, but deep enough to get bothered. Women, that was another matter. He liked to talk to women. He liked to move around women, and they liked to watch him move, but these two, or was it three, they weren't impressed.

"So, you want to get even with this guy you had a fight with?" McBride said, lighting his cigar. He was sitting there in his frilly white apron and his nigger-black wig, and the big coon, he was wearing a jacket like you might expect to see on one of those guys had a wand, waved it around in front of a band, an orchestra. He had on a bowler hat too.

"That's one thing, yeah," Hillbilly said. "Another is, I thought maybe I could make some money."

"You know all about the oil deal, to hear you tell it," McBride said. "You know everything."

Hillbilly nodded.

"Knowing everything, that could get you in some shit, couldn't it, Two?"

"It could," Two said. And then, in another voice. "That's the facts, my friend."

"Show him just a little bit of shit, Two," McBride said. Two squeezed Hillbilly's kneecap so hard, Hillbilly thought it would pop off. He reached down with both hands and got hold of Two's wrist.

Two said, "Let go." And his other voice said, "Yes, do."

Hillbilly let go, and Two, he kept squeezing, and Hillbilly, without even realizing it, put the side of his hand in his mouth and bit down on the flesh to keep from screaming. Just when he thought he was going to bite through his own hand or his kneecap was going to come off, Two let go, gave Hillbilly's thigh a pat.

"That's a little shit," McBride said. "I don't like someone

knowing my business, and me not telling it to them. I don't like you getting it from Rooster, cause I don't like Rooster. He ran off, you know. Smarter than he looked. I didn't have much more use for him and I guess he knew it, figured what was coming. You, maybe I got some use for. That face of yours, it heals up, bet it looks pretty good. It look good?"

"Yes," Hillbilly said. "It does. But my nose, it ain't never gonna be straight again."

McBride burst out laughing, and Two, he grinned, big and wide and white.

"I fought Jack Johnson once, before he was anybody," McBride said. "He broke my nose. I didn't even know it till later. It hadn't been for a hurricane coming, messing up our fight, I think I'd have won. Never got to find out. We had to stop it before it got started good. A nose, it's a funny thing. It'll break easy. Let me show you."

McBride leaned out of his chair very fast and hit Hillbilly in the nose with a short right. Blood sprayed and Hillbilly dropped his head and moaned.

"You just thought it was broke before," McBride said. "Wasn't nothing before. Now it's something. You come to me, and you tell me things I don't think you ought to know, and I'm thinking, thing to do is have Two give you the big nigger job. He can twist your head off like you was a chicken, fuck your neck stump while you bleed out. He could do that, and he wouldn't bat an eye. I could do it, but I don't want to get blood on my dick. You hear me, Used To Be A Pretty Boy?"

"Yeah," Hillbilly said. "I hear you."

"Good. I'm gonna let you live, but take what we done here as a kind of lesson, a message. You twisted on that gal, come to me, and that's all right, but you twist on me, I'll twist you. Hear me?"

"Yeah. I hear you. Loud and clear."

"That's good. That's damn good. Now let me tell you what you're gonna do, and at this stage of our association, you ain't got no say anymore, hear me?"

"Yeah."

Two slid over and put his arm around Hillbilly's shoulders. When Hillbilly turned, Two was real close, his white teeth grinning, his green eyes bright as emeralds.

He turned back to McBride, and McBride began to talk.

While Sunset and Clyde were gone, Lee and Goose and Karen, using Clyde's pickup, had moved the tent and all the belongings, making four or five trips, to Clyde's place.

When Sunset and Henry and Clyde pulled up at Clyde's place, the tent was up, and out to one side of it was the tarp Clyde had erected, and to the other side, the house he had burned down. Out front of the tent a large post had been cut and there was a thick chain fastened around the post, fixed so that it ran through a place drilled in the center. The chain was pretty long and Ben was fastened to the chain by means of a collar made out of an old belt. Lee and Goose and Karen came out of the tent and Lee was carrying a chair with him.

"What in hell are you doing?" Henry said.

"Jail," Sunset said. "You're going to jail."

"What jail?"

Sunset put the car in gear and pulled up the hand brake, turned in the seat to look at Henry, who sat in the back with Clyde. Clyde had used a short piece of rope to tie Henry's hands together, and Henry looked as mad as a hornet in a fruit jar.

"That's exactly what I got to thinking," Sunset said. "What jail? I need a jail for Henry, but I haven't got one. And I got to thinking too, you got friends, and I take you to my place, leave you there, they might come and see me. So, we've moved. People know where I live, that's got around, but Clyde, they might not think of his place, and if they do, well, Clyde, he's lived out here pretty much by himself for years. Right, Clyde?"

"Oh, yeah. And except for Hillbilly for a while, I ain't had any visitors, so anyone might matter to you, I doubt they know where I live. It could be found out, but that's what shotguns are for, nosy bastards."

"You're gonna regret this, girlie," Henry said.

"I already regret it," Sunset said. "Regret the day I took this job and found out anything about you."

Henry looked puzzled. "Then let me go. Drop the job. Take off. Hell, the money offer is still open. We can toss Clyde in too."

"I regret the day, all right," Sunset said, "but there's this thing about having a center, and damn it, I got one, and I don't want it to shift."

"Do what?" Henry said.

"You wouldn't understand," Sunset said.

They took Henry out of the car. When they got to the post in front of the tent, Sunset spoke to Lee, said, "Well, Daddy, is the post in solid?"

"Ben thinks so. He tugged for a while, then laid down."

"All right, then."

Clyde went in the tent, came out with a pair of handcuffs and a padlock. He used a knife to cut Henry loose, then put the handcuffs on him.

Sunset took the collar off Ben, who came over and sniffed Henry's crotch like he might like to bite it off.

"What in hell are you doing?" Henry said.

"Putting you in jail," Sunset said. She looped the chain through the cuffs and used the small padlock to stick between links.

Lee put the chair up against the post.

"This is your jail," Sunset said.

"Out here?" Henry said.

"It's kind of shaded," Sunset said.

"You can't do this."

"Sure I can. Just hope I haven't lost the keys to the cuffs or the padlock. Sit down, or I'll have Clyde sit you down. Karen, go get Henry some water, would you?"

"You are going from bad to worse," Henry said.

"Sit down, Henry."

"How long you going to keep me here?"

"I don't know. I got to figure what to do with you, which lawman will not let you go, which ones aren't with the Klan or got Klan connections, or who won't change their minds by letting money touch their hands."

"You may find that a difficult person to find," Henry said.

"Not everyone's crooked," Sunset said.

"I believe they are," Henry said. "I believe, it comes to push or shove, everyone's crooked, or at least willing to compromise. It's the way of the world, girlie."

"Sir," Lee said, "call my daughter girlie one more time, and we'll see how many times I can chase you around that post before the chain seizes up."

Henry sat in silence. Karen came with a cup of water. Henry took it and threw it on the ground.

"Damn, Henry, and that's all you get until nightfall," Clyde said.

"Can I sic Ben on him?" Goose said.

"Not just yet, honey," Sunset said.

35

The tan Plymouth hummed through the darkness like a bee, and though it was hot, the windows were mostly rolled up because of the grasshoppers. The grasshoppers were everywhere. Even now, at night, they were hopping in front of the lights and making little messes against the front of the car.

Plug pulled the car to the side of the road and picked up the bottle on the seat, twisted off the cap and took a sip and the smell of whisky filled the air. Hillbilly, sitting on the front passenger side, said, "You don't need none of that."

"I've already had plenty."

"That's what I'm saying. You don't need any more."

"I don't get why you're sheriff. Never even heard of you before, and now with Rooster gone, they make you sheriff. Just seen you once, with the redhead, and now you're sheriff."

"For one thing," Hillbilly said, "I'm not stupid."

"You better watch it," Plug said. "You don't want me on your ass."

Hillbilly laughed.

Tootie, who was sitting in the backseat, shifted the shotgun on his lap, said, "I think we all ought to have some. We're gonna need it. I could get out right now and start walking, and that's what I ought to do, start walking, but if I'm gonna stay, gonna do this thing, I'm gonna need some of that. We all ought to have some."

Two, sitting beside him, a shotgun across his lap, said, "No one walks anywhere."

"That's right," Two's other self answered. "We all stay. Get the car moving."

"I want a drink," Tootie said. "I don't think a brain-kicked nigger talks to himself ought to tell me I can't have a drink. A nigger ought not tell a white man anything."

Two lifted the shotgun in his lap casually and put it to Tootie's right ear and pulled the trigger. The blast took off the top of Tootie's head and took out the window and peppered the inside of the car with shot. There was blood all over the back of Hillbilly's neck, all over the backseat, all over Two and his black jacket and his black bowler hat and the inside of the car smelled like sulphur.

Plug jerked open the door and leaped out. He raced around to the front of the car and put both hands on the hood. He said, "Goddamn. Goddamn."

Hillbilly hadn't moved. He felt Tootie's blood running down the back of his neck.

"I don't like people who don't want to finish what they start," Two said.

"Me neither," said the Other Two.

"No," Hillbilly said, his hands trembling on the shotgun in his lap. "I don't like them either."

"Open the back door," Two said. "Drag him out."

Hillbilly placed the shotgun carefully and slowly on the seat. He couldn't have been more slow and careful if it was an egg that already had a crack in it. He didn't look back at Two. He got out and opened the back door. When he did, Two said, "Stand back," and lying with his back against his door, he put both feet on Tootie and kicked him out. Tootie fell to the side of the road in a sitting position. Grasshoppers were everywhere, and soon they were all over the body.

Two got out and came around and laid his shotgun on the ground. He lifted Tootie's head, fanned at grasshoppers with his big hand, leaned forward until his mouth was close to Tootie's. Two reached behind Tootie's head, his long thumb and longer forefinger locking into the hinges of Tootie's jaw. He squeezed and Tootie's already open mouth went wider and Two bent close and put his mouth over Tootie's mouth.

"Good God," Hillbilly said, "what in God's name are you doing?"

Two sucked at Tootie's mouth for a moment. Then he dropped Tootie in the dust.

"What God wants," said Two.

"I ate his soul," the Other Two said. "Ate it and it was sweet."

"Good God," Plug said from the front of the car.

Two picked up the shotgun and stood, said to Hillbilly, "Drag him off."

The Other Two said, "Pull him in the woods there."

Hillbilly did as he was told, and promptly. As he dragged Tootie away, grasshoppers leaped in all directions and when he got to the edge of the woods he saw the foliage was all eaten away by the hoppers and the brush was just sticks. Hillbilly pulled Tootie through the bare brush, back where there were some big trees, and left him lying on some pine needles.

Two walked over to Plug, said, "You got trouble doing what you're supposed to do?"

"Wasn't no cause for that," Plug said. "He was just talking. We all got second thoughts. He didn't mean nothing by it. Wasn't no need in that. We ain't like you—either of you. We ain't done this kind of thing before."

The big man stood silent, the shotgun cradled in his arms. He tilted his head to one side.

Plug said, "I'm over it. I ain't got no second thoughts."

*

346

Hillbilly cut off a piece of Tootie's shirt, used it to wipe the blood off the back of his neck. He dropped the cloth on the ground, went back, got in the car. The sound of the shot going off had not been right in his ear, but he had a ringing in it. Everything he heard, he heard well enough to understand, but it was as if the words were being called up to him from inside a cave.

Plug started the engine, said, "All I'm saying, Two, is you didn't have to do that. He didn't mean nothing. He was just nervous. He's got a wife, a kid."

"You think these others don't?" Two said. "Think he's any better than them? There's no need to put good or bad or wives and kids into it. That sort of thing doesn't matter. It's not in God's universe. Babies die all the time. Old folks die all the time. God isn't concerned with dying. He's concerned with souls."

And the Other Two said, "You think it matters to me? You think anything matters to me? Wives and kids, they die like anyone else. We hold all the souls we can, and when God calls us, we give them to him. Our death will be worth more than the multitude, because we are the multitude."

"I can see that," Hillbilly said, and cocked an eye at Plug.

Two said, "When we get through, this car is gonna take some real cleaning."

"And we got to order a glass," the Other Two said. "And get some paint. Brother McBride likes this car and he'll want it fixed."

When they came to the place where Sunset lived there was only the floor of the house where the tent had been and the outhouse and the tall post where Marilyn had started a clothesline.

"They done run off," Plug said. "We ain't gonna have to kill nobody."

"I don't think they run off," Hillbilly said.

"Sure they run off," Plug said. "They didn't, where are they?"

347

"They don't know I'm with you," Hillbilly said. "They don't know I got some ideas about where they are. They're hiding all right, but not the way you mean."

"Tell us," Two said.

"I think we should try Clyde's," Hillbilly said. "I was them, that's where I'd go, take my tent with me, start over."

"Clyde?" Two said.

"Deputy," Hillbilly said.

"What about Henry?" Two said. "Brother McBride said he was arrested today. Said some maid told someone and someone told another someone, and then Brother McBride got the news."

The Other Two said, "That's what this is all about, you know. Henry. And the woman."

"And the others?" Plug said. "It about them?"

"It is," said Two. "It's about them and this Zendo."

"But Zendo, he don't know nothing," Plug said.

"He may know something now," the Other Two said. "But what about Henry?"

"He's with them," Hillbilly said. "Ain't nobody around here gonna help them. They got to have him with them. If they're at Clyde's, he'll be there too. They got to be at Clyde's, or Marilyn's, Sunset's mother-in-law, and I don't think they'd go there. Too obvious, too easy. But Clyde's, that would be the place."

"That's good," said Two. "And the mother-in-law?"

"I don't know she's a problem," Hillbilly said.

The Other Two said, "We'll consider on that. I'll tell Brother McBride, and he'll consider on it. Hillbilly, you direct us. And Plug, drive us, please."

"I ought to have to do something important," Goose said. "Good as you been to me, miss. Good as Lee's been."

"What I want you to do," Sunset said, "is help Clyde out. Me

348

and Daddy, we're going over to Zendo's, see how it's going with Bull. I've had an idea I think might be good."

"I just want to help," Goose said.

"I know, and thanks for asking. Stay with Clyde and Karen and Ben, watch old Henry here and the tent. That's your job and it's important."

They were standing outside the tent, near the post where Henry was chained, sitting in his chair in the moonlight.

A plate he had eaten off of was on the ground and Ben was licking it.

"Can't you make this dog go on?" Henry said. "He peed on the post a while ago. I don't like having him around. He keeps sniffing me."

"If I wanted to do something about him, guess I could," Sunset said.

Lee came out of the tent. Sunset and Lee got in Sunset's car. Lee said, "Sure we should leave them here?"

"No one knows about this place, not even people that know Clyde. He doesn't have visitors. It's a good idea, being here."

"Living under a tarp, I can see that he doesn't have visitors," Lee said.

"Actually," Sunset said, "it's nicer than the house he burned down. And now, there's the tent."

"That tent is getting pretty crowded," Lee said. "When this is over, back on your land, we ought to build a house, help Clyde build one here."

"We'll see," Sunset said.

After they hit the main road the lights were full of grasshoppers and a tan Plymouth passing them.

"Slow here," Hillbilly said. "It ain't so easy to see the place in the dark. Right there. Turn there. Road ends at his place."

"How far?" Two asked.

"Not real far," Hillbilly said. "A piece. But not far."

"Go down a ways, pull over and park," said Two. "We'll walk down and see them."

"We'll take what God needs," the Other Two said.

Plug took the turn and the road was dusty and the dust rose up as they went, like a heavy mist, and grasshoppers jumped out of it, splattered against the windshield, which was already greasy with them. Plug drove a short piece, pulled in where there was a stretch of clearing, turned off the lights and parked.

Hillbilly and Two had twelve-gauge pumps. Plug had a .45 revolver. Two said, "We'll say what and when and how."

"Yeah," Hillbilly said, "you fellas are the boss."

"You say we, you mean, you, right?" Plug said.

"I mean the both of us," Two said.

Plug nodded. "All right. I see that—I think."

They got out of the car, walked down the road a ways, then Two stopped them.

"We'll go ahead," Two said. "You come down the road walking. When you hear us cut down, you come running."

"Why don't we just sneak up on them?" Plug said.

Two turned his head slowly. He took off his bowler and shook out the sweat. The horseshoe scar looked raw in the moonlight. "We'll sneak."

"We as in . . . you two?" Plug asked.

"Correct," the Other Two said. "Understand?"

"Sure," Plug said.

Two nodded, went down the road quickly, then went into the woods and was gone.

Plug said, "I say we go back to the car, drive away and keep driving."

"There's lots of money in this," Hillbilly said.

"Wasn't saying there wasn't money in it. I'm saying I don't care anymore. Tootie was supposed to get money too, wasn't he? He ain't getting no money now. So what's money to him?"

"Nothing to him," Hillbilly said, "but maybe it's more for us. We could ask McBride about Tootie's share. We could maybe split it."

Plug looked at the dirt road. "Don't know I want to kill no woman. Don't know I want to kill nobody. Tootie . . . dying like that, that was bad enough. I once shot a deer and got sick."

"You can't think of them as people. Got to think of them as targets. That's the way you do it, Plug."

"You was her friend," Plug said.

"I don't feel any different about her now than I did before. I don't care for her daddy, or Clyde, cause of what they done, but her, I don't feel any different. It hasn't got anything to do with the way you feel."

"The hell it doesn't."

"You going in, or not?"

About that time they heard a shotgun blast, and Hillbilly said, "That's Two. Means it's time for us."

Hillbilly started trotting down the road, and Plug, after a moment's hesitation, went after him.

Way it went down was Two came up on the left side of Clyde's place, came through the woods with his shotgun ready, quiet as a dead mouse in a cotton ball, moving toe heel, and when he got where he could see Henry chained to the post, he thought about what McBride had said. He said, "Brother, Henry ain't no good to us. He's got too big a mouth, and he ain't ever gonna be happy having a nigger get part of it. Henry don't need the money he's supposed to get. Me and you, we do. Henry, he's played his string and he's just another soul for you to gather."

Two went out of the woods and started walking toward Henry. Henry looked up, smiled, said softly, "Good to see you, Two."

"Good to see you," Two said, lifted the shotgun and fired, knocked Henry out of his chair, drove him back against the post.

Two pumped up another load as Ben came running, growling. He shot Ben and Ben's legs went out from under him. Ben skidded in the dirt, yelped and fell, his side puffing up and down in big motions.

Inside the tent, the first shot caused Clyde to poke his head out, then pull it back in as the second shot was fired and Ben went down. Clyde wasn't near a gun when the shots went off, and when he pulled his head back in, he grabbed his shotgun. When he looked back out the colored assassin was much closer, putting the finishing touches on Henry, shooting him a second time in the body, leaning over him, putting his face close to Henry's face. Clyde was about to shoot, looked up, saw trotting down the dusty road Hillbilly and Plug, Hillbilly with a shotgun, Plug with pistol drawn, and he knew then how they had found them.

"Out the back," Clyde said, and pushed Goose, who was trying to come forward with one of Clyde's pistols, toward Karen, who was already at the back of the tent.

Clyde pulled out his clasp knife and flipped it open. Just before Two lifted the front tent flap, he cut the back of the tent open and they all three went out and started running through the woods, grasshoppers exploding all around them with a beat of wings. Behind them they could hear running, and when Clyde looked over his shoulder he saw the big colored man in the bowler was gaining, running fast for a big man, so smooth it was like he was part of the night itself.

"Go left," Clyde said, knowing a trail was coming up. "Go left."

And Karen did. It was a narrow trail through the woods and the moonlight was not as bright there. Karen was wearing a dress and blackberry vines tore at it and Clyde could hear it rip and hear her grunt as the blackberry thorns tore her flesh.

Goose fell behind Clyde as they ran, and Clyde turned to look for him.

Goose wasn't there.

Goose thought: Sunset told me to watch after things, and I ain't done it. I just turned and ran. We all turned and ran.

And with the big pistol hanging heavy in his hand, Goose started running back toward Two, thinking: I will surprise him. I will shoot his ass before he realizes I'm on him.

And just as Goose was turning the trail, lifting his pistol, ready to surprise Two, the big colored man surprised him by being there suddenly, as if he had sprung up from the ground like a giant grasshopper.

And Goose stopped and pointed the pistol with both hands, pulled the trigger, thought: How can I miss? I'm close. But he did miss.

Two didn't. The blast lifted up Goose and knocked him back and slapped him to the ground. Goose tried to lift the pistol, but found he wasn't holding it anymore. He wasn't holding anything anymore. In fact, the shot had cut off his right thumb and some of his fingers and had gone on and hit him in the stomach. He didn't feel pain. He just felt hot and stunned and breathless.

Now the big man in the bowler was standing over him. He dropped to his knees beside Goose. The man took off the bowler and put it on the ground. "You're real fresh, son," he said. "Real fresh."

"That's the way we like them," said the Other Two.

Goose tried to figure that, the two voices, the one man, but

353

he couldn't, and he couldn't think of anything but what an idiot he had been, running back like that, and he was dying now, and he knew it, and he hadn't never had any pussy or done much of anything but work hard, and it was all over now, and then the man had his mouth over Goose's mouth, sucking, and Goose tried to fight but his hands wouldn't lift and he tried to bite, but he couldn't have chewed snow, weak as he was, and he didn't feel hot anymore, he felt cold, and now he felt pain, but that didn't last, cause a moment later, he didn't feel anything.

Clyde wanted to go back, started to, but he had Karen to protect, and Goose, maybe he'd taken another trail, though Clyde couldn't think of one, knowing these woods like he did, but he kept running after Karen.

The trail came to an end. They stood on the bank of the creek, and here the bank was high up with lots of trees growing out from it, their roots exposed, and Clyde grabbed Karen's arm, said, "I'm going to lower you down."

She took his hand and he leaned out and lifted her as if she were a doll, eased her over the edge, and lowered her, said, "Take hold of that limb, and swing under there. There's a place."

It was a washout under the roots, and from where they had stood on the bank, you couldn't see it. It was pretty big, and as Clyde lowered her down she got hold of one of the roots, let go of his hand and swung herself out of view. He thought: Hope there ain't no moccasins in there.

When she was out of sight, Clyde bent down close to the bank, called softly, "Can you hear me?"

"Yes," Karen said.

"I'm handing the shotgun down. Be careful. Reach out and take it. I'll swing it on my belt."

"Okay," Karen said.

Clyde took off his belt, fastened it around the stock of the shotgun, bent down close again, swung it out and back into the hole. Karen grabbed it and he let go of the belt.

He got hold of a root and swung out and down, got hold of another, lowered himself so he could swing inside the wash with Karen. He had to bend his head slightly to fit, but it was the way he remembered. One time he had gone fishing and had waded out in the creek to get his line untangled, and he had seen the wash. It was almost half as tall as a man and very wide and pretty deep. The only difference now was that the creek had been high a few times and it had washed it out even more.

When he felt Karen close to him, squatting, leaning against him, he reached in his pocket, got a matchbox, took a match out and struck it.

A beaver was at the far side of the indention, and it hissed at them and bared its teeth. It looked like a big hairy rat there in the light of the wavering match.

Karen huddled closer to him.

"Hold this match," Clyde said, took the shotgun and used it to poke at the beaver until it sprang past them, made Karen squeak slightly, leaped into the water and swam away.

The match went out.

"Be quiet now," Clyde said. "Up against the back of the wash, and be quiet."

"I'm scared," Karen said.

"Then we're scared together."

"Goose?"

"We can't think about that now. Be quiet, I said."

They eased back until they were as far as they could go, and quit squatting, sat down, waiting, listening.

*

355

At the front of the trail Clyde and Karen had taken, Two could see blackberry vines had been ripped and disturbed where they had once grown tight on either side of the trail.

As he stood there looking, Hillbilly and Plug came up, Plug pushing his revolver into its holster.

"You're slow," Two said.

"You done killed everybody?" Plug said. "We seen that boy. He wasn't nothing but a kid."

"Silence," the Other Two said. "They went this way."

"Sunset?" Hillbilly asked.

"A big man and a girl," Two said.

"Probably Clyde and Karen," Hillbilly said.

"Henry, you shot him too," Plug said. "I thought we just come to get him."

"We got him all right," the Other Two said.

"You got him, and Tootie. What's to keep you from getting us?" Plug asked. "You might want to suck our faces too. Did you suck the dog?"

"No soul," Two said. "God didn't give animals souls."

"What about you?" Plug asked. "You got one?"

Two grabbed Plug by the shirt and shoved him back. Plug dropped his hand to his gun, but didn't pull it. He said, "All right. All right."

"No more," Two said. "Not a word."

Plug nodded.

Two started trotting down the trail, Hillbilly and Plug behind him.

Clyde and Karen sat in the wash and listened to an owl hoot and the creek water run. They saw a coon cross in the moonlight, splashing water, clambering to the other bank, melting into the brush and trees. Grasshoppers were rattling and rustling through the brush and they could see hundreds of dead ones in the water, washing by.

After a while they heard the crunching of leaves and such and the sound of running feet coming nearer. Karen tensed and grabbed hold of Clyde. Clyde sat with his legs crossed, the shotgun lying across one thigh, listening. It was hot in the wash and sweat ran down his face and stuck to the inside of his shirt, and he could feel dampness from Karen and he could smell something too. Fear.

The running stopped above them and there was the sound of someone breathing heavy. Clyde guessed Plug. Thought: They stopped right here? Why? They see some sign?

No. No sign. These guys, they wouldn't know sign.

Or would they?

Could they read where they left the trail, dropped over the side into the creek?

And if they could, would they know there was a wash here? Maybe they'd come down into the creek, and from here, he would have a shot.

Still, there were three of them. And he had the girl.

But they could have stopped because the trail widened here, there was room to spread out, take a breather. Maybe—

"There ain't no use," he heard Hillbilly say. "Clyde, he knows these woods good as a goddamn squirrel."

Then Clyde heard someone, the big colored man, he figured, though he sounded very educated, very smooth, a Yankee colored, say, "Brother McBride isn't going to be happy."

"We should go back and wait on them," another voice said, and Clyde didn't know who it was. He didn't sound colored or Southern either. Maybe it was the other white guy, but he had seen him around, knew he was from around here, and that didn't sound like a local's voice. Was there a fourth person? Someone he hadn't seen?

"No," said the first voice, the one he thought must be the colored man. "They won't come back. They won't do that."

Then there was movement, followed by silence, and they sat for a long time listening to nothing. Then there was an explosion. So loud Karen made a little yip.

She put her hand over her mouth, bent double. Clyde reached out and patted her gently on the shoulders.

Clyde found that he was breathing heavy. He took a deep breath and let it out slowly through his nose.

Easy, now, he told himself.

Easy, now. It didn't sound that close. It was just loud. It might have been a gun, but it didn't sound like one. No. It wasn't a gun. The more he thought on it, the more certain he was it wasn't a gun.

But what was it?

They waited about five more minutes, Clyde counting out what he thought was five minutes in his head.

Clyde thought: No, don't go up there. That could be just what they're waiting for. Us to show our faces. Maybe that's what they're doing. Lying in wait.

But the explosion? What was that?

Clyde rested the shotgun across his knees, wiped his damp hands on his shirt. He used his hand to wipe sweat from his eyes, dried his hands on his shirtfront again.

They waited. Twenty minutes or so went by. Again, Clyde figuring it in his head, deciding maybe twenty or so was long enough.

Clyde leaned over and put his mouth over Karen's ear.

"You take the shotgun. I'm going to slip out and into the creek. Go up a ways."

"No," Karen said.

"I'm going to go up a ways and cut back, see if anyone is up there. If not, I'm going to call down to you. If I don't call, if anyone shows their face over the edge, starts to come into the wash, you shoot to kill."

"Clyde."

"Keep it soft," he said.

Karen lowered her voice again. "Just wait. I'm scared. Just wait."

"We'll wait a while longer, but just a while," he said.

They did wait, and it was a long wait, and finally Clyde slipped out of the wash and dangled off the roots and down into the water. He was quiet about it, but still the water splashed as he waded through it, the dead grasshoppers washing along as he waded. He took to the bank on the side the wash was on, climbed up and flipped open his knife.

He was down some distance from the wash, and he could see along the moonlit trail, could see where they had been standing, but they weren't there anymore. He crept down that way, and through a gap in the trees, high up, he could see a lick of brightness as if the sun had risen early and blown up.

It was a fire.

He went over to the bank, got down on one knee, said, "It's me, Karen. Hand up the shotgun if you can."

Karen's hand poked out and took hold of a root, and she swung out with her back to the water, one hand holding her up, and she extended the shotgun to him with the other. He took it, and Karen swung out on the root and got her feet on other roots, started working up the bank. Clyde grabbed her wrist and helped pull her the rest of the way up.

"Are they gone?" she said.

"From here. They've gone back to the tent."

He pointed toward the brightness shining through the trees.

"Lord—what about Goose?"

Clyde shook his head. "I don't know."

They crept back the way they had come and found Goose lying in the trail. His mauled hand lay close to his chest and the revolver he had tried to shoot Two with lay busted by his side.

Karen got down on her knees and touched his head and cried softly. "They didn't have to do that. They didn't have to do none of this. Why?"

"Money, dear," Clyde said. "I'll take care of him later. Leave him."

Karen bent forward and kissed Goose's cold forehead.

They waited out in the woods for a time, and Clyde finally slipped back by himself. He saw there was a terrific blaze, and he realized now what the explosion had been. They had set fire to his truck, probably a rag in the gas tank, and that had blown it up. They had set fire to the tent and his tarp as well. One thing about them, they didn't just do a thing halfway.

He eased up that way, the shotgun ready, but there was nothing to shoot. Henry's body still lay by the post, and Ben's nearby.

Clyde went back to find Karen and when they came back they got the well bucket, some pans from under the tarp, and went about trying to wet the ground down around the fire, keep it from spreading to the kindling-dry woods beyond.

36

The house in the woods that had been Pete and Jimmie Jo's was small but much nicer than the one Zendo and his family had lived in.

"You trying to tell me this is our house," Zendo said to Sunset.

"I'm saying when it all works out, it will be," Sunset said. "Ain't no one else using it now, and no one would expect you to be here, so it's safer than your place. And I'd stay out of the fields for a couple days. You can afford that, can't you?"

"I suppose."

"Just a couple of days," Lee said.

"And Bull will be with you," Sunset said. "Right, Bull?"

"Right," Bull said, and he found a chair and sat, the ten-gauge across his lap.

"I just feel funny being in someone else's house," Zendo said.

"Your dog's on the front porch and he's happy," Lee said. "He knows it's home. And the pig, he's here in the room with you."

The pig lay on its back on the floor, its feet in the air, happy because it didn't know what its future was, couldn't foresee itself as bacon.

"Look here," Sunset said, "they built this place on land that's yours. All that oil under the ground on this land, it's yours, Zendo. You're rich."

"I'll be dead, that's what I'll be," Zendo said. "Rich don't do a man no good if he's dead."

"That's what we're going to change," Sunset said. "You getting dead and this land not being yours. We've got Henry arrested, and when I figure how to go from there, we'll do the rest. In the meantime, I think you're safer here. And it's built on your land, and that makes it yours as far as I'm concerned."

"And she's the constable," Bull said.

Zendo's wife, the toddler clinging to her leg, said, "We didn't know about all this, we wouldn't be hiding. We wouldn't have no oil, but we wouldn't be hiding."

"Eventually, they would come for you," Sunset said, "you knew about it or not."

"I don't like it none," Zendo said.

"I'm sorry it's this way," Sunset said. "But that's how it is. Me and Daddy, we got to go back now. I got to figure what to do with Henry, who to go to so I can be backed up. Bull, you need anything?"

"Outside of being twenty years younger," Bull said, "I don't reckon so."

The first thing Sunset saw through her bug-splattered window were roaring flames licking high at the sky and the shapes of high-flying grasshoppers. Then she saw Clyde's truck, or the blazing skeleton of it; the windows had blown out, the doors had been knocked open by the blast, and the truck bed was torn off; the remains of the bed lay nearby, the ass end of it pointed toward the sky.

"Jesus," Sunset said. "Karen."

She drove faster and would have driven right up on the blaze had Lee not yelled at her to stop. She slammed on the brake, leaped out of the car and started running, screaming Karen's name. Lee slid over and took the rolling car out of gear and pulled the hand brake, got out.

He began to call. First for Karen, then for Clyde. He saw Sunset bent over something on the ground. When he got close, he saw it was Ben and where Sunset had put her hands on the dog, they came away red.

They found Henry. The blaze had gotten to him and burned off one of his legs and it was working its way up. Lee stamped on him until the flames went out. They walked around the blaze that was the tent, and Sunset, seeing there was nothing left of it but fire, lost the strength in her legs. She sagged and Lee caught her.

"It don't mean she was in there," Lee said.

There was movement, shapes seen through the fire. Then the shapes came around the fire, one carrying a syrup bucket, the other a large pan.

Karen and Clyde.

"It was Hillbilly," Clyde said.

They all went to Sunset's car and she drove it away from there, down the road a piece, and pulled over on a narrow logging road.

"I knew he was a piece of shit," Sunset said. "But this—Jesus. It's all my fault. Everything is all my fault."

"It's that sonofabitch's fault," Clyde said. "He brought Plug here, and that big colored man. Big as Bull. The one you told me about."

"Two," Sunset said.

"Poor Goose," Lee said. "I was more than fond of him."

"Me too," Karen said. "Oh, Mama, I can hardly breathe."

"I've got to go back and bury him," Lee said. "I got to do that now. I got to see him."

"No," Sunset said.

"What do you mean, no?" Lee said.

"I've tried to go about this slow," Sunset said, staring into the fire. "Tried to put all my ducks in a row. Like arresting Henry. But they killed him. And they killed Goose and Ben and they tried to kill Clyde. That's my fault. I shouldn't have thought we were safe. It's time we end this. It's time we arrest them. You saw them, Clyde. You're not only a witness, you're a deputy constable. And you saw them, Karen. We know who they are, and what they did. I have to arrest them. I got the right. They were in my jurisdiction."

"This colored fella," Clyde said. "He don't look like no pushover. And Hillbilly, I found out he wasn't neither."

"Daddy whipped his ass," Sunset said.

"He certainly did," Clyde said.

"We're going to get Bull, and we're going to go into town and we're going to arrest them."

"Goose?" Lee said.

"He'd understand a bit of a wait," Sunset said. "He'd want us to get them. And McBride, his bunch, they won't expect us to come so soon. We go get Bull, make them open up the company store, and get some guns and ammunition, go get McBride and Two and Plug, and especially Hillbilly."

"All those guns," Clyde said. "That doesn't much sound like an arrest."

"We got to persuade them," Sunset said. "Way they are, they might need a lot of persuading. But we'll arrest them if we can. We ain't like them. First, we got to try and make sure this fire don't spread."

The fire burned itself out and they damped all around it using pans filled with water from the well. Then they drove to Camp

364

Rapture first, to the sawmill store. Sunset didn't bother with finding the store manager to open it. She took a tire tool out of the trunk of her car and jimmied the back door and they went in. By flashlight, they got what they needed—ammunition, guns, all shotguns. They went over and got Marilyn out of bed, then they all stuffed into the car. They drove over to where Bull and Zendo's family were.

"But you said Bull would be with us," Zendo said.

"I know what I said," Sunset said. "But things have changed."

She told them what happened, said, "They won't be thinking about you. They do, they don't know you're here. If you want, you can hide out in the woods. But I got to have Bull. Some reason you don't hear from us, say by tonight, you ought to leave."

"And go where?" Zendo's wife asked.

"I don't know," Sunset said.

Bull stood up, said, "Keep the ten-gauge, Zendo. That'll be good company. I think the constable's right. We take it to them. It was me, I'd have done that from the start. Then again, I ain't no law."

"They'll be so busy with us," Lee said, "they won't be thinking about you, Zendo."

"If I didn't feel you were safe, I wouldn't ask you to keep Karen with you," Sunset said. "But again, we don't come back, go, and take Karen away from here too."

"Oh, Mama," Karen said.

"We'll be back," Sunset said. "I'm just saying."

"Goose, he ain't gonna be back, now, is he?" Karen said.

"You got to be strong," Sunset said.

"I'm scared," Zendo said. "I won't lie to you none."

"We're all scared," Sunset said. "And I'm tired of being

365

scared and confused, accused of things I didn't do. Tired of bigwigs and tough guys cheating and stealing and killing, and I'm tired of my not knowing one of my own constables was a liar and a bastard. They killed a boy, Goose. A good boy. They killed one of their own, shot him while he was chained to a post. And they killed my dog."

They gathered round and passed out guns. All of them took twelve-gauge pumps and a box of shells. They took some of the shells and loaded the guns and put spare shells in their pockets.

Sunset made sure her .38 had six shells in it. She and Bull were the only ones with handguns. Sunset gave hers to Karen, said, "Don't shoot yourself."

Sunset turned to Bull and Lee, said, "Bull, Daddy, by the power invested in me, you are now deputy constables."

"Damn, that count for a colored?" Bull asked.

"Does today," Sunset said.

The pig grunted. Clyde said, "That is one swell pig. I was you, I wouldn't eat it."

When they came out of the little house to get in the car, there was a sound in the air like a great sigh. Looking up, they could see the moon was hidden by a flow of grasshoppers, and the sound of them grew louder, from a sigh to a buzz to a hum that reminded them of the great saw up on the hill in Camp Rapture. They couldn't know it at the time, but the grasshoppers had already descended on Zendo's field. There would be no need for him to work it again this summer, for in a matter of minutes, the dark wave of insects had come down with the moonlight and eaten out the field, leaving nothing but roots and dirt. Then they had moved on, filling the sky above Sunset and her posse.

Sunset drove, Clyde beside her; in the backseat were Bull and Lee. Daylight was coming and the black sky was lightening, and as they drove the windshield became so littered with bugs Sunset had to stop and get a stick and scrape them off. She used a rag she had in the glove box to wipe the glass, but all it did was smear. As she cleaned the windshield, bugs hit her, stinging her flesh. They had to stop three times so they could clean the windshield, taking turns, Clyde next, then Lee.

When the sky became lighter they saw an amazing sight.

The landscape had changed and the world was void of greenery. The trees were like the skeletons of giants that had fallen from heaven, poking bones every which way. Low down was the same. Green had gone to gray and brown and the song of the hoppers ebbed and flowed as they ate their way through the dry summer morning and the bugs struck the car so hard Sunset could see paint chip off.

They fought the road and fought the bugs and drove on slowly into Holiday, where the first strong light of morning showed the streets and buildings were entwined with waves of insects, and up on the hill, the overhang above the drugstore, even as they watched, the greenery disappeared, like some kind of conjurer's trick.

They drove past the apartment, over to the sheriff's office, jumped out. They ran a gauntlet of bugs that was like an ocean wave. The wave knocked Sunset down and staggered the others, except for Bull. They went in the front door of the sheriff's office, one at a time, guns ready.

Plug sat behind his desk, as if waiting on them. His hands were in plain sight, resting on the desktop. Sunset yelled and stuck the shotgun under his chin.

Plug said, "Go on. Do it. I didn't hurt nobody, but do it."

"I saw you," Clyde said.

"But I didn't want no part of it. I got away from them when we got back to town. But I didn't know nowhere to come but here. I don't got nowhere to go. And I didn't shoot nobody. Nobody at all."

"Consider yourself under arrest," Sunset said. "I'm the law now. And be damn glad of it."

Plug got up, lifted by the shotgun barrel at his throat. Sunset pushed him backward toward the cells.

"Where are the keys?" she asked.

"In the drawer," he said.

Lee got them. They put Plug inside and locked the cell door. Sunset said, "I want to just cut down on you. I want to kill you, Plug. Goose, he wasn't nothing but a boy."

"I didn't kill nobody and didn't want to," Plug said, sitting down heavily on a bunk. "I thought I did, but I couldn't. I didn't shoot nobody. The nigger done it. He done it all. That Hillbilly, he would have, but he never got the chance. The nigger, he's crazy. He blew Tootie's head off. Almost blew mine off. No money's worth that. But I couldn't get away from them. I had to stay with them. They threatened to kill me."

"So did I," Sunset said.

"Go on ahead. I don't mind if you do it. I just didn't want that nigger sucking on me. He shoots you, then he sucks on you. He thinks he's taking your soul out of your mouth," Plug said. "He got kicked in the head by a horse. He's got the mark. It made him crazy. He thinks he's two people. Maybe he is. Jesus, he's one crazy nigger."

"Where's Hillbilly?" Sunset said.

"I think he's up at the red place," Plug said. "I think he's with the nigger and McBride. They got a whore over there. I was gonna run off, but the bugs came. I thought they passed on, I'd run off. But I don't know what I'd have done, where I'd have gone."

"You aren't going anywhere, Plug," Sunset said. "What's the red place?"

"Apartment over the drugstore. Just across the street there."

"All right, then," Sunset said. "We go get them. The whore, we don't want to hurt her. She's not in on this."

"There's a front way and a little back stairs," Plug said. "Remember I tried to help you. Remember that."

They fought bugs and got in the car and sat. They could see the apartment across the way. Close enough to walk to, but in this storm of bugs, not a good idea.

Sunset said, "I'm gonna drive right up close. Daddy, you and Bull, you take the front. Me and Clyde, we'll take the back. We surprise them, away from their guns, we got a good chance. Much as I know you'd like to, don't shoot you don't have to. Try to arrest them. But they try and hurt you, then shoot to kill."

"What do we do?" Clyde said. "Knock?"

"That's one way," Sunset said.

Sunset drove across the street. The insects were rising and falling in waves. The grasshoppers were so close together they looked like a great speckled ribbon of green and brown and gray and black. They wound around the town, the buildings, the cars, the oil derricks that poked up willy-nilly here and there.

No one was on the streets except them and the bugs.

Sunset drove them right up to the front stairs, then she took a ribbon from her shirt pocket and tied her hair back.

"I don't know what more to say," she said. "You're through the front, we're through the back."

"That's all I need," Bull said.

"Personally," Lee said, "I'd like something a little more specific."

"Sorry, Daddy. I'm not Robert E. Lee on the war plans."

"It'll do, then," Lee said.

"Everyone, please come back," Sunset said.

She and Clyde got out of the car and ran around to the side of the drugstore. The insects were less there. They went along the side until they got to the back of the drugstore, the smaller set of stairs there. The bugs were thick again. They got low and went forward. Sunset had to raise the shotgun stock to cover as much of her face as possible and she could feel the little legs of the bugs working in her hair, in the long tail of it tied back behind her.

Pretty soon they were at the stairs and going up, Clyde pushing to try and get in front of her, but she didn't let him, kept the lead, and finally they came to the back door.

Bull and Lee went up the front way, quick and ready, shotguns pumped full of a load, ready to cut down if need be, or simply ready to knock on the door, arrest all volunteers.

The insects were so thick they could hardly climb the stairs, and just as they were about to reach the top, a smear of insects splattered on the top stair caused Lee's shoe to slip, and he slid and one leg went through the railing, and he did a kind of drop, as if the ground opened up below him, and there was a cracking sound like hot fire eating a dry stick, and Lee just sat, his one good leg poking through the railing, the other coiled under him like it had no bones. He let out a yell so loud it almost drowned out the plague of locusts.

"My leg. Goddamn it! It's gone, Bull. It's gone."

Bull knelt down, said, "Sunset, she's gonna be going through that back door. She's gonna need right smart help. You gonna have to wait."

"Oh, Jesus, it hurts. Go on. Do it, Bull."

And as Bull went away from him, Lee jerked off his belt and stuck it in his mouth and bit down, trying not to scream again.

Bull went up and didn't knock. Knocking was out. He went

at the door with his foot and hit it hard and it flapped back like a nag's tongue. He went in and it was dark in there as the door swung back in place, and there was nothing to see, but suddenly he felt something, something hot and at his spine, low down, and it took him a piece of a second to realize there was a knife sliding into him from behind.

Clyde hit the door with his body, but it was a good door, and it knocked Clyde back and almost made him fall down the stairs.

"Damn," Clyde said, and he went at it again.

This time the door frame gave, but not completely, and Clyde hit it again, and Sunset hit it with him, and it went back, throwing splinters, and they went in, pushing the door closed to keep out the rush of grasshoppers.

Bull swung his shotgun butt back and around and caught something. The pressure on the knife went away. But the knife stayed with him, and he thought: Goddamn, taken from behind, that's not right, not me, I'm always ready, but goddamn, I feel it, a knife in my back, tight as a bull's dick in a chicken's ass.

Now he turned toward his attacker and was grabbed by the front of his legs, and he knew, there in the dark, he had hit someone with the shotgun stock, knocked them down and they had hold of his legs and he was going to fall on the knife.

Bull twisted his body as he went down, tried to hit on his side, and did. Mostly. But the hilt of the knife caught some of it, and he felt it go in, like John Henry driving a railroad spike. Inside of him was all the fire of the world, then someone . . . or something . . . was crawling up him like a cockroach. And now with his eyes adjusted, light from outside coming in through the edges of the door where it had not quite closed, the light of morning filtered through the bodies of millions of locusts, he saw a black face, a head wearing a bowler hat. Then powerful hands were at his throat. He tried to bring the shotgun around, but the cockroach slapped at it so hard it was knocked from his hands, and the cockroach dropped all its body weight on him (one big roach) and it drove him down and onto the hilt of the knife and he let out a scream and there were black dots swimming in front of him and the light from the doorway went dim, then he was back, but not fully, seeing everything now as if through a piece of gauze. He tried to reach out and grab the cockroach by the throat, but all he did was knock the bowler hat off. He grabbed at the man's head, trying to push him back. His thumb ran over something there. A scar. And now he was going weak, and he could feel something warm beneath him, his blood, running all over the floor, and he felt as if it were a great pond and he was falling back into it. He slipped his thumb around and caught the big roach in the eye, and the man twisted away, but it wasn't good enough. Then the big man, the giant roach, wide as him, was pushing down again, making that knife really work. The face came close and Bull could see the man's teeth as he opened his mouth and laid it over his own, began to suck, and he thought: This, this will make me mind my own goddamn business from here on out. Then he felt a wave of laughter, but couldn't laugh. From now on. Yeah. I will mind my business. I won't have any more business, mine or anybody else's. And with the last of his will, Bull clamped down on Two's bottom lip with his teeth and bit so hard he could feel his back molars crack.

Two leaped back and Bull reached at his belt, pulled his pistol and fired. The pistol kicked and flew out of Bull's weak hand, but the shot hit Two in the stomach.

Two stood up.

Bull thought: Goddamn, and I thought I was tough. He had lifted his head a bit, but now he let it lie down, closed his eyes, thought: What's gonna come is gonna come, cause I'm done.

Two put one hand on his stomach, stepped over Bull, toward the door, shoved it open. Insects hummed into the room. He stepped out on the stairway landing, and closed the door behind him, did it softly, like there was nothing the matter with him. He saw Lee on the top steps, his leg twisted up under him as if it were rubber, a belt in his mouth.

"We've been shot," Two said.

Lee lifted his shotgun and let off a round. It hit Two and knocked him back and Two slammed against the railing and the boards cracked and went away and he went through, fell the long drop to the ground. Using one hand, Lee flicked another load into the shotgun, crawled over to look down, the belt clamped in his mouth like a hawk with a snake.

Two wasn't there.

Lee wheeled as best he could, the pain in his leg making his vision waver, saw from his new vantage point that Two was up and walking down there, staggering up against Sunset's car, holding his bowler in his hand. He opened the door, put on his bowler, got in behind the wheel.

Lee worked at getting turned better, so he could get off another shot. He could feel the bone in his leg jamming against the inside of his skin. He heard the car start. He got turned around, but the doing of it was so painful, he spat out the belt, screamed, blacked out for a moment.

When he came to, he had dropped the shotgun to the ground below, and the car was driving off with Two at the wheel. Lee ducked his head, passed out.

*

Just inside the back door, Sunset and Clyde heard Bull's pistol bark, then the shotgun blast. Sunset's whole body was shaking. She said, "Go left, I'll go right."

"I'll go where the shot was," Clyde said.

"I'm the constable, you're the deputy. You do as I say."

Clyde nodded, went left, down the long room. As he passed the windows, the light from them wavered and heaved with the blocking and unblocking of the morning sun by waves of grasshoppers.

When he got to the end of the hall there was a door there, and he went through it, the back of his neck feeling as if someone had laid an ice-cold towel there.

Sunset went right, and as she came to the end of the short wall, there was enough light from the windows she could see Bull lying there, not moving, and she could see to the left of that a shelf, and on the shelf all manner of things, but among them a silver platter next to a kerosene lantern, and in that platter, which was tilted slightly, she could see a shape coming down the hall, on the other side of the wall. Even seen in the platter, from that distance and with the bad light, she knew it was McBride. He was wearing what at first she thought was a dress, then decided was an apron.

Clyde moved through the dining room with its chandelier and well-set table, and there was plenty of light in there, but it was a funny kind of light, like he was looking at it from the inside of an egg yolk. Clyde slipped along, listening. He heard the floor creak.

Clyde stopped.

The blond whore stumbled into view, out from an open doorway in the back. She was half dressed.

"Don't shoot," she said. "He's behind the wall. He don't want a shoot-out."

"Who?" Clyde said.

"Hillbilly."

"You sent a woman out, Hillbilly?"

"You ain't got no cause to shoot her," Hillbilly said from behind the wall. "You'd have come right in on me and I didn't want her shot."

"He don't care about me," said the whore. "He's just buying time . . . Hillbilly, it's one of those men whipped your ass."

Clyde motioned her over to him. "Get behind me," he said, then to Hillbilly, "Throw out your gun."

"Ain't got one."

The blonde shook her head.

Clyde nodded.

"I ain't wanting to get killed over all this," Hillbilly said.

"You go on out the back way," Clyde said to the whore.

"McBride, he went through that door there, down the hall," she said.

"Go on out the back way," Clyde said again. "And thanks."

She went away and Clyde said, "I know you got a gun, Hillbilly. Throw it out."

"Naw. I do that, you might shoot me."

"I'm gonna shoot you for sure, you don't."

"Let me think on it."

Clyde slid forward, stood near the wall, Hillbilly on the other side.

"Last chance," Clyde said.

"Or what?" Hillbilly said. "I watch myself pretty good. You come get me."

Clyde lifted the shotgun and pointed at the wall, where he thought he heard Hillbilly, and fired, pumped another round into the chamber, dropped low, waited.

"Goddamn," Hillbilly said.

Clyde slid around to the doorway, staying low, poked his head and gun around on the other side. Hillbilly lay on his back, a pistol nearby. He wasn't hurt bad, but the shot had surprised him and he had been peppered with pellets. A piece of the wall, a splinter, had gone back and into Hillbilly's shoulder.

"You ain't bad off," Clyde said, picking up Hillbilly's pistol, sticking it in his belt.

Hillbilly took hold of the splinter and pulled it out of his shoulder, took a breath, turned his head toward Clyde. "Guess you can get even now."

Sunset heard the shotgun blast to her left, in the rooms beyond. The blonde came through a door stepping lively, saw her, waved at her, went out the back way, into the grasshoppers, closed the battered door.

Sunset turned, looked back at the wall where McBride was. She could see him in the platter, still easing forward. She slipped backward until she was between the windows, her back against the wall. She let her ass slide to the floor, pulled her knees together, propped the shotgun on them, braced the stock against her shoulder.

McBride poked his head around the corner, poked it so fast the stupid black wig he was wearing shifted dramatically.

Sunset cut down on him.

Most of the shot hit the wall, but stray pellets lit into McBride's face and he let out a yell, disappeared back behind the barrier.

Sunset pumped up another load, braced herself again. Thought: He hasn't figured I can see him in the platter. She could see him leaning against the wall, picking at the pellets in his face.

"You damn bitch," he said. "You hit me some."

"I was trying to hit you a lot," Sunset said. "Surrender, and it'll go better."

"Ha."

"You always wear an apron?"

"You messed up my breakfast, bitch. I'm gonna shoot you until you can't be made out for a person."

Sunset was trying to decide what to do, like maybe break and run, because here she was, just sitting, nothing to protect her but hopefully being quicker than McBride, and she was thinking this when McBride stepped out quickly from behind the wall, took hold of the lantern and stepped back.

She fired.

But it was too late. Her shot hit the far wall and the silver platter fell, hit on its edge, came rolling toward her, whirled and fell flat.

Goddamn, Sunset thought. I was looking at him in the platter, and he still beat me to the punch.

The lantern, lit, appeared on McBride's arm from behind the wall and was tossed at her. Sunset leaped away. The lantern hit behind her. A burst of flame ran up the wall, ate the wallpaper like cotton candy. Sunset felt its heat, felt her hair crinkle. She rolled away from it as McBride stepped out from behind the wall. He had a double-barrel shotgun, and when he cut loose, Sunset, already rolling, threw herself flat. The shot tore above her. She felt some of it nip at her heels and heard the window behind her blow. Then there was a sound like something growling from beyond the grave.

Sunset lifted her head, tried to put McBride in her sights, but what she saw was his amazed face. He had broken the gun open, having fired both barrels, was ready to reload, but his expression caused Sunset to turn her head, look over her shoulder.

The flames on the wall were licking out to taste the air and

377

the grasshoppers flooding in were catching fire. They washed in a burning wave toward McBride.

McBride dropped the shotgun, covered his face as they hit him, a mass of bugs aflame. His wig burst alight, and he tried to dive to the floor, but the grasshoppers followed him down, were all over him. He rose up screaming, batting at the air, his apron on fire, and Sunset thought: You dumb sonofabitch, just roll. You ain't on fire, it's your apron, that stupid wig.

But he didn't roll. The wig had become a fool's cap of fire. He snatched it off his shiny bald head, tossed it and ran. Ran straight at Sunset. Sunset was so amazed, she didn't shoot, and he kept going, running hard, went right past her and through what was left of the window, flames flapping behind him like a cape, insects on fire, whizzing around his head like a halo. Then the cape of fire dropped through the window and was gone and the air crackled with flames and exploding grasshoppers.

Clyde appeared to her left. He had Hillbilly with his hands tied behind his back with a twisted pillowcase. Hillbilly looked bloody and bowed, but not too bad off.

"You okay?" Clyde called.

"Almost," she said. "He hurt bad?"

"Got some pieces in him, mostly wood from the wall. He'll live."

The entire wall behind Sunset was on fire and the fire was spreading. She said, "Out the front."

"Is that all of them?" Clyde said. "Did we get them all?"

"God, I hope so."

Sunset stood, slapped flames off her skirt where the kerosene had splattered and caught. Clyde kicked Hillbilly in the ass, said, "Move it, songbird."

When Sunset got to the doorway, she stopped and bent over Bull. She said, "Bull?"

"Is he gone?" Bull said.

"Who?"

"That big nigger in the bowler?"

"I don't see him anywhere."

"That's good."

"I'm sorry, Bull."

"Don't let the peckerwoods have my body."

"You're gonna be all right."

"Got a knife in my back. My legs, everything from my pickle down, gone cold, won't move no more. We on fire? I smell smoke."

Clyde was there with Hillbilly now. He said, "Yeah. There's fire, Bull."

"Let me burn," Bull said.

"You ain't gonna burn. Clyde, go down and put Hillbilly in the car. There's rope in the trunk, you need it. Use it to tie his legs to his arms, throw him in the backseat, better yet, the trunk. Come back and help me with Bull—Jesus, where's Daddy? Bull, can you hear me? Where's Daddy?"

But Bull didn't answer.

A moment later, Clyde came back in with Hillbilly. "There ain't no car. Your daddy, he's hurt."

"Hurt?"

"Yeah. Leg is broke." Clyde looked down at Bull. He wasn't moving and his eyes were closed. "Bull?"

"Bull's gone," Sunset said, coughing at the smoke.

"Yeah, and so is this place," Hillbilly said.

The far wall was fire, and the fire, fed by kerosene on the floor, was creeping toward them.

"Leave him," Clyde said.

379

Sunset thought about that, about how he lived and what he told her, said, "Reckon so."

Sunset took Hillbilly down, her shotgun in his back, and Clyde picked up Lee, carried him.

When they were at the bottom of the steps, Hillbilly said, "I didn't mean for it to go this way, Sunset."

"I have a feeling you don't never mean for nothing to happen, but it always does."

"I'm kind of cursed."

"Hell, you are the curse."

The flames were licking at the apartment and smoke was pouring out the open door and the drugstore below was starting to catch fire. The flames were so hot and bright, the grasshoppers had finally started to recede. Sunset looked up, saw them like a dark rainbow against the sky, going south, and fast, dimming the sun.

When Clyde came down the steps carrying Lee like a baby, Sunset said, "Watch this piece of dung a minute," and left him with Hillbilly. She went around back, looking for McBride, still cautious, the shotgun at the ready.

She found McBride face forward against the overhang. There were burn marks on the ground where he had dragged himself. He was a blackened shape now, his hands like claws where he had scooped out some clay as if trying to climb up the overhang to God knows where, or maybe burrow through it.

They went across the street to the jail, Sunset with her gun at Hillbilly's back, prodding, and Clyde carrying Lee. They put Hillbilly in the cell with Plug, and Clyde laid Lee on the bunk in the other cell, called up the town doctor, who came and looked at Lee and said he was bad.

"He's gonna need a hospital," the doctor said. "That leg. It might have to come off. I ain't up for that kind of thing."

"I got use for this leg," Lee said, his face covered in sweat.

The doctor, who was a short fat man wearing a plaid shirt and pants that looked as if they could use a wash, said, "Yeah, but it might not have any use for you anymore. I'm gonna do my best to set it, but we got to get you over to Tyler. There's people there better at this kind of thing than me. This ain't no simple break. This one's all twisted up."

"We'll get you to the doctor, Daddy," Sunset said. "He don't know that's what will happen for sure."

"If I mess with it much, it is," the doctor said.

"Can you take him to Tyler?" Sunset said.

"I can," said the doctor, "but it'll cost."

"He's a deputy constable."

"He's your daddy."

"And he's still a deputy constable. You see he gets there. You bill Camp Rapture—better yet, you bill Holiday. And give him something for pain."

"For Christ sakes, yes," Lee said. "Knock me out. Give me some dope. Something."

"Daddy," Sunset said, liking the sound of calling him that better and better, "still believe what you said, about the union of everything in the universe, us and everything in it all being part of one big thing?"

"Not so much," Lee said.

"What about these two?" Clyde said, nodding toward Hillbilly and Plug.

"They're for the law," Sunset said.

"There ain't no law," Clyde said.

381

"Today there is. And you're it. Stay till we figure something out. I'm gonna check on Karen."

"What then?"

"We'll cross that bridge when we get to it."

When it was done and Lee was on his way to Tyler, courtesy of the doctor and his car, Sunset got the keys to the sheriff's car, went out and cleaned the windshield free of bugs and got in. She sat there and thought about the fact that she and Clyde were unhurt, her dad was the worst off and he hadn't even gotten inside the apartment. And Bull. Poor Bull. He was dead, and all she had was a few bangs and cuts and some little shotgun pellets in the back of her heels, pellets she could pick out with tweezers.

She sat and looked at what was left of the fire across the way. The fire department, such as it was, was trying to put it away, but mostly they were running around the fire truck and cursing. They had succeeded in flushing the building with a lot of water from their big red engine, and what was left of the apartment and the drugstore was nothing but some charred timbers you could stir with a stick.

She thought about Bull, burned up in there, and it made her think of the story she'd heard about Greek heroes, how they put them on piles of lumber and burned them up and sent their souls up in smoke and flames.

On the way home, Sunset saw the sky had cleared and it was full of nothing but a crow. The trees, grass, anything that had been green, was gone. It was as if green had been a dream. Now that the storm of wings and legs had departed, there was only desolation. Even the bark had been stripped off the hardwoods. All about were dead grasshoppers, victims of collisions and fights with their hungry partners.

She drove along until she came upon her car. It was beside

the road, the driver's door open. Sunset stopped near it, took the shotgun lying on the seat and got out. The morning had come in full now, and it was hot, but she felt more cold than hot as she moved alongside her car, looked inside. Nothing but dried black blood on the front seat.

She walked along the road slowly, crunching dead grasshoppers under her feet, looking right and left. Then she saw him. He was sitting with his back against a great pine tree that was stripped of its needles. He had his hands on his thighs and he was looking at her. His bowler hat was on the ground, the crown touching the earth. Flies were so thick on the front of his shirt they looked like a vest. His coat was pushed back over his shoulders, as if he had tried to give himself a little breeze. The scar on his head looked raw and stood out, like an actual horseshoe was inside his skull, working its way to the surface.

Sunset kept the shotgun pointed at Two, moved toward him slowly. When she was standing over him his vest startled and flew away. She saw part of his bottom lip was bit off, and she thought: Good for you, Bull. His green eyes were filmed over and still and a fly was on one of them.

"I guess the both of you are dead," Sunset said.

37

They buried Goose in the same graveyard where Pete and Jones and Henry's wife lay. They didn't know Goose's last name, and since he hadn't liked his first name, they put on the wooden cross GOOSE. A GOOD BOY.

Lee couldn't attend, but from his hospital bed he wrote out some words and Sunset read them. They were simple and nice and there were Bible quotes.

Ben was buried at Sunset's place, near the big oak where he liked to lie. Sunset said her own words over that grave. "You're home, boy."

Two weeks later, in her bug-scarred car, Sunset drove over to see Marilyn. She drove past Bill and Don working their mules, other men working oxen, driving trucks, doing this and that.

There were a lot of trees to work. The grasshoppers' short reign had caused a large number of them to die and they were being cut fast and furious, hauled in, put on the belt, run through the saw.

Bill looked up from his work as Sunset drove by. "She ain't treated that car right. See how it's all cut up."

Don nodded. "She looks all right herself, though, don't she?"

"I got to go with that," Bill said. "I don't like her none, but me not liking her ain't hurt her looks. And she's got some guts, things she did, her and that Clyde. I knowed that Hillbilly wasn't worth the steam off shit when I first seen him."

"You didn't know no such thing," Don said.

"I did. Just didn't say so."

"Watch them mules," Don said.

Sunset drove past the mill, on up into Marilyn's yard. She went up on the porch and knocked. While she waited she looked at the haze of sawdust over the mill, listened to the sound of the great saw.

Marilyn opened the door with a smile. She looked splendid and young in a white housedress with blue designs.

"Good to see you, Sunset. After all that business I haven't seen you much. And you're all dressed up. That's a nice dress."

"I bought it in Holiday. I wanted something green, there not being much green left."

"I ain't never heard of such a thing as them grasshoppers acting that way. Not here. North and West Texas, Oklahoma maybe, but I ain't never heard of them here, not doing like that."

"They ate all there was up there, so they came down here."

"Here now," Marilyn said, pushing back the screen. "Don't stand on the porch, sweetie. Come on in."

Inside Sunset took a chair. It was the same chair Marilyn had slapped her out of some weeks ago. She could hear the big clock ticking away.

"Where's Karen?" Marilyn asked.

"At Uncle Riley's."

Marilyn considered this for a moment.

"She there because of the baby?"

"Aunt Cary helped her on that."

"She . . . she got rid of the baby?"

"She didn't want his child. Not after all that."

Marilyn nodded, sat silent for a time.

"I suppose that's right. I don't think God would judge a girl on that."

"No," Sunset said. "I don't think he would."

"And Clyde?" Marilyn said, trying to change the subject.

"Holiday. He's still being the sheriff. Think they're gonna hire him for real."

"And your daddy?"

"Still in the hospital. Gonna keep the leg, but it'll be stiff. Going to Tyler to get him when I leave here."

"I'm sorry to hear about his leg, but it could have been worse."

"Could have. Though Bull might disagree."

"I didn't even know he was real."

"He was real all right."

"There was a deputy involved—"

"Plug. He'll see trial. He tried to help me some, so that might make it a little easier for him. I don't care if it does, really."

"After all that," Marilyn said, "I heard Zendo moved off, and him owning all that oil. All that happened, and he moved off."

"He moved up North, and he still owns the oil. Clyde manages the place for him. People around here will leave Clyde alone, but they wouldn't like a colored man owning all that oil. Zendo can be rich up North easier than he can be rich here, and he gives Clyde a little cut to manage it. The house, the one Zendo lived in, the one on the oil land, Clyde's got them both. He's gonna live in one, rent the other. That's okay with Zendo."

"Clyde sure is sweet on you. He'd be a catch. Especially now."

"I suppose he would. I wanted it to go that way, but when it all settled out, going through what we all went through—I just don't feel like that about Clyde. I don't have that feeling, you know? Something missing. After all the killing, nearly being killed, I don't feel like wasting a moment, making a mistake that'll hurt me or him."

386

Marilyn smiled. She had taken a chair herself. "I know. You got to have that. That feeling. Jones, when he was young, like Pete with you, he made me feel that way."

"Hillbilly made me feel that way. I guess, in the end, it isn't enough. Clyde didn't like me telling him, but I think he understood. Best he could. In the end, I think he's more of a bachelor anyway."

"There's some fellas in prison gonna like Hillbilly," Marilyn said. "You know what I mean, him being all pretty and everything."

"Not yet," Sunset said. "And I don't know if he'll heal up so pretty. Daddy sure gave him a beating. Thing is, he got loose. In Tyler, where they took him for the trial. The jailer had a daughter."

"I'll be damned."

"They caught the daughter. Hillbilly run off, left her in an unpaid room in Texarkana. They figure he's in Arkansas somewhere."

"He is one dog," Marilyn said.

Sunset nodded.

"You act like something is on your mind," Marilyn said.

"Didn't know I was gonna bring it up for sure. I didn't come here knowing I was gonna say anything. Not really. But I am. Woke up yesterday morning, and I was thinking about something. It's been with me a while, and I couldn't let it go. Back of my mind, buried back there. Yesterday it come floating up, and I let it go. Today, I'm not feeling like I can."

"What in the world do you mean?"

"How did you know Jimmie Jo had a baby?"

"What?"

"You told me she had a baby, but I didn't tell you."

"I guess it was around the camp. Preacher Willie."

"That she was shot with a thirty-eight."

"It was around—Sunset, what are you getting at? I'm sure everyone knew about that business."

"That's what I thought, it was just around. But there were other things. You showing me how to use posthole diggers, saying how you could dig with those better than a shovel, even straight down. That's how Jimmie Jo was buried. Straight down. And the baby—where's the flowerpot that used to be on the porch, Marilyn?"

"It broke."

"Yeah. I saw pieces of it out at the baby's grave."

"You're going wrong here, Sunset."

"I'd like to be, but I don't think so. McBride, he knew about the oil on Jimmie Jo, but he didn't know about the thirty-eight. I think he had, he'd have told me. He didn't care. He didn't know what I was talking about. Pete, when he came to you, crying, did he come to you and tell you about Jimmie Jo?"

"He didn't kill her, if that's what you mean."

"It isn't. You let me think he might have, but he didn't."

"It didn't matter. Not right then. Jimmie Jo was dead, so was Pete."

"Just tell me, Marilyn. Why?"

Marilyn was silent for a long time. The grandfather clock chimed noon.

"I didn't do what you think I did," she said.

"What did you do?"

"Pete was upset about you. He cried about you. He didn't think you were the kind of wife you could be, and he'd met that woman, that whore, Jimmie Jo—I was protecting you. And him. But I didn't—it isn't what it seems."

"What is it, then?"

"My plant, the one that was in the pot on the back porch. It

388

died. Everyone knows Zendo has the best soil around. I thought I'd take the back road, the one that's on the oil land, the one I thought was someone else's. Just forgotten land. Thought I'd go out there, see if I could get some of that dirt. I meant to ask Zendo, but if he wasn't around, figured I'd just take some. I got out there, saw the house, the one Pete built for his whore. He told me about it, but when I seen it, I was sick. It was better than the one you lived in, Sunset. I was mad, and I went up there to see her, but she wasn't there. And when I left, driving home—I'd forgot about the soil, you see—well, I seen her. There was an oil pool and she was lying out there beside it. She had on an orange and green dress. A gaudy whore's dress. I could see it good, the part wasn't covered in oil. You couldn't miss her lying there. I pulled over for a look. She was lying there, and she was just the same as dead. She had drowned, like. Her brain was dead, but her body was still moving. She had been drowned but wasn't all of her dead. Whoever done it, they'd left her for dead, but she wasn't. And she was having the baby, Sunset. Even after she was by all reason dead, her body was giving that baby life.

"I had seen Aunt Cary deliver a baby, and I knew whose baby that was. My grandchild. And I delivered it, cutting it out of her cause she wasn't alive enough to worry about doing it the right way, did it best I could remember how, but it was born dead, Sunset. Dead baby from a dead mother. I just made sure she was all dead. I didn't do her any harm wasn't already done. Shooting her like that, it was merciful.

"I took the baby then, put it in the jar. I had posthole diggers with me to get dirt at Zendo's, and I stuck the baby in the jar and buried it over there on his land."

"Why, Marilyn?"

"The child was gone. Wasn't anything gonna bring it back, and it wasn't something you needed to know. I was trying to protect you, Sunset. Really. I buried Jimmie Jo too, using the diggers. I just wanted them out of the way. I thought maybe Pete did it—I thought that then. I know now it was that other man—McBride, you called him. But I thought if Pete killed her, and the baby died because of it, and people heard, then no matter how much he was liked, that was too much. And you and Karen, you'd suffer. I made a mistake, though. I left my posthole diggers. I carried them back to the truck, leaned them against it, then I forgot—upset, you see. Drove off and they just fell to the ground. Pete knew who they belonged to. He came and asked me about it, brought the diggers with him. He asked me about Jimmie Jo. I think he thought I killed her."

"You did," Sunset said. "When you shot her, you killed her. Figure that's why Pete wrote out the file the way he did, buried the baby as a colored. To protect you."

"Jimmie Jo was already dead. That McBride, or one of them working for him, they drowned her."

"McBride wasn't as good at killing people as he thought. In the long run, he couldn't even fight grasshoppers. If he'd been good, you wouldn't have had to finish the job."

"Why would I kill the baby?"

"Maybe you wouldn't. Maybe you didn't want Pete having a baby by some whore he wasn't married to. I don't know."

"It was perfect, Sunset. Really. She was out of your way, out of Pete's life, and out of my life. The baby—I don't know, maybe it's like Karen's baby—it was best. The way it ought to be. Way God wanted it. Pete, I told him where they were buried. Zendo found the baby first, moved it, and Pete found it, moved it to the colored graveyard. Guess he did that until he could put it in a white cemetery. I don't know. We never got the chance to talk about it. You killed him."

"He hid the land business with the body," Sunset said.

"Marilyn, you didn't mind me taking the blame for killing Jimmie Jo and the baby."

"I did mind. I just couldn't say anything."

"You know what I think?" Sunset said, standing. "In the long run, you thought it would work out fine, me taking the blame. You knew Pete wouldn't end up taking it, not the way everyone felt about me. That way, you had me too, for killing Pete. And you could stay in good graces with Karen."

"I done a lot of good by you, Sunset. I got you that car. I helped you."

"Maybe so. Maybe you really did it all for Karen. And yourself. Thing is, I'm nervous around you, Marilyn. You might get moody. I might wake up sewed to my bed, you standing over me with a rake. A shotgun. That thirty-eight."

"You did some things yourself."

"I defended myself against your son. I went to arrest some men who were breaking the law and who tried to kill my daughter and my deputy and killed a boy I cared about. A dog I liked. They would have killed me, Daddy. My conscience is clear. What about yours, Marilyn?"

Sunset started out the door.

"You gonna arrest me?"

"I'm not wearing my badge. Or my gun. I don't intend to put them on again. I don't need them anymore."

Sunset pushed the screen door open and let it fly back. Marilyn came out and stood on the steps as Sunset reached her car.

"You're quitting?"

"I am."

"You're not going to arrest me, then?"

Sunset shook her head.

"What are you gonna do?" Marilyn said, and she had to

strain to hear Sunset over the buzz of the great saw that had started up again.

"I'm gonna pick up Karen, say good-bye to Clyde, go get Daddy, then—I don't know. Maybe just keep going."

"Do you believe me, Sunset?"

"I don't know. Don't know it matters anymore. Not enough, anyway. But I got some doubt, and that much is too much. Important thing is, I got my center."

"Do what?"

"So long, Marilyn."

Sunset got in her car and drove away and Marilyn stood on the front porch and watched until she was out of sight and all that was left to see was the road and the dust from the passing of the car.